TALGORIAN PROPHECY

Melissa Alvarez
writing as
ARIANA DUPRÉ

ADREMA PRESS

To shifts in perspective.

TALGORIAN PROPHECY REVIEWS

Winner: Speculative Fiction Romance in the Dream Realm Awards

Finalist in the Colorado Romance Writers Award of Excellence

4 STARS - Dupré's well-plotted and exciting novel grabs the reader. At its center is a wonderful story about lovers reconnecting. This is surrounded by a suspenseful paranormal adventure with several twists that will continually surprise. ~ Romantic Times

5 CUPS - Ms. Dupré has created a mind blowing tale that grabs you right from the start, throwing you into a maelstrom of action and keeping you on the edge of your seat all the time. With superb ingenuity the author pens a breathtaking adventure with some astounding characters and sensual romance. Without missing a beat the author takes you from a normal hunt into a spectacular paranormal world where you learn the key to what is happening. This is one of those stories that at the end the reader feeling like they had just run a marathon. To sum all of it up would be to say one phenomenal read. ~ Wateena, Coffee Time Romance

5 STARS - Talgorian Prophecy is filled with suspense, love, and fantasy. The plot will keep readers on the edge of their seat. The emotions in this story run deep, I was wiping tears several times before I finished reading. The characters are well-defined. Fans of suspense, romance and fantasy will love this one. ~ Ann Boling, ReviewYourBook.com

SRR GRADE: A - "I really loved this book, it had a couple of really great surprises and it was never slow.... One warning, make sure when you start Talgorian Prophecy you have plenty of time to read, you won't want to put it down until you have turned the last page. I can't wait to read more by this very talented author. ~ Lynda, Simply Romance Reviews

NIGHT VISIONS REVIEWS

Winner of the CataRomance.com Reviewer's Choice Award for Best
Single Title Paranormal Romance

ForeWord Magazine's Book Of The Year Award Finalist
Category: Romance

4 STARS - This book is brisk and entertaining, with someone attempting
to sabotage the construction of the hotel, kill Angie and even hurt Jared.
The road to the end is exciting! This is a marvelous story about
developing trust and a sensuous expression of love, despite the fear that is
reinforced by unexpected forces. The secondary characters are
interesting, and their roles occasionally draw on their connection to the
early inhabitants of the property. ~ Romantic Times

5 STARS - This first installment of the Visions Trilogy has me pulled so
far in I couldn't dig my way out. I am salivating for more. I need to read
the next book more than I need my next breath. Ariana Dupré has
written a mystical story of characters so real they can reach out and grab
you. FIVE stars for a lovely story. ~ Paula Beaty, The Romance Review
Spot

5 STARS - Ariana Dupré has masterfully created a scintillating romantic
suspense story with eerie paranormal elements and roller coaster
episodes that compel you to hold your breath with fright and then sigh
with desire in NIGHT VISIONS, the first story in THE VISIONS
TRILOGY. . . . Things that go bump in the night will never seem the
same after reading this mystical love story. I whole heartedly recommend
Ariana Dupré's NIGHT VISIONS for a thrilling read and I am anxiously
awaiting the next installment of THE VISIONS TRILOGY.
~ Donna Zapf, eCataRomance & CataRomance Reviews

Other books by Melissa Alvarez

365 Ways To Raise Your Frequency
Your Psychic Self
Simply Give Thanks
Analyze Your Handwriting
Your Color Power
Ghosts, A Spirit Guide and A Past Life
Chakra Divination® Cards & Charts Activity Book
The Essential Guide To Chakra Divination
Chakra Divination Ultimate Balance Journal
The eLink Directory of Paranormal Investigative Groups Around the World
Homemade Recipes for Horse Treats plus Fly Sprays & Tips for Owners
The Phoenix's Guide To Self Renewal
Christmas Desserts
Penelope Panda's Shooting Star

Writing as Ariana Dupré
Paranormal Romantic Suspense

Night Visions
Paradise Designs
Briar Mountain

Websites:

MelissaA.com,
BookCoversGalore.com,
BookCovers.Us,
APsychicHaven.com

Published by Adrema Press

ISBN: 978-1-59611-108-0

Cover Design © 2013 Melissa Alvarez at BookCovers.Us/BookCoversGalore.com
Cover Art ©Depositphotos

PUBLISHING HISTORY
Cerridwen Press trade paperback / October 2008
Adrema Press trade paperback / May 2013

Third Edition

10 9 8 7 6 5 4 3

Trademarks Acknowledgement - The author acknowledges the trademarked status and trademark owners of the following wordmarks mentioned in this work of fiction:
    Buick: General Motors Corporation
    Ford: Ford Motor Company
    Gummy Worms: Ferrara Pan Candy Co., Inc.
    Mothman: Austin, Michael W. Individual Stoneking's Island, Inc.
    Mustang: Ford Motor Company
    Scrunchie: L&N Sales and Marketing, Inc

CHAPTER ONE

"WOULD YOU GO HOME IF A SERIAL KILLER ABDUCTED your child?" Megan Cassidy slammed her fists hard against the desk. "Would you?" Her angry stare bore into the steel gray eyes of the officer, emotions raging past better judgment. "How dare you dismiss me. You have no idea what I'm going through."

Lieutenant Randal rose from his chair and walked around the desk. He grabbed Megan's elbow, propelling her toward the door. "We'll call if there are any developments."

"I'm not going anywhere, you coldhearted—" She yanked her arm free from the tight, uncomfortable grip and faced him. She searched his eyes for some shred of understanding, any emotion she could connect with. His features were like a brick wall, cold and rough. "Don't you understand? I *need* to help you find my son."

A mangled, bloody scene flashed through her mind. The glint of a knife, the pitching roar of maniacal laughter rang in her ears. A hooded man stabbed a lifeless body again and again.

The killer's emotions radiated from him. The spark in his eyes reflected joy in the kill, yet the snarl of his lips held contempt for the victim. He looked up. His evil glare slammed into her.

Megan shrank back in terror, her pulse raced.

Anger. Pure and uncontrollable fury. His rage coursed through her. She trembled but couldn't pull her gaze away. She tried to see his face but the hood covered his features. Red crazed eyes stared at her from the darkness.

Locked within his hypnotic trance, Megan waited for some clue to the maniac's identity.

The scene vanished.

Megan dug her fingers into the hard flesh of Randal's arms. Her voice lowered, straining with emotion. "We have to find my son *now!*"

"Ms. Cassidy!" Randal jerked his arm away.

"I saw…" Her heart pounded. Fear rose up her spine at the thought of the Mangler with her son. She stepped between Randal and the door. "I can help you. We must search now before it's too late."

"What do you mean we?" Lieutenant Randal laughed. "I've told you I won't have some half-cocked celebrity in the middle of my investigation, especially one who claims to be psychic."

"I can use my abilities to find Robbie. I've assisted other police departments throughout the country in missing persons cases." She'd encountered resistance before but Randal had closed his mind to anything he couldn't see or prove with facts.

"Do you think I give a damn about what you've done with other departments?" Randal snorted.

"I'll stay behind the scenes. The media will never know I'm around. The Clarkston Police Department and West Virginia State Police can take all the credit." Despite her bravado, her voice cracked. Tears stung her eyes. "It's how I always work."

She braced her hands against the doorframe to keep Randal from pushing her out of the office. "This is my son we're talking about, Randal," she said, blinking back the tears. "Put yourself in my shoes. I'm begging you."

Randal sized up the woman blocking the door. Straight hair hung below narrow shoulders. Its honey color shimmered in the sunlight streaming through the window beside them. If the Mangler had abducted his son he wouldn't leave the station either but damn if he'd act like this. Maybe he was too hard on her but he didn't like her type.

"I understand your feelings. In abduction cases, hysterical mothers often exhibit your type of behavior. Raving like a lunatic about psychic powers doesn't do anything for you, your son, or our investigation."

"In each of the previous abductions the Mountain Mangler took the child first and then its parent, who had psychic abilities, like I do." She clung to the doorframe. "An hour after he killed the kid, he murdered the parent. The bodies were all found in the West Virginia portion of the Allegheny Mountains. He's going to come after me now that he has Robbie."

"I know his MO. As we agreed, when the time comes, we'll use you as bait to lure him to us if we can ensure your safety. If not, we'll try a different approach. We have men looking for your son." Randal rubbed the stubble on his cheek and blew out a heavy breath. "Until that time comes, you can wait over there if you'll stay out of the way." He pointed toward a navy blue chair sitting near the wall beside his office.

"When that time comes?" Her voice raised an octave. "We can't sit around and wait for something to happen. We need to find him now! Your men are looking in town, not in the mountains. Why won't you let me help?"

"Ms. Cassidy, I can't investigate your son's disappearance if you keep antagonizing me. We're working as fast as possible. Now please, have a seat."

Megan frowned. He wasn't going to give in. A new thought crossed her mind. What if he let her secret about Robbie slip? She couldn't deal with any more stress. She fought against the panicky anger Randal fueled in her. "You haven't told the press, right? I've worked hard to keep Robbie's existence a secret in my public life. I don't want them to find out about him now, in the middle of a serial killer investigation, or have the paparazzi coming after me to get a story."

"I promised not to release names unless it was necessary. You don't have to keep asking me. Regardless of what you think of my integrity, my word is my bond. Now, Ms. Cassidy, please, will you go sit down?"

Megan dropped her hands from the doorframe and stepped aside. "What are you going to do first?"

"Let me handle the investigation." Randal grabbed some papers off the fax machine, returned to his office and shut the door.

"Six people are dead, Randal." Megan yelled at him through the window. "My child isn't going to be next!"

She stared as the Lieutenant closed the blinds on the office door.

His word better be his bond.

One slip from Randal and her secret would be national news. Only a handful of people knew of Robbie's existence. She kept it that way to protect him. It had been difficult to go out in public together but they'd managed with Carmela's assistance. A lot of good it did.

She'd been lucky to find Carmela, Robbie's babysitter since birth. She was loyal and, as far as Megan knew, had never told anyone about him. A couple of times, they'd even pretended Robbie was Carmela's son when the paparazzi got too close.

She even chose the private school he attended because of the strict code of silence it maintained. Several other celebrities' children attended Cross Meadows. She'd always thought it was a necessary expense, until today when the serial killer abducted him from the school grounds.

This is my fault. If I hadn't chosen to use my abilities to support us, this never would have happened.

Working the television talk show circuit had thrown her into the limelight because her readings were so accurate and now, Megan Cassidy was a household name.

It had gotten to the point where she couldn't keep up with the hundreds of reading requests she received every day. Once she hit the talk shows the numbers increased. She spent her days conducting readings on the phone or in person and she was booked seven months in advance. Granted, she now made enough money to afford everything she and Robbie needed but why had success come at such a high price?

If only she could control the way she received the information maybe Robbie would be with her right now instead of in the clutches of a killer.

Wandering over to the chair, she couldn't keep the Mangler's vileness from her thoughts. That madman had her only child. She dropped into the seat. Leaning forward, she rested her elbows on her knees and held her head with cold hands.

Hours ago she'd seen Robbie's abduction in a vision while waiting in the school's car line to pick him up. Anger ripped through her at the memory.

"Your mom called and asked if someone could bring you home today. She's sick with the flu," the man had said, walking Robbie toward the front doors. Robbie saw the school's volunteer badge stuck to his shirt and believed him.

Upon receiving the impression, she'd thrown the car door open and run to the school's entrance, pleading, *Not my child—not Robbie. Oh God, please don't let this happen to my son.* Panic wound around her making it difficult to breathe. Her stomach clenched into a knot of sick desperation. Her heart beat at a frantic pace.

"Robbie!" Megan started, realizing she'd screamed his name out loud, as she had when she ordered the teachers to search for him before racing to the parking lot.

"Ms. Cassidy, are you all right?" Gentle fingers moved her hands away from her face.

Megan looked into the soft green eyes of a female officer with short brown hair.

"I was too late," she whispered, "I didn't save my son."

The officer's expression melted into one of deep sympathy. "We're doing all we can to find him."

"What damn good are psychic abilities if I couldn't use them to protect my child? I ran as fast as I could but I wasn't fast enough. If only I'd sensed the abduction sooner."

"You can't blame yourself." The officer gave Megan's hands a squeeze. "I've seen you advise so many people on television. Don't you always say if you're meant to have a vision you will?"

Megan withdrew her hands. "Yes. Only this time it came too late."

Why can't I be right all the time? Why don't I see the visions far enough in advance to do the most good? No, I'm not doing this to myself again. It's out of my hands.

She always worried about her accuracy. There wasn't any point in doing readings if the accuracy wasn't there. Then she wouldn't be any different from the frauds that gave real psychics a bad name. Long ago she'd realized no psychic was ever one hundred percent. *It is a gift, not something I can control.*

A vague vision had destroyed her impending marriage to Brody. Now this one came too late and Robbie could lose his life.

The horrible, violent vision wouldn't undermine her determination. Megan straightened in the seat. He would not win. She'd use all the psychic abilities at her disposal to find Robbie alive.

"I've been a fan for years," the officer said. "Your secret is safe with me. I'm sure your abilities would be invaluable to us if only Lieutenant Randal wasn't so stuck in his ways." She stood. "We have a couch in the lunchroom. You're welcome to sleep there."

Megan nodded. "Thank you."

"Anytime. I've got to go back to work."

As the officer strode away the memory of a dream flashed through Megan's mind. Robbie was in a cave, crying for her while she fought with an unknown assailant, the previous victim's bodies lay around a clearing. She hadn't understood at first but she'd

had violent, struggling dreams about each of the murders the night before. She froze in place—the dreams were like her recent visions.

A nauseous feeling rose in her throat, sweat broke out on her forehead as a chill trembled through her body. She tried to tamp it down by taking deep breaths but the shaking wouldn't stop. Her stomach pitched and rolled.

The Clarkston and State Police assured her the killer would hold Robbie captive while he stalked and terrorized the second victim—her.

Please, God, she prayed, *don't let the Mangler change his MO.* This time, it was personal.

She scanned the large open police station bustling with activity. Desks filled the main room while individual offices lined the walls. Phones rang, the water cooler gurgled and the copier clicked and hummed along with the low drone of people talking. There must be something she could do. Her nerves were too on edge to sit in a stupid chair.

She glanced at Randal's office, stood and took a casual stroll along the narrow outside corridor, which followed the four walls of the station's main room. She pretended to inspect the different posters on the walls while she listened to the conversations behind her, hoping to overhear any discussions about Robbie.

Halfway around she paused beside an open door. The plaque underneath its window read Detective Paul Archer. She peeked inside. One of the officers who had responded to Cross Meadows emergency call sat behind a wooden desk reading a file.

Even sitting he looked tall, with black hair and tanned olive skin. When he glanced up, she moved away from the open door and feigned interest in a wanted poster.

"Brody Phelps is on line two," a voice said over Archer's

intercom.

Brody? He'd been on her mind since the abduction.

Archer lifted the receiver. "Archer here."

She stepped closer to the doorframe, listening intently.

"What conflict of interest?"

Another long pause.

"You're the best tracker in West Virginia. If we have any hopes of finding this boy alive, you're it. Let me know if things change."

Anger ran through her like fire. Was Brody refusing to participate in the rescue because of their past? Well, it was time he got over it. She stormed into Archer's office. "Let me talk to him."

"Sure. Bye." The detective laid the receiver in its cradle. "I'm sorry, Ms. Cassidy. Can I help you?"

"I wanted to talk to Brody."

"He's gone."

Just like my son. She frowned and spun around. Facing the loud buzz of activity coming from the central room, she strode out of Archer's office.

A dark shadow moved through her peripheral vision. She looked toward it and found herself staring at people walking around. They were carrying files, talking on the phone, speaking in hushed tones. None of them was the person she'd seen. She realized it hadn't been a person at all but a spirit.

The shadow spirit triggered a deeper connection. The buzzing softened, sounding distant. Her vision darkened as if a tunnel was closing in around her. She waited for the psychic scenes to play out in her mind.

The tunnel's black walls led to a pinprick of light at the end. The white circle grew closer as the walls sped by. She traveled through its brilliance and into a forest clearing.

Megan glanced behind her. The police station had disappeared. Instead tall evergreens surrounded her. The smell of pine hung heavily in the air. The forest was strangely silent. She looked up at the sky through an opening in the forest canopy. It appeared to be early afternoon.

She stood in a clearing. The mouth of a cave was on the rockiest side and an old miner's cabin on the other.

Why am I here? she thought as she waited. Her heartbeat raced. She held her breath in anticipation.

A man exited the old wooden shack. He stepped over a dead tree as he crossed the yard, stopping several feet in front of her. She sensed danger and death around him. His dark hair hung in limp dirty strands past his shoulders. He wore a flannel shirt with black jeans and boots. His face was bony, his eyes bulging.

He laughed. The maniacal sound echoed through the silence. His lips curled back in a snarl.

Megan recognized his laugh. *He's the serial killer who abducted my son! The Mountain Mangler.*

Which meant, if the dream was right, she'd find Robbie in the cave.

She stepped sideways in sync with the man in front of her, matching his stride, watching his every move. She imagined a brick wall blocking him from getting into the cave where Robbie hid.

Small rocks, from the boulders surrounding the mouth of the cave, crunched beneath her feet until she stepped onto a small grassy area. She positioned herself so the cave and Robbie were behind her and the shack was behind him. She planned to keep it that way.

Bright sunlight streamed into the small clearing through the forest canopy. The Mangler intentionally slanted the knife in his hand against the sunlight and reflected it into her eyes, blinding her in an instant.

She looked down, blinking against the yellow spots left in her vision and saw a large branch lying on the ground near the forest's edge. She returned her gaze to the thin man.

A sword hilt stuck out of a scabbard secured to his back and there was a knife casing strapped around his leg. The antique weapons looked out of place with the red flannel shirt and black jeans. Had they been there a moment ago?

He lunged forward.

She ducked and rolled, sprang to her feet and ran for the stick. Grabbing it, she whirled to face him but faltered. She wasn't prepared for the pure evil in his eyes.

She couldn't wimp out now. She had to fight him. Robbie's life depended on using every skill she'd learned from her teacher, Zangar, in martial arts class.

His lips curled and a low growl rumbled from his chest. Her stomach lurched. A shudder of fear rocked her body. She'd seen that look before in her nightmares.

Robbie emerged from the mouth of the cave.

"Get back inside!" She lunged forward putting her body between the killer and her son. "Robbie! Go now!"

"Mommy!" Robbie cried, before darting back into the cave's depths. She turned back to the Mangler.

He shifted his weight and tapped the knife blade against his open palm. The leer on his angular face made him look gaunt. His lips curled in a smile, revealing yellow, rotting teeth.

She couldn't think about her actions. She rushed him swinging the stick. He twisted away and took the blow on the scapula. The impact sent a bone-jarring tremor up her arm. The sword rattled in the scabbard. Despite the pain from the last blow, she pivoted for momentum, swinging the stick full force at his head. It cracked when she connected.

He fell back a step.

Her confidence surged as he moved further from the cave and her son. She would not let him kill Robbie like he had the others.

He grabbed at the stick, missed and lost his balance. He retreated under her assault. She landed blows to limbs and head, driving him away further and further away.

Laughter rumbled deep within his chest. He rotated. She swung the stick but he blocked it with his forearm and slashed the knife down, gashing her hand.

She cried out as hot searing pain shot up her arm.

He pinned her with a stare. Yanking the stick from her grasp he slung it away. "Did you really think I'd let you win this little game?"

She stumbled backward searching frantically for another weapon. Blood flowed down her hand, dripping off numb fingers.

He grabbed her shoulders. Cold steel ripped into her skin right below the rib cage. He pushed the sharp blade down, slicing through the flesh to her hip. The burning hot

pain seared through her abdomen. Her shrieks of pain echoed through the forest. She couldn't breathe, her body shook and she gasped for air. She screamed again as he slowly pulled it from her body, laughing at her agony.

Megan clutched at the wound, a gush of warm blood filled her hands. Gurgling sounds rumbled in her throat and sweat broke out across her forehead. Wrapping around her, Death prepared to take her soul.

She looked at the killer.

She stared into dark brown eyes filled with concern, not evil intent. Detective Archer held her by the shoulders, not the Mangler. She was bent forward clutching her abdomen. She glanced down but blood didn't stain her stomach or hands. The vision had ended.

She straightened, dropped her hands and peered past Archer. Everyone in the police station had stopped working to stare at her. Lieutenant Randal watched her from his office doorway. Tall, muscular, black hair in a crew cut, Randal's wide stance and intimidating stature made him look more like a military commander than a policeman.

"Are you okay, Ms. Cassidy?" Archer asked, releasing her.

"Yes… I'm fine." She rubbed her eyes, pressing against the lids, trying to clear the scene from her mind without being obvious that this was a routine process.

"Come. Sit down," Archer said.

"No, really, I'm fine," Megan said.

"I insist." Archer guided her inside his office, shutting the door behind them.

Megan collapsed into a chair. The intense fight during the vision had exhausted her. Which was weird. Normally, she saw the scene play out. Visions took some energy but not a lot. They never affected her like this one had. Tired as she was, she could have been an active participant in the fight.

She looked up. Archer's stare bore into her.

"What happened out there?" he asked.

"You don't want to know." *You won't believe me any more than Randal did.*

"Yes, I do." Archer slid a chair over to sit beside her. "Why were you pressing on your eyes?"

He'd noticed? "To release a violent vision. I press my lids to clear my psychic third eye. If I clear it and project a calm happy scene I can let go of any negativity left from the vision."

"Very interesting. What was the premonition?"

"Does it make any difference? No one in this department will listen to anything I have to say, even when it's my son who's missing."

"I'll listen."

She studied him for a moment. He seemed sincere. "I saw where the killer is holding my son. It's in the mountains. There's a clearing with an old miner's shack and a cave. I fought with the Mountain Mangler. I'd die before I let him hurt my child."

Detective Archer studied her. "Are your visions always this intense?"

"What do you mean?"

"It's as if you weren't here. You moved, screamed even but I couldn't get you to respond to me."

"I'm connecting deeply because he has my child, so yes, the visions are more intense." She stood and walked to the door.

"Will you tell me the details?"

"Why?" Megan scrutinized Archer.

"I know Randal is giving you a hard time about the psychic stuff. I, on the other hand, have had some experiences of my own. I'm more open to things of a psychic or paranormal nature than anyone else in this department."

He might have some pull with Randal. Megan returned to the empty chair. She gave Archer all the details of every metaphysical incident she'd had about the case up to this point. He'd stopped her at the beginning to get a pad and pen for notes. When she got to the latest vision, she held back.

"I fought with the Mangler but he won the round." She wouldn't tell him she'd seen her own death.

"You're not going to give me the specifics of this latest vision are you?"

Megan shook her head. "Speaking words give them the power to manifest. I know I'm being superstitious but it's my belief. Let me use my abilities with the search teams."

"That's out of my control. Randal gave specific orders that you aren't allowed to work with them."

"Why not? What has he got against psychics anyway?"

"He's never said so I don't know," Archer laid the notepad on the desk.

"If we're done here, may I leave?"

"Where are you going?"

To find my son if I can get out of here. She pointed to the chair Randal had indicated earlier. "Right over there."

Archer nodded. "If you change your mind I'd like to hear about the vision."

"If I change my mind. Thanks for listening, Detective Archer. It's more than anyone else in this station would do." She strode across the room and plopped down in the chair. Archer watched her from the open doorway, Randal from another desk in the middle of the room. After a few moments both men went back inside their offices.

Hours later, there wasn't any more news. Randal and Archer had managed to keep her in their sights but now they joined several officers in a conference room. Megan glanced at the wall clock. Five a.m.

An officer shut the door to the meeting. Megan grasped the opportunity and headed for the exit. When Randal realized she'd left town, instead of going home as he'd instructed, he'd be furious. He'd probably want to kill her too. If the Mangler didn't do it first.

CHAPTER TWO

"MOMMY!" ROBBIE SCREAMED.

"Oh no!" Megan slammed on the car brakes and swerved onto the grassy shoulder. She threw the car into park. At least she'd gotten off the road this time before the vision hit her full force.

She gripped the steering wheel and laid her head against her hands. Behind closed lids, the blackness turned gray. Its fuzziness resembled a television station off the air. Suddenly, full color images filled the screen.

Looking down, Megan gasped at her blood-soaked hands and a wide gaping wound in her abdomen. Weakness wobbled her legs. Nausea rose in her throat, the taste of bile gagged her. She fell to her knees.

The killer stood over her. Horrible images of mangled bodies flashed through her mind. His burning anger at the previous victims overwhelmed her. He despised them, thought they were weak, useless, just because they were not the one he sought. Fury consumed his deranged thoughts. He spun away to stalk toward Robbie who stood at the cave's entrance.

Megan screamed, "Run, Robbie! Hide!"

Robbie fled into the darkness. The Mangler stopped. Turning around he settled an enraged gaze on Megan. "Now, you die."

Plunging the hunting knife into its sheath he yanked the sword from the scabbard on his back. The slick grating of metal on metal sent a shiver down her spine.

I must keep him from the cave.

The panicked thought drove her forward. Her eyes rolled upward with the pain and she almost passed out. Weak from the loss of blood, she clawed the ground, frantic to reach her son, to save him. Excruciating pain pierced her with every movement. She crawled forward, pushing her body to the limit.

A hard kick in the side knocked the breath out of her. Gasping for air she lost her balance and landed face first on the ground. He dug the toe of his boot under her rib cage and in one powerful movement flipped her onto her back. He pressed a booted foot against her chest.

Holding her down, he raised lanky arms high above his head, both hands clutching the sword's hilt. Muttering foreign words, he moved his foot from her chest to straddle her. She scooted backward on her elbows, pushing with her feet to escape. In two swift strokes he drew the sword down.

Her screams ripped from her. Intense pain racked her body under the slicing blade. He cut an X across her torso from shoulders to hips. Jerking her onto weak knees, he pushed her head forward and raised the sword high in the air to decapitate her.

If he kills me, I can't protect Robbie.

I won't let him hurt my only child.

Love and protectiveness for Robbie washed over her, pushing away the pain, filling her until she thought her heart would explode. Anger at the serial killer for abducting Robbie deepened, fought for a place in her heart.

Her eyesight expanded. Colors became more vibrant. Something shifted inside. Suddenly, she was floating above her assailant and could see everything around her.

This must be what death feels like.

Dark wings beat the air, giant talons dug into her assailant's shoulders, lion's claws ripped his chest. The flurry of motion spun her out of control. Her anger surged into a furious rage. Moments later the man disappeared beneath the animals' combined attack.

The scene changed to a fuzzy screen.

Megan jerked away from the steering wheel. Wave after wave of nausea churned her stomach.

Air. I need fresh air. When did it get so hot in here?

Her stomach heaved.

She popped the latches on the convertible top. Holding down the release button the motor whirred, the top lifted and bent back. The fresh chilly air cooled her skin.

Death waited within that madman.

She sensed an evil presence and twisted in the seat, peering over her shoulder, seeking the unknown. Only an empty road lay behind her. She looked into the trees. She couldn't shake the feeling that someone, or something, watched her.

Megan faced forward. Her imagination was working overtime, that's all it was. She rubbed her eyelids. The coldness of her fingertips took her mind from the murderous scene. She pressed down until she saw blackness. Moments later the lights in fuzzy shapes appeared. Darkness wiped her mind clean of the horrible scene.

She projected a new scene on the psychic screen within her third eye, one where she held Robbie in her arms, comforting him. She envisioned a glowing blanket of white light wrapping around his tiny body, protecting him, wherever he was. When it surrounded both of them she imagined it turning into a strong shield that could deflect any vibrations from entities wishing them harm. When the process was complete, she removed her fingers.

She'd never get used to violent premonitions but clearing the screen in her mind's eye grounded her. She didn't know if Robbie would feel her or not. She hadn't been able to connect telepathically with him since the abduction. It gave her hope to know that she'd tried to connect with him while erasing the negative images.

She opened her eyes. A large white wooden sign announced the entrance to town. She hadn't noticed it when she'd pulled over. Squinting against the early morning sun, she read the faded words.

Flatrock Creek.
Where Man Meets The Mountains.
Population 239
Home of the Talgorian Shifters
State Basketball Champions

They'd changed the name of the high-school mascot? The new name sent shivers down her spine. She couldn't think about that now, saving Robbie was the only reason she'd ever return here. Flatrock Creek had been her birthplace, her home and her heartbreak. Now it must be her salvation.

She looked into the valley at the sleepy little town. Old buildings lined Main Street. The forest butted up to their back doors. Its proximity was a little too close for comfort with a killer running free. She knew from experience how easy it was to slip in and out of the woods unnoticed.

A couple of city blocks outside town sat the ranger station. Wildcat Mountain's rounded peak rose into the sky. It was small compared to the other dominating peaks filling the skyline.

Megan needed the best search and rescue ranger in the state, someone with instincts bordering on psychic, even though he'd never admit it.

Brody Phelps.

I'm taking one hell of a chance.

He probably still blamed her. Otherwise why would he have refused Detective Archer's request? Even though the accident wasn't her fault, after all these years she still couldn't shake the remorseful feelings. She dreaded facing Brody. Since she'd left she'd tried to get up the courage to call, or write a letter. She'd been a coward and now it was time to face the consequences.

She wouldn't let Brody walk away from her again. Not this time, not when Robbie's life was at stake. And her own.

Shaky hands held the wheel. The sun warmed the leather but the chill of the premonition lingered. Slipping the car into gear, she eased it on the paved road and drove down the hill toward Flatrock Creek.

The breeze blew her ponytail, the pure scent of pine rode the crisp air, yet she grew even tenser. The clock on the dashboard said seven a.m. as she entered Main Street.

Everything looked the same. Frye's Pharmacy where she'd bought bubble gum, the malt shop that made the best chocolate shakes she'd ever tasted and the old farmers' hangout, Harvey's Hardware.

The dual lane road split on either side of the Town Hall, which sat on an island of land between the north and sound bound lanes. Recent construction had created a one-way circle around the old white building. The black sections of new pavement were in sharp contrast to the faded gray street. Flowers bloomed in decorative designs on either side of the wrought iron railings leading up the stairs to the front door. Megan glanced up at the bell tower on the Town Hall's roof, only to find a clock in its place.

Her heart sank. As a teenager she'd loved the bell tower. She remembered the first time she'd snuck up there. Brody had to convince her to be adventurous, playfully tugging when she resisted. They'd shared their first kiss beside the tarnished, old bell.

Life had been fun and carefree. She hadn't had any worries. In the seven years since she'd left Flatrock Creek, she'd struggled to make a good life for Robbie. It had been hard work but she'd succeeded, alone. Her thoughts drifted back to the police station.

Randal would be furious when he found out she'd heeded her

visions and snuck away to the Allegheny Mountains to find Robbie instead of waiting in Clarkston as bait. Archer might take her side though. She hoped he could make Randal understand why she'd left. That is, if Archer even got it.

I couldn't sit there, wasting time, any longer.

If only she didn't need a tracker she could find Robbie by herself. She couldn't find the clearing alone. She no longer knew these woods by memory. A lot of landmarks would have changed in seven years.

She glanced at the Town Hall in the rearview mirror. Turning her attention forward, Wildcat Mountain loomed on the horizon. The ranger station was a short distance away. Brody would be at work. She knew calling first would destroy any chance she had of gaining his assistance.

That was the problem. She knew. The police wouldn't listen to her. No one believed her.

Sadness washed over her. A good mother would never let anything bad happen to her child. She couldn't connect to Robbie and that worried her even more.

"Oh, Robbie. I love you, baby. Mommy's coming, you're not alone," Megan whispered.

Her stomach tightened and tears stung her eyes. *How could I fail my child?* She was strong in the face of adversity but this was the worst crisis she'd ever faced. When Brody broke off their engagement she'd gone into hysterics. Losing control hadn't gotten him back and it wouldn't save Robbie now.

Brody's words still hurt. *I hate you, Megan. Don't come near me again.* If she revealed the secret she'd kept from him the hatred would only deepen. She had to avoid that at any cost.

She wiped away an escaping tear, yawned and stretched her arm across toward the passenger seat. Her body ached from hours of high tension and lack of sleep. Even a catnap would lose valuable time. She had to force her body to stay awake.

The ranger station came into view beside a long narrow sign announcing the entryway into Edgewood National Forest. It reminded her of a ranch entrance. She turned into the building's parking lot, choosing a space away from the town-owned vehicles. She noticed the building sported new signage. It was now called Flatrock Creek Police and Ranger Station. She turned off the car, glanced at the clear sky and decided to leave the top down. She grabbed her brown purse from the passenger seat, exited the car and hurried toward the building.

BRODY PHELPS SIPPED coffee, which had gone cold long ago, while he flipped through the file lying open on the desk. The only excitement all week had been Owen Henderson's regular Friday night binge at Sheridan's Bar. He set the cup down to jot a final detail in Henderson's report and took the folder to the records room, filing it the tan cabinet labeled H-J. The bell over the front door jingled.

"Be right out." He slid the drawer closed and walked down the dimly lit hallway into the main office. Saturday morning sunlight poured through three large windows overlooking the mountains.

He blinked, waiting for his eyes to adjust to the brilliant light. A faint, fresh scent drifted to his nostrils, triggering a sliver of memory he couldn't place. It reminded him of springtime.

A slender woman stood with her back to him, looking out the windows. Tight jeans hugged curvaceous hips and a narrow waist. Her straight honey-colored hair with golden highlights was pulled back in low ponytail.

"What can I do for you, ma'am?" Brody asked, stopping a few feet behind her.

Instead of turning, she stiffened. Slender shoulders squared and her head lifted slightly. Brody frowned. Something about her was vaguely familiar.

Realization shot through him. *No, it couldn't be.* His heartbeat lurched and scorching heat seared through him.

"Megan?"

The woman cleared her throat and turned to face him.

"Megan!" Stunned, his jaw dropped but he quickly clamped it shut. Brody stared at her. The memories flooded back, making love, their engagement, the accident and the breakup. She didn't say a word but watched him with those brilliant blue eyes as if she had the power to penetrate him and see into his soul.

There was little resemblance to the glamorous psychic who appeared on television talk shows. Dark circles shadowed doe eyes and worry lines marred her classic beauty.

Brody shoved his hands into his pants pockets. "It's been a long time, Megan."

"How are you, Brody?"

Her voice sounded tense, not the carefree silky tone he remembered. Hearing the husky way she said his name made him think of the past and the desire they'd shared. Desire he buried years ago, that he'd rather not remember now. Her body was no longer the slim tomboyish figure of a teenager. Her curves begged to be touched.

Megan smiled softly.

Can she read minds? "I never expected to see you again. What brings you back to Flatrock Creek?" he asked.

"I need you, Brody."

"You need me?" He crossed his arms over his chest. "What the hell for?"

"It's Robbie. My son."

A son? So she had moved on, married and had a family. She'd been able to forget him so easily? She'd told him they'd be together forever, yet she'd wasted no time in finding someone else to love and have a family with. Resentment and jealousy stabbed at him. It was a feeling he hadn't experienced in years. "You have children?"

"Robbie…" She choked on the name. Her eyes filled with tears but she blinked them away. "I've kept him a secret from the media. I didn't want people to know about him because I was afraid someone would try to hurt him because of my job."

Brody stepped back. He had to distance himself from the memories, yet he couldn't stop staring at her.

"Why did you refuse Detective Archer's request?"

He frowned. "Robbie Cassidy is your son?"

Despite their past, or maybe because of it, her pain washed over him, clenching at his heart. He'd never forgotten how Megan had stood by him when his cousin, Arial, disappeared. When the police discovered the body he'd been devastated and angry. People shouldn't hurt little kids. He'd sworn to help children in danger and, as an adult, had become a ranger and a police officer. Arial's disappearance had upset Megan but she'd stayed strong for him.

Now her son was missing. He fought the unexpected longing to hold her the same way she'd held him back then.

He couldn't get involved with Megan again—not even to comfort her. Even though he'd sent her away, she'd always possessed his heart in a way he could never escape. Getting involved with her on any level would only bring pain back into his life. The accident had been Megan's fault because she'd misinterpreted her vision. If she'd been accurate he would have been able to repair the car and prevent the accident. His parents would still be alive.

He remembered the car's twisted metal. His heartbeat pounded harder thinking about the day his parents wrecked and the sadness of losing them both at the same time. His breathing quickened.

Megan's tired gaze held his. She wet her lips with the tip of her tongue. The feelings they'd shared had been nothing more than first love. It didn't matter how soft her skin looked now or how much her full lips begged to be kissed. She'd betrayed him and he wasn't ready to deal with Megan or her visions again. "Archer didn't tell me about you."

Megan stepped forward and grasped his wrist. The look in her eyes held a plea for help. "Brody, I need you. I'll even pay you to be my guide."

His skin burned under her touch. He wanted to pull her into his arms, plunge his tongue into her mouth and reclaim what had once been his. He should send her away and keep his sanity. "Archer will find someone to search for your son. I'm afraid you've wasted your time. Now, if you'll excuse me, I have to get back to work."

It took all of his self-control not to change his mind. He was acting like a jerk and couldn't stop. He tried to justify his actions by thinking of the wedding he had to attend this weekend. He really couldn't miss it. Besides, he never took time off work.

"Please don't send me away until you hear me out. Give me a chance to explain why you're my only hope."

Brody looked down at the slim fingers squeezing his wrist. She death-gripped his skin, her hold so tight the tips of her fingers had turned white. He looked into her eyes. The fear and pain he saw there pulled at his heart. His resolve slipped. How could he not lend a hand?

He pried her fingers from his wrist and then held her hand, caressing its softness. Looking up he examined her face. Something in her eyes captured his attention. Why did she have to stare at him as if he were the only person she could count on?

God help him, he was about to make the worst mistake of his life.

CHAPTER THREE

"OKAY, MEGAN," BRODY NODDED TOWARD THE lounge area, "sit down and tell me why you're here."

She entered the room. An overstuffed brown couch with two matching chairs, a plank coffee table and end tables added a sense of coziness to the police station. She sat on the couch clutching the purse against her abdomen.

What was Brody thinking? Had he wondered about Robbie's father? Or what her life was like now? Maybe he felt indifferent about seeing her again. She took a deep breath to calm her nerves.

Brody lowered all six foot two inches of his toned physique into a chair. She let her gaze move over his broad chest and down strong arms as the shirtsleeves tightened around muscles bunching beneath the fabric. A utility belt holding a two-way radio and other items clung to his narrow waist. *Man, he sure fills out that ranger uniform.*

Her heartbeat increased watching him settle into the chair. She fought the urge to go to him, bury her head against his neck and let him comfort her. It was all she could do to keep her seat. She wanted to lean on him, to feel his strength protecting her. She hadn't realized seeing him again would be this difficult.

Years ago he had wanted her love and she'd willingly given it. She remembered the time he'd playfully tickled her at the community barbecue, chasing her into the forest until they'd both tumbled onto the grass and into each other's arms. The day he'd asked her to marry him had been the happiest of her life, a joy eclipsed only by Robbie's birth. Brody had been her most trusted confidant until that fateful morning when the accident ripped their world apart.

She'd tried to get over Brody by dating other men but none had compared. She'd even convinced herself she didn't need a man in her life and Robbie's love was enough. Now she realized she'd only kidded herself. A love like theirs was rare. For a moment she allowed herself to wish for love again.

Brody watched her.

Instead of the baby-faced teenager who caused her to spin out of control, the man staring at her with such intensity was a stranger. His features were more sculpted and laugh lines creased the outer corners of his eyes. She knew she'd never be able to deny her feelings, even after all this time or the pain she'd experienced when he'd broken her heart. How much had he changed after his parents' deaths?

She searched for any softness in his eyes, an unclenching of his jaw, anything to indicate he'd forgiven her. She saw nothing to offer even a shred of hope.

Not that she'd expected forgiveness.

"I'm waiting, Megan."

She stared at Brody and twisted the purse strap. "It started eight months ago. A girl was kidnapped and two weeks later her mother was taken. They found both of them murdered in the Allegheny Mountains about twenty miles north of Clarkston. Two months later, a man and his teenage son disappeared. When, again two months later, a woman and her daughter were abducted, the Clarkston police realized they had a serial killer on their hands. They called in the State Police but neither department is saying much. The victims are always a parent and child, with the parent having some type of psychic ability and the killer cuts an X across their chest and decapitates them."

"The Mountain Mangler?" Brody crossed his arms over his chest.

"You have heard of him?"

"Archer wanted me on the search and rescue team with this case but you know that don't you? You came back to Flatrock Creek to see me because…"

"Yeah, I knew Archer wanted you on the team." She rubbed her face with her hands. "Brody, you're the best Forest Ranger in West Virginia and a trained police officer. You've been tracking these mountains your whole life. You know this area better than anyone and have proven it by finding eight missing people. If anyone can find Robbie, it's you."

"Have you been keeping tabs on me, Megan?" His eyes narrowed and the muscles in his jaw twitched.

Megan jerked her gaze from him. Heat rose into her cheeks under his scrutiny. She couldn't admit that was exactly what she'd done. "I saw you on television when you found the Anderson boy in the Allegheny's."

She met his stare but his expression remained cold. "You were quite a hero."

"This is out of my jurisdiction."

"Not as a ranger."

"What does Robbie's father say about your coming to me?"

"I'm not married so there isn't anyone else to consider. Please help me."

Brody stood and paced over to the desk.

Megan waited. She knew better than to pressure him. And because this concerned her, it wouldn't be anything less than monumental for him to agree.

He turned to face her. Indecision and something else flitted in his eyes. Images from their youth flashed through her mind, the accident, his anger.

Crap. I'm reading him. Megan tried to break the connection by imagining a brick wall between them. It didn't work. She looked away and thought of the serial killer taking Robbie. Anger took over and broke her psychic link to Brody.

"I'm sorry, Megan." He frowned. "I'm going out of town tomorrow. I can give you the names of other rangers who are good trackers. I hope you find your son."

"What? You must be kidding!" She wouldn't settle for a ranger who wasn't a natural tracker and didn't have the intuitive ability, instincts and dogged determination that Brody had. "This is unacceptable. Couldn't you cancel your trip?" Megan rubbed her temple. "You still resent me, don't you? I did not kill your parents."

"I don't want to talk about it."

"No." Megan stood. "We will talk about it."

She moved to stand in front of him, in case he decided to walk out on her—again. "My son's life is in danger. He may die. What about your promise to Arial? When she was murdered you swore you'd always find a way to help a child in danger."

"There's too much in our past. You'll be better off with someone who doesn't have our history."

"I don't want any other ranger. I want you. You're the best. You've got an instinct about this sort of thing—intuitiveness—even if you don't agree. Please, Brody. I haven't bothered you in all these years. The one time I ask for your professional expertise, not for myself but for my child—how can you refuse?"

"Because I have other commitments. I can recommend Ranger Thompson in Calgory. He's an excellent tracker." Brody reached for a pen and wrote something on a notepad. He ripped the page from the pad and held it out to her. "Here's his number. Tell him I referred you." He tossed the pen on the desk.

Dark brooding eyes bore into her. "Dammit Brody, Robbie needs you." Her anger swelled.

Brody turned away. When Detective Archer asked him to work this case it had been a hard decision to choose his cousin's wedding over work. He'd let her complaints influence him.

Now Megan needed him.

He wanted to be there for her, he really did but the risk to his heart was too great. Megan had torn his world apart once. He couldn't let history repeat itself. Not now, not ever again. "You only want to use me for my tracking skills just like everyone else. You only came to me because I know these mountains. You said so yourself."

Tracking was his job and he loved it. He didn't mind being used for work but with Megan it was different. He'd always hoped if he ever saw her again it wouldn't be work related.

"Brody, there's something—"

He threw up his hands. "I don't want to know, Megan. Whatever it is, it won't influence my decision. For once, why don't you accept you've made a mistake?"

"A mistake?" Megan stared into his eyes as she stepped toward him. So these were his true feelings. "I'm not too proud to admit when I'm wrong. But there's not a psychic on this planet who is right one hundred percent of the time."

For a moment he watched her. Megan hoped he was reconsidering his decision. Maybe he'd change his mind and search for Robbie.

"I know you're under a lot of stress. I'm not going to put myself in a position to be hurt by your *visions* again." He took her hand and pressed the piece of paper with the phone number into her palm. "I'm sorry."

"I don't want your sympathy, Brody." Megan backed toward the door, crushing the paper in her fist. "You told me how you felt seven years ago. I should have believed you. I don't know why I ever thought you would feel differently now. I'll handle this situation like every other one in my life—alone."

Megan jerked the front door open and slammed it behind her. She ran down the steps, fumbling with her keys. They slipped through her fingers, clattering onto the sidewalk. She scooped them up but dropped them again.

Anger boiled in her stomach, mixing with the ever-present fear. Tears clouded her vision. She snatched up the keys. Her heart beat so furiously she thought a heart attack was imminent. She paused to take a deep breath while visualizing her heartbeat decreasing. Once the rapid pounding and her breathing slowed, she continued down the porch.

And stopped dead in her tracks a few feet away from the car.

Her gaze narrowed on the child-sized, blue baseball cap lying on the Mustang's dashboard. The letters NY were stitched above the brim.

Oh God! Panic tore at her, catching her breath and shattering her. She ran to the driver's side door and leaned into the car for a better look.

Robbie, in capital letters, was embroidered in white above the adjustable clasp.

The killer's here!

"Give me my son!" Megan screamed and spun around, looking for him. "Damn it, show yourself, coward! Give Robbie back to me!"

Fear rose along her spine. The Mangler had followed her to Flatrock Creek! It was too soon. This meant his MO had changed. He wasn't waiting to come after her, which meant he could have already harmed Robbie.

Megan halted her frantic circling. Only a few feet separated the station from the trees. The Mangler must have disappeared into the forest.

She willed herself to slip into a semitrance and tapped into the psychic part of herself. She stood immobile, allowing her physical vision to go out of focus as she searched the woods behind the buildings across the street psychically, setting her mind free. In her third eye she moved quickly through the trees, watching them speed by in a colorful blur in her peripheral vision while she focused on the clear view directly in front of her. She searched everywhere for any trace of the killer's darkness or the sight of him fleeing through the forest.

She dropped the invisible wall she kept around her own emotions, making her vulnerable to others' feelings. She tried to connect with the killer's emotions. Apprehension and uncertainty immediately enveloped her, jerking her back into the ranger station and Brody. She imagined a wall around him to keep his emotions at bay. She'd deal with him later.

Megan traveled back into the forest, searching for any other negative emotions that might belong to the killer. If he were nearby, she'd be able to sense him.

Nothing! She turned and performed the same search in the forest behind the station. Projecting her mind forward again, she found an eagle feasting on a kill in a clearing, while a rabbit hid beneath a nearby bush—he'd narrowly escaped being the bird's breakfast. A little farther away, a large black and gold iguana peered at her from the top of a boulder. Her mind sped past the animals but the feeling of being watched caused her to backtrack in her mind's eye to the iguana's rock. The odd-colored reptile had disappeared. How did an iguana get out of its natural tropical habitat and into the Allegheny Mountains anyway? It probably escaped from the pet owner's cage. Megan scanned past the rock and further into the forest.

Megan's frustration melded with fear in her mind. How had the killer disappeared without a trace? At every turn she hit a dead end. It was as if he'd somehow blocked her psychic attempts to find him. She'd sensed this before, from other psychics. She did it herself to keep other psychics from reading her. If the Mangler could block her that meant...

The mental connection severed. She slipped from the semitrance to full consciousness. Refocusing her vision she examined the cap.

She fought the deep knowing filled with unthinkable possibilities. Was the killer psychic too? Moisture beaded her forehead, her body started to shake. The taste of bile filled her mouth, her stomach pitched and rolled. She pushed the feelings back down. She wouldn't throw up.

Megan slid down the side of the car and collapsed on the gravel beside the wheel. She covered her face with her hand. It was wet from tears. *When did I cry?*

The weight of the past hours—worrying about Robbie, arguing with the police and facing Brody had been tough. The Mangler had followed her, changing his MO. The possibility of a psychic killer—it was overwhelming. She grabbed her knees. She couldn't take any more. What had she done to deserve such a horrible fate? Pain and loss took control of her emotions. Tears poured down her face. She couldn't hold back anymore.

"My baby, my poor baby," she cried, rocking her body like she rocked him to sleep. "Someone, please, anyone! Help me find my son!"

CHAPTER FOUR

WHAT'S GOTTEN INTO YOU, PHELPS? BRODY WALKED back to the file room. He had to stay in control of his emotions. The shock of seeing Megan again made him weak.

He could easily cancel the trip. His cousin would get over it.

What am I afraid of?

Certainly not Megan. He should try to find the boy. If Megan's son ended up dead, he would wonder for the rest of his life if he could have prevented his murder. The guilt that he hadn't helped the boy would be more than he could bear.

Megan must have gotten pregnant right after leaving Flatrock Creek. She'd wasted little time in finding a new lover. The thought hurt. He'd always believed the love they shared was special but she'd never tried to come back to him once she left town. He realized now he'd expected her to.

Why hadn't she married the boy's father? Or was she divorced? Why did she feel that she handled everything in her life alone? Weren't her parents a source of support and comfort? Suddenly he realized there was a lot more to *this* Megan Cassidy than the young girl who left Flatrock Creek.

Screams tore through his reverie, sounding like they came from the parking lot. He bolted through the building and out the front door to find Megan on the ground shaking and crying hysterically.

He knelt down and grasped her by the shoulders, which were

slimmer than he remembered. He pried her hands loose from the hold she had on her knees, checking to see if she was hurt or bleeding anywhere. He released her and she clung to her knees again, rocking back and forth, sobbing uncontrollably.

"What the hell happened out here?" he asked. *She's not physically hurt. Something must have upset her.* Megan was a flaming spitfire minutes ago and now…

Brody's heart pounded. He stood and scanned both directions of the empty street. Everything appeared normal.

He knelt beside her again and searched her face. "Megan, why are you crying?"

Maybe it was a delayed reaction to his decision. She'd always been strong-willed and happy unless she cried over some poor stray she was trying to save. She never took unnecessary chances but was more the dependable, reliable type of girl next door. You could always count on Megan to do the right thing. In all the time he'd known her, he'd only seen her this upset once. It was when he'd broken up with her seven years ago. Overcome with his own pain and loss, he never listened to anything she'd said because he'd wanted her to suffer too.

Maybe he still did. Was that why he'd refused her?

What a jerk I am. How can I think of myself when she's in such pain? A feeling of revulsion swept through him. He'd always thought of himself as a stand-up guy. Someone others counted on. He hadn't treated Megan right but he wasn't willing to let her back into his heart yet.

Her sobs broke through his thoughts. Brody looked down. She shook so badly her teeth chattered. Her whole body spasmed in response to her choking sobs. He gently ran his hand up and down her back. "Megan, you have to calm down."

She broke into a coughing fit.

Was she strangling on her tears? Brody thought.

"I'm sure the officers working on your son's case will find

him." He trailed his fingers down her arm. Her skin was soft, as he remembered. When she stopped coughing, he lifted her chin. Glazed eyes stared past him. Damn. "Megan, don't do this to yourself."

He clasped her cold, trembling hands within his. He wanted to gather her in his arms and dry her tears. Tell her it was going to be okay. But he'd forfeited that right years ago. Now all he could do was find out what had happened to make her this upset. His pulse hammered. He noticed Megan's heartbeat throbbing in the hollow at the base of her throat.

Her sweet fragrance drifted on the air, awakening memories of their past. He remembered buying a bottle of honeysuckle body mist at Frye's Pharmacy for Megan's thirteenth birthday. He'd never known her to wear any other fragrance.

For a moment, he forgot the reason for their breakup and how empty life had been without her. He hadn't cared about her feelings when he sent her away because his own pain and loss had been so traumatic.

He hated seeing her cry like this, it was breaking his heart. He brushed a stray strand of hair out of her eyes. Even with her face flushed and wet with tears, she looked beautiful.

"Come here, ladybug, it's going to be okay." He drew her head against his chest, wrapping his arms around her shoulders.

Megan sobbed against him.

"Please don't cry. Everything will work out. Take slow breaths," he said.

His deep voice droning in her ears made her remember all the times he'd held her like this. The comfort of his embrace reminded her how much she loved him.

She raised her head.

Watery blue eyes filled with terror stared up at him. She shook and quivered in his harms. He ached to take away the fear. Holding her, breathing her scent, brought back feelings of the love they'd shared.

Brody hurt for her. He couldn't stand to see her suffering. He could only imagine how it felt to have your child abducted.

"Bro—Brody...he's here..."

"No, Megan, your son isn't here. You've been under a lot of stress."

"Not Rob...Robbie," she stuttered between sobs, "The Mangler."

"What?" Brody glanced around the parking lot. "I don't see anyone."

"He's come for me."

Panic stabbed at him. She was talking nonsense. He pulled Megan to her feet. When she stumbled, he slipped an arm around her waist, holding her close.

"Come on, we're going inside." He led her toward the station but she pulled away.

"No!" She swiped at the tears. "Not without the cap."

"What cap?"

"On the dashboard. It's Robbie's..." She looked toward her car and he followed her stare. Brody saw the Yankee's cap and moved toward the Mustang. "I'll get it for you, we'll take it inside."

"No!" Megan screamed and jumped between him and the car.

"Don't touch it, Brody," she whispered. "Robbie was wearing that cap when he disappeared. The Mangler put it in there while I was inside." Her lower lip quivered. "It's Robbie's favorite. He put it on every afternoon when he got to the school's car line where I picked him up."

Brody stared at her in disbelief, watching a tear trickle down her cheek. "The Mangler is in Flatrock Creek? You're sure about this?"

"Positive." Megan held his arm, searching his eyes for some sign he believed her.

The touch of her icy hand sent a chill over him. "Give me the keys," he said.

"I had them in my hand." She inspected the ground. "I must have dropped them."

"Check your purse and your pockets."

Megan reached in her pockets and seconds later pulled out a keychain.

"I don't remember putting them there." She dropped the keys into his palm but not before he saw how badly her hand shook. His heart wrenched. Another tear slipped down her cheek.

"You forgot. That's all." Brody used his most soothing voice. "Why don't you sit on the porch while I secure your car?"

Megan nodded. He picked up the purse from the ground and wrapped an arm around her waist. She leaned on him while he walked her to the steps. She stumbled but he kept her from falling.

Once he settled Megan onto the porch step, he headed back toward the car, removing the radio from his utility belt. He held it to his mouth and pressed the button. "Lancaster."

"Yeah, Chief?" The radio crackled.

"The Mountain Mangler could be in the vicinity, notify the deputies and contact the neighboring ranger stations—get the word out. I need you at the station and park on the street. I'll fill you in on the details when you get here."

"Ten-four."

Brody leaned into the car and opened the door with the interior handle being careful to barely touch it. It would be more likely that fingerprints would be found on the exterior handle so he didn't want to touch the car anymore than was necessary. He placed the key in the ignition and turned it but didn't start the engine. Using the top of his fingernail, he hit one button and the roof started moving into place. Holding down two window controls at a time the same way, he stared out of the windshield at Megan while the glass rose.

My God, she might lose her child. Truth was, the boy was

probably already dead. Brody's fingernail slipped from the control at the thought. He pressed it down again.

He couldn't even begin to imagine how she felt. Losing a child must be worst than losing a parent. *If I don't find Robbie while I have a chance, I'm neglecting my responsibilities like Megan did.* Thinking back on his parents' accident he realized she had tried to prevent the outcome she'd seen. He wasn't even making an effort to find her son.

She sat on the steps, rubbing her temples. A feeling of sadness for her washed over him. Maybe he'd been wrong to lay the blame on her all those years ago. She warned him and he'd believed her. In the end she had been wrong in her interpretation. In his eyes she'd used her so-called ability recklessly and because of her irresponsibility both of his parents were dead.

That situation solidified in his mind that psychic visions weren't real. If they were she would have known which car was going to wreck and his parents would be alive today.

Regardless of what her fans thought, Megan didn't have psychic abilities. No one did. She had an overactive imagination. How could he continue to hold her responsible for predicting what was impossible to know? He realized he had been too hard on her in their past.

He locked the top into place, removed the keys from the switch and locked the doors. Lancaster parked as Brody shoved the keys into his pants pocket.

"Sam, get the parking lot taped off and guard this car." Brody said when Lancaster approached. "The Mountain Mangler could be in Flatrock Creek so stay on the alert. Watch for anything unusual."

"Ten-four, Chief."

Brody went to Megan and tugged her to her feet. "Let's go inside."

She leaned against him until they reached the office.

Maneuvering her to the couch, he noticed her face was pale with harsh lines creasing her forehead.

"Wait here."

Brody brought back a soda from the refrigerator and hurried to the storage room, returning with a blanket. He was surprised to find Megan was no longer crying. She'd put the hair scrunchie around her wrist and was finger combing her hair.

"Drink this," he said, handing her the soda. "How are you feeling?"

"I'll be okay. My scrunchie gave me a headache" She reached in her purse took out a small, individual dose package containing two pain relievers and then twisted the soda top. "It's hard to think of Robbie alone with a murderer. I'm sleep deprived and tired but I'll make it through this. There isn't another choice."

He wrapped the blanket around slim shoulders, drawing it to her chest. She took the pills with a sip of soda.

"Look at us." Megan laughed halfheartedly. "You're wrapping me up in a blanket like you used to when we were together. Only this time it's not some poor animal I'm crying over."

Large eyes stared up at him, full of apprehension. He wanted to wrap his arms around her. Long ago he would have but not now. He no longer felt comfortable hugging her on impulse.

"Do you think…" She looked away. "Never mind."

"What?" He sat down beside her. "You can say it, Megan. Whatever it is."

"Could I have a hug?" Her voice wobbled.

Brody touched her cheek. He turned her face so he could look at her. Those beautiful eyes welled with tears again. He took the soda from her hand and placed it on the end table. "Come here."

She molded against him, wrapping her arms around his chest. He held her, savoring the sweet honeysuckle perfume. Her uneven breathing gradually steadied as she relaxed in his arms. The rapid pounding of her heart slowed. He ran a hand down her back, soothing her. She nuzzled her head in the bend of his neck, her breath hot against his skin. A familiar hunger swept over him. He wanted her, wanted to explore every inch of her.

Disgust ripped through him. How could he fantasize about Megan when her son was in such danger, maybe even dead? All she asked for was a damn hug and he couldn't stop thinking about how they'd been together.

He cared about her. Which made him vulnerable, weak. He reluctantly broke the embrace. "Better now?"

Megan nodded. Some of the tension had left her face.

"I need to call Clarkston so they can get someone up here."

"Do what you need to do. I'm fine now."

Brody went to his desk, sat down and dialed. When the call connected he gave his name and asked for Detective Archer. He watched Megan staring out the window into the mountains while he waited for dispatch to put the call through.

"Archer here."

"Hi Paul, it's Brody."

"Does this call mean you've changed your mind?"

"Not exactly. Megan's here."

"Oh boy. Randal reported her missing. He was pissed when Megan didn't go home as he'd instructed."

"I'd imagine so," Brody said. "We've had an incident here. The boy's cap was planted in Megan's car while she was in the station talking to me. She swears it wasn't there before. She said the kid had it in his backpack."

"*Shit.* The killer is there. She told us the same thing about the cap. I'll let Randal know and we'll have someone up there before noon. Meanwhile, keep an eye on her, Phelps. She isn't above putting her life on the line for her son."

"I know."

"Phelps?"

"Yeah?"

"Watch your back. This guy has no remorse. He isn't going to think twice about killing anyone."

"I understand. Goodbye."

He disconnected, dialed Doc Warner, explained the situation and asked him to come over and examine Megan. He watched her for a moment after he hung up. She'd always been so feisty, so full of fire. Now, she seemed beaten, the life gone out of her.

Picking up a notebook and pen from the desk he went to sit beside her on the couch. "A Clarkston detective will be here by lunchtime to examine your car. I know you're upset, Megan but I have to ask you a few questions about what happened out there."

"I understand." She nodded and drew the blanket tighter about her shoulders.

"Did you see anyone who could have put the cap in your car?"

"I didn't see anyone outside. The cap was just there. The killer planted it. I know he did."

Brody jotted down her answer. "Are you sure Robbie had the cap with him when he went to school?"

"I'm positive. He took it with him every day. It's his favorite. He put it on when he came outside to wait for me. I've already told the Clarkston PD all of the contents of his backpack." Her bottom lip quivered, a tear slid down her check.

"All right. Try to stay calm." He waited for a response but she was lost in thought. "Okay?"

She nodded.

"Did you drive straight through from Clarkston this morning?"

"Yes." Megan picked up the can to take a sip of soda.

"Did you notice anyone following you here?"

"It was pretty desolate. There wasn't anyone who drew my attention."

"Anything else you can tell me?"

"No, that's it." Megan's deep blue eyes met his gaze without reserve. "I'm sorry, Brody. For everything. I never meant to hurt you, ever. I loved you."

Several tears spilled before she looked down at her hands.

Brody's heart ached. She hadn't forgotten. Even now, with her child missing, she thought of the past between them. He laid the pad and pen down on the coffee table took her shoulders, turning her toward him. "Megan, you're in danger."

"I know."

She looked so devastated.

Brody lifted her chin. He knew what he had to do. "Look, I was a jerk when I broke up with you because I held you responsible for my parents' deaths. I understand that now. You couldn't have prevented the accident. I shouldn't have hurt you."

Megan set down the soda and wrapped her arms around his neck. She didn't believe him. He said the words but in his heart he still hadn't let go of the pain, he really didn't mean what he said.

Brody held her to him. Her scent and the softness of her hair against his cheek drifted over his senses reminding him of the summer days they used to spend together.

"Does this mean you'll go with me?" She pulled away.

"I think you'd do better with another ranger."

"I understand." Megan stood to leave.

Brody caught her and gently pulled her back down to the couch. "Sit down. You've been threatened and are probably in shock. Doc Warner is on his way over to check you out. I don't want you to leave until he says you're okay."

"I'll be fine."

"Don't be reckless, Megan. I can't let you go out there alone. If the Mangler is here, you're not safe."

"You really don't have a choice do you, Brody? You can't hold me here." She muttered, "This nightmare has just begun," as she stood and walked to the door. "I need time to think. I'll be back around ten to speak with the Clarkston officer and pick up my car."

"You've changed, Megan. You were never like this when we were together."

Megan laughed. "Did you really think I'd stay the same?" She suddenly became very serious. "Having a child changed me, Brody, especially when I raised him alone. Robbie is the center of my universe. Now a serial killer has taken him from me. I want him back and I'll do anything and I mean anything, to get him away from the murderer. Reckless or not."

"Megan—"

"I need some time alone, Brody. Don't worry, I promise to stay nearby." She offered him a small smile before walking out the door.

Dammit. The hardheaded girl had grown into a stubborn woman. He couldn't keep her at the station without reason.

It bothered the hell out of him.

He went to the window and watched her walk toward town. He pulled the radio from his hip.

"Lewis, what's your twenty?"

"Breakfast at Ernie's."

"Are you sitting in your usual spot?"

"Ten-four."

"Look for a blonde walking down the street from the direction of the station. She's wearing jeans and a green t-shirt. Bring her back here."

"What's going on, Chief?"

"I'll explain later."

"Do I know her? Is it someone local? Must be something exciting going on if both Lancaster and I are doing surveillance."

"Lewis!" Brody raised his voice. The young officer's excitement grated on his nerves. "It's not surveillance. Just do what I asked and get her back here, okay?

"Ten-four."

She's too stubborn for her own good. He'd protect her even if she refused to stay with him.

When he could no longer see Megan he dialed Doc Warner. Brody told him Megan was headed into town so he should go there instead of coming to the station.

Of all the people to reenter his life, why did it have to be Megan Cassidy? She was the only woman who could get under his skin and bring his emotions to life. He'd done a damn good job of burying all thoughts of loving her. After all these years, in a matter of minutes she'd taken his heart on a rollercoaster he hadn't ridden since she'd left town.

CHAPTER FIVE

MEAGAN KICKED A STONE TO RELIEVE THE BUILT-UP frustration. The Mangler had made his first move. He'd made her lose control and that made her hate him even more.

Then there was Brody.

Even though he said he released the grudge he'd held against her, it didn't mean he believed in psychics. If he thought of her the same way Lieutenant Randal did, he'd never look for Robbie. There was only one way to convince him for sure. She didn't want to go that route yet.

It was time for her to take back control of her emotions. Okay, granted, she'd had a small breakdown a few minutes ago, well, it had been more like a big scene but she had to move past the negative emotions, refocus and connect to her inner strength.

She'd let this serial killer get into her head. She'd reacted to him and it had drained her. It was time to reclaim her strength from this crazed lunatic who was mentally sucking her dry. She needed a quiet place to be alone for a few minutes so she could connect with her higher self within the light.

She glanced around to make sure no one followed her before darting between two buildings. She ran behind them and into the forest. Locating a sunny spot underneath the tall pines she stood in the center. *This place will work.*

She tilted her head back, letting the sun's warmth drift over her. She called for protective white light from the Universe.

Imagining it close around her, she leveled her head to face forward. With her eyes shut, she allowed the light to penetrate through the crown chakra at the top of her head. As she visualized her body filling with white light, she grew stronger. A slight breeze drifted over her bringing with it the crisp clean scents of nature. Through her feet the power of the earth crept upward, flowing into her. She psychically called to her spirit guides for assistance and protection.

She focused her attention to opening the doorway to the psychic realm by clearing all other thoughts from her mind. She asked her guides to deliver the vision that would lead her to Robbie.

Blinding currents swirled around her. She slipped to a trancelike state filled with emotions.

Love. For Robbie.

Energy. To hunt a killer.

Power. To defeat the enemy.

Megan waited. Moments later her psychic screen became fuzzy with swirling colors as the vision unfolded.

The mouth of a cave appeared, fifty yards ahead was an old shack with vines covering one side. A dead tree lay in front of the door.

She saw him through the small broken window of the shack He wore an oversized dark flannel shirt with a hood and tight black jeans. He stood with his back to her, leaning over a makeshift table.

The sound of metal striking against flint as he sharpened a knife contrasted with his low whistling.

She watched as a dark, negative power swirled around him. Raising the knife into the air, he observed his handiwork and drew the weapon back, slicing the air with the steel blade, creating waves in the energy.

A sense of satisfaction exuded from him, twisting the aura around him until its color became pitch black. His body became the vortex in a whirlpool of evil power. Suddenly she realized the knife was meant to kill her. She tried to get a look at his face but he turned away.

As if he knew she watched him.

He couldn't. Could he?

Unless...

She had sensed him blocking her psychic search earlier. Could his psychic abilities equal or surpass her own? Chills shook her from head to toe. Deep bone-jarring chills that only came in response to truth.

She took a deep breath, watching the scene in front of her, knowing now with certainty the Mangler was a powerful psychic too.

Bony fingers with black fingernails caked with dirt grasped the edge of the hood. He pulled it lower over his head.

Dirt? Or is it dried blood? Megan thought.

Turning in her direction, he exited the shack, raised his arms and began to waltz alone.

Let's dance, Megan. He laughed, deep and hollow, its evil intonation echoing through her mind. *Three have failed the psychic challenge. Are you the one the Prophecy predicted? Can you save your son?*

If it's a challenge you want, Mangler, Megan sent the thought telepathically, *you have it. What prophecy?*

Ah, you don't know.

Where is my son?

He gestured toward the cave then back to the shack as he continued to dance around.

You're crazy. You won't win, Megan shouted. *Why in the hell are you dancing around like a lunatic? Stop it! Answer me!*

He jerked the hood from his head, revealing only darkness where his face should be. *Don't be so sure of yourself, Megan Cassidy. The others called themselves psychic too but couldn't defeat me. It's your move.*

The scenes vanished from the screen in her mind's eye. All that remained was the gray static.

Megan pulled the protective light closer. Its heat moved through her, rushing to her shoulders and up the back of her neck. It traveled into deep muscle tissue as it massaged and worked away the tension held within her body. Leaving her invigorated and refreshed.

Somehow he was affecting her visions, connecting to her on a psychic level, only allowing her to see what he wanted her to see. She pushed away his negativity, visualizing it being replaced by a force field around her, which couldn't be penetrated.

She opened her eyes and headed back toward Main Street. It was time to gather the few supplies she needed and then, with or without Brody, she was going after that son of a bitch. The thought of him putting his hands on Robbie enraged her.

Empowered and feeling full of life, she left the forest intent on defeating a killer.

TEN MINUTES LATER Megan pushed open the door to Frye's Pharmacy. A bell tinkled. The store smelled lemony clean. The scent immediately threw her back to summers spent confiding in Auntie Faye about the crush she had on Brody, which had blossomed into full-fledged love.

The drugstore hadn't changed. It was as if time had stopped. She moved through the aisles picking up several items. In the back corner sat the old pinball machine. Megan ran a finger across the cool glass top. She and Brody had played this game for hours. She'd been so excited the first time she'd beaten him. In the midst of her celebration dance he'd blurted out, "I love you." She smiled at the happy memory.

Megan made her way to the cash register. She laid down baby wipes, eye drops and a small container of tissues on the counter, pulled out her wallet and waited.

A head full of gray hair passed by the little glass window of the pharmacy. A few moments later a short, sturdy woman in her early seventies walked around the corner to the register.

It was Mrs. Frye, the local pharmacist, whom she always called Auntie Faye.

"Nice morning we're having, isn't it?" The older woman smiled at Megan and wiped her hands on the flowered apron covering a blue striped shirt and brown khakis.

"Yes, it's beautiful." Megan nodded.

Would Auntie Faye recognize her without her glasses on? They hung around her neck on a silver chain. She was as blind as a bat without them.

She set the glasses on her nose, picked up each item and rang the price into the register. "That'll be five-twenty."

Megan fished out the money and handed it over.

Auntie Faye took the bill, glanced at Megan as she made change. She put the change in Megan's palm. Recognition lit up her eyes. Auntie Faye grabbed Megan's hand, money and all. "Well, land sakes alive!"

Smiling softly, Megan stared at Auntie Faye. "Yes?"

"In all my born days, I never thought I'd see you again, Megan Cassidy." She scooted around the counter and wrapped Megan in a big bear hug. "Child, you're a sight for sore eyes. Where have you been? You're looking good. Well, maybe not too good. What's wrong, honey? Your eyes are puffy. Have you been crying?"

It was as if she'd never left.

"A little."

"Well, you ain't been in Flatrock Creek that's for sure! Come on over here and sit with me, like you used to do. I'm in the middle of filling Landsley's blood pressure medicine but you go right ahead and tell Auntie Faye all about whatever brought tears to those pretty blue eyes."

Auntie Faye walked into the pharmacy behind the counter. When Megan didn't follow she came back to take her by the hand. "I said come on, child. We've got some catching up to do."

Megan allowed herself to be dragged along by Auntie Faye, as she'd always done.

Even though Auntie Faye wasn't blood related, she'd always been like a second mother and best friend. Megan could sure use a friend about now.

"There's your stool, now sit," Auntie Faye said.

Megan ran her fingers over her name engraved on the top of the seat. Auntie Faye had let her carve it with a buck knife when she was ten years old.

The woman pushed her down onto the seat and scrutinized every inch of her. "How you been, sweetie? I've missed our chats."

"Auntie Faye, you haven't chatted with me in seven years." Megan laid her package on the worktable.

"That doesn't mean I haven't missed you." The older woman put her palms on either side of Megan's face. "You were like a daughter to me until your family left town. I never heard from any of you... Well, it doesn't matter. I'm so happy you're home."

Megan squeezed Auntie Faye's hands. "I'm sorry I didn't write. I had to make it on my own. I missed you too."

It was the truth.

"We womenfolk need to talk this out." She released Megan, pulled up another stool and sat. "Now you tell Auntie Faye what's wrong."

"I'm sorry, I don't want to burden you. It's been a rough day."

"Hogwash. There's more to it than that. You're just not telling me."

Megan examined Auntie Faye. She'd aged gracefully. Her hair was nearly white except for the back, which was a darker shade of gray, not the dark brown she remembered. Wrinkles lined a jovial face, round from excess weight. Auntie Faye's green eyes held concern as she peered over the deep rose frames of her reading glasses. They'd never had secrets between them. She'd talked to Auntie Faye about everything, including Brody.

"Brody still lives here," Auntie Faye said, as if reading her mind.

"Yes, I know." Megan nodded. "I saw him this morning."

"How'd he take seeing you again?"

"Not well, I'm afraid."

"Menfolk! Sometimes I wonder why they are the way they are." Auntie Faye winked at her. "They're like grapes, sometimes sweet, sometimes sour. You never know what you're gonna get until you taste 'em. It's what I always say."

Megan grinned. "Yes, you've always said that."

"Don't let him upset you. He'll come around." Tipping her head a bit to the side, she pushed her glasses back on her nose, so she could study Megan. "He's the reason you came home, isn't he?"

"Not the way you think." She didn't really want to get into details with Auntie Faye. "I'm here because I asked Brody to track my son."

"Your son? I didn't know you had a boy."

"I've kept him out of the media. A serial killer has abducted him. The police are trying to find him but they won't let me use my abilities to search for him."

"Your child is missing? Oh my word, Megan!" Auntie Faye grabbed her hands. "This is terrible, terrible news, honey. What can I do?"

"There's nothing you can do, Auntie Faye. It's up to the police. Thanks for the offer."

"Brody's our Chief of Police now and he's still working as a ranger. Nothing much goes on around here so it's easy for him to handle both jobs. He's dang good too. Nobody messes with him. Especially when he gets all broody." Nodding her head to agree with herself, Auntie Faye stood up and went back to work on the prescription. "If you've got Brody on your side, you'll find your son. What's his name? How old is he?"

Megan hesitated. "His name's Robbie."

Auntie Faye stopped to stare at her. "And he's how old?"

She'd never known Auntie Faye to sidestep an issue. Megan looked down at her shoes. Lying only created problems. She lifted her gaze and met Auntie Faye's knowing stare.

"Brody's middle name is Robert. Robbie wouldn't be short for Robert, would it?"

Megan swallowed.

"That boy of yours is six ain't he?"

Megan glanced away.

Auntie Faye nodded. "Well, never you mind. Brody said yes, didn't he?"

"No, ma'am." The feeling of being thirteen years old again filled her. She remembered when Auntie Faye had explained the facts of life at her mother's request.

"Megan Cassidy, you look at me, child."

Megan turned her gaze back to the older woman. Auntie Faye stood a few feet away, hands propped on ample hips.

"You were never good at keeping secrets from me, Megan. Don't you worry. I'm not going to tell anyone. If you need Brody don't you give up, you hear? He's too stubborn for his own good. I've been telling him since he was born. Don't let his standoffish ways bother you. He's too macho for his own dang good sometimes."

"Yes, ma'am." Megan's mouth tilted in a grin. "You haven't changed a bit."

"Who me?" Auntie Faye wiped her hands on her apron out of habit. "I'll never change. Who'd run this town?"

She put the lid on the plastic bottle, dropped it in a bag and tossed it into a nearby bin. "You're world famous now aren't you?"

"No, not quite." Megan picked up her package.

"Can't you use your psychic powers to find Robbie?" Auntie Faye leaned her hip against the counter and using both hands, pushed stray hairs away from her face.

Megan grimaced. When people referred to her abilities as powers it made her uncomfortable. They were a gift. While they were empowering, the term powers reminded her of superheroes.

If the last vision was any indication, she would need superhero powers this time.

"That's the problem, Auntie Faye. I can see the area where Robbie is but I can't get to him. That's why I need Brody. He knows these mountains."

Auntie Faye leaned in to whisper, "That's not all you need from Brody." Merriment danced in her eyes. She gave Megan an exaggerated wink.

"Auntie Faye!" Megan shook her head but grinned at the older woman. "All I need from Brody Phelps are his tracking skills. Besides, he already refused so I'll find Robbie by myself. I just need a plan."

"You shouldn't be traipsing around those mountains alone. It's not safe, especially with the poacher problems we've had lately. Larry Tate, our local animal rights activist, said this is the worst poaching he's seen in years. He goes out every day trying to catch them on film so Brody can arrest them, bless his heart. So you can't be too careful out in those woods. Now if you had a gorgeous hunk of a man with you, I bet you'd find your son and a few more things, like love, along the way."

Auntie Faye was already matchmaking. "I don't think I'll find love again." *And definitely not with Brody.* "I'd like to stay and talk all day, Auntie Faye but I've got a few more stops to make. I just arrived in town and have more supplies to purchase."

"Okay, sweetie. Where are you staying?"

"I'm not staying in town. I have to find Robbie. The only reason I'm not in the mountains already is because…never mind."

"Oh, Megan. I hate to see you hurting so. Why don't you come to my house, I'll cook you up some lunch before you head out. I'll call in someone to run the store so I can take care of you like I used to do."

Megan glanced at the clock on the wall. She was losing valuable time now that the Mangler had made his move. "I'm sorry. Maybe another day? I wanted to be in the mountains by lunchtime."

The pained look and the love shining in the old woman's watery eyes grabbed Megan's heart and twisted. She missed the feeling of family, of belonging, of just being important to someone.

"I have to find my son, Auntie Faye. I can't live without him." Her voice cracked, its tone husky with emotion. "I have to go."

"If you change your mind, or if there's anything, anything at all I can do, you just let me know." She pulled Megan into a tight embrace. "It's so good to see you. Even under these horrible circumstances."

"It's good to see you too." Megan stood, picked up the package and turned toward the exit.

"I'll walk you out." Auntie Faye stepped around Megan. "How're your parents?"

"Fine." As far as she knew.

"You tell them Faye Frye said hello. They should come see me sometime."

"The next time I talk to them, I will."

Who knew when that would be? She rarely talked with them anymore. Their strict code of ethics prohibited a baby out of wedlock. It was against all they believed in. They didn't even acknowledge her career as a psychic. None of their friends even knew they had a daughter much less a grandchild.

Except for Robbie, she'd had been alone in the world since leaving Flatrock Creek. Auntie Faye's sincere welcome warmed Megan's heart.

"Howdy, Faye." A gruff voice said.

Megan recognized Doc Warner's booming baritone.

Both women looked toward the sound. Sure enough, Doc Warner waited in the main aisle. His tall thin physique didn't fit his deep voice. In jeans and a dress shirt his thinness was very apparent. Megan thought he looked a bit like a scarecrow. He held a black medical bag by his side.

A vision flitted though her mind. Brody had sent Doc Warner to check her out. Beside him stood a deputy in a dark green uniform, hat in his hand. He nodded when Megan looked at him.

"Hi there, boys. Lovely morning isn't it?" Auntie Faye hooked her arm through Megan's.

"It sure is, Faye," Doc Warner said. "It's great to have you back in town. I was beginning to think a Monocath had taken you."

"Oh fiddlesticks! Why would those monsters want me?" Auntie Faye gave Lewis a slow knowing look. "Besides, they surely wouldn't stoop to killing elders."

"Good thing it's a myth then. I'd hate to see one of them go up against your feistiness. They'd be sure to lose." Doc Warner laughed and moved closer to Megan. "Look at you, Megan Cassidy, all grown up. Don't let this talk about the area myths and legends bug you. Since we changed the school mascot it seems that's all anyone wants to talk about. It's a running joke around here. So, you're a famous psychic now aren't you?"

"Psychic, yes. Famous, sort of. Brody shouldn't have called you." She reached out to shake his hand. Joke or not, thoughts of the myth sent chills over her. She couldn't remember how the story went and she wasn't about to ask.

"Now, now, did I say Brody called?" He held her hand for a moment too long, as if assessing her condition without being obvious.

"I sense he did." She raised an eyebrow at the deputy. "You too?"

The deputy nodded. "Yes, ma'am. Chief Phelps wants you back at the station."

"How about I take a quick look at you first, Megan? I want to make sure you're not in shock," Doc Warner said.

He was one of the best doctors she'd ever known. Kind and caring. "I'm feeling much better. Talking with Auntie Faye helped."

Auntie Faye went behind the counter and brought out a small chair. "Here sweetie, you sit down." She guided Megan down into the seat. "I'm glad you stopped by, Doc. She looks mighty pale to me."

"You're not going to let me out of this are you?" Megan handed the parcel to Auntie Faye.

"It'll only take a few minutes." Doc set his bag on the counter and then removed a stethoscope and penlight. He listened to her heart, examined her pupils, checked her pulse, pressed her fingernails and looked inside her mouth.

"All done?" Megan started to stand but Auntie Faye pressed down on her shoulder with a firm hand.

Doc Warner put his equipment back into the bag. Leaning against the counter, crossing his arms, he appraised her. "Tell me why you were so upset earlier."

"I'm sure Brody already filled you in." Without a full rundown from Brody, Doc wouldn't have come looking for her.

"Yes but I need to assess your emotional state. And the only way I can is if you talk to me."

Megan stared at the three people watching her. Suddenly the room seemed very small and crowded. The air grew warm and stale. Its weight bore down on her, suffocating her. Her heartbeat pounded in her ears. She took a calming breath, working hard to control the claustrophobic feeling.

The state of her emotions would stay buried deep within, not shared with people who meant well but no longer knew the woman she'd become.

She patted Auntie Faye's hand. She stood and took her package from the older woman. "My son's missing, Doc. I appreciate your concern but I can't discuss the investigation. I really should be going."

Megan strode to the front door but paused to glance over her shoulder to find the Deputy on her heels. She looked past him to the two people who, long ago, had been important influences in her life. "Auntie Faye, Doc Warner, thank you for everything. It really is great to see you both."

They smiled and nodded.

Once outside, Megan started toward the station. Buying supplies would wait.

"Ms. Cassidy, my patrol car is this way."

Megan stopped to face him. "What's your name?"

"Deputy Lewis, ma'am." He placed the hat on his head and waited.

Megan sensed he was a man of high morals and ethics. He was tall, muscular and handsome. "What's your given name?"

"William but most folks call me Bill."

"Well, Bill, I appreciate you're following orders but I walked here and I'll walk back. You go on ahead. I'll meet you there."

"Sorry, Ma'am, I can't. I have strict orders to accompany you back to the station."

Megan studied him for a moment. His hands rested easily against his leather utility belt, obviously a very patient man. A crisp breeze ruffled her hair. "I respect your orders, Bill but I'm walking."

She took a step away but stopped to face him. "The transfer you've been considering, Bill?"

His eyebrows raised in surprise. "Yes, ma'am?"

"It's a good move for you. You'll find love with a brunette named Ria."

Deputy Lewis pushed his hat back on his head. "How'd you

know about my transfer request?"

"I'll meet you at the station, Deputy." Megan smiled at him then walked off at a brisk pace, leaving Deputy Bill Lewis standing on the sidewalk with a puzzled look on his face.

CHAPTER SIX

BRODY PACED ACROSS THE PROCH, WAITING FOR THE Clarkston Forensics team to arrive. A half hour ago he'd sent Lancaster back on patrol and taken over the watch. He glanced down the street for what must have been the hundredth time.

Lewis should be back with Megan by now.

He lifted the radio from his utility belt, held it to his mouth and pressed the button. The FCPD patrol car came into view, rolling slowly down the street. Megan walked along beside it. Her long strides ate up the sidewalk, her hair blew behind her in the slight breeze and she had a bounce in her step. She looked full of life.

He returned the radio to the belt. This was the strut he remembered. Megan had always bounced when she walked.

One thing hasn't changed, he thought, glancing at the patrol car she refused to ride in. She's still stubborn.

What had happened since she left the station to cause such a change in attitude? A strong air of confidence radiated from her. The defeated woman he'd seen earlier was gone.

This was the Megan from his past. His Megan.

Who am I kidding? She quit being my Megan the day I sent her away.

Brody thought back to the day before his parents died. She'd gotten a vision and been adamant to check the brakes in his old tan Buick. They'd taken it to the mechanic only to find the car was in good shape.

If she had forced him to check his parent's tan Ford too, the failed brakes wouldn't have sent them spiraling off the mountainside. Megan should have realized she'd misinterpreted her vision when the uneasy feeling hadn't gone away.

After their breakup and hours of research, he'd developed a better understanding of how psychics were supposed to receive their information. He still wasn't convinced any of it existed in reality. He'd never known anyone who could give him an accurate reading. God knows he'd tried.

None of the readings he'd gotten after their breakup had been accurate or proven psychic abilities were real. In fact, they'd only solidified his opinion that all psychics were frauds.

Deputy Lewis parked the car and walked to the porch, stopping beside Brody. "Why would Ms. Cassidy tell me that my transfer request would lead me to Clarkston and love with a brunette named Ria?"

Brody stared at Lewis. "Megan told you that?"

"Yes. Maybe I should look her up online."

"Look up Ria?"

"No, her—Ms. Cassidy."

"Don't bother. She's a world-renowned psychic if you put any credence in all that New Age mumbo jumbo."

"Really?" Lewis grinned. "My grandma had the sight but she used the cards. I've never known anyone who just blurted it out like that. Cool."

Brody scowled at him. "I don't want to hear it."

"You knew my grandma. Didn't she tell you the past would come back to you twofold?"

Brody remembered the reading all too well. It had been a trying day and he'd had a couple of beers at Sheridan's. Mrs. Lewis saw him leaving the bar and convinced him to come to her house for a reading. After the breakup with Megan, he'd been curious if the old woman could tell him anything with accuracy. She lived nearby so he'd agreed. "Yeah, she said it would be my own fault. Don't be gullible, Lewis. That stuff isn't real."

"The hardheaded woman walking toward us, was she in your past?"

Brody watched Megan getting closer, noticed the quick sashay of her hips, the fluid motion of her body. He'd never seen a more beautiful woman. "Don't you remember Megan?"

"Can't say I do. I'm five years younger than you. I recall grandma's reading though. Overheard the whole conversation from the living room."

Brody scowled but kept Megan in his sights. "What your grandma said was a generalization that could be true for anyone."

"You didn't answer my question."

"I was engaged to Megan when we were in high school." Brody jiggled the coins in his pocket. "Satisfied?"

"No. Grandma said it was your fault. What'd you do?"

Brody glared at him.

"Never mind." Lewis held his hands up in defeat, chuckling as he backed toward the door. "Be careful, Chief. I've never known grandma's predictions to be wrong."

"I've never known any psychic to be right."

"Well, we'll see. Some predictions take a while to happen. She's a pretty one. I'll be inside, finishing some paperwork, if you need me."

Megan took the steps two at a time and stopped beside Brody as Lewis shut the front door. "Have you heard from the Clarkston officer?"

"Should be here any minute." A sweet scent drifted on the breeze to tantalize his senses.

Megan's perfume.

The sooner she left town the better. These constant reminders of times past interfered with his concentration.

Megan laid a steady hand on his arm. "Brody, we have to talk."
Words he did *not* want to hear.

Crystal blue eyes, serious and focused, gazed at him. "Megan, we've been through this already."

"No, there's more. You have to know everything before I leave, in case something happens to me."

Brody's pulse leaped. What else could there be? From the intense look she gave him, he wasn't sure he wanted to hear what she had to say. Megan spoke as if she knew the Mangler would succeed in taking her. He wouldn't let anything happen to her, of that much he was sure. "We can go inside."

A dark sedan pulled up in front of the station with West Virginia tags and stopped beside Deputy Lewis' patrol car.

"No, not now," Megan said. "After the Clarkston team leaves."

Brody walked down to meet the officers with Megan. A tall muscular man with a dark crew cut stepped from the car. His features hardened when he looked at Megan. A thin man exited the passenger side.

"Good morning, Lieutenant Randal." Megan fisted one hand on her hip and held the paper bag in the other. "I didn't expect to see you here."

"There's no way I'd let some so-called psychic mess with my officers' minds. You should have stayed in the station."

Randal grasped Brody's hand in a firm shake. "Chief Phelps, I'm Lieutenant Travis Randal and this is forensics specialist, Officer Michael Tanner. I told Detective Archer I'd personally see to this. What have you got here?"

"The Mangler put Robbie's hat in my car." Megan stepped closer to Randal. "He's here and I'm next. Have you gotten any more leads? Anything to lead you to Robbie?"

"I was not talking to you, Ms. Cassidy. Now, if you'll please excuse us, this is a crime scene. We can't have civilians contaminating the evidence. I need to discuss this case with Chief

Phelps."

"I'm not going anywhere." Megan stepped closer.

Brody grabbed Megan's arm and pulled her back beside him. "Why don't you go inside while I talk to these officers? We can do this faster if you don't antagonize Lieutenant Randal."

"I'm staying right here."

"Okay, Megan," Brody said, "but you have to be quiet and let us work."

"Doesn't mean I'll like it." Megan stared down the Lieutenant. "His MO has changed, you know."

"I realize that, Ms. Cassidy." He opened his cell phone. "Should have known there wouldn't be any reception up here in the boonies." He pressed some buttons and held the device to his ear.

Brody stared at Megan. God, she was beautiful. He'd forgotten how those blue eyes could throw daggers. She stuck her voluptuous chest out, ready for a fight, accentuating her curvy figure even more. His heart beat a little harder as he watched her. A brief image of her naked underneath him clouded his mind.

"The boy's hat is in the car?" Randal said, putting the phone back into his pant's pocket.

"Cap. His *cap* is in the Mustang on the dashboard." Megan snapped the words at him. "When I arrived I only had the few items you see lying inside my car and a trunk full of camping supplies. Robbie's ball cap wasn't in there. I told you about it in the statement I gave when he was abducted."

Megan's voice pulled Brody back into the moment. "I secured the car and had a deputy tape off the perimeter until you could get here."

"Keys, please." Lieutenant Randal extended his hand.

Brody took them from his pants pocket and dropped the small ring into Randal's outstretched palm. Officer Tanner retrieved a black case from the sedan's trunk. As Tanner turned toward the

Mustang, Megan's words sank in. "How has the Mangler's MO changed?"

"Once he kidnaps the child, he usually waits two weeks before abducting the parent. In each of the past cases he's waited exactly seven days before he started terrorizing the second victim. It's how this guy gets his thrills." Randal jiggled the keys. "Robbie was taken yesterday afternoon around two. We're within the first twenty-four hours and he's already on the move for Ms. Cassidy. He's not waiting a week like he did in all the other murders. It's not a good sign."

"You're sure he'll target Megan?"

"Obviously he already has." Lieutenant Randal put on a pair of gloves and went to assist Tanner.

Brody stayed with Megan behind the tapeline. The fewer people on the crime scene the better until all the evidence had been collected.

He scanned the area in case the Mangler was hiding out nearby, watching the activity. He radioed his staff to check on their progress but they hadn't found anything or anyone out of the ordinary.

A while later the Clarkston officers began packing up their gear, returning it to the trunk of the sedan. Lieutenant Randal approached Brody and Megan. "We found some fibers and a few prints which probably belong to Ms. Cassidy. I'm taking the cap, a tissue, soda and a small stick we found in the car."

"May I touch the cap before you take it?" Megan asked. "I might pick up something."

"You're kidding, right?" Randal rolled his eyes.

"I wouldn't joke about trying to find my son." How could Randal be so ruthless? He didn't consider her feelings at all and in her mind that made him a terrible cop. He hadn't even proven to her yet that he could do his job right.

"You'll contaminate the evidence if you touch it. Sorry."

"When will you have your report?" Megan crossed her arms in front of her.

"Like I've told you before, Ms. Cassidy," Randal said in an even tone, "if we have a break in the case I'll notify you. Meanwhile, I suggest you return with me to Clarkston so we can put you in protective custody until you're needed."

"For bait? You know... I've changed my mind about that. Robbie is not in Clarkston. He's here in these mountains." Megan flung her arms in the air, indicating the towering range around them. Frustrated, she paced between Randal and the dark sedan. "I've told you where he's is a hundred times if I've told you once. I don't understand why you refuse to listen to me."

"We're not going over this again. I don't believe in your harebrained psychic abilities, period. They do not belong in any investigation I'm conducting. You need to accept the facts because I'm tired of hearing about what you imagined happened to your son. If you refuse our protection you're on your own. We'll be in contact when we're ready to lure in the perp."

Megan stiffened. *This is like talking to the air.* No matter how hard she tried, she couldn't get through to Randal.

Brody grasped her arm. Her stance suggested she might attack Randal any moment. He didn't need her to assault an officer. Even though, right now he wanted to do the same thing. Why would Randal even consider using Megan as bait? Especially after she said she'd changed her mind?

"Thank you," Brody said between gritted teeth, stepping in front of Megan.

"It's my job. Here's my card if anything else comes up." Randal scowled at Megan. "You'd do best to follow my advice and let me escort you back to Clarkston."

"There's no way in hell I'm going anywhere with you."

"Suit yourself." Randal nodded at Brody. "Chief Phelps." He climbed back into the sedan with Officer Tanner. They pulled out of the parking lot, heading toward Clarkston.

Brody released a breath and slipped the business card into his shirt pocket. One situation resolved one more to go. He walked up the steps, opened the front door and motioned Megan inside. "Let's get this over with."

DEPUTY LEWIS GLANCED up from the computer screen. He smiled at Megan before returning to his work.

"Let's sit in the lounge." Brody led the way across the room.

Muscles flexed under his shirt. He'd grown into a powerful man. Strong, sleek, sexy. Megan's stomach fluttered. She wished there could be a future for them but fairy-tale endings were for storybooks. Besides, she'd seen her own death. Brody may have forgiven her for the death of his parents but he'd never forgive her for what she was about to say. A wave of sadness rushed over her.

Regardless of what Brody Phelps thought about her, a little boy needed him. She had to convince him to find Robbie. There was only one way. She hadn't wanted to tell him like this but she'd run out of options. "Could we talk in private?"

Brody shoved his hands in his pockets. "You can talk about the case in front of Deputy Lewis."

"Believe me, what I have to say you'll want to hear in private."

He shifted his weight. His intense stare never left her face. "Lewis, I'll be in back if you need me."

"Yes, sir," Lewis replied.

"This way, Megan."

She followed him down the hallway, past several doors and into a small room. A table and chairs sat in the center. File cabinets lined the walls.

"Have a seat." Brody motioned toward a metal chair as he walked around the table to sit facing the door.

Megan's heart pounded at the thought of what she was about

to do. Her stomach twisted in knots. She hadn't wanted to use her secret to force his hand but after the last vision it was imperative Brody know the truth.

This confession would change everything. Her hands began to tremble but she pushed the fear back and concentrated instead on remaining calm. She could not lose her courage now.

She quietly closed the door, lingering a moment before turning to face him. "There are some things I need to tell you before I leave Flatrock Creek. Things I should have made myself say years ago but I was young and afraid."

Megan sat down across from him, placing her purse and package on the table. She didn't have to use her psychic abilities to tell his defenses were up.

"At eighteen I didn't understand my abilities. Even now I don't always understand every vision I receive. When a situation is serious and I make a mistake, it sticks with me. I was wrong about your car having the brake problem. It has haunted me for years. All I can say about your parents' deaths is I'm so very, very sorry."

"You're about seven years too late." Brody leaned back in the chair and crossed his arms over his chest. "Is that all?"

I wish it were.

"After you called off our wedding, you made it clear you never wanted to see me again. You didn't love me because hate had replaced any love you felt…" The words caught in her throat. She looked down at her hands clasped together on the table, noticing the whiteness around her fingernails. She released the tight grip.

After all these years, Brody's words still ripped at her, tore her heart open and exposed old wounds that had never healed. Megan took a deep unsteady breath.

She had to get through this. If the visions came true and she died, her son deserved at least one parent in his life. Shame and regret filled her. Robbie would never know a family with both a mother and father.

"After you called off the wedding, I couldn't tell you. God knows I wanted too. I picked up the phone a thousand times, I wrote you a hundred letters that ended up in the trash. I'm so sorry I haven't told you before now." She looked up at Brody's hard expression and stormy eyes. His jaw clenched as he drew his arms even tighter across his chest.

"If the Mangler succeeds in killing me—"

"Spit it out, Megan."

She took a deep breath and stared at him, needing to see his reaction. "When I left Flatrock Creek I was seven weeks pregnant with your son. Brody, Robbie is our child."

Megan waited for the volcano to erupt. Instead Brody's eyebrows knitted together. "Impossible. You couldn't have been pregnant when you left town."

"I don't lie. I didn't tell you Robbie's age because I didn't want you to figure it out until I could tell you myself. I did a home pregnancy test a week after you broke up with me. You wouldn't answer my calls, you refused to speak with me." Megan's voice cracked. Tears welled in her eyes as she reached inside the purse and pulled out Robbie's birth certificate. She glanced at the document before handing it to Brody. "Robbie's birthday is January twenty-first. He turned six this year."

Brody unfolded the paper. His lips thinned into a straight line, jaw muscles clenched while he read the paper. He didn't speak, didn't look up.

Megan's heart broke with the pain she knew she'd brought on him. He'd never forgive her for keeping his son from him for six years. It was very possible that he'd never see Robbie alive. The thought chilled her soul.

"I brought a duplicate of his birth certificate because I knew you would need proof. I don't expect your forgiveness. You hated me. I knew you wouldn't want a child I'd given birth to. I couldn't bear it if you hated your son because of me."

"Why should I believe you, Megan? It's easy to put a man's name as the father on a birth certificate."

"Because every time I look at Robbie I see you." She took a picture of Robbie from her purse and slid it across the table toward him. "If you need more proof, you can request a DNA paternity test once Robbie is rescued."

"Damn." Brody picked up the photo. Resting his elbows on his knees, he held the photo in one hand, birth certificate in the other.

Megan knew any other man would have been angry and sent her packing. She'd really expected the same reaction from Brody, especially after the way he'd blown up at her seven years ago. Instead he stared at the items in his hands.

She hadn't anticipated such an opposite reaction.

"If anything happens to me, there's a document on file with my attorney. It gives you all parental rights regarding Robbie as his father. My parents will never be able to take him from you, not that they'd even try. They never accepted Robbie and disowned me because I insisted on having our baby. Here's my lawyer's business card."

Brody picked up the card, slid it in his shirt pocket without even looking at it. He stared at Robbie's picture.

Megan waited a few more minutes. When he didn't speak she picked up the purse and paper bag and walked out of the room.

A SON?

Megan had kept their son from him?

Your past will come back to you twofold and it will be your own fault. Megan and Robbie were two.

Brody stared at the photo and certificate in disbelief. The blood rushed through his veins and pounded in his ears, deafening all other sounds.

Robbie's small face grinned at him, a gap in his smile where he'd lost two front teeth. Dark straight bangs accented ears that stuck out a little. Short fingers wrapped around a T-Ball trophy. The picture could have been him at six years old.

Tightness banded his chest. His eyes stung.

This child is my son.

A son who, for six years, had not known his father. He'd missed his birth, his first words, his first steps.

Did Megan even tell Robbie about me?

Had Robbie ever asked?

Anger replaced shock.

She should have found a way to tell me during the past seven years. Not thrown such a revelation on me while Robbie is missing.

I may never meet my son.

"Why did you do this?" His tone was slow, deliberate. "How could you keep him from me?"

When Megan didn't answer he looked up to find she'd left the room.

Where did she go?

He couldn't think straight. What were the reasons she'd given earlier? Had he even heard?

"Damn it, Megan! Get back here!"

The metal chair clattered to the floor as he bolted from the room. He got halfway down the hall when a loud explosion from outside rocked the building. He broke into a run. In the front office, Deputy Lewis ran in from the opposite hallway.

"What in the hell happened?" Lewis shouted.

The front window was shattered and black smoke poured in from outside.

"Oh my God!" Lewis said.

"Megan…" Brody dropped the picture and certificate on the desk and ran across the broken glass. He jerked open the front door. The silver convertible burned furiously.

"Megan!" The flames licking into the air kept them from

getting close. Brody yelled over the roar of the inferno. "Lewis, get the fire extinguishers!"

The deputy sprinted inside the building. Brody ran around the car yelling Megan's name, looking for some sign she hadn't been in the car or any evidence of the perp who'd done this. The fire blazed so hot he couldn't tell if there was a body inside or not.

He grabbed his radio and shouted into it. "Tim! Get your guys to the police station! We've got a car fire with a victim trapped inside."

"Ten-four!" a man's voice replied.

Brody shoved the radio into his belt. Calling out for Megan again, raw emotion clawed at him. His heart hammered out his deepest fears. She couldn't be dead. Not when she'd brought his son into his life.

He'll terrify the second victim before abducting them. This nightmare has just begun. Megan's words rang in his ears.

Wrong again.

Like she'd been wrong about his parents. Damn her stupid psychic impressions! The Mangler wasn't trying to scare her. He wanted her dead.

Had he succeeded?

CHAPTER SEVEN

BRODY HEARD THE SIRENS APPROACHING AS THEY sprayed the car with extinguishers. The white foam did little to control the blaze. Lewis threw a red canister to the ground when it sputtered empty. He ran to the side of the building, turned on the outside faucet and aimed the garden hose at the fire.

"Lewis, soak the driver's side. The fire department is on the way." Brody called out over the roar of the flames. The fire extinguisher emptied. He threw it down and picked up the last full canister. The sirens grew louder as the fire truck pulled into the parking lot. Two firefighters jumped into action, pushing Brody aside as they pulled a hose from the truck toward the car.

Brody ran to the fire chief. "What can I do, Tim?"

"Stay out of the way," he said, unrolling a second hose. "We'll take it from here."

"Let me do something!"

Tim glanced at Brody as he ran past.

Brody's feet wouldn't move. Images of Megan's defiant stand against Randal and her tears flashed through his mind. The warmth of her smile, her throaty laughter, her embrace all lost to him forever. His heart ripped apart. This was his fault for turning his back on her, for leaving her alone to raise a child he'd never even known about. He thought he knew pain and loss but he didn't.

Not until now.

His son may never be found alive...and Megan... He forced himself to turn away from the burning car. He stared into the sky as he walked back to the porch.

Why this? Why now? No one could survive that explosion.

The sun disappeared behind a cloud. A chill rolled over him despite the balmy weather. How much darker would this day get?

The old boards creaked under his weight. He collapsed onto the step. His gaze fixed on the flames that took Megan from him. Why had he been so hard on her? He hadn't given her any more of a chance now than he had seven years ago.

If only he'd listened to her back then maybe his life wouldn't have been so hollow and consumed with work. How he regretted having been such a stubborn teenager. He'd unleashed his pain by lashing out at her. He hadn't cared if his uncompromising actions hurt her, her family and himself.

Heat from the fire scorched his skin. Brody squeezed his eyes shut against the sight of the raging inferno.

It took this to force him to face his feelings? In the couple of hours since Megan's return she'd rekindled emotions he thought he'd buried long ago.

Now, it was too late.

If he hadn't been so quick to blame Megan for his parents' death, if he had accepted it was an accident and nothing more, he could have enjoyed a life with the woman he loved and their son.

Had Megan seen her own death? Was his family lost to him because he chose not to listen to her, not to believe in her abilities?

Dammit, it *was* his fault. Even with the heat from the flames a chill rose up his spine. Grandma Lewis' prediction had just come true.

If he accepted what she'd said as truth it meant all this metaphysical crap was real. Brody hung his head, pressing his forehead against clasped hands. His eyes stung with tears, his chest constricted.

He didn't know what to think or believe anymore. Even with the sounds of crackling fire, people yelling and the pungent smell of smoke in the air, there was one truth he could no longer deny. He loved Megan.

Who am I kidding? I've always loved her. Now she's lost to me forever. I didn't even redeem myself when I had the chance.

Brody heard the step creak as someone sat down beside him.

"That noise was my car blowing up?" a voice whispered.

Brody jerked his head up. "Megan?"

He blinked to make sure his imagination wasn't working overtime. She stared at the burning vehicle, eyes wide.

"The Mangler did this." She glanced at him, steel determination in her eyes. "It's a game to him. Where is he? Did you catch him?"

Brody thought he'd never seen a more welcome sight. His heart soared. *I have a second chance!*

He grabbed her and held her tight. Brushing the hair from her face, he lost himself in those big baby blues now full of surprise. "I thought you were…"

At that moment, he resolved Megan Cassidy would never leave his life again. He lowered his lips to seal the promise in his mind.

WARM LIPS CARESSED HERS.

What in the world? His fingers threaded into her hair, pulling her closer to him.

She didn't care why Brody was kissing her, only that he was. Megan opened her mouth slightly, wondering what he'd do. Brody deepened the kiss, tangling his tongue with hers with an unexpected urgency.

Megan sensed the sudden, wild need in him. *For God's sake, we're on the front porch, people are watching.*

Brody's hand slid from her waist to her shoulder, brushing the side of her breast. Heat raged, melting her, burning a path down her stomach and between her thighs.

Suddenly, she didn't care if anyone was around. It didn't matter that her car exploded. The only thing that held any importance was Brody's kiss.

A kiss she had given up any hope of ever experiencing again.

Brody's fisted his hand in her hair. He gently pulled her head back while deepening the kiss even more. Megan met his urgency with an intense hunger, moving closer to his body, sliding her hands up his back until they rested on broad shoulders. She pulled him closer, wanting more.

As suddenly as he'd taken her mouth, Brody released her. His ragged breathing matched hers. Brown eyes dense with desire seared her with their passionate heat.

"Brody?" she whispered. Lifting her hand to his face she palmed his cheek, eyes questioning and pulled him back to her. "Again…"

He fluttered a quick kiss over her lips. "That always was your favorite word."

"Only with you." *Always with you.* Brody took her body to places she only remembered in dreams. Places she would love to revisit once she found Robbie.

"Let's go inside." Brody took her hand, stood and pulled her up from the step. He yelled out over the noise of water spraying from the fire truck's hose. "Lewis, stay here. I'm calling Randal. He'll have to turn around."

"Ten-four, Chief," Deputy Lewis said, a broad smile on his face as he wound the garden hose back onto the plastic holder.

Megan looked from Lewis to the smoldering remains of her car. The firefighters had put out the fire during Brody's blazing kiss. She touched tender lips, mentally reliving every detail.

A tug on her arm and the thoughts fled. Megan allowed Brody to guide her into the station, his large hand on the small of her back, a reminder of the pleasure those hands had once given her.

His words came crashing through her memory, *I hate you and I never want to see you again.* Those words changed her life forever and killed her trust in love.

At the desk Brody took the business cards from his shirt pocket, picked up the phone and dialed. Moments later he explained the situation to Randal.

Megan waited, pacing the floor while Brody's voice droned in the background. Why had he kissed her as if he couldn't get enough of her? Like his life depended on it? Did he think she was in the car? He must have. Brody's reactions to her, to the situation, were confusing.

Psychically, she could look, take a little peek and know what he felt. She wouldn't invade his privacy with her abilities but man, it was so very tempting.

At the sound of the receiver clicking into the handset, Megan stopped in front of the desk. "What was the kiss about?"

Brody studied her, his eyes dark but lacking the desire they'd held earlier. "I thought you died in the explosion."

"Oh." He didn't want her, it was a natural response to the realization she hadn't died.

An odd impulse but an impulse just the same.

"Where did you go?" Brody crossed his arms over his chest.

"The restroom." *To refocus, center myself, splash water on my face.*

"Why didn't you tell me about Robbie?" The lines between his eyebrows deepened with a scowl, anger flashed in his eyes, yet he remained calm and in total control. "How could you keep him from me all this time?"

"Let me ask you something, Brody." Megan sat down on the sofa exhausted from the emotional roller coaster she'd been riding. "If I had told you about Robbie before now, what would your first reaction have been?"

"I'd have said he wasn't mine." Brody sat with one hip on the chair's arm. Megan remained motionless under the intense scrutiny of his stare.

"And you hate me, remember? You told me so. Regardless of that amazing kiss we just shared, you blame me for your parents' deaths." Megan rested the back of her head against the cool leather, knowing she'd never be forgiven. She closed her eyes against the momentary weariness and Brody. "I wanted to tell you about Robbie but as hard as I tried, I couldn't bring myself to face you."

She thought his kiss was amazing? Her hungry response was pretty incredible too. He pushed the feeling of delight aside. "You should have told me. You could have found a way." His voice tensed with emotion, carrying a raw edge.

Megan looked up at him. He'd moved from the chair to the middle of the room, his back to her. "Don't be so quick to walk away from me, Brody. You know as well as I do how you would have reacted. You would have told me to get the hell out of your life. Oh but wait—that's exactly what you did without knowing about the baby. You despised me."

She rose from the couch and walked to stand behind him. "You would have felt I'd trapped you, which is the last thing I wanted."

"Damn it, Megan." He faced her. "You show up after seven years, tell me I have a six-year-old son who has been kidnapped by a serial killer who's after you too. What do you expect?"

"Honestly? I'm really surprised you're not freaking out. Yelling and throwing a fit like you did when you broke up with me. I don't understand how you can be so calm about this." Megan picked up her purse from the couch. "I guess I'm not the only one who has changed. I didn't *expect* anything from you, Brody. I had only hoped."

What a mistake. Flatrock Creek only held bitter memories. Had she actually thought the answer to her problem could be found within Brody Phelps? "I had hoped you would go with me to find Robbie."

"Do you regret telling me about him?"

"Of course not. Telling you the truth is a weight off my shoulders. The killer has intensified his efforts to abduct me. After my most recent vision, time is of the essence. I have to find Robbie before he succeeds and I've already wasted three hours here. Since you're not going with me, I'm heading into the mountains as soon as I replace the supplies I had in the trunk of the car."

Megan waited. Hoping he'd change his mind. Tense moments passed, Brody's scowl deepened, emotions she couldn't pin down reflected in his eyes but words never came.

A vision flashed on the dark screen in her mind. Brody lay crumpled on the ground, Robbie stood in the entrance of the cave crying. The Mangler, knife in hand, stood between her and Robbie.

Brody will be there when I die.

She didn't want him to get hurt. She sucked in a deep breath. "I've never depended on anyone since I left Flatrock Creek. I don't know why I thought I needed anyone now. Goodbye, Brody."

Holding her head high, Megan turned her back on her past and looked toward the immediate future—finding Robbie.

BRODY WATCHED HER walk away. Like he had seven years ago and earlier today. Only this time Megan was in control. No begging or pleading, she'd just shut him out. Anger and confusion threatened his self-control.

He wouldn't let her walk out of his life again. He caught up to her in a few quick strides. Reaching over her shoulder as she started to open the door, he placed his palm on the wood and slammed it shut.

"You're not going anywhere," he said.

"You can't stop me." She glanced up at him, determination

shining in her eyes.

"I can and this time I will." He grabbed her arm and whirled her around to face him. "Until we find Robbie, you're staying with me. The Mangler isn't trying to scare you, Megan, he's trying to kill you. Which means Robbie may—"

"Don't say it." She clamped a hand over his mouth, "don't even think it. Speaking thoughts give power to them. Robbie is alive. I sense him. I won't accept any other alternative."

The coldness of her hand against his lips surprised him. Fear had always made her fingers turn to ice. He covered her hand with his, trying to warm her. He kissed her palm before moving her hand away. "Your earlier impression was wrong."

"I said I was sorry about your parents, Brody. I was eighteen. I didn't understand how my abilities worked."

"The one today, when you told me the Mangler would try to scare you before he attempted to abduct you. He's skipped right to killing you."

"That wasn't psychic. The police told me he followed the same pattern. It's his MO."

"What *do* you sense about him coming after you?"

"I can't tell you."

"You believe it's so bad you can't talk about it?" How superstitious had she become?

"Yes." Megan pulled her hands away, clasping her fingers together.

"Before today, I thought all psychics were frauds."

"Has something changed your mind?" Her eyes narrowed.

"When you left, Deputy Lewis' grandmother told me something I thought would never happen. Today her words came true. I'll admit you were right about the brakes failing on a tan car even though you thought it was mine instead of Dad's. I don't believe in all this stuff but if you say your visions can lead us to Robbie I'm willing to try using them to find him."

"What did Grandma Lewis say?"

"My past would come back to me twofold."

Megan nodded. "That's true."

Brody turned his back to her. "She said it was my fault."

"It's not altogether your fault, Brody." Megan walked around him and looked into his eyes. His forehead wrinkled with worry lines. "I should have told you about Robbie long ago. If anyone is to blame, it's me."

"Regardless, we're in this situation and we need to work together to find our son."

Our son. The impact of those two words hit her right in the gut. She'd longed to hear Brody accept Robbie. Tears stung her eyes, a knot formed in her throat from a moment of happiness in this otherwise screwed up day. A soft smile caressed her lips. Joy soared through her. She flung herself into his arms and hugged him tightly. "The timing sucks but I've wanted to hear you claim Robbie for so long. I wanted to tell you so much. I couldn't bring myself to face you."

He hugged her and leaned back to look into her eyes. Blood rushed to her face, changing her pale skin to a light pink, she released him and took a step away.

"Maybe your visions will lead us to Robbie. I'm going along with this because Grandma Lewis' prediction happened after all these years. If I'm going to assist you, I need to know everything about your visions. Where do you think Robbie is being held?"

He watched her struggling with the decision to tell him about the visions. He saw the confusion in her eyes.

"Will you at least try to believe what I'm saying?" she asked.

"What am I supposed to believe?"

"Believe in me. What I'm telling you is real to me. My visions are second nature, a part of my daily life. I can't control them."

"You do readings for people for a living. If you charge money for the service then you must be able to control how you receive impressions."

"I charge nominal fees to give my abilities value. I may not receive what my client wants to hear but instead I'm shown what they need to know." Megan walked over and sat down on the couch. "Whether you realize it or not, Brody, psychics have a great responsibility. I'm very skeptical about my own abilities. Sometimes it's a burden I'd rather not have. If you're going to laugh at me, or make fun of me, make snide comments, or do any of the things I have to deal with from every nonbeliever on the planet on a daily basis then I'd prefer to keep my visions to myself. Robbie's abduction is stressful enough." She blew out an exasperated breath.

Brody joined her on the couch, grasped her hands. "I'm not going to make fun of you, Megan. At this point I'm willing to try anything."

"Even if doing so puts your life in danger?"

"Yes, even if I'm in danger." She actually believes she knows where the killer has Robbie. "Where do you think he is?"

"It could be anywhere," she hedged. Megan pulled her hands away and rubbed the palms against her knees.

Why the hell is she hesitating? "Megan—"

"I see a cave," she interrupted. "Beyond the entrance is an old shack with vines covering one side. It's in a small clearing. The grass is thick near the shack but thins out toward the cave and becomes very rocky. A dead tree has fallen in the front yard near the door. The shack has a broken window with shards of glass sticking out of the frame. Inside is some sort of table. I saw the Mangler sharpening a hunting knife on it."

Brody blinked. Damn. She was right. What she described could be anywhere. "You saw all that in one vision? Are you sure you're not imagining something you saw when you lived here?"

Megan's stare pierced him. He stared right back, then, realizing he hadn't believed her at all, cleared his throat and looked away.

"It sounds like an old mining shack. There are hundreds of them in the mountains." He gave a sarcastic laugh. "You wouldn't happen to know which one, would you?"

Megan's complexion turned paler. He instantly regretted the comment. *God, what is wrong with me?*

"You'll never understand," Megan said. "I can't blame you."

"Megan, I'm trying. This goes against everything I believe. It's going to take some adjustment on my part." Brody leaned back against the couch. *Believing in her visions is harder than I thought.* "I apologize for laughing. Seriously, do you have any idea where we should start?"

"Not yet." Megan said, staring across the office.

"Did you see anything else?"

"Yes." She shifted on the couch to face him. "You'll probably laugh again but this is important. I think the Mangler is psychic too. He's looking for a challenge, someone who can test his abilities. He said, *'Let's dance'* and told me the other psychics hadn't come close to winning the game."

"Does Randal know this?"

"No. I had the vision on the way to Frye's. Randal doesn't believe anything I say anyway, so there's no point even telling him."

Brody nodded. *She thinks the same thing about me.* "Have you had others about the Mangler?"

Megan rubbed her temple. "There was another one, I fought with him."

"What happened?"

"A fight."

"Who won?"

Megan gazed into his eyes. Her brows pinched together. "He did. Can we please stop talking and get into the mountains? I feel like time is running out. We need to go."

Brody realized she wasn't telling him the entire vision but he'd have to get it out of her later.

"We'll need supplies." He stood and started toward the hallway but suddenly turned around almost bumping into her. "One more thing. Don't wander off. We stay together otherwise the risk is too great for both of us."

"But what if…"

"If you want my help, Megan, you play by my rules."

"Okay." She nodded.

"Follow me." He led the way to a storage room where he grabbed two of the pre-packed search and rescue survival backpacks. Unzipping each one he added flashlights, five water bottles each and food rations. In one pack he placed extra radios, batteries and secured a lightweight dome tent to it.

He had a job to do and Robbie's life depended on him doing what he did best. He thought about the photo Megan had given him. Robbie looked like a mischievous little imp. Hurt ripped through him. He'd missed so much in Robbie's life.

He glanced at Megan standing in the doorway, noticed the clock on the wall above her head and the anger turned to a sense of urgency. She was right. Time was running out. The Mangler's MO had changed. He'd already had Robbie for nearly twenty-four hours. If past missing person cases were an indication, Robbie could already be dead.

Brody pushed the thought aside. Megan's superstitions were rubbing off on him. God forbid if thinking something made it happen. Working quickly, he finished gathering the supplies.

He handed Megan the lighter backpack. For an instant he thought he saw love in her eyes but it quickly disappeared. All this psychic talk was making his imagination run wild. "Can you carry this?"

She shoved the purse and small bag inside.

"Sure can. Ready?" she asked, shrugging the yellow pack onto her shoulders.

"Yep." He strode past Megan to his desk, picked up Robbie's photos and certificate. "May I have these?"

Megan nodded. "I brought them for you."

He placed both items in his wallet as he headed toward the front door. Outside Deputy Lewis stood by the smoldering car talking to one of the local farmers. "Lewis, a word?"

"Coming, Chief." He shook hands with the older man and met Brody on the porch. "What's up?"

"I'm putting you in charge for a few days. All the information about my trip is in the top desk drawer. Will you call my cousin, explain the situation and cancel my reservations?"

"Sure. Where are you going?"

"I'm going with Megan to find our son. You know what to do when Randal gets here. I have my satellite phone and radio if you need me. They should both work up there. I'll keep in touch."

"Did you say *our son*?"

"It's a long story."

Lewis glanced at Megan. "That only leaves one part of Grandma's prediction to come true."

Brody shook his head. "No. It doesn't."

"Really?" Lewis slapped Brody's shoulder several times. "Be careful, Chief."

"I will." Brody walked down the steps around the side of the station.

Opening the backpack, then the purse, Megan took a lavender envelope with Brody's name printed on the front. She zipped the pack closed.

She handed the envelope to Deputy Lewis as she slung the pack over her shoulder. "If I don't make it back, promise you'll give this to Brody. It's important."

Lewis frowned at her but accepted the envelope. "You have my word, Ms. Cassidy."

"Thank you." Megan ran to catch up with Brody. Rounding the side of the building, she slowed to a walk. Brody was leaning inside the truck, moving things around to make the backpack fit. His pants tightened over muscular glutes and thighs.

Megan's pace slowed. Her heart beat faster as she noticed how strong he'd become. He grabbed the side of the cab for support and angled himself further inside, his muscles hardened under tanned skin.

Suddenly, she saw gray lines on a black screen. The lines cleared and she watched as Brody's large hands slid up her bare legs, grabbed her behind the knees and pulled her toward him.

"Megan, what's wrong?"

Brody's voice pulled her out of the vision.

"Nothing, I…" She realized she'd stopped walking and quickly hurried around to the passenger door.

He pushed the seat in place and climbed inside. Megan slid into the truck, placing the backpack between her feet.

Leaning over her, Brody opened the glove compartment, searching inside until he found three maps and dropped them in Megan's lap. His arm brushed her thigh as he straightened. The contact sent an electric shock through her.

Megan grabbed his hand between both of hers. It was firm, rough and calloused. Had she realized being in contact with Brody would raise her emotions to such heights, she might have thought twice before returning to Flatrock Creek.

"Brody," she whispered. His warmth soothed her. She flattened her palm against his, feeling the pulse at his wrist, steady and solid. They would find Robbie, together.

"What is it?" He wrapped long fingers around her hand, his gaze so intense it touched her deep inside.

"Thank you." She lifted his hand and placed a kiss on the palm before releasing him. She had sealed the words with the gesture from their youth.

Brody nodded and reached over to squeeze her hand. "These maps represent the mountains though West Virginia. Can you pick out a smaller region using your psychic stuff?"

His voice sounded deeper, a bit raspy. A rush of emotion hit Megan but she blocked it. She didn't want to empath his feelings, not now when she sensed them simmering just under the surface. Brody felt things passionately. He'd never forgive her. It was enough he gotten past his anger and agreed to search for Robbie.

"I'll focus on the maps while we drive to your house."

"I didn't say we were going to my house."

"Aren't we?"

"Are you reading my mind? *Can* you read minds? This psychic crap is making me question everything. I don't like it." His eyes blazed, long fingers gripped the steering wheel as he turned in the seat to face her.

"I can't read minds. I don't read people without their permission either." This was the reason why she didn't read people without their specific request. Brody looked as if he was about to explode.

"What do you mean?"

"Sometimes I just know things. I wasn't reading your mind, I knew we were going to your house." Megan shifted in the seat. "I pick up information all the time. From people, the environment, anything can bring it on. I can't control them, they're part of my everyday life. A reading is when I tap into someone's energy to search for answers to their problems. I don't do readings unless I've been asked to. Instead, if I feel like I'm getting too much information I try to block it. I close myself off to the vision if I can. I wouldn't want my privacy invaded by another psychic so I don't do it to anyone else."

"Have you read me today?"

"No. I blocked your emotions a few minutes ago because they were so strong. I'm sorry if you're angry with me, I shouldn't have kissed your palm. It's just…" Looking away she gathered her hair and twisted it in a knot. "Are we going to your house or are we going to sit here talking all day? My—our son needs us."

Brody turned in the seat and started the truck with a frown on his face. He backed it out of the driveway and pulled onto the main road, heading north. "Yeah, we're going to my house. I have to get my ATV."

Megan laid the maps out on her lap, passing flattened palms over each one. "And the rifle."

CHAPTER EIGHT

BRODY DROVE ALONG THE WINDING MOUNTAIN ROAD in silence. Several times he glanced over at Megan. The maps lay across long slender legs, her eyes unfocused as she moved her hands, holding them about an inch over each map. Sometimes she'd look up from the maps, cock her head to the side and close her eyes before opening them to look down again.

This is too weird.

The woman had read his mind. Twice. Even though she said she couldn't read minds. A coincidence or lucky guess? Strange either way.

A wave of intense desire had engulfed him the moment her lips touched his palm. He's almost come undone. All he wanted was to kiss her senseless, again. It was neither the time nor place.

Megan had been wrong though. It wasn't anger she'd blocked—it was desire.

Now that he knew she could pick up on his feelings, he'd be more careful to hide them.

He turned from the pavement onto a dirt side road. The truck rumbled down the half-mile driveway shadowed by thick maple trees.

A two-story log cabin home came into view. Its rich brown wood accented a deep green tin roof blending it into the setting. A high pointed central gable stretched across the roofline. The tall windows in both the front and back of the home gave a three hundred and sixty degree view of Flatrock Creek in the valley and the Allegheny Mountain Range.

"We're here." Brody parked the truck in front of the porch. "Bring the maps. You can look at them inside."

Megan returned two maps to the glove compartment. "I've got the location."

Brody circled the truck to open the passenger door but Megan met him in front of the cab.

"Nice house," she said, following him onto the porch.

"Thanks." He never thought Megan would be in his home. Would she recognize it? Judging by the surprised look on her face, she did. He unlocked and held the door open for her.

She stepped over the threshold.

How many times had he pictured her in a wedding gown with her arms wrapped around his neck while he carried her inside?

That dream died with his parents.

Megan gasped as she moved further into the large living room. The back wall, made of glass, allowed an open view of the valley behind the house. A wide stream flowed through the dale. A sliding glass door beside the windows led to an oversized deck, empty of furnishings.

"Brody..." Megan spun around, the utter shock in her eyes dug into him. "You built *our* house?"

"I liked the design." He shrugged and turned away. *What was I thinking? I should have made her wait in the truck. I'm not in the mood to answer all the questions she is sure to have.*

Stepping up to a small landing, he pulled a keychain from his pocket, unlocked the gun cabinet and took out a rifle, ammunition and a military issued knife. He secured the cabinet and put the gear on the couch.

"We might be out there a couple days. I'll get some extra clothes." He bypassed Megan, who looked around the house in wonder. He took the stairs two at a time.

The faster he could get the clothes together, the quicker they could get out of the house. He could only imagine what was going through her mind right now.

In the bedroom he dug through the drawers, grabbed an extra shirt and pair of jeans. For Megan he found a brown pair of pants he'd accidentally shrunk in the wash but never got around to throwing away, a t-shirt and long-sleeved jacket. He grabbed several pairs of socks and underwear. Megan probably wouldn't wear his boxers but he grabbed a pair anyway.

Inside the walk-in closet, he retrieved a round bag that attached to the bottom of the backpack and two pairs of lightweight shoes. They would be too big for Megan but she could wear double or even triple socks in an emergency. Brody exited the closet to find Megan standing in front of the dresser. She turned a small Dalmatian figurine over in her hands. "Lazlo…"

She'd made it for him in eighth grade during an after-school pottery class.

"You kept Lazlo?"

"Yeah," he said, packing all the items inside the bag.

"Why?" she asked.

Brody straightened. Her blue eyes pierced through him again. He hated that she made him feel as if she knew his darkest secrets.

"Mom always liked it." It wasn't the whole truth. The figurine was Megan's first gift to him. Seven years ago he'd packed up every reminder of her but had never been able to throw any of them away. Last summer, he'd found the box.

Now he wished he'd left it packed up. He had to get her out of the house before she noticed any more mementos he'd held onto. He zipped the bag closed. "Come on. Let's go."

Walking downstairs, a shrill ring filled the air as he stepped off the staircase and into the living room. Brody removed the cell phone from his pocket and flipped it open. "Phelps."

"Chief, Lieutenant Randal is back. Wants to speak to you—"

Brody heard the shuffle of the phone before he could even reply to Lewis.

"Phelps, where is she?" Lieutenant Randal demanded.

Brody glanced over at Megan walking down the steps. "With me."

"Damn lucky she wasn't in the car when it exploded. Bring her back here pronto. I want her in protective custody."

Brody's gut clenched. *Lewis kept the fact Robbie is my son from Randal. Good.* "I understand. I can't bring her back to the station. I'm heading into the mountains with her to try to locate the boy. I'll protect her."

Randal blew an exasperated breath into the phone. "Don't tell me you've fallen for her psychic mumbo jumbo?"

Brody lowered his voice. "I don't believe in it any more than you do. But she does. If it means finding the boy she needs to try. I'll be in touch. If anything turns up I'll let you know immediately so you can send backup."

"I don't like this. We can't keep her safe in the mountains."

"I understand. Can you send officers to Flatrock Creek? I'll have Lewis alert the locals we use for search and rescue."

"I hope you know what you're doing, Phelps."

So do I. "Understood. I'll be in touch. Put Lewis on." Brody listened to the shuffle again as Lewis came back on the phone.

"Chief?"

"Here's what I want you to do, Lewis. When Randal leaves for Clarkston, get the S&R guys ready to roll. If I find anything up there, I'll radio in. Get Gamby to head up the team and you stay put at the station. Troy's fishing down by old Quarry Mill this weekend. Send someone out there to get him to work while I'm gone. Lancaster is on patrol but you can bring him in. I want every extra man ready and available."

"Why the sudden urgency, Chief?"

Brody turned his back to Megan, lowering his voice. "Did you hear what Randal said?"

"Yeah. You think the Mangler's done something to your boy?"

"I don't know but we've wasted enough time. If Megan's right the Mangler is closer than we think."

"Consider it done, Chief."

"Lewis?"

"Yeah?"

"Thanks, man."

"I'd do the same for my boy. You find him. Okay?"

"Ten-four."

Brody flipped the phone shut. Megan's hand slid over his shoulder. "What is it?"

He resisted the urge to touch her, kiss her, hold her and tell her everything would be all right. He hated the turmoil going on inside him. Stepping away he turned to look at her. "Randal wants to put you in protective custody."

"No way. I'm looking for Robbie and Randal isn't going to stop me."

"That's what I told him." He gazed into those blue eyes so full of mystery. The massive valley outside drew his attention. Somewhere out there a killer held his son hostage. Megan paced the floor, distracting him. "Did you ever tell Robbie about me?"

She stopped pacing. The determination in her eyes softened. "Yes. Robbie knows all about his dad. He knows you're the most famous ranger in West Virginia. He knows you care about people and how important your work is. He even saw you on television when you found the Anderson boy."

"He did?" Brody rubbed his chest. His heart ached hearing this.

Megan nodded. "Yes. He said that..." Her voice cracked but she cleared her throat. "That if he ever got lost you'd find him too."

The teary eyes and broken words touched him. "Has he ever asked why we weren't together?"

"Once. I told him sometimes mommies and daddies have to live apart. Things happen in life to send them on separate paths. I told him we both loved him very much and one day he'd get to meet you."

"Your answer satisfied him?"

"Yes. He's six, Brody, not sixteen asking for details."

She was right. Nothing could make up for the time he'd lost. "I should have been there for him, Megan. If you'd only told me. I don't know if I can ever forgive you but for now I'm putting my feelings about what you've done aside. I will bring our son home alive and I *will* be a big part of his life whether you want me to or not."

"I want you in his life. Robbie needs his father."

Brody studied her. Did she mean it? He decided only time would tell. "Where'd you put the map?"

She pulled it from her back pocket and held it out.

Taking the folded paper, Brody spread it out on the coffee table. "Okay, where are we going?"

"I sense Robbie's in this section, near the top." Megan pointed and drew a circle with her finger.

"Are you sure?"

"Yes. Do you know the area?"

"Unfortunately. They found Arial's body there. You've chosen Monocath Mountain. It's the highest point in the West Virginian Allegheny Mountains. The terrain is rocky and rugged. There are a few rumors of paranormal activity going on up there."

"Great. Just what we need. What activity?" Megan's voiced dripped with sarcasm.

"Ghosts were sighted, I think someone said they saw a UFO. Oh and there's the one guy who swears Bigfoot lives up here."

"Oh brother. How long will it take to get there?" she asked.

"About twenty minutes to the base. Getting to the top will take a few hours. We can make it most of the way with the ATV but when the old mining roads turn into trails we'll have to walk." Brody folded the map and picked up the supplies from the couch. He walked to the front door, holding it open for her. "Let me get the ATV loaded and we'll be on our way."

Megan stopped as she passed him and took the bag of clothes and knife he handed her. "I really am sorry, Brody. I hope one day you'll be able to forgive me for keeping Robbie from you."

He watched the slow sway of her hips as she walked away. Maybe she'd be able to forgive him too. Forgive the hurt he'd caused by walking out on her when she needed him the most. He hurriedly closed and locked the house. "Megan, wait! Don't open the door until I can check the truck."

"The Mangler hasn't been here," she said over her shoulder.

"You don't know if he has or not. He planted the cap and blew up your car when you were in the station. Just let me check it out."

She tapped her temple. "I'm psychic remember?" She jerked open the passenger door. "See, nothing happened," she said, placing the supplies inside.

"Damn it, Megan!" He darted to the truck, threw the items through the open door and pinned her against the vehicle. "You have to follow orders. I can't have you blatantly going against me because you think you know some psychic thing. You're not always accurate. If you can't go along with me on this I'll turn you over to Randal and find Robbie myself."

Her eyes widened.

Brody realized he pressed against her. He could feel her taut nipples against his chest. He released a breath to calm himself but he didn't move away. The blue shade of her eyes matched any Caribbean ocean. Flawless skin, its creamy ivory hue set off by the sprinkling of freckles over the bridge of her nose and cheeks. Her full lips silently begged to be tasted. Megan Cassidy had grown into a beautiful, vibrant woman.

"Promise me, Megan. Promise you'll follow my lead, do as I

say. If you can't give your word and stand by it, the risk is too great for everyone involved." He leaned into her even more until she gasped.

"I scanned the area first."

"Promise, Megan!"

"I…can't…"

"Then you go back to Clarkston."

"No…wait." Megan sucked in a deep breath. "All right. I promise."

"Good. If I know anything about you, a promise is your word. Or has that changed too?"

"I'm bound by it." She wiggled against him. "Brody, you're squashing me."

"Um…hum…" His voice sounded thick and raspy, even to him. "I hate you for what you've done to me, Megan."

She dropped her head back against the truck to look up at him. "Brody, I…"

His lips covered hers fast and hard. She gasped but kissed him back with such force and intensity he forgot the reason she was back in Flatrock Creek.

Breaking away, he leaned his forehead against hers. "Damn." This was how they'd once been together. Passionate. He'd been happy with her in his life before. He stepped away. "Get in the truck."

He went to the storage shed, unlocked it and took out two wide planks. Two kisses in four hours weren't acceptable.

Feelings of anger, betrayal and desire consumed him. How long before he burst into flames like the damn car? He needed to be emotionally distant with Megan, as he would in any other police case.

He lowered the tailgate and wedged the wood against it. He glanced at Megan standing by the passenger side, watching him. Back inside the shed, the ATV roared to life and he drove it up the planks into the truck bed. He wedged a full gas can beside the ATV and secured two helmets. Jumping to the ground he slid the boards into the bed on either side of the wheels and tied everything down. He climbed into the cab. Shoving the supplies behind the seat, he leaned down and looked out the open door at Megan. "Let's go."

MEGAN GLANCED AT Brody as the truck rumbled down the dirt road. "I don't know what's going on between us, Brody but I'm going to forget that just happened."

She unfolded the map and laid it across her legs. What kind of mother would she be if she let feelings for Brody interfere with finding her son? "Do you know a place called Talgor Ridge?"

"Yeah. It's remote."

"Good. We need to be there."

"Make up your mind, woman. Either we're going to Monocath Mountain or Talgor Ridge." His eyebrows lifted in confusion. "Which is it?"

"I keep hearing Talgor Ridge. We should go there first. I don't know why but we should."

"Don't lead us on a wild goose chase, Megan."

"Do you really think I'd do that?" She looked at him.

Brody pulled out onto Highway 55. He picked up the police radio handset. "Lewis. We're in route to Talgor Ridge."

"Ten-four, Chief." The radio crackled, Brody released the button and put it back in the casing. From the speaker Lewis laughed and said, "Watch out for the Talgorians."

Megan jerked her gaze from the map to the radio. Talgorians. She'd forgotten about the myth. "Do you believe in the Talgorians, Brody?"

"About as much as I believe in the Monocaths, Bigfoot and the Mothman. I think it's a myth passed down by the superstitious."

"The Monocaths." Chills shivered through Megan's body. "Do

you remember the story?"

"Don't you?"

"Sort of but I haven't heard it since I was a kid. Would you tell it to me?" Maybe if Brody recounted the myth something else would come to her.

Brody glanced at her. "Well, okay, it'll pass the time anyway. It's said that long ago the Celestial League, a spiritual group similar to the Greek gods who kept order and peace within the world, bestowed immortality upon a group of shapeshifters called the Talgorians. It was a reward for living good lives and protecting humans. One day a Talgorian woman married an evil tyrant who chose to break away from the Talgorian ways.

"Soon his followers separated from the original race and called themselves Monocaths. While the Talgorians led a peaceful life and chose to blend in with humans, the Monocaths were brutal, savage killers who would do anything for power or money.

"To punish them the League took away their shapeshifting ability. This caused them to hate the Talgorians even more. The Monocaths declared war on the Talgorians and hunted them down like animals. The Monocaths developed their skills in magic to compensate for losing the ability to shift.

"The Monocath King ambushed the royal family and murdered the queen. The king escaped and took the Talgorians into hiding.

"People say you should never visit Talgor Ridge or Monocath Mountain during the crescent moon because the Monocaths are scouring the mountains searching for Talgorians to kill."

"Or so the story goes," Brody chuckled and glanced at Megan. She sat spellbound, shivering uncontrollably. "Are you okay?"

She nodded.

"Are you sure you want to hear the rest?"

"Positive."

Brody slowed down for a sharp curve. "Supposedly the queen's spirit delivered the Talgorian Elders and Monocath Ancients a series of prophecies handed down by the League. When the last one is fulfilled, only one of the immortal clans will survive. To protect themselves, the Talgorians spread throughout the world with only the Elders hiding at Talgor Ridge."

Megan turned off the air-conditioning and rolled down the window. Warm wind blew against her face but her body still shook from the chills.

"Are you going to be sick?" Brody slowed down as they approached a lookout point. "I can stop so you can walk around."

"No, I'm cold. It happens sometimes when I hear a Universal Truth. Let's keep going. It'll pass."

"It's a myth. It's not true."

"Let's just get there."

Brody pushed the gas pedal and drove in silence until he took a right onto a single lane dirt road shaded by tall pines, maples and oaks. "It's odd the two places you chose to look for Robbie are connected to an old myth."

It's weird the Mangler mentioned a prophecy in the vision. Megan looked out the back window toward the highway. "Why did we turn here?"

"I'm taking the back way. You warm yet?"

Megan nodded.

Brody hit the automatic switch to raise her window and turned the air on. "This serial killer could be playing off the mythology. Maybe in his sick mind he believes he's a Monocath. It's possible he's committing the murders based on the fantasy of how an ancient cold-blooded race would kill. Monocaths are perceived in the myth to be barbarians so he mangles the body to be the same way."

Megan turned in the seat to face him. "Why an X across the torso? And why decapitate them? There seems to be some purpose to his madness. If he's deranged, wouldn't the wounds be random instead of the same each time?"

"Not necessarily. Serial killers often use the same pattern on all the victims. In the Mangler's case, the pattern is one psychic parent with the child's murder first, an X on the torso and decapitation."

"He's using the child to challenge the parent." Megan realized she'd said the thought in a whisper. She glanced at Brody, hoping he hadn't paid attention.

They exited the forest into a clearing. As Brody put the truck in park, Megan looked out across the valley. They'd stopped high on the back half of Talgor Ridge.

Brody's fingers laced through hers, with the other hand, he turned her face toward him.

"Tell me the rest of the vision, Megan." His eyes darkened.

"No." She couldn't bring herself to say the words.

"I need to know what you saw." He released her chin but held her hand tighter when she started to pull away.

"Brody...I..."

"Saying it doesn't really make it true, you know."

"Yes, it does." She'd always believed speaking thoughts gave them power and brought them to you. But if she didn't tell Brody, he wouldn't know what to do when the time came. He wouldn't know how to care for Robbie. She hung her head. "You're right. You need to know."

Megan tried to pull her hand away and this time he let go. She looked out over the valley again, searching for the right words. "When we save Robbie, you'll have to take responsibility for him, be the father he's always wanted. Hold him when he's hurt, teach him how to play ball and never, ever let him forget how much I love him."

"You're acting like you'll never see him again."

"I won't. I saw Robbie alive in my vision. We have to make sure he stays alive. We have to get there before the killer hurts him. I saw myself fight the Mangler and lose. He's going to cut an X and decapitate me like he did the other three parents. I swear I'll take him out with me. I'll die trying to save our son." Megan paused to look out of the window. "You have to promise me you'll always be there for him. Don't let your anger with me interfere with giving Robbie your love."

"Your visions haven't always happened as you've seen them. I'll protect you, Megan. We'll all be okay. You'll see."

"You may not be able to protect me when the time comes. In my vision I saw you lying crumpled on the ground. I don't want you to get hurt either. You made me promise to follow your rules on this search. I need you to promise me you'll take care of Robbie when I'm gone."

"I can't, Meagan, because you're not going anywhere."

"Promise, Brody." She faced him, the tears in her eyes about to spill over and whispered, "Please…promise."

He could only nod.

"It's settled then." Megan wiped at the tears with her fingertips, wishing things could end differently. If only they could be a family.

It wasn't meant to be.

CHAPTER NINE

BRODY TIED THE HUNTING KNIFE TO HIS THIGH AND slung the pack and rifle on his back. He pressed a button on the remote to lock the truck as he walked toward Megan. She stood on a large rock facing the ridge with her eyes unfocused. He'd seen the look several times in the past few hours.

Standing there unnoticed, he watched and waited. A wisp of hair blew across her face. She didn't flinch, instead she kept staring straight ahead toward the ridge. Her expression was one of deep concentration. Naturally pink lips pursed together. He'd never seen anyone look more beautiful—or more alone.

Several minutes later she blinked a few times and her eyes refocused. She jumped down from the rock.

"This way," she said, passing him as she walked away from the ridge.

"I thought you wanted to go to the ridge?"

"So did I but now we have to go this way."

"Wait." Brody caught up to her, grabbing her elbow he spun her around. "You can't go running off in any direction. We need to methodically search this ridge. Why do you want to go west?"

"I feel a pull. I can't really explain why."

"A pull toward Robbie?"

"I don't know." Megan shrugged her shoulder. "Can you let go now?"

"This isn't logical."

"You're right. Nothing about this is logical. I have to follow my feelings."

He released her.

She seemed agitated. Rubbing her temple, she headed into the forest. For the next hour he followed, noticing the sway of her hips as she climbed the incline leading away from the ridge.

His thoughts drifted back to high school. They'd hiked to the springs near Monocath Mountain and gotten stuck there after dark with only a sliver of moonlight to guide them. Had she forgotten? The chilling description of her death interrupted the memory.

"Megan, hold up a sec."

"What's wrong? Can't keep up?" She waited by a boulder for him. Her gaze moved from his lips to his eyes.

He noticed her cheeks were flushed from the exertion. She had dirt on her forehead.

"You need to hydrate." He slid the rifle strap from his shoulder and flipped the pack to the ground. Fishing through it he found and handed Megan a bottle of water. "Sit down and sip this. We only have five bottles of water each so don't waste it."

"I can walk and drink."

"Please sit."

"Fine but only for a minute." She sat on the ground.

Kneeling beside the pack, Brody drank deeply from his own water. "Do you remember the time we hiked up to Monocath Springs?"

"When you scared me silly with those ghost stories so you could ease my fears by making love to me." Megan's gaze caught his. "I'd forgotten the springs were near here."

Brody stared into her blue eyes, as he had that night. The memory of their lovemaking was vivid in his mind. They'd done it everywhere—standing against the rock cliff, on the blanket under the trees, even on the tailgate of his truck. Megan had suggested skinny-dipping in the springs to cool off. They'd had sex in the water and again on the moss covered ground. It had been impossible to get enough of each other.

Megan looked away first. "I'm sorry... I didn't mean to bring that up. Why did you ask?"

Why had he asked? What had he asked? His brain wrapped around the images of her naked against him, her moans of pleasure and the intensity of their combined release. He took a large gulp of water. He thought hard about what he had wanted to say. *Oh yeah.* "Do you remember those noises?"

He had heard them first. Shrieking whines over the sound of something running through the forest. They were lying on the moss and he had been enjoying Megan's soft, succulent kisses. His gaze drifted to her lips. He remembered her sweetness. If he leaned forward now, he could taste her again.

"Yes, some were like deer grunts. Those other cries—I could have sworn someone was being chased." She took another long drink of water.

Brody reached out and rubbed the pad of his thumb over a spot on her forehead. She darted her gaze toward him, lowered the water bottle and stared.

"You had dirt on your face."

"Oh. Thanks." She rubbed the area he'd touched with her palm. "I'm a mess, huh?"

"You've been through a lot. We both have." Brody recapped the water bottle and returned it to the pack. "Do you think those noises had anything to do with the story of the Talgorians and Monocaths?"

"Do you?" she asked.

Just like her to turn the question back on him. "No." He got up, slung the pack over his shoulder and picked up the rifle. "It's a myth."

He grabbed her hand and helped her up. She hadn't even taken off the pack to rest. He pulled too fast and she lost her balance, falling forward. She slammed into his chest. Her breasts crushed against him. He could feel her heart pounding.

From hiking or from being so close to him?

He searched her eyes and saw a flicker of desire. It was quickly replaced by pain. In that instant he understood why she'd kept Robbie from him. He'd never known how much his immature reactions had hurt her until this moment.

"Right," Megan said, pushing away, "a myth."

Minutes later, they emerged into a thinly wooded area which opened into a valley.

"Stay away from the edge, Megan."

"No problem. Besides, we're here." Megan turned north and went about a hundred yards through the sparse trees and stopped beside a thick grove of underbrush. "May I have the knife?"

"Wasn't there a reason you wanted me here? Something about my tracking skills?"

Megan rubbed a hand over her face, wiping the sweat away. "I'm sorry. You're right. There's such a sense of urgency around this feeling. Whatever we're supposed to find is through this underbrush."

"Is that why you practically ran here?"

Megan nodded.

"Maybe we can find a way around." Brody started to follow the edge of the thick underbrush.

"No. We have to go through here." She glanced toward the sky. "It's already afternoon. We don't have a lot of time before nightfall."

He looked back. Sweat beaded on her brow, darkened her shirt. It was madness to try to cut through this mess. "You haven't eaten. Why don't we have a ration pack? Afterward I'll start cutting this down."

"I'm not hungry." She stood with a wide stance and her hands fisted on her hips.

"I sure hope this feeling leads to Robbie."

"So do I."

He unsheathed the hunting knife. "Stay close behind me."

"I will." Her hand rubbed between his shoulder blades sending an unexpected shock through his muscles. "Thanks, Brody."

He nodded and pushed through the brush, cutting the tangled vines and bushes. A few feet into the growth he held a large sapling to the side. "Here, hold this back."

When she didn't answer, Brody looked over his shoulder. Megan's backpack lay on the ground. He hurried down the newly cut path. A few yards away a tall thin man dressed in black jeans and a flannel shirt ran through the scattered trees toward the cliff with Megan hanging limp over his shoulder.

"Dammit!" Panic tore at him. Years of training kicked in. He slammed the knife into the sheath, jerked the rifle from its case on his back and readied it as he ran out of the brush and through the trees.

It's the Mangler! Why didn't I hear anything?

He stopped, aimed at the man's leg and fired. He staggered but didn't fall.

Brody aimed for the other leg and fired again. This time he fell to his knees, dropping Megan on the ground. He crouched beside her for a moment before sprinting toward the cliff.

"What the hell?" Brody lowered the rifle as the man jumped.

He ran to Megan. Blood stained her hair. An egg-sized knot raised along her temple. He felt for a pulse and found it. Relief washed over him. Unconscious but alive.

He approached the edge of the cliff, looking over the deep drop-off. He expected to see a dead man lying at the bottom of the rocky crag. A wide creek ran through an uneven terrain flanked by bushes and overgrowth following the shoreline. Brody scanned the area for a body and came up empty.

No one could survive such a jump.

He looked through the scope to examine the area better. On the other side of the ravine, beside a large oak, he saw the man— smiling and swaying with his hands held out as if he were dancing a waltz.

"Impossible!" Brody took aim and fired.

He ran to the side, looked up at Brody and laughed. He tipped an imaginary hat and disappeared behind the oak before Brody could get off another shot.

What was so damn funny? Why had he laughed and danced like an idiot? Brody rubbed his forehead. He hadn't expected the killer to act anything other than serious and deadly.

He searched through the scope, waiting for the man to reappear. When he didn't, Brody rushed back to Megan. Laying down the gun he shrugged off the pack to retrieve the smelling salts from the first-aid kit. He lifted her into a sitting position to cradle her head in the crook of his arm and broke open a capsule, waving it underneath her nose several times. He wrinkled his own nose against the strong smell of ammonia. "Come on, ladybug. Wake up."

Megan's eyes fluttered. She jerked away from him in terror.

"Hey! Hey! Megan. It's me, Brody." He held her arms, staring into terrified eyes as he tried to get her to recognize him. "Are you okay?"

"Where's the Mangler?" Megan rubbed her head, wincing when she accidentally touched the bump.

He ignored the question. "Let's get ice on that." He took an instant cold compress out of the kit, squeezed to activate it and held it against her temple. She flinched at the touch. "Sorry."

"Is it bad?" Megan looked up at him.

"No, only an abrasion over a goose egg." Brody examined the wound, moving her hair away from the knot before replacing the compress. "What happened?"

"I was about five feet behind you. I didn't sense him coming. A hand covered my mouth and he hit me in the head with something hard. Everything went black."

"You're lucky I turned around when I did. I didn't hear him attack you." Was he so deep in thought that he'd been oblivious to any sound? There was no other explanation.

"Where is he? How'd you save me?"

"I shot him in the legs. He jumped off the cliff."

"Then he's dead? Oh God, what if he did something to Robbie?"

"He's not dead."

"What?" Megan sat up straighter. "Could he have survived the fall? How far down is it?"

"About five hundred feet."

"He has to be dead. We should look for his body. Maybe there is a clue in his clothing."

Brody shook his head. "He didn't die. I saw him dancing and laughing at the forest's edge. He tipped an imaginary hat at me before disappearing into the woods."

"He did the same thing in my vision. What does this mean? How could he survive?"

"I don't know but the sooner we find Robbie the better." He handed her the compress. "Can you walk?"

"Yes. Help me up please." Megan reached out and took Brody's outstretched hand. Once on her feet, she didn't let go, instead, she squeezed his fingers and wrapped her other arm around his neck.

"You saved my life," she whispered.

"I'm not going to let anything happen to you." *Even though I almost let the Mangler abduct her.* He checked the bump on her head with a gentle touch. "Keep the compress on to reduce any swelling."

He put on the gear but kept the rifle in his hand. Reaching over he linked his fingers with Megan's. She jumped at his touch.

Brody caught the surprise in her eyes. "I'm going to hold on to you in case you stumble. He gave you a nasty blow."

"Okay," she said quietly.

He led her toward the underbrush. Moments later he let go of her hand to pick up her backpack. He held it while she slipped it on. He pointed toward the path. "Are you intent on going through here?"

"There's no need. I have come to you."

They spun around toward the voice behind them. A man wearing leather pants, a loose-fitting shirt and shoes resembling moccasins stood near a tree. His arms hung by his side. Pale skin contrasted sharply with straight raven hair cascading past broad shoulders.

Brody stepped in front of Megan and aimed the rifle. "Who are you?"

"I can be of assistance," the man said. "Come with me."

"We're not going anywhere with you," Brody said. "What in the hell is going on around here?"

"I sense he's safe. I don't think he'll hurt us." Megan walked several steps toward the man before Brody grabbed her arm. She looked at Brody, her eyes pleading. "He's the presence I felt earlier. We must go with him."

"We don't know anything about him. You were attacked. How can you be so trusting?"

"Because I can sense he isn't going to harm us, just like I sense the Mangler wants me dead."

"You will be safe from the evil ones with me." The man nodded and began to walk away.

"Come on, Brody." Megan followed him through the trees.

"I don't like this one bit." Brody lowered the rifle, caught up with Megan and took her hand. If anyone intended to harm her again, they'd have to go through him first.

. . .

THEY FOLLOWED THE stranger past tall firs and large boulders until he finally stopped in front of a vertical flat rock embedded into the side of the mountain. He ran his fingertips across the slate. It shimmered and vanished revealing the mouth of a cave.

What is this? Magic? A chill swept over Megan. She wrapped her arm around Brody. She needed to feel the safety of his protection.

The man went inside but Megan hesitated. She sensed entering this cave would change her life forever.

Everything always happens for a reason, she told herself, even if we don't know what the reason is at the time.

She took a deep breath. Psychically she scanned the area. There wasn't any negativity here. Taking a leap of faith she released Brody to step forward into the darkness.

Walking slowly until her eyes adjusted, Megan focused on the stranger who was now holding a torch.

Brody snaked his arm around her waist and pulled her close to his side. Tenseness made his muscles tighten against her. Anxiety radiated from him. His body was on high alert.

"I don't like this," he whispered, "stay with me."

Always. But that wasn't what he meant. Brody only wanted to keep her safe.

"I will," she whispered back.

They followed the stranger deeper into the darkness keeping the torchlight in sight. He walked down a narrow pathway through the cave. The passageway twisted from side to side, the torch's glow disappeared momentarily with each turn. After several minutes they emerged into a large, well-lit cavern.

Three men and four women, all dressed similarly to the stranger, sat cross-legged on mats in a line. A fire burned in front of them and a wooden table and box were behind them.

The stranger turned to them. "Please sit, Megan, Brody. We have much to discuss."

"How do you know our names?" Brody insisted, blocking Megan with his body.

"We have known you both from birth. Now that we are safe within the earth, I may talk freely. My name is Asari and I am a Talgorian Elder."

"Yeah, right," muttered Brody. "A cult freak is more like it."

Megan jabbed her elbow into his ribs.

"As are they," Asari said, moving his arm away from his body to indicate the people sitting on the mats. "Please sit."

Asari waited. Megan sat down opposite the Elders. Each one smiled at her.

They practically ooze power, she thought.

Brody stood behind her.

"What I am about to tell you, Megan Cassidy," Asari said, sitting near her, "will be hard to understand. Know I speak the truth. Believe and you will save your son."

Megan glanced up at Brody. His intent stare was glued to Asari.

"May I call you Asari?" Megan asked.

The Talgorian nodded.

"Thank you." Megan adjusted her legs to a more comfortable position. "Asari, I thought the Talgorians were a myth."

"Thousands of years ago my wife Selda, the Talgorian Queen, was murdered."

"What do you mean, thousands of years ago?" Brody said.

"You're the king?" Megan asked at the same time.

"Yes, I'm King Asari Zenalt, leader of the immortal Talgorians. Thousands of years ago, we lived in peace among the humans. The Monocaths, a group of immortals that were once part of our race became envious of our women and our ability to shapeshift. Because they were once Talgorian they knew the secret to taking our life force. When they discovered they could absorb our essence upon our deaths, they began to kill our people. Their king made me watch while they murdered Selda. I barely escaped with my life. I had no choice but to send the remaining Talgorians into hiding."

"Can you really shapeshift?" Megan asked.

"Of course not," Brody said. "This is absurd. We don't have time for fairytales, myths or legends. We have to find Robbie."

"Please sit," Asari said.

"A serial killer has our son, Asari." Megan leaned forward. "He could die."

"I understand. The ritual is necessary if you want to save him."

"What are you talking about?" Brody asked.

"She must be trained to glimmer before she can fulfill the Prophecy," a female Elder said.

Megan looked at the woman who'd spoken. "What's does that mean?"

"I am Nia. To glimmer means to shift your body into your birthmark totem. Simply put it's shapeshifting."

"Hang on." Megan stood and backed up against Brody. She needed to touch him to ground herself. Her mind whirled. What if this were true? No, Brody was right. These people had to be crazy. They'd wandered upon a group of cult members.

Megan's head ached near the bump. A dull pain throbbed behind her eyes. She rubbed her temples but the pounding only increased. "What are you saying?"

Asari rose and held his palm up to the Elders to keep them quiet. "After Selda's death, her spirit visited me and delivered The Talgorian Prophecies, which were given to her by the Celestial League. For thousands of years we watched for the birth of the prophesized Griffin. Because of the threat against you, your parents and the League agreed to keep you hidden and to delay the transformation ritual in the hopes that we could prevent the Prophecy from happening. Despite our precautions, it has begun, putting both your life and your son's in danger."

"Are you saying I'm a Talgorian?" Megan asked. *This can't be true.*

Asari nodded. "Welcome home, *broeistar.*"

"What does that mean?" asked Brody.

"Beloved," Megan said, rubbing her head, which suddenly felt as if it would explode.

"How did you know the word?" Brody's voice edged with anger.

How did I know? Have I heard it before?

"I don't have a clue." Megan addressed Asari. "What does it mean?"

"*Broeistar* is Talgorian for beloved."

"No. You're wrong." *He's lying. What he says is impossible. This can't be true.* "I'm not Talgorian. I can't shapeshift and neither can you because immortals, shapeshifters and griffins don't exist. This is some kind of sick game to keep me from looking for my son. I'm leaving."

Megan spun toward the exit. The quick movement sent the cave walls spinning around her. She stumbled. Brody caught her by the arm. She glanced up at him but he stared past her to the Talgorians. Megan turned around to see what he was looking at so intently.

The Talgorian Elders stood naked behind Asari. They radiated surges of power. It pulsed in reflective waves reminiscent of those left by a pebble dropped into a pond. Flowing outward from the Talgorians, an electrical charge zinged through her as it passed by.

Asari gave Megan a knowing smile. "Sometimes the only way to believe is to have the experience yourself. Watch your heritage unfold, Megan Cassidy, Talgorian Griffin."

CHAPTER TEN

THE RIPPLES BEGAN TO GLOW A FAINT YELLOW. Astonished, Megan watched as, one by one, the Talgorian Elders changed into various animals and mystical creatures she'd thought only existed in myths.

A Centaur, Unicorn and Dragon stood beside a deer, bear, eagle and wolf. How was it possible? Her eyes weren't lying but was she truly Talgorian? *How did I know a Talgorian word?*

Asari smiled and nodded. "Now you will understand."

His body began to change. He shrank until a black and gold iguana sat on the ground where he'd stood.

"Oh my God." Megan recognized the animal from her psychic search through the forest. Her knees buckled. Brody's arm slipped around her. He held her close and kept her from sinking to the ground.

We are your people. You are one of us. Asari's voice entered Megan's mind.

How can I hear you? Megan thought.

Telepathy.

If what you say is true I'm not even human.

You are Talgorian. It will take some time to adjust to your immortality.

I'm really immortal?

You are. Unfortunately, time is not on your side. If you are to save your son from the Monocaths you must embrace your heritage and you must do it now. Do you understand?

I hear what you're saying. I don't believe this.

Telepathy is the Talgorian mode of communication. I am only a thought away.

Asari shifted from iguana back to his human form and began putting his clothes back on. The other Elders followed his lead, shifted and dressed.

Megan pulled her gaze from them to look up at Brody. His eyes were wide, his jaw slack. Judging from his shocked expression, she knew he'd seen the same thing. It wasn't her imagination.

Which meant the thoughts were real too.

She closed her eyes. Maybe when she looked again, the people would have disappeared.

Megan peeked through barely parted eyelids. They were there, smiling at her. What's the use? She opened her eyes and pried Brody's fingers from her waist. She sat down on the cavern floor.

Megan cradled her head in her hands. People couldn't shapeshift, yet these eight men and women had done it.

A warm hand touched her knee. Fingers lifted her chin. Through watery eyes she looked into Brody's face. She tried to read his expression but her mind wouldn't focus.

Her thoughts scrambled with the memory of her visions. The beating wings and lion's paw ripping the Mangler apart imprinted on her psychic screen.

Am I that beast? The Griffin?

She looked past Brody to Asari who stood a few feet away.

"The myth is real?"

"Yes, *broeistar,* we are real. It is time to take your place with our people. You must go through the tenth-year ritual. Only then will you learn of your birthright and save the child."

This is all wrong. I'm not a freak. "I can't do this," Megan said. "I'm not your griffin, Asari. You've got the wrong person. I'm human—not immortal. Griffins don't exist."

"Denial is understandable in your situation. I can prove your birthright." Asari stepped closer. "Every Talgorian is born with a birthmark in the shape of their shifting totem. Your mark is below your bellybutton. The top half is an eagle, the bottom a lion. You, Megan Cassidy, are the Talgorian Griffin."

Megan shifted her gaze from Asari to Brody. His eyes held the same confusion she was feeling. He had often teased her about the birthmark. He'd said it fit her perfectly because she was free-spirited like the eagle and ferocious as a lion. The Griffin never entered her mind.

"How do you know about my birthmark?"

"Your parents showed it to us when you were born. Because of the prophecies we all agreed to protect you."

"How?" Brody asked, his voice flat, as he faced Asari.

"When Talgorian children are ten years old and in rare cases younger, they go through the transformation ritual and are taught to glimmer. There are two ways that Talgorians use the shifting energy. Any time we shift, we glimmer. We also use this same energy to Soul Merge. To answer Brody's question—"

"I think you better explain Soul Merge first." The urgency in Megan's voice surprised her. If she were Talgorian she really didn't want to screw this one up, if she hadn't already.

Asari nodded. "Soul Merging is our mating ritual, the merging of our souls. When a Talgorian falls in love with someone not of our race, they may tap into the glimmering energy to mate with them for eternity. When we Soul Merge the other being takes on their lover's shifting abilities and their immortality. It is against Talgorian law for us to enter this ritual unless the one we love requests it."

"Could I have already mated with someone and not known?"

The question froze Brody's heart. The thought of another man touching her, caressing her, loving her...

"To Soul Merge you must have completed the transformation

ritual, which you have not. However, I must warn you. From this day forth you must remain in control. After today, if you tap into the glimmering energies during sex, you will Soul Merge and be mated for eternity." Asari looked from Megan to Brody. "It is not to be taken lightly or to be done without permission from your potential mate."

"Understood." Brody glanced at Megan.

"What happens if one of the mates is killed?" Megan asked. "Does the other live on? Is the surviving mate allowed to Soul Merge again or is it a one-time deal?"

"When death comes to one of a mated couple they both do not die. Any time a Talgorian has sex they are capable of Soul Merging. We control the power." Asari said. "It is our responsibility to maintain control during the sexual act so that we do not unintentionally Soul Merge. There have been cases when Talgorians had more than one mate at the same time. To Soul Merge is your right as a Talgorian but you must deal with the consequences of your actions."

"Why wouldn't you turn it off after you found your mate?" Megan asked.

"It is a gift from the Celestial League. They chose to give us the ability to Soul Merge more than once," Asari said. "To answer your question, Brody, we protected Megan by isolating her from other Talgorians so the Monocaths wouldn't discover her true identity." Asari shook his head. "It didn't work because the Talgorian Prophecy started anyway."

"What about Robbie?" Brody asked. "Is he Talgorian too?"

"No, he can't be. If what you say is true he's half human." Megan stood up, brushed the dirt from the back of her jeans.

"Oh God, I'm not even human." She spoke the words on a breath.

Brody shrugged the backpack off. He got out a water bottle and gave it to Megan. "Here, drink this."

"Children born of a Talgorian mother are Talgorian, regardless of the father's race." Asari clasped his hands behind his back. "When you gave birth, your Guardian inspected your son. He has the mark—a hawk."

"You saw Robbie's birthmark when we were in the hospital?" Megan asked.

"No, your Guardian did."

Megan took a sip of water, recapped it and dropped it into Brody's backpack. "Who is my Guardian? I want to know who you've had watching me all these years."

"And you shall know. From the time of your birth, the Guardian has watched over you, even when you thought you were alone. I have called your Guardian to us."

Megan shook her head, rubbed her fingertips against her temples. "This can't be happening to me."

Brody grasped Megan's wrists and gently pulled her arms down. "We'll get to the bottom of everything. Is what he said true?"

Megan looked into Brody's eyes. Immediately a warm wave of calmness passed over her. She nodded. "Yes, it's true. Robbie has a birthmark resembling a hawk near his right ankle."

Brody released her and walked away. It didn't take psychic abilities to tell he was upset.

Asari placed his hand on Megan's forearm. "If you need confirmation of my words, contact your parents."

"My parents? We don't talk anymore. Besides, my cell phone doesn't work up here."

Asari smiled.

The thoughts entered Megan's mind immediately.

You are Talgorian. Use telepathy.

What could it hurt? If she couldn't reach her parents Asari was a liar. She and Brody could get back to searching for Robbie. Megan nodded at Asari. "Okay. I'll give it a go."

Mom? Dad? Can you hear me? It's Megan. I've met a man

named Asari. He's telling me some pretty wild stories. Can you verify what he's saying without me telling you what it is?

She waited a few minutes and tried again. Nothing.

"You're a liar, Asari." Megan waved her hands toward the Elders. "All of this is your fantasy. Somehow you got into my head but this fiasco is over. I won't be a part of it any longer."

Brody stepped close beside her.

"Come on, Brody, we're out of here."

"Not yet, Megan." Brody's baritone voice echoed behind her. "We need more answers."

Megan spun around. A mixture of worry and determination etched his features. "Brody, we have to find Robbie. You're right. This is some cult wasting our precious time."

"I'm not finished here yet." Brody shoved his hands into his pockets. He stared past Megan to Asari.

"You're kidding me right? You can't believe I have psychic abilities yet you'll consider the possibility I'm not even human? You've lost it, Brody. I never thought you, of all people, would even consider that I'm an immortal shapeshifter."

Megan grabbed her backpack and started from the cave. "I'm going to find my son." Halfway to the exit a voice entered her mind, stopping her mid-step.

What King Asari said is true, Megan. You are the Griffin of the Talgorian Prophecy. Megan's father's voice echoed with clarity in her mind. *We tried to protect you from the Prophecy because we feared for your life. The Monocaths are ruthless in their war against us. Should you face them in battle there is a chance you will die.*

We love you too much to let that happen, Megan. Her mother's soft tone followed. *When we pulled away from you it was because several Monocaths came into town. We moved and cut off communications with you. You don't know this but we even changed our names and gave them reasons to follow us in order to lead them away from you. They didn't know who you were and we wanted to keep it that way. We thought we could keep you away from them and the Prophecy. It worked, until now. Breaking contact with you and Robbie hurt us more than you'll ever know. I hope someday we can make it up to both of you.*

Oh God. It's true? Megan stumbled but somehow Brody caught her before she fell. She held onto his arm for support.

Yes, broeistar, it is true. You are Talgorian, as is Robbie, her father said.

You both put your lives on the line to save us? You did that for me?

We'd do anything for you and your child, honey, her mother said. *You're our only child, the love of our lives.*

I'm so sorry that I harbored hard feelings against you. Megan sobbed. *I'm so, so, sorry. I didn't know. I love you both very much. Can you forgive me for doubting you?*

There's nothing to forgive, Megan. Nothing at all, her father said. *Just save our grandson so we can all be a family again when this is over.*

"Robbie," she whispered. It explained how he connected with her telepathically. Suddenly afraid because she hadn't been able to link to him since the abduction, Megan panicked and projected her thoughts. *I'm coming Robbie, Mommy's coming. I know you're scared. I'm scared too but be strong honey. Be strong.*

"I have to get out of here." Megan stumbled forward, out of Brody's grasp. "Robbie needs me."

"Megan, wait." Brody blocked her path and gathered her in his arms.

Asari touched Megan's shoulder. "Your parents confirmed what I told you?"

"How could they confirm anything? They're not here." Brody said.

"Telepathy." Asari glanced up at Brody. "I know you do not believe but Megan's psychic abilities are real. All Talgorians are psychic. As are the Monocaths."

Megan tugged from Brody. "The Monocaths are psychic?"

"Yes. They are powerful in their psychic and magical abilities, which is why you must go through the transformation. It is your only hope."

"The Mountain Mangler is a Monocath?"

Asari's brow lifted. He turned away to walk over to the other Elders. He sat down to confer with them.

"That's why I feel like the Mangler's blocking me," Megan whispered to Brody. "It explains why you didn't hear him take me. I wonder what he did to you."

"I don't know, Megan. At this point it seems like anything is possible. I don't know what to believe." He released her as Asari approached.

"We have decided to tell you everything," Asari said, "but first, you must perform the transformation ritual to claim your birthright as a Talgorian."

Megan glanced from Asari to Brody. His sculpted features bore his confusion. *He's gorgeous. Such a good man. This must be so much harder for him to believe than it is for me.*

Robbie's life depended on her decision. She could walk out of here right now but they both might die. If she accepted her destiny she could save Robbie even if she couldn't save herself.

There wasn't a choice to make. Robbie would always come first.

Megan nodded to Asari and turned to Brody. "The only way to save our son is to claim my immortality as a Talgorian. I have to do this, Brody. The transformation will change things between us forever. I don't know what will happen afterward, so while I consider myself human, I want you to tell you again how sorry I am about your parents' accident. I never meant to hurt you. I only wish my love had been enough to carry us through."

"Megan—"

"Let me finish." She stepped closer. "I shouldn't have kept Robbie from you. It was wrong, regardless of my reasons. I was a coward not to find some way to tell you. Maybe one day you'll find it in your heart to forgive me."

She reached up to caress his cheek. "He looks like you. Please take care of him after my death. Don't ever let him forget me or how much I love him." Megan's voice, thick with emotion, cracked.

She held Brody's hands and kissed both palms. "I'll always love you, Brody, even if I'm not human."

"Megan, I—"

"No, don't say anything. It'll only make this harder on me." Megan released him and faced Asari. "I'm ready."

"Come." Asari led her toward the Elders.

"You don't have to do this," Brody said, following them.

Asari held out his hand, palm facing Brody. "Wait there. You are only being allowed to stay because you are the Key."

Brody took several steps forward. "Megan. Are you sure this is what you want?"

She stared at him, nodded and turned her attention back to the Elders who were retrieving items from the box and placing them on the table.

"What do you mean, I'm the Key? Megan, stop. This isn't a good idea."

"Brody Phelps. You stay right where you are and keep your dang big mouth shut. You hear me?"

Megan turned around at the familiar voice. "Auntie Faye?"

"Hey there, sweetie," the old woman called and waved to Megan. She stopped to give Brody a hug. "Now you hush and let us get on with it, Brody. Gotta save your boy, you know."

"Mrs. Frye, what are you doing here?" Brody asked.

"You'll see in a minute. Now, be quiet. I know you hate it when you can't jump into action but this is one time you have to stay out of it. Okay?"

"I—"

"Promise, Brody. This is important."

"I'm not going to promise because I have to protect Megan," Brody said. "For now, I'll do as you ask."

"That's a good boy." Auntie Faye patted his arm and walked over to Megan. "Well, Asari, is our girl ready?"

"Auntie Faye. Why are you here? Are you Talgorian?"

Asari took Auntie Faye's hand and placed it in Megan's, palms together. "Megan, meet your Guardian."

"Impossible. Auntie Faye can't be my Guardian. I haven't seen her in years. You said my Guardian was with me all the time."

Auntie Faye nodded. "You see, Megan, Guardians are different from other Talgorians. Our shifting isn't limited so we can protect those in our care."

"What does your birthmark look like?" Megan asked.

"It is a spiral within a triangle within a circle and it is always on the small of our backs," Auntie Faye said.

Show me. Megan asked telepathically.

The birthmark? Auntie Faye responded in kind.

"I didn't think that would work," Megan whispered.

"I know. It's a lot to understand." Auntie Faye rubbed Megan's upper arm. "You'll do fine."

"I want to see you change. I need to know who's been guarding me."

Auntie Faye glanced to Asari. "Do we begin now?"

Asari nodded and addressed Megan. "Are you ready for the transformation ritual?"

"As ready as I'll ever be." Megan looked over at Brody and wished their lives had run a similar path instead of opposite. "Let's get this over with."

The Elders formed a large circle around them, the fire, box and table. In soft tones they began to sing a slow song.

Megan didn't understand the words but the tune sounded

familiar. Didn't Mom hum something similar? Her heartbeat pounded in anticipation of the unexpected.

"The first time you shift," Asari said, "we will assist you. Then you will shift again, without us."

Megan nodded.

"We will communicate telepathically once you've glimmered." Asari picked up a bowl from the table and handed it to Megan. "Drink this."

"What is it?"

"A brew that aids in glimmering. Usually it is not necessary but at your age you will need it."

Megan glanced at Brody and drank from the bowl. The liquid was bitter with a sweet aftertaste. She grimaced and lifted her gaze from the bowl to Asari. "All of it?"

He nodded.

She drank the remainder down in a few gulps. "Okay. Now what?"

Asari picked up another bowl. He placed his thumb into the bright blue mixture and rubbed it across Megan's forehead. He repeated the process, creating orange horizontal lines under her eyes and a red vertical line on her nose and chin. With each stroke Megan's stomach tightened more. She couldn't see in her mind's eye what would happen. Had her psychic abilities shut down?

"It is time," Asari said to Auntie Faye.

The older woman stepped forward to stand directly in front of Megan. "I love you as if you were my own daughter. As your Guardian I have been with you throughout your life to protect you."

Positive surges washed over Megan. Moments later Carmela, Robbie's nanny, stood in Auntie Faye's place, wearing jeans and a t-shirt. How much of her life had been a lie?

"Carmela?" Megan shook her head. "This is impossible. How can you be two different people?"

"I am a Guardian, a Talgorian protector."

"That is all you need to know, Megan." Asari retrieved a piece of fabric from the table.

"No, I'm not going further with this ceremony unless I get some answers." Megan balled her hands into fists. "Do you understand how upsetting this is? Two people I love and trust are the same? No, I know there's more. I want to see your true self."

"Guardians are the elite force of our race. Their secrets cannot be divulged outside the Elder Circle. I'm sorry. We cannot give you details of their abilities but because you are the Griffin of the Prophecy, we will allow you to know your guardian as her true self."

Carmela stared at Megan. "I'm sorry, *broeistar*. I know this is difficult and upsetting for you."

She shifted again. A young woman with shoulder length hair stood in Carmela's place. She wore dark brown pants of thin leather with a matching top, which showed off six-pack abs. Her straight auburn hair, cut blunt, brushed against muscular shoulders. She appeared about Megan's age. "My Talgorian name is Varici."

"You should be in an action movie." Megan looked at Brody to see his reaction to the bombshell Varici. He watched with a scowl on his face.

Pain from her fingernails digging into sweaty palms caused Megan to unclench her fists. "I understand about Carmela but Auntie Faye... the whole community knows her. She's an integral part of Flatrock Creek. How could you be here as Auntie Faye when you were with me in Clarkston as Carmela?"

"She left town a few days after you moved away," Brody said from a few feet away.

Megan peered over at him. When had he gotten so close?

"Now that I think about it, she returned around the same time the Mangler killed the first victims and has been in and out of town since."

"What about the store? Wasn't it open?"

"Yes," Varici said, "we left someone in charge of the daily operations."

"Mark, a pharmacist from Alaska," Brody said.

"Talgorian?" Megan asked.

Varici and Asari nodded.

"That doesn't explain how you were with me every day as Carmela and here too since you returned to Flatrock Creek."

Varici smiled. "Auntie Faye visited with family in Clarkston. She was out of town a lot."

Megan realized that Varici wasn't going to give her the details she so desperately wanted to know. Auntie Faye and Carmela had always watched out for her, had always loved her.

They were both Varici. Megan knew that she would have to trust in the love the others gave her over the years to trust Varici.

"We should continue." Asari held out the piece of fabric he'd removed from the box.

"What am I supposed to do with this?" Megan accepted the silky lavender material.

"After you undress, you will wrap this around the back of your neck and let both ends hang to the front. It has special micro-fibers that act as a conductor when we add our energy to yours to help you shift the first time."

"I have to undress?" Megan tightened her hold on the silk. The Elders had undressed before they shifted, except for Asari who was the only one who had changed into a small creature but Varici hadn't. "Why didn't you undress to shift?"

"It's a perk."

Megan shook her head. "I can't."

She really couldn't strip down in front of Brody. Her body had changed after having Robbie. The flat abdomen she'd worked so hard to keep as a teenager now had a small bulge she couldn't lose.

She wasn't about to let Brody see in her in the buff after all these years. How could she undress in front of strangers?

"You must learn to change if you want to save your son." Asari picked up another bowl from the table. "Your clothes will be destroyed if you don't undress."

Megan cast another glance in Brody's direction. How embarrassing. Asking him to turn around would be even worse. Besides, he'd never agree to miss any of the weirdness happening to them. She had to do this to save Robbie.

She pulled the t-shirt over her head. When the last of her clothing lay in a pile beside her, she put the silk around her neck and lifted her hair from underneath it.

She warmed under Brody's heated stare. It scorched down the length of her body but she didn't dare take her eyes off Asari.

Varici lifted one side of the fabric, Asari the other with his free hand. Muttering words she couldn't understand, they crossed the fabric in an X between her breasts. Varici tied it at the small of her back. Asari stuck his fingers in the bowl and drew designs on her sides, chest and stomach with gold glittering paint.

He stepped back, replaced the bowl and wiped the paint from his hands with a small towel that lay on the table. "To glimmer, you must tap into the passions deep within you. Your thoughts, feelings and emotions make you who you are. Once you are comfortable with how the process of glimmering feels, you need to connect to your totem, the Griffin."

Asari grasped Megan and Varici's hands. "When the circle is connected, we will assist with our emotions. You only need to feel. Now, close the circle."

Megan reached for Varici but paused when she noticed Brody, hands fisted by his side, legs spread slightly apart. He looked ready to spring into action. Worry tensed the muscles in his face. Megan offered him a soft smile as she took the Guardian's hand.

The force generated by the Elders traveled to the interior of their circle of three. Megan turned her gaze upward. Her body absorbed each powerful surge. Suddenly, she longed to stretch her muscles. She thought of Robbie, of Brody, of the Talgorian's protection.

The Elders spoke to her telepathically, saying foreign words, which filled her with a deep sense of love.

Her arms and legs tingled as if they'd fallen asleep. "Asari?" she asked.

"You're doing fine, Megan. Concentrate."

"I am. I feel you with me."

Such intense love and they didn't even know her. Megan closed her eyes. She heard soft popping noises that reminded her of the way electricity sounded when you stood under power lines. She visualized the Griffin in her mind. Its mighty wings, lion paws and magnificent face of an eagle.

An intense need to be the Griffin filled her. She opened her eyes to find that the Elders seemed further away, smaller. The dark colors of the cave came alive. The fire was especially vibrant. Her vision had somehow expanded. She could see the Elders, Brody and most of the cave at the same time.

Varici and Asari no longer held her hands. *When did they let go?* Both smiled up at her.

Brody's mouth hung open, his eyes were wide in disbelief.

"Did it work?" Megan asked. Instead of her voice she heard the screeching call of an eagle.

Oh my God! I changed?

CHAPTER ELEVEN

MEGAN LOOKED DOWN TO SEE PIECES OF THE SILKY fabric lying on the floor near huge black talons emerging from yellow, leathery claws. Several inches higher black feathers covered her arms. She raised her hands to look at them and the claws rose causing her body to rear up with the motion. She almost fell over so she lowered them back to the ground. She stuck her head between her arms, which were now legs, to look backward. Her body was shaped like a lioness and her feet had become huge paws.

"Come." Asari said telepathically. "Now you shall know your greatness."

She raised her head to see the Elders walking toward her. They formed a circle around her. Varici took Brody by the hand and brought him in front of the Talgorians. He never took his gaze from Megan even as Varici led him toward a dark area of the cave.

Where are we going, Asari?

You shall see in a moment. You've done well, Megan. We are all proud of you.

She stepped forward and stumbled. *What the?* Maybe crawling would be easier. She tried and her new body moved forward. *It worked.*

The sensation was strange, lumbering. A twitch tickled her shoulder blades so she looked back. Wings! She squeezed the tickling muscles and the wings spread wide. Very wide. She looked at one side then the other and back to Asari.

Impressive isn't it?

I don't know how to work this body.

It will become easier. Follow me. The transformation ceremony isn't complete.

Megan wobbled after him as they passed the table and followed a pathway until they entered another large, bright room. Mirrors were fixed onto wooden beams lining the passageway. Torches protruded from sconces attached to the cavern walls.

With her expanded vision, she could watch herself in the mirrors as she walked to the center of the room. As the Griffin, she was massive.

Why did I think Griffins were small? She couldn't recall but this beast in the mirrors was the largest animal she'd ever seen. It even had a lion's tail.

How can I be this creature?

Brody stood at the far end of the cavern. His expression of shock had changed to one of wonder.

Will I understand him if he speaks? So far no one had uttered a word except in her mind.

Fear stopped her in the center of the mirrors. If Brody couldn't believe in her psychic abilities what did he think of her now? He'd never believe this even though he'd watched the transformation with his own eyes. She could hardly believe it herself. The mirrors didn't lie though.

Megan stared at her reflection. Golden eyes gleamed back at her. She opened her mouth and looked at the pointed tongue inside. Wicked. She turned her head to admire the white feathers. They overlapped black plumes, which covered the front half of her body until they turned into a sleek, golden fur. A long tail hung behind her, the tip a golden brown. She wiggled her butt and the tail swung. *Amazing.*

She caught Asari's gaze in the mirror and turned away from inspecting the Griffin to face him.

The Elders stood evenly spaced around the perimeter of the room. They started to chant in Talgorian, their tones low and steady. As the Griffin, Megan understood the words. *The time is now, change has come, fly high and soar, claim all that is yours.*

Asari and Varici held hands. Taking small steps they danced forward, repeating the Elders' chant. Each placed their free hand on either side of her face.

To complete the transformation you must fly, they said to her in unison.

Fly? I can't fly. I can barely walk. Panic seized at her heart. *I can't do it. I don't know how.*

Energy radiated from Asari, Varici and the Elders. *To defeat the Monocath and save the child, you must. Draw from our power, feel the essence of flight. Look up, Talgorian Griffin.*

She did and saw the high cavern ceiling.

Can I do it?

Robbie needed her. She let the love for him fill her heart, mind and spirit. She twitched her shoulder blades and focused on a high ledge.

A surge of adrenaline accompanied the power of love in her heart. Megan lifted from the ground and flew toward the ledge. Twitching her shoulders again she heard the beat of wings in the air. She kept her eyes trained straight ahead on the ledge. Focused and concentrating she soared higher until she landed on the target.

Rocks broke and crumbled under her weight. Resting only a moment, she soared away into the ebony depths of the cavern.

Except it wasn't dark. She could see almost as well as she could in the light.

It was an incredible feeling, flight. A sense of freedom and power surged with each downward thrust of her wings. She claimed the power, accepted her destiny in her heart.

Talgorian Griffin.

Megan slowed to land on the top of a large stalagmite. This whole situation was incredible. Here, alone in the depths of the cave, she wanted to cry her eyes out, to cry for her son, for the love she'd lost with Brody and for herself.

Her heart ached. Her whole life had been a lie—she wasn't even human. The tears didn't come. Instead strength from somewhere deep inside her overwhelmed the sadness. She stretched feathered wings and spread them wide. She looked back and examined them. She had the wingspan of a large pterodactyl.

I'm not a dinosaur, she thought, *I'm an amazing mystical being who happens to live in modern times on Earth. I must be strong. I must save my son from the Monocath and defeat the monster before he kills again. Too many have lost their lives in the Mangler's search for me. Now, he's found me and I will not rest until he cannot harm another.*

Noticing a pool of water, she flew down and with a soft thud landed at the edge. She peered into its depths. A beautiful eagle stared back. A sense of peace overcame her.

This is my destiny, my heritage, my new life.

Her heart warmed with acceptance as she embraced the Talgorian Griffin into her life. A renewed sense of determination filled her. She lunged forward, lifting feathered wings into the air and leaving the fear behind.

Angling around a natural cavern wall, she flew back into the mirrored room.

"I am the Talgorian Griffin!" Meagan shouted the words as she landed but heard only a piercing screech of the eagle again. *This is really going to take some getting used to.*

Asari smiled as the Griffin lumbered toward him. "You have done well, broeistar. Now change back by thinking of your human form and glimmering. We'll practice one more time to make sure you can change alone."

I can understand the spoken word in this body. She nodded and pulled the power inward. Moments later she stood naked before them.

"I...I did it! I can't believe I actually changed into a huge beast."

"Now, try again," Asari said, "without us."

"Okay, here goes nothing." Megan nodded.

The room pulsated as she glimmered and changed back into the Griffin.

"Megan," Brody whispered.

She faced him. And saw the pain, wonder and confusion in his eyes. He reached out and stroked her neck feathers. His touch was gentle, almost loving. She lowered her head and leaned against his shoulder.

If this change hadn't happened, they might have had a chance for a future together. Now they never would.

"I don't understand how this is possible." Brody slid his hand down the Griffin's back. The beast was noble, proud and inside, it was Megan. "You're magnificent."

"Isn't she?" Asari joined Brody. "The Talgorian Griffin is one of the elite few, similar to the Guardians, who can defeat the Monocaths. More powerful than most of our race, with stronger psychic abilities and, well, we're not even sure what all of her capabilities will be."

Brody stroked the Griffin's neck and across her back, threading his fingers deep into the soft, thick fur of the lion. "You said I am the Key. Exactly what does that mean?"

Asari turned Brody to face him, looking the human in the eyes. "She is to be protected always. The Monocath will stop at nothing to defeat her once he realizes she is the Griffin of the Prophecy. The few Monocaths left are the oldest and most powerful of their race. They have only two goals and those are to Soul Merge with a Talgorian female to regain the ability to shift and eliminate every one of us from the face of the earth. It is only in this form and with the power of love and fire that she shall defeat the Monocath Ancient, the Mountain Mangler. You must protect her while helping her meet the challenges she will face."

Megan lifted her head to look at Asari. *Can I defeat him? Or is this a hopeless battle?*

"We must never lose hope, *broeistar*. Our entire existence depends on the ultimate defeat of the Monocaths."

"Can she understand us when she's the Griffin?" Brody asked, noticing Megan's movements indicated she followed the conversation and Asari seemed to be responding to unasked questions.

"Yes. She can also communicate telepathically with other Talgorians."

Brody reached up and maneuvered the eagle's face to his level. "I promise I won't let anything happen to you, Megan. I don't really understand what I'm expected to do as the Key but I will do my best. We will find our son and we will save him—together."

"I take your word as truth." Asari held out his hand and waited.

Brody clasped Asari's hand and gave a firm shake. "How will love and fire defeat the Mangler?"

"I cannot tell you, because I do not know." Asari stepped back and held his hands out, palms up. "You are ready, broeistar. It is time to return to your human form."

Powerful surges rocked through the room. Brody watched the waves radiate outward from Megan. The Griffin disappeared. She stood before him, naked. He saw the amazement in her eyes, before letting his gaze drift downward pausing at her large breasts with taut rosy nipples. He remembered their weight in his hands, the softness of sucking them into his mouth. Further down the mark of the Griffin on her lower abdomen drew his gaze to the tuft of blonde hair between her legs. He grew hard in response. He drank in every nuance of her body, committing it to memory until he reached her eyes. She blushed but didn't move, her gaze glued to his face.

"I'm sorry, Brody. I never knew I was a Talgorian." She headed toward Varici. The Elders left their positions and followed her.

Brody watched Meagan walk away. Her firm buttocks swayed with each step. *God, she's beautiful.*

"Are you in love with her?" Asari asked.

Brody didn't answer. Instead he watched the way Megan's hips moved as she stepped into her pants.

"As the Key, you must be willing to forfeit your life to save hers."

"He'll do no such thing." Megan turned toward the two men, tugging down her shirt. Brody hadn't answered and she really didn't want to know if he'd responded to Asari's question. "My hearing is keener since I've glimmered. All of my senses are heightened. Robbie will need his father if anything happens to me."

Asari smiled. "It is time for you to find your son. Varici will show you the way out."

"Can't I just fly there and save Robbie?" Megan asked, as she put on her shoes.

"Do you know where he's hidden?" Asari said.

Megan shook her head. She left the Elders to rejoin Asari and Brody. "I can search the area where I sense he's held."

"I cannot tell you what to do. It is your choice. Remember the Monocaths have had thousands of years to perfect the use of their abilities." Asari held her hands. "You have just come into yours. If there is any chance of defeating the Monocath, it will be through your courage and cunning. Unfortunately, according to the Prophecy, we cannot help you. Only the Key can be by your side."

"Exactly what does the Prophecy say?" Brody asked.

"When the Monocath kills in pairs, the Griffin and Key together must seek the salvation of the innocent. In this quest only four exist, no other shall assist. The Griffin, Key, Monocath and child—good and evil shall collide. Only change will bring acceptance. Only fire will end the rampage. Only love challenges death." Asari released her hands.

"Why would the Monocaths abide by the Prophecy and not assist the Mangler?" Megan asked.

"Long ago only the Talgorian race existed." Asari said. "Immortality was given to us by the Celestial League as a reward for our good deeds in protecting the humans. They warned us it was an honor and privilege, which could be taken away."

Asari's gaze traveled over the Elders before returning to Megan. "One of our females was fooled by a human who disguised his evil intentions to Soul Merge with her. He proclaimed himself the Monocath King and led over half of our population away with the promise of riches and power. Instead of following our peaceful ways, they used deception and violence to gain what they wanted. The League warned them but they didn't listen so their ability to glimmer and Soul Merge were taken away. This made them infertile. They could no longer bring humans into the race or create offspring with the women they had. Eventually all the females were killed. It was rumored some even had a pact to kill one another to be free of the Monocaths."

"How sad," Megan said.

Varici nodded. "If a Talgorian Soul Merges with a Monocath it will restore the ability to shapeshift and procreate to their race. They try to trick our females into Soul Merging with them. It is imperative that we are always aware of their illusions. We must never let it happen. Only their Ancients are left and without the ability to Soul Merge they can't reproduce. We have stayed hidden but now we must fight this war with them. If we are successful, we will eventually eliminate the remaining Monocaths."

"How do you kill them?" Brody asked.

"With the X and decapitation, just like they kill us," Asari said. "The League said they will remove either race's immortality if we interfere in the prophecies. They won't risk it, nor will we. The outcome will determine who wins this war and who retains their immortality. We all must follow the rules set forth by the Celestial

League."

"We live in a series of caverns the Monocaths cannot penetrate. Varici will show you how to open and close the gateways." Asari stepped backward. "I am only a thought away, Talgorian Griffin."

A surge of energy filled the cavern. Asari changed into the black and gold iguana and disappeared into the shadows. His clothing lay in a pile at their feet.

"Come." Varici said, walking toward the exit.

Megan picked up her backpack and followed. Another forceful surge moved over her. She looked back into an empty cavern. How had the Elders disappeared so quickly?

Varici laid her hand on the cave wall and turned her wrist to the right. The rock disappeared. She turned her hand to the left and it reappeared.

"How does this work?" Megan rubbed her hand over the entrance. She expected her hand to disappear into an illusion but it met hard rock.

"Underneath these mountains are an interconnecting series of caverns. When the Monocaths separated from us, we devised these doors using our Guardian powers. Give me your hand."

Varici took Megan's outstretched palm and laid it against the rock. "To open, you turn your hand to the right and think the word, zulante, to close, turn left and think *drantar*."

"What keeps the Monocaths out?" Brody asked.

"The Guardians' protection on the gateways picks up the difference in touch. Talgorians have shifting atoms, the Monocaths don't."

Megan followed Varici's instructions. Moving her hand while thinking the words she was able to open and close the entrance. "Interesting."

"If you need to hide quickly, use your psychic abilities to find a door." Varici opened the gateway again and walked out.

As they emerged from the cave Megan expected to see filtered sunlight shining through the forest canopy. Instead, a full moon had replaced the sun. She hadn't noticed while learning how to operate the gateway. Varici stepped a short distance from the cavern opening, raised her hand into the air and the rock slid back into place, securing the opening.

"Do you use magic too?" Brody asked.

"No, only my Guardian abilities. Remember, Robbie is telepathic but should you speak to him in this manner you run the risk of the Monocath overhearing the conversation. He is tapped into Robbie's mind in case he's found the Griffin. He doesn't know you're the one prophesized and you should keep this information from him for as long as possible."

"I can't connect with him right now." Her voice cracked. Overwhelming sadness brought tears to her eyes. Brody's hand rested on her shoulder. A simple touch but his strength enabled her to regain control of the emotions.

"It may be a spell blocking Robbie's ability to link with you," Varici said. "Be careful, *broeistar*."

"I don't know why I didn't recognize you." Megan looked deep into Varici's eyes. "Your eyes are the same as Auntie Faye and Carmela now that I think about it. Are you still my Guardian?"

"Always, *broeistar*." Varici grabbed Megan in a strong hug. "As Asari said, we are only a thought away. This is your quest, your destiny. Only the Griffin and the Key can save the innocent."

"Thank you," Megan whispered.

Varici released her, smiled and disappeared.

"I'm never going to get used to this," Megan muttered.

"Me either." Brody handed her one of two flashlights. "Let's get moving."

"I think we should take five minutes to talk about what happened in there," Megan said, as he walked away. "Don't you?"

· · ·

I CAN'T TALK. I need to think.

"Not now." Brody ran a hand through his hair. "We've got to get back to the truck so we can drive to Monocath Mountain. After all I witnessed, it's the most logical place for the Mangler to hold Robbie."

What he'd heard was insane. What he saw unbelievable.

If he hadn't been there to see the transformation ritual for himself, he would never have believed it. Even now it was difficult to comprehend.

How did two groups of immortals exist in complete secrecy from the rest of the world?

By learning to blend into the human race. He'd never look at people in the same way again. How could he serve the public when at any given time he could be up against an immortal who could easily kill him?

He glanced back at Megan. He'd never think of her in the same way either. She was strikingly beautiful in human form and magnificent as the Talgorian Griffin. *But she isn't human, she's immortal, which changes everything.*

She walked with her head down. He could only imagine how the transformation affected her. To feel her body change into a mythological creature must have been traumatic. Or exhilarating.

Words wouldn't even begin to make her feel better. He didn't know how to comfort her. She'd been alone in the world since they broke up, making a life for their son with the only gift she thought she had. He could no longer blame her for keeping Robbie a secret. Her parents pushed her away, he'd pushed her away and the only one who had been there for her through it all was a shapeshifting Talgorian Guardian.

How could I have been such a jerk?

As much as he hated to admit it, the problem was his. He was the one who couldn't deal with this, not Megan.

She'd done everything asked of her without the slightest

hesitation. Sure she'd wanted reasons and he could tell she really didn't want to undress in front of him but she'd complied.

It had nearly been his undoing.

He hadn't been prepared for the memories seeing her naked brought to the surface. Days of crazy lovemaking in any private spot they could find. He'd never been able to get enough of her. He kept seeing her standing naked in the cave with nothing more than a blush on her face, knowing he was inspecting her from head to toe. Even in her embarrassment she hadn't tried to cover herself or look away. It made him want her more.

How could he accept Megan's immortality and ability to shapeshift into a huge Griffin? If he could only wrap his mind around the whole situation and figure it out. Everything he believed in, truth, justice and humanity, had been thrown right out of the window in the past few hours.

The path curved alongside the mountain. Moonlight cast eerie shadows against a cliff on one side and a ravine on the other.

"Megan, be careful through here. It's getting narrow," he called over his shoulder. "The truck is parked up ahead."

A pebble fell, then several more and the next thing he knew the sound of rocks crunching against brush grew louder. He stopped, looked up while turning around to locate the noise and saw a huge boulder headed straight for Megan, who wasn't paying attention, still walking with her head down.

"Megan! Watch out!" He sprinted at full speed, grabbing her around the waist, spinning her out of the way and taking care to hold her close. If they fell, he'd take the brunt of the impact. Her feet slipped and they careened into the ravine.

Twisting and turning, he managed to land on his back. The backpack kept the rifle from digging into his skin. He planted his heels into the earth as they slid, holding Megan on top of him and slowed to a stop.

The sound of the boulder tumbling further down into the

ravine drowned into the distance as the Mangler's maniacal laughter filled the air.

Brody rolled Megan off him, sat up and pulled the rifle off his back. He shot toward the laughter. When the crack of the gunshot dissipated into the night, the Mangler's laughter could be heard from deep within the forest.

"Are you okay?" Brody picked up a dropped flashlight and pointed it upward. Megan's brows were drawn tight, eyes narrowed and her lips were a straight line. He'd seen the look many times in high school. "Megan, this is not the time to lose your temper."

"He has my son." She pulled away from Brody and stood. "I'm going to transform and kill that son of a bitch. I'm tired of this game."

"No, you're not." Brody rose beside her, grabbed her by the upper arms and turned her so he could look into her eyes. "He has *our* son. You can't let your anger get in the way. You need courage and cunning to succeed. You can't let the Mangler know who you really are. Not yet."

"Hell, I don't even know who I am anymore." Megan jerked away. "My whole life has been a lie, everyone I love is not who I thought they were and I'm being targeted by a killer. Right now it sucks to be me." She turned away, picked up the other flashlight and headed out of the ravine to the path. "I'll meet you at the truck."

Brody retrieved his flashlight and followed. "I know how you feel but you have to keep your cool too."

Megan whirled around. "You know how I feel? How could you possibly know how I feel, Brody? You threw me out of your life before I could even tell you I was pregnant and until a few minutes ago I thought my parents turned against me because I refused to give up our baby. I had to beg you to help me find Robbie. Now I find out about this Prophecy while I'm with you—the one person in the world who will never, ever believe in me. You can't possibly know how I feel right now so don't even try." Her voice cracked and she turned away.

"Megan, I care about you. Don't do this—"

"No, don't *you* do this. You really don't have to worry about protecting me. I'm immortal, I can shapeshift into the almighty Griffin. I can take care of myself."

She headed down the path toward the truck. Brody let her go. She was right. He really didn't know what she was going through. Anger must be part of it, like in the grieving process. He'd give her the space she wanted.

In the few short hours since Megan's return to Flatrock Creek, she'd crawled right back under his skin. Maybe she'd never really left. He'd been wrong to let her go.

At the truck Brody did a quick check around the exterior. He unlocked and held the door open for Megan. She avoided looking at him as she climbed inside. He shut the door, pulled the radio from his hip and pressed the button. "Lewis."

The radio crackled. "How's it going, Chief?"

"Not good. I'm going to need backup on Monocath Mountain."

"Sorry, Chief. There's been a mining accident. We've got three men trapped."

"Do you have the situation under control?"

"Yes, they weren't in too deep. They've got air but it's going to take some time to remove the rocks and dirt to get them out. It's not national news."

"All right. Radio me with updates. I'll need backup as soon as you've resolved the situation. We're leaving Talgor Ridge and driving to Monocath Mountain."

"Ten-four. Make sure you leave your radio on this time though. I tried to reach you earlier and couldn't."

"I was in a cave." Silence filled the airwaves for a few brief moments. After what happened in the cave, Brody found himself doubting everything. Could Lewis' silence mean he was Talgorian too?

"Okay, Chief. Be careful up there."

"Will do." He'd give Lewis a chance to come clean about the Talgorians. He'd joked about them earlier but was it a ruse? "Is there anything else you want to tell me, Lewis?"

"Nothing you don't already know."

Damn. That wasn't an answer. "Ten-four. Phelps, out."

Brody slid the radio back into its holder and opened the driver's door. Once inside he turned to Megan. "Are you all right?"

"Fine. Let's get to Monocath Mountain." She looked out of the window. "I don't want to talk."

Brody saw the tear tracks on her cheek clearly outlined in the moonlight. His heart ached to soothe her, to take away the pain. He didn't know what to say to make it better. Maybe she needed more time to adjust to what Asari said.

He twisted the key in the ignition, turned the truck around and headed down Talgor Ridge toward the monster waiting for them at Monocath Mountain.

CHAPTER TWELVE

THE FOREST TURNED INTO AN OPEN ROAD AS BRODY turned onto Highway 55. Megan watched the white centerlines move by in a blur. What a horrible day it had been. Her past, present and future were out of control.

She listened to the hum of the truck engine. God, she needed sleep. If this nightmare was over she could go home to life the way it was before the Mountain Mangler, Monocaths and Talgorians.

A dull ache crept to her temples. She closed her eyes and rubbed the area with her fingertips. She sensed a presence close by, dark and menacing. She pushed the feeling away. Visualizing a wall of white light around them she blocked against any negative forces. If the Mangler tried to connect with her psychically right now, he'd drain any strength she had left.

"Look in the glove compartment. I keep some pain reliever in there."

"Thanks. I ran out." She heard him digging around behind the seat.

"Here's some water."

Megan lifted weary lids to find a half-filled bottle of water in front of her.

She took it from him, retrieved the pain relievers from the glove box and washed two tablets down with a sip of water.

"Why don't you try to get some sleep? It's a half-hour drive from here."

"I can't. Robbie needs me to find him."

"You're not going to do him any good if you're exhausted. Besides, what can you do while we're driving? Take a short nap, you'll feel better." He glanced over and brushed a stray strand of hair from her face. He took the bottle of tablets from her and threw them back in the glove compartment and flipped the door shut. "When was the last time you slept?"

"Before Robbie's abduction."

"Come here, ladybug." Brody placed his arm around her shoulder, pulling her close.

She started to resist but then, with a sigh, laid her head against him. Maybe it would be okay to relax for a minute. She should stay alert but she was so tired, mentally and physically.

She wanted to be held, needed to be comforted by someone. She'd been the strong caregiver for far too long without anyone to care for her in return. Sometimes the helplessness and vulnerability were hard to deal with and even harder to hide.

This is one of those times.

A protected feeling soothed her within the circle of Brody's strong arm. The stress and lack of sleep pulled at her, taking her to the place she'd been fighting.

Megan's breathing deepened. The steady rhythm filled the silence inside the truck.

She slid down his chest until her head rested against his thigh. Adjusting her body, she snuggled into the crease of his hip wrapping her arm around his leg. She molded to him like she had all those years ago.

Why had he let the angry hormones of a teenager banish her from his life? He couldn't blame it on being a teenager. Even as an adult, he'd never tried to repair their relationship because of her psychic abilities. It had been really easy and immature, to blame Megan for his parents' deaths instead of accepting it for what it was—an accident. *It's not Megan's fault you missed six years of your son's life. She did what she thought was best, based on your actions. You have to stop blaming her for having psychic abilities. It's not like she asked for them. She was born with them, like every other Talgorian. Her visions could save your son.*

Damn conscience.

It was right. He couldn't keep blaming Megan for his own fears. He had to accept her, all of her, even the immortal Talgorian Griffin, because he loved her.

He stroked her hair as she slept, its softness a gentle reminder of tender moments they'd shared. Not only had he lost six years with his son, he'd lost seven with Megan. He needed her. Now he knew how much.

The moonlight shadowed Monocath Mountain looming in the distance. Whatever happened there would change all of their lives forever. He didn't understand what he could do. When Asari told him he was the Key he hadn't taken it lightly. He knew the part he would play in this situation was important. If only he could live up to the expectations Asari put on him. Could he die for Megan?

She stirred in his lap. Her hand tightened around his leg. Her body jerked. He ran his hand up and down her arm to soothe her into a restful sleep.

SHE SOARED ABOVE the cliffs. Moonlight lit the rocks and crags, casting eerie shadows across Monocath Mountain. Rabbits ran into their holes. The crickets were silent. Only an owl didn't show fear.

Was it Talgorian too?

A large pine tree lay at an angle near a rock shaped like a house. Megan memorized the landmarks as her wings beat a steady rhythm through the night air. She followed an old trail around the left side of the mountain. She dived down lower, flying underneath the forest canopy, following her instincts in search of Robbie.

A clearing with a small shack came into view. Brody leaned

against the door, his arms crossed in front of him. Megan circled and landed a few yards away.

"Ah, my Talgorian Griffin. You have finally come to me."

Megan answered and the eagle's cry filled the air.

"I can't understand you. Please, change for me so we can talk. I want to see you in all of your beauty."

She shifted and stood naked before him. "What are you doing here? This is the shack where I saw the Mangler."

"I've been waiting for you. Hoping you'd come back to me. I was a fool to let you go." He strode toward her, grasped her shoulders. "You're so delicious. I've missed touching you."

He slid his hands underneath her breasts, caressing their fullness. Leaning down, he sucked and teased her nipple, flicking his tongue over the protruding nub while he tweaked the other nipple between forefinger and thumb. His tongue laved her skin, moving from her breast to her neck. He sucked the tender flesh there. Nibbling, and biting.

Her body flamed under his attention. She'd had many dreams of him in the past seven years but none had ever been this real. She'd always wanted to be a couple again. He'd needed time, maybe she'd stayed away too long.

"Stop. You're going to give me a hickey."

A low laugh rumbled in this throat. "It's okay, baby. I'm claiming you," he said against her skin. "You're mine. I'm never letting you go again. I need your love...your energy...your power." He slid his hand between her legs, cupping her mound. He parted the folds of her sensitive flesh as he sucked harder on her neck. Dipping his finger inside, he rubbed his thumb in slow circular motions.

Passion coiled within her. Every movement of his hand tensed her body tighter, bringing her closer to release.

He withdrew his finger to pinch and tease her. He licked her neck with his tongue until he reached her earlobe. The sensations of his fingernails and tongue grazing her flesh combined with the chilly night air caused goose bumps all over her body.

"Brody."

"Soul Merge with me, Megan."

Yes, she would make them one for all eternity.

This feels wrong.

Why would he ask her to Soul Merge, knowing the repercussions? She couldn't ask him to give up his humanity for her.

"Why would you say that?" Megan pushed him away.

"Because I want you." He grabbed her again.

An evil grin spread across his face. Megan jerked out of his grasp as realization pulsed in her, clearing the fog caused by his lovemaking.

The scratch of steel slipping against steel filled the air as he pulled a sword from its casing on his back.

Where did that come from?

"You're not Brody!"

"No I'm not. If you don't give me the power to glimmer, you will die." The Mangler swung the blade.

Megan ran, glimmering as she fled until she lifted into the air as the Griffin.

"You'll die by my hand," the Mangler screamed from behind her, "as will your son!"

"Never!" she yelled and the eagle's cry filled the night.

MEGAN OPENED HER eyes with a start. *Where am I?* Disorientation became recognition.

Her head was on Brody's thigh.

They were in the truck.

Her arm was wrapped around his leg like she'd slept on him as a teenager. She pushed up, he grunted and she realized her hand was on his crotch. She jerked it away, lost her balance and scrambled to sit up.

She remembered the dream. *Oh God, what was I doing in my sleep?*

"How long was I out?" She tried to appear nonchalant but her voice sounded raspy.

"About half an hour. I decided to wait until we got to the trail to wake you. We'll have to take the ATV from there."

"Umm...did I do anything strange in my sleep?"

Brody grinned and looked over at her. "Nothing I didn't like."

"I'm sorry." Her cheeks were hot with embarrassment. In the dark, maybe he wouldn't notice.

"It's all right. You must have had some dream."

"Yeah but it wasn't a good dream. It was a nightmare." She turned to him and a pain shot through her neck. "What the—"

She pulled down the sun visor and flipped up the mirror cover. The light came on. Megan pulled her hair away from her neck. A huge red mark stained her skin. "Stop the truck!"

"Why? What's wrong?"

"Stop the truck!" Panic raced through her. How could she get a physical mark on her skin from a dream?

"There isn't anywhere to pull over."

Megan looked out of the front window to see a winding road going up Monocath Mountain. They were rounding a sharp curve. She saw a scenic viewing area for tourists to look over the valley in her minds eye. "There's a lookout up ahead—pull in there."

"What's the matter?"

"Magic. He used magic on me."

When the lookout came into view, Brody pulled in and put the truck in park. "You're not making any sense. Who used magic on you?"

"The Mountain Mangler."

"How could he?"

"Turn on the interior lights." Impatiently she pressed the reading light. "Look at my neck."

"What the hell?" Brody pulled her toward him to get a better look. "Where did this come from?"

She told him about the dream in detail. "He's marked me, said he claimed me. I swear, I thought it was you. He knows I'm the Griffin."

Jealousy tore through Brody. "Why would you think it was me, Megan? We haven't had sex in years. I'm sure the men in your life since me made you forget all about us."

Megan turned away to stare out of the window. Her whole life was upside down right now and Brody worried about her sex life. She might as well tell him the truth. "There hasn't been anyone since you."

"Don't lie to me. I've seen you on television draped over different men's arms."

"Sure, eye candy. I dated but none of them was ever in my bed."

"In the past seven years you haven't had sex with anyone?"

"The first year I was pregnant and then I had a newborn. Taking care of Robbie took up most of my time." Why was she explaining her reasons? She didn't owe him an explanation at all. Why was he questioning her sexual activity anyway? "Ah hell, that's exactly what I'm saying. Right now I really don't care if you believe me or not. All I know is this maniac got into my dream, pretended to be you, touched me, marked me and tried to kill me." She looked into the mirror. "Do you think this will go away since it was put there by magic?"

"Why don't you ask Asari?" Brody opened the door and stepped out into the night air and slammed the door. He couldn't deal with anything else right now.

The temperature had dropped, creating a chill in the air. The crispness of the night cleared his mind. If Megan hadn't been intimate with anyone else could she still love him? She said so when she changed but he hadn't thought she meant she was in love with him.

He thought of her raising Robbie alone, without any support from him or her family. She probably didn't have the time to be involved with someone else. It was foolish to think she could be in love him after all this time. He pushed all thoughts of love and sex out of his mind.

When Megan had told him about the dream she said she found the Mangler by going to the left side of the mountain. He thought about the roads and trails on that side. He knew of two fitting her description. They'd check them both. He'd have to trust that she would lead them the right way.

Imagine that.

He would have to put his faith in her clairvoyance.

He knew he'd need backup now. Asari said only the Talgorians and Monocaths weren't allowed to interfere. He never said anything about humans. He rubbed his hand over his eyes. *What a day.*

He pulled the radio from his hip. "Lewis, what's the status of the miners?"

"We're halfway through the rubble, Chief. Most of the men in town have come out." The sound of voices, machines and the clattering of rocks being thrown filled the background as Lewis spoke.

"We're heading up Monocath Mountain now. I'm taking the ATV toward the peak. We're checking the two mining roads on the West side of the mountain. Radio me when you have men available."

"Ten-four, Chief."

Brody held the radio for a moment as he stared out over the valley. He considered the miners and his own situation before shoving the radio back into his utility belt.

The Mangler knew Megan was the Griffin. He'd pursue her more than ever, putting them in greater danger.

Thunder rumbled, echoing behind the mountain. A storm was on the way.

"Damn." He got back into the truck and shut the door. He stared out of the windshield. A streak of lightning flashed above the mountain peak. "Megan, we have to talk whether you want to or not. This could easily get out of control and we don't have any plan to stop this lunatic."

"I know."

The soft tone of her voice gave him pause. He twisted in the seat to face her. Such sorrow reflected in those big blue eyes. She didn't need his anger. "Let me start over. This is stressful for both of us. To be successful, we need to prepare.

She nodded. "You're right."

"What did Asari say about the mark?"

"It's never happened before."

"So we're in new territory here, even for the Talgorians." He held her hand, interlacing his fingers with hers. "What else did he say?"

"We need to be extra careful now the Mangler knows I'm the Griffin."

I thought the same thing. "How could he know? It was only a dream."

"Asari said it was real. The Mangler used magic to enter my dream so he experienced it too." She shuddered. "I can't believe I let him touch me."

"How could you have known?"

"I shouldn't have slept." Megan leaned her head against the seat.

He lifted her chin with his fingers. "We'll get through this." He tucked a piece of hair behind her ear. "I promise."

Megan nodded. "So. What's your plan?"

"Asari said they don't know exactly what you're capable of. I think we should try to figure out what abilities you have. Maybe we'll discover some talent we can use."

"Exactly how are we going to do that?"

"How much do you know about Griffins?"

"Only what I learned in school. They look like I did when I transformed. They hated horses, protected gold and precious stones, could fly and were monogamous. I don't remember anything about them having any special abilities like dragons breathing fire."

Monogamous. That explains why she's never taken another man to bed. I was her first and last. "As a Talgorian, you have psychic abilities—"

"That you don't believe in." Megan removed her hand from his grasp.

"You're right. I didn't believe in them. Today's events have changed my mind about a lot of things. I guess Asari was right when he said sometimes you have to see it to believe it."

"So now you're a believer?"

"Do I have another choice?"

"Sure you do. We always have choices in life."

"Not this time we don't. I believe in what I know as fact. What I see and can prove. My experiences solidify the facts for me." Brody caressed her arm. "I believe in you, Megan. I know there is more to the Griffin than what you learned in class or in the cave. You're special. If you weren't, there wouldn't be a prophecy about you fighting a Monocath."

Her eyes brightened a bit. "Where do we start?"

"How about the legendary abilities of superheroes and mystical creatures?"

Megan chuckled. "If you think it'll work."

"At this point, it can't hurt."

"What should I try first?"

"Let's start with things you might be able to do in human form." He looked out the window. "Try to raise yourself from the seat."

"Levitate?"

Brody nodded. "Sure, why not?"

"Okay." Megan closed her eyes and sat there a few minutes. "Did I move?"

"No. Scratch that one."

"Can you create a force field around us?"

"I'll try. How will we know if this works?"

"I'll get out and throw a branch at the truck. If you're able to do it the stick should bounce off." Brody exited the truck, searched for a dead limb and nodded when he was ready.

Megan imagined a domed force field around the truck. "Throw it."

Brody drew the stick back and slung. It didn't get close to the truck but ricocheted against an invisible wall and hit him in the chest.

"You did it!" He walked toward the cab and suddenly jerked backward. "You can stop now." He tried again, this time reaching out to feel for a barrier with his hands. He returned to the cab but left the door open. "We can use this. What about your hearing? You heard me whispering to Asari in the cave."

She cocked her head to the side. "Where is the Alexander's house? I hear a woman cooing to her baby."

"How do you know the name? What is she saying?"

"I see the word clairvoyantly. The baby is crying and she's saying, 'It's okay Jesse. Mama's here.' She's humming a lullaby now."

"Is this a vision or do you actually hear her?"

"It's both. I see the picture in my mind's eye and I hear her the same way I'm hearing you. This feels different from clairaudience though."

"They live about ten miles from here. So we know you can hear at great distances. Good. We can use this too."

"Come on." He got out and leaned in to look at her.

"Why?" Megan didn't move.

"Let's try some other things you wouldn't be able to do in the truck."

"What if someone drives by?"

"This road isn't traveled much, especially this late at night. If a car comes we'll stop."

"All right." Megan climbed out and went to the edge of the overlook. Lightning flashed behind the mountain. "There's a storm coming."

"I saw it a few minutes ago. We'll make this fast so we can get up there before the storm."

Megan faced him. "So what do you want to try?"

"Can you shoot lasers from your eyes?"

She put her hands on her hips and stared at him. "You have got to be kidding me."

"Well, no, I mean…" Brody shoved his hands in his pants pockets. "I know it sounds stupid but they do it on television."

"Yeah, it's called a special effect."

He watched her.

"Fine, I'll try. I don't expect this to work though."

She looked out across the valley and up into the night sky. She closed her eyes in concentration. A breeze blew her hair back from her face. The moonlight gave her skin an ethereal glow. She practically radiated power.

Brody watched the energy gyrating around her. Pride and love pulled at him, filling his heart and twisting the pit of his stomach. He couldn't take his eyes off her. She slowly lifted her eyelids and stared into the sky. Brody realized he was holding his breath and released it.

"Nothing." She turned toward him. "Should I try to shoot fire from my fingertips now? Or if you have a truth lasso…"

"Very funny. Do you have a better idea?"

"I seem to be able to control the energy around us. So maybe…"

She held her arms out to the side, then brought them together in front of her hips. She raised them up, smiled and lifted them a little more.

Brody looked down. He floated several feet off the ground. "Megan?" The further up she lifted her arms the higher he rose into the air. "Okay, put me down."

"Cool. I wonder how far I could take you?"

"We don't need to find out. You proved your point, now put me down now." Hovering in the air, he watched her power radiating in pulsating circular waves. Her eyes glinted with mischief. She was teasing him on purpose.

"You're going to make me beg aren't you?" Just like she had in school whenever she found a way to get one up on him. "Fine. Will you please put me down?"

She lowered her arms until his feet touched the ground.

"Could you do this before the transformation?"

She shook her head. "Of course not. When I tried to shoot the lasers I could feel the energy building. I thought I might be able to manipulate it."

"Let's go." Brody climbed back into the truck.

"Hey, this was your idea. Don't you want to find out what other new talents I have?"

"Those will do quite well for now." He clicked the seat belt into place. "Come on."

Megan got into the passenger side, shut the door and put on her seat belt. "You really don't have to be so bossy you know."

"You're right, I'm sorry. It's so much. Seeing you looking like some warrior princess ready to go into battle. It made me feel…"

Awed, amazed, horny. He imagined her in a tight leather outfit as a beautiful vigilante.

She reached over and squeezed his shoulder. "Everything that's happened today is a lot for me too. If we can use my new abilities to save Robbie it's worth it."

How could she be so calm in light of the crisis they were in? It was as if these new abilities gave her more confidence. She was nothing if not determined. He had to admit he admired her strength of character. "I'm proud of you, Megan."

She reached over and kissed him on the cheek. "Thank you for pushing me and for believing in me, for not shunning me even though you know I'm not even mortal. Let's go find our son."

He nodded and turned the key in the ignition. Looking both ways, he pulled onto the mountain road. Out of nowhere headlights rounded the curve.

"Watch out!" Megan screamed.

Brody slammed his foot against the brake pedal.

Tires squealed as he jerked the steering wheel to turn the truck away from the oncoming vehicle.

CHAPTER THIRTEEN

THE TRUCK SHOT STRAIGHT UP INTO THE AIR AS THE oncoming car careened underneath them and down the road.

Energy pulsated through Megan, strong and powerful. She waited until the car was out of sight before she lowered the truck back to the ground.

Her heart pounded against her chest. Adrenaline surged through her. She laid her hands back in her lap. Trembles shook her fingers so she interlocked them. She looked over at Brody.

"Oh my God." He stared at her, eyes wide.

"You were right." She said quietly. "It *was* a good idea to find out if I had any special abilities since the transformation ritual. I guess I can levitate things."

"Megan, look in the mirror."

"Why?" From the way he was staring something was wrong. She flipped the visor and mirror cover in two quick moves.

"Your eyes."

She looked at her reflection. Peering back at her were the yellow eyes of an eagle. "What in the world? I didn't glimmer. I only manipulated the energy like I did a few minutes ago. Were my eyes yellow then?"

"Not at all. It must have been the adrenalin surge. Or were you about to change?"

"I don't know. I wasn't trying to." She watched her eyes return to their normal shade of blue. "Let's get out of here. I bet you anything the Mangler was driving that car. I can smell his stench from here."

"Enhanced sense of smell. Another ability." He pulled the truck back on the road in the opposite direction to the car they'd avoided.

Bolts of lightning slashed the night, giving Monocath Mountain an eerie feel.

The silence in the truck was deafening. Megan fidgeted in her seat. What was Brody thinking? She refused to tap into his thoughts and called telepathically to Asari instead.

I am here, broeistar.

Megan explained the ability tests and the color change of her eyes.

You have tapped into the eternal power of the Talgorian Prophecies and the essence of the Griffin.

Which means?

It is our nature to use the energy around us when we shift. You were able to do this at a much higher frequency because you are the Griffin of the Prophecy. You are manipulating it on a

much deeper level by drawing on the power of the Griffin at the same time. The Griffin has to emerge in some form when you tap into its power so your eyes changed.

I understand a little better now, thanks. You said prophecies. Are there others besides mine?

I cannot say what will pass. The outcome of the first determines if more will occur.

In case I fail?

There are more Monocaths than the one you fight who will continue to try to destroy us. If you fail, they will kill you and use their magic to take your essence as you die. When your essence transfers to them, they become stronger making our race weaker. Our protective fields will be disrupted. It will be harder for us to hide or win battles against them. Essentially, they will drain our life force.

Whatever happens during your quest, you must never Soul Merge with them which will give them the power to glimmer.

Talk about pressure.

You are strong and learning to use your abilities quickly which is most important. As in your dream, the situations you encounter may not be as they appear. Always think before you act and be suspicious of everything and everyone. Not only is your son's life at stake but the entire existence of the Talgorians are in your hands. If you win, your power will grow tenfold. You will gain his virility upon his death without the evilness. Your success will make us stronger and one step closer to defeating those who wish to destroy us.

I want to succeed but I have seen my death.

Understood. Be careful, broeistar.

I will.

Megan broke the connection and gazed at the headlights leading up the mountain. The light bounced as the truck ran over a small bump in the road.

How had her life come to this? Her son was in the clutches of a maniac, the people she loved weren't who she thought and she'd never have true love again.

Megan glanced over at Brody, his face serious and intent on the road. He'd been in her dreams and in her heart since the day she'd met him. Any future she'd secretly hoped for with him had died when she'd discovered her immortality. She wouldn't ask him to Soul Merge. It would be selfish on her part. Even if he agreed she'd always feel she'd trapped him into a relationship with her.

The Talgorians expected her to defeat the Monocath Ancient. Regardless of what happened in battle, she would save Robbie.

She imagined his dark hair, tousled and messy, his easy grin and high-pitched giggle. Her heart clenched, pounding harder against her ribs.

My child, my son, my baby.

He had been her whole world since his birth. They'd been

through so much together. When money had been tight, his small warm arms wrapping tightly around her neck had taught her unconditional love. She looked out of the window, a tear trickled down her cheek. She wiped it away.

Resolve filled her. The Mangler would not get away with this. She would stop him one way or another. With her recently acquired abilities she'd fight the Monocath to the death. His or her own.

Brody slowed and turned the truck from the pavement and onto a dirt road.

"Where does this lead?" Megan asked, straightening in the seat.

"You said you found the Mangler's hideout in the dream by going to the left. I know two ways to get to the top of Monocath Mountain by going left. This is the first."

Megan projected her mind through the forest, following the trail. "It's the correct one."

"Are you sure?" Brody glanced at her.

"This is it." She nodded. "We're going to run out of road soon though."

"That's why I brought the ATV. We've got about six miles before we reach the narrower mining roads. We'll go as far as we can on the ATV but I don't think it'll reach the summit." Lighting flashed across the sky. Brody frowned. "This storm might catch us."

"It will but we can handle it," she said with certainty. "You know, this would be so much easier and faster if I flew up to where Robbie is and saved him."

"You can't."

"Well, I could. The Mangler knows I'm the Griffin of the Prophecy now. I want to get this over with. I want my son back."

Brody stiffened beside her.

"I'm sorry. I mean our son."

"It's okay." He navigated the truck over a section of the dirt road filled with potholes. The movement jostled them in the seats. "You've only shifted twice. I think it would be wise to take the time to practice before you go flying up there without a plan and without knowing what you can do as the Griffin. Look at all we learned by taking a few minutes to research your abilities when you're not the Griffin."

"You wanted to see me naked."

"What?" Brody turned to look at her. "That's not true."

Megan raised her eyebrow and smirked at him.

He quickly looked away. "I thought you couldn't read minds."

"I can't. I get feelings, visions and impressions. Like the one I had of me standing in front of you naked. I know it didn't come from my mind. It must have been from yours."

"I thought you didn't read people without their permission."

"I don't. I told you reading someone is when you're specifically looking for an answer to a situation or a problem within them. Clairvoyance doesn't always involve a structured reading. I can't control the images and flashes of knowledge I get or

information that comes to me when I'm not trying. It's a daily occurrence and a normal part of my life. Admit it. You imagined me naked a minute ago."

"So? I was thinking about you changing into the Griffin. You have to get naked to change. It was a normal thought process."

"Don't you mean a lingering thought process?"

Brody stopped the truck at the end of the road and put it in park. "Are you teasing me, Megan? If you are you might be in for far more than you can handle."

"I can handle you just fine or don't you remember?"

Brody stared at her a long moment.

Megan's body warmed. He was so close. The male scent of him filled the truck. She breathed in deeply, inhaling him, filling herself with his essence. He gave her strength, empowered her. She longed for his touch. She realized Brody was the reason she'd never made love with anyone else. He was her life force, her Key. She needed his strength now more than ever.

"Oh, I remember all right, Megan. Did you really think I'd forget? Or seeing you undress in front of me wouldn't bring back the memories of being with you? I know you feel the connection between us. You were embarrassed to strip down in front of me in the cave but you did it anyway. You've accepted this hand fate dealt you without a complaint. To me, your actions speak volumes."

He reached over and ran the knuckles of his fingers down her cheek. "I was a fool, Megan."

Her breath hitched.

"What are you saying?" she asked.

"I never should have let you go."

Megan's heart raced. This was what she'd dreamed of, what she wanted but she couldn't handle it right now. It was too much. She needed his strength but not a full confession of love.

Not that he'd even offer one.

She could deal with the kisses he'd given her since arriving back in Flatrock Creek but the deeper emotional parts of their past needed to stay buried. Before today she'd hoped for his love.

He couldn't love her.

Not anymore.

She didn't expect love from him and wouldn't ask for it. She was a freak of nature, a shapeshifting immortal.

"You did send me away. Now isn't the time to rehash the past." She got out of the truck.

Sweat had broken out between her breasts and across her forehead. The coolness of the night sent a shiver down her spine. It was as effective as a cold shower in clearing the thoughts from her mind and the heat from her body.

Brody climbed out of the truck and came to her. "I know you have a lot to deal with but you can't carry the weight of the world on your shoulders. I'm here for you now. Don't go it alone. Let me in."

"You're the Key. I think the next thing we need to figure out is how you fit into all of this." Megan walked toward the back of the truck. "Do I need to get a flashlight so you can see how to get the ATV out, or is there enough moonlight?"

Brody joined her and lowered the tailgate. "I can see. Evading the issue isn't going to make what we're feeling go away you know. The timing sucks but we have to deal with this sooner or later." He slid the planks out and leaned them against the tailgate creating a ramp. Climbing into the bed of the truck he untied the ATV.

"Let's talk about it later. Right now I..." Megan cocked her head to the side, listening.

"What is it?"

She held her hand up for him to be quiet and took several steps away from the truck. Then she took several more.

"Stay where I can see you." Brody said in a loud whisper.

Megan slowly moved forward and then broke into a run. She disappeared into the darkness of the dense trees.

"Dammit, Megan!" He bolted off the ATV and jumped to the ground.

A flurry of sound filled the forest. The swish of a sword. Grunts and thuds. Brody grabbed a flashlight from the truck and ran toward the noise.

Suddenly an eagle's cry shrieked through the night. The beating of large wings had Brody looking upward.

The Talgorian Griffin soared through the night sky with the Mangler in her claws. Brody watched her fly higher. Several hundred feet above him, she slung him toward the ground. As he plummeted she swooped down, caught him in her claws and slung him again. Brody heard him yelling out, the words a foreign language. This time the Griffin let him fall until his body pounded against the ground. Moments later his laughter echoed though the forest.

Brody looked up at the Griffin circling in the sky and wondered if he could communicate with Megan. If the Talgorians used telepathy maybe, as the Key, he could too. He sent a thought to her. *Megan, come down.*

What a weird feeling.

He'd never tried to project his thoughts to someone else before. Obviously, it hadn't worked. She still circled the sky, looking for the Mangler.

He tried again. Megan, come down.

This time she flew toward him, shrieking. Had she heard him or was it a coincidence she'd given up the search at that moment?

She passed by and headed toward the top of Monocath Mountain.

What is she doing? In the moonlight the Griffin looked like a dragon flying through the night sky. Suddenly she propelled backward as if she'd hit an invisible wall. She plummeted to the ground.

"Megan!" Brody yelled. Damn it, she was going to get herself killed doing crap like this. He watched the treetops, listening for the sound of her crashing into the trees. He needed to know in what direction to search.

A distant thumping noise came from where she'd fallen. Brody's heart soared as she flew over the pines and toward the truck. *Thank God she's okay!*

He knew the Griffin was large but watching it hover above the truck put its size into perspective. Especially when it lifted the ATV out of the truck bed with enormous claws and placed it on the ground.

He wanted to test Megan as the Griffin but it wasn't fair to ask when he didn't know what had happened in the forest.

"Change back, Megan. The Mangler's gone."

She landed beside him with a heavy thud and glimmered.

Standing naked before him, her golden hair shimmered around narrow shoulders, covering her breasts. She stretched out a hand to him and collapsed with her head tilting backward. He lunged forward, catching her before she hit the ground.

He lifted Megan and carried her to the truck. As the storm started to break, rain splashed against his arms. Looking down he saw a reflection in the raindrops dotting Megan's creamy skin. He glanced upward. The clouds hadn't covered the moon yet.

Brody struggled with the door handle for a moment before pulling it open. The light inside the cab gave him a clear view of the perfection that was Megan. Her breasts were full, with rose-colored nipples hardened against the chill of the night air. Her stomach was flat and muscular right down to the thatch of blonde hair. He stared at the Griffin birthmark. It looked more defined than he remembered or maybe it was because she'd changed.

Laying Megan on the passenger side of the truck he shut her inside, went around to the driver's door and opened it. Reaching behind the seat he dug through the backpacks to find the extra clothing he'd packed. Once he'd located the extra clothes and shoes he climbed inside and hit the automatic lock. He looked out into the darkness for any sign of the Mangler.

The rain beat down. The moon disappeared behind the clouds. He'd been out in many a dark night but tonight, without the moonlight, the eerie blackness seemed menacing. He couldn't shake the feeling that someone watched them. After several moments of staring out the window he turned his attention back to Megan.

She lay awkwardly on the seat. Her legs were together and resting against the door. Her arms hung limply by her sides.

What had she heard to draw her into the forest?

He laid the clothes between them and turned on the overhead lights. The cab filled with a soft glow.

Megan shifted and groaned.

Golden hair fell away from her breasts. Her left leg dropped toward him. Creamy thighs led to the soft blonde curls between her legs.

Brody swallowed. He shouldn't be staring at her like this. She was vulnerable. He should wake her so she could dress.

His body throbbed. She excited him so much. Even in the cave he'd had to push back the desire when she'd disrobed.

This is wrong.

He reached over and touched her forearm. "Megan, wake up."

She didn't stir.

He grasped her shoulder and shook a little. "Come on, Megan. Wake up."

She still didn't move.

Why wasn't she coming around? Had the Mangler somehow hurt her?

He reached over the seat, found one of the first-aid kits and got the smelling salts out of it. He opened the package and moved it under her nose.

Even though the ammonia smell bothered him it had no affect on Megan.

"What in the hell is going on?" Brody frowned, reaching for her neck to check her heartbeat. It pulsed strongly against his fingertip. He put the ammonia pack back inside the first-aid kit.

He thought of what Asari had said. The Key, love and fire, will save her.

This definitely wasn't the time for fire.

Love.

Brody struggled with the word. He'd loved Megan once. When her car blew up, he'd accepted that she still held his heart. Would love bring her out of this?

He looked away, tried to calm the pounding of his heart and the throbbing in his pants. This was a big step and there would be no turning back even if she was the immortal Talgorian Griffin. He turned back to her listless form.

This feels like the right thing to do.

He let go of the negativity he'd clung too since his parent's death. It wasn't Megan's fault any more than it had been his. It had just happened. He lifted her hand and kissed the palm. "Megan…come on, ladybug…open your eyes."

Holding her hand, he waited. "Megan? Can you hear me? We need to save our son together." He pushed her hair back and ran his knuckles down her cheek. "Megan, please wake up."

The feelings of desire had disappeared. Now the only thing filling him was love for her pounding in his heart. "Megan, please. I need you."

Full to bursting with the acceptance of his feelings for her and the thought she may never come out of this, he turned her face toward him. "I'm not going to lose you again."

Leaning in, he kissed her lips softly.

She didn't respond.

He kissed her again, more firmly this time. "Come on, baby. Kiss me back."

A breath shuddered from her.

He kissed her once more, this time, opening her mouth and slipping his tongue inside. The sweet taste of her enveloped him. He allowed his love to pour into her. Gathering her in his arms he held her tightly as he let the strength of his emotions escape through the kiss.

Megan raised her arm and grasped his shoulder, pulling him closer. She returned the kiss, softly at first. As his love awakened her, the kiss affected her like a drug. She needed more.

His sweet taste drove her into a frenzy. She crushed her body tight against him, drawing on his essence to regain her strength.

He continued the exploration of her mouth. He'd give her everything she needed to survive whatever the Mangler had done to knock her out like this.

She broke from the kiss and stared up at him. "Brody…"

"Shh, it's okay, ladybug. You're going to be okay now."

Her hand slipped down his side and to the front of his pants. Immediately he came alive under her touch. She stroked him through the thin material.

"Make love to me." She fumbled with the utility belt until it fell from him to the seat. "I need you to love me—to make me complete."

He pulled her hand away from his crotch. "This isn't a good idea. You've just woken up, you could have a concussion."

"I need you to make love to me like you used to. I've lost so much. I need to feel you inside me, loving me." She pulled her arm away, unzipped his pants and pushed them down enough to expose him.

Warm fingers wrapped around him, slipping up and down. He grew harder under her attention. She pumped him until he thought he would explode. "Megan…"

She claimed his mouth, kissing him deeply. Sucking his tongue inside her mouth, she stroked his erection in rhythm with each pull on his tongue.

Brody broke away. His ragged breathing filled the cab. "We should get moving." If they didn't go now he'd make love to her.

"I can't change into the Griffin. The Mangler chanted a magic spell as he fell. Once I changed back to human form, my ability to glimmer became dormant. I know this is absolutely the worst timing in the world but the power of making love with you will restore me. I can't fight the Monocath if you don't." She leaned forward, sucked his earlobe and whispered in his ear. "Your essence is part of me. I need to feel you, to hold you, to love you. Don't you want me, Brody?"

The warmth of her breath sent shivers over him.

While kissing his neck she unbuttoned his shirt and pushed the fabric back exposing a muscular chest dusted with black hair.

Megan slipped her fingers into its softness. Massaging his muscles she tweaked brown nipples between her fingers. Inching down, replacing her fingers with her mouth, she sucked and nibbled on the taut flesh.

Brody turned to shove the utility belt to the floorboard.

When his hips lifted she pulled his pants down to his thighs, trailing kisses along his legs until the trousers were down around his ankles. She licked the tender area behind his knee and gave the inside of his thighs the same attention. She moved back up his body, pausing at the thick length of his erection.

"Megan…"

He trembled in anticipation. Sex was the greatest energizer in the world. She'd dreamed of being with Brody again since the day he'd sent her away. Right now she needed him.

She looked up into dark eyes, smoldering with desire. Cupping him in her hand she massaged and smiled at his quick intake of breath. She scooted down onto the floorboard so she could watch his reactions. She licked her lips and blew warm air against him before slowly sliding her tongue up the silky shaft. From base to tip she licked, over and over again, her eyes never leaving his.

Brody's breathing quickened. The warm musky smell of him radiated through her, giving her strength and power. She licked again but this time broke eye contact to take him in her mouth.

"God, Megan…" Brody groaned as he drew in a deep breath.

Stroking up and down she sucked and licked. The more she tasted him the stronger she became.

"Come here." Brody lifted her onto him. Her breasts flattened against his chest. "You're driving me insane."

"I've missed you. Let me show you how much."

"Not yet." He captured a rosy nipple in his mouth and sucked as he slipped his fingers between her legs, caressing the damp folds of her flesh. He slid a finger inside and her muscles clamped tightly around it. Memories of the same sensation on another part of him raced through his mind.

He kissed her neck and laved his tongue against the mark the Mangler had left on her earlier. He wanted to cleanse away any claim put on her by another. She didn't know it but in his heart she belonged only to him. He moved to a tender earlobe and drew it between his lips before following her jawline to her mouth.

Brody's large hands slid up her bare legs, grabbed the backs of her knees and pulled her forward. Like he had in the vision.

"Brody, I need you now," she panted. Straddling him, she reached between their bodies, guiding him to her core.

Her gaze locked with his. She slid down his length and back up. His fingers dug into her flesh, drawing her back down against him. *God she feels good.* Her muscles tightened around him. He wanted to thrust into her, to bring them both to release but he held back, enjoying the slow silkiness of each movement.

Megan rolled her hips and he nearly came undone. She undulated above him. Short fingernails dug into his shoulders. Gripping her firm hips, he slammed into her tight walls. Her body squeezed, bringing him closer to release.

Megan's breath came out in quick bursts. She'd waited so long for this. The scent of him, the feel of him inside her touched deep within her inner spirit. She ran her fingers over his muscular chest, leaned forward and quickly kissed him. She drew him deep inside, relishing the way his hardness scraped against her flesh. The friction increased the pressure, driving her further toward the edge.

Closing her eyes she drew his essence through the vigor of their lovemaking, allowing it to flow into every cell of her being. Her body tensed, rocking closer to the edge of ecstasy. "Brody."

She opened her eyes and watched as he pounded into her harder. "Now!" She held onto his shoulders as the pulsating spasms coursed through her body. Her heart pounded as heat engulfed her.

He'd never seen a more wondrous sight. Golden hair flowed

around her shoulders, her breasts bounced with each movement of their bodies and eagle eyes blazed yellow.

Light pulsated from her, its radiance and brilliance glowed lustrous white around them. She tipped her head back and he noticed the Mangler's mark on her neck had disappeared. He smiled with pride. He'd taken the mark from her with his lovemaking. He'd erased any claim the killer made on her. She belonged to him. Again.

As her body tightened and clamped around him, he fought to hold back, to take her to the fullest extent of her orgasm before he gave in to his own. She drew heat up his shaft with each thrust of her hips. She pressed down and wiggled against him. The orgasm burst from him. He pulled her down against him, chest to chest, heart to heart.

"Et amoran vel, broeistar," she whispered her love for him in his ear.

Brody cradled her in his arms. He didn't understand what she'd said but it didn't matter. The pounding of her heart matched his. They were one.

Suddenly Megan sat up and stared at him in horror. "Brody. I didn't…oh my God! Did I Soul Merge with you?"

CHAPTER FOURTEEN

THE MANGLER STOOD AMONG THE TREES, WATCHING the brilliant glow radiating from the truck's cab. Damn if she hadn't found a way around the spell.

The vixen was smarter than he'd thought. She'd met every obstacle he'd placed in front of her, especially surprising him when she'd levitated the truck.

He'd finally found the Talgorian Griffin. Now he had to find a way to regain the ability to shapeshift before he killed her.

At least he'd uncovered one weakness.

Imitating the child had brought her into the forest but using force to make her Soul Merge had been a mistake. He hadn't been prepared for the power of the Griffin.

If the radiance shining from the truck cab was any indication, she grew stronger.

He sensed Zangar's approach before he heard the squish of wet leaves under the other man's shoes.

"Fly much, Mangler?"

"My name's Alten. Use it." He turned. Zangar wore all black down to his leather gloves. A long black coat covered a tight t-shirt and jeans tucked into boots which nearly reached his knees. A sword hilt protruded from a scabbard on his back. With his long dark hair hanging past his shoulders and dark good looks that drove the women wild, he looked like the vigilante he was. He hated Zangar because he always got what he wanted including women, power and the king's favor.

"What are you doing here?" Alten asked.

"The Ancients sent me to get an update on your progress." Zangar looked toward the truck. "She's the one?"

"Yep." Alten nodded. "The Talgorian Griffin."

"And?"

"And why didn't you contact me telepathically?" Alten asked. "You really didn't need to go to the trouble of finding me."

"There are rumors." Zangar faced Alten.

Alten stared at the other man. "What kind of rumors?"

"The king is worried you will not be able to handle her. He thinks you will lose this battle and the Prophecy will empower the Talgorians." Zangar reached in his pocket and pulled out a cigar and lighter.

Alten stepped back. "The king assigned me to this frigging Prophecy. Why would he do such a thing if he didn't feel I could accomplish the mission?"

Zangar puffed on the cigar several times. He glanced back to the truck before blowing the smoke into Alten's face. "He's having second thoughts. He thinks I would do the job better."

"Too late now. None of you can interfere. This is my mission. If he didn't think I was the best warrior for the job he shouldn't have assigned it to me." Alten turned back to the truck. Anger started to build inside.

Not only had the wench had sex with the ranger, she may have even Soul Merged with him. Now his own people doubted his ability to succeed, like they always had in the past.

"Maybe the king should have chosen you, Zangar. I'm sure you'd have been able to seduce her with that big ass scar on your face and neck." He laughed. "Maybe she would have loved your movie star looks despite your scar."

"Don't kill the messenger, man. This affects all of us even though you have to fulfill the Prophecy alone. Hell, the king only wanted you to shut up that blabbering psychic he bedded when he was drunk. He was stupid to believe he could tell her all about us and the Talgorians and think she'd keep our secrets. Shutting her up was your mission, not to bring the Prophecy down on us by killing children and psychics. As usual, you had to go rogue. If the king had known sending you out to find her would have led to this…" He took a long drag on the cigar. "I don't understand why he even gives you chances to redeem yourself. You always screw up."

"If you're finished insulting me why don't you leave?"

"Listen Alten, we need to have the ability to glimmer again before this situation plays out. Then we can Soul Merge with some human women and ensure the survival of our race. You've got to trick her into Soul Merging with you." Zangar took another puff from the cigar.

"You think I don't know this?" Alten smacked his fist into his other hand. "Who are you to question my methods anyway?"

Zangar blew smoke into the air on a slow exhale. "What are you gonna do?"

"I don't know yet." Alten rubbed his chin. "I got into her dream. Maybe I can again, only this time, be there in the flesh too. I'll use magic to make her think she's with the ranger. Once we Soul Merge, I'll kill her."

"What about the boy?"

"He's in the cave. I'll deal with the mother first. Not like the other times."

"You better be damn sure you know what you're doing. If you fail and she doesn't kill you, the king will."

Alten rolled his eyes, laughed hysterically and suddenly stopped. "I don't think it will be a problem."

Zangar pushed the end of the cigar into his palm. The red ambers sizzled against the leather glove. "We'll see. It's not like you've never screwed up a mission, you crazy bastard. You went after all the others without any thought on how to proceed. It's time to use your brain for once."

"I've got it already!" Alten spat the words at Zangar. "Is there anything else you wanted?"

"Nope. We're done, *Mangler*."

"Don't call me that." He hated the name the humans had dubbed him. He didn't really know why, since it was how he killed but it grated on his nerves.

"Or what?" Zangar laughed. His deep baritone sliced the night. "You think you can take me on?"

Alten growled and took a step back.

"That's what I thought." Zangar shoved the rest of the cigar into a coat pocket and walked into the inky blackness of the forest.

Alten seethed at the truck. He couldn't fail. He would prove the king wrong. As the light dimmed in the cab, he started to formulate a new plan of action.

MEGAN PULLED THE spare pants over her bare hips, grabbed the extra shirt lying on the middle of the seat and slipped it on.

Making love with Brody had restored her strength and given her focus. She watched him in her peripheral vision as she pulled her hair back with a scrunchie and then put on two pairs of Brody's socks and then his extra shoes. The man was delectable in every way. The flexing of his muscles as he pulled his clothes on, the tousled hair, all made her want to make love to him again. Now that she had been restored, they needed to get moving again.

Megan twisted in the seat to face him. "I know I was forward. I apologize." Reaching out a hand, she stroked his cheek. "Thank you for saving me from the Mangler's spell. Without you I'd never have come out of it."

Brody pulled her close and kissed her. "You don't have to thank me for making love to you."

"Do you feel different?" She leaned back.

"Satisfied, yes. Different, no."

"Can you change into a Griffin?"

"I don't think so." Brody chuckled.

"I wonder how Soul Merging is different. There's never been a glowing light around me when I changed."

"Your eyes changed again too."

"They did? Maybe we did Soul Merge." Megan broke from his embrace and leaned back the seat. "It's all so confusing."

"We couldn't have."

"Why not?"

"I didn't ask you to Soul Merge with me. I don't feel a change has taken place within me that would make me immortal or give me your abilities."

No, he hadn't asked. He'd never ask to be an immortal and share her life. What had even made her worry about it? She'd only managed to hurt herself by hoping he might want more.

"True. I couldn't imagine you would want such a thing. Then again any man would be tempted by the Griffin's power and immortality."

"Megan…"

"It's okay. Really. You're right. I didn't feel I was sharing anything on a soul level with you. Just my body. That's all I needed anyway—to break the spell and restore my strength. You gave me exactly what I needed." Megan slid over to the window. "It's stopped raining and the moon is out again. I think the best thing to do is to unload the ATV and get up the mountain."

"You already unloaded the ATV."

"I what?" Megan asked.

"Don't you remember? As the Griffin you lifted the ATV right out of the truck bed and placed it on the ground."

"I did?" How could I move it and not remember?

"I'd already untied it and you took it out. So if you're ready, let's go since you don't want to listen to what I have to say."

"Fine." Megan climbed out of the truck and slammed the door. She looked at the ATV sitting beside the truck. She could only surmise the Mangler's spell had kept her from remembering. She realized her backpack was inside the cab. She opened the door to find Brody holding the pack out to her, a frown on his face. She took it and shut the door.

She knew she wasn't being fair. She just couldn't deal with his rejection on top of everything else. If he kept quiet she didn't have to face the situation yet.

Brody climbed out of the truck, gathered the rest of the supplies and kicked the door shut. Megan watched him as he tied everything to the ATV and wiped the rain off the seat but he never even glanced at her.

She'd hurt his feelings after all he'd done for her, even the incredible sex.

He took keys out of his pocket and pushed the remote to lock the truck before returning them to his pants. As he started to climb onto the ATV, Megan grabbed his arm and turned him toward her.

"Ready?" he asked.

She ran her fingers along his hairline. The moonlight reflected on his face. Even now, he looked wounded.

"I'm sorry I've been such a bitch. I shouldn't cut you off. I don't want to discuss our past right now. After we've found Robbie we will but not now. Okay?" She apologized silently in her mind. They wouldn't talk because she'd be dead but at least this might appease him for the moment.

Brody frowned down at her. "I guess I don't have a choice in this do I?"

"I'm sorry, Brody. I can't cope with any more emotions than I'm handling right now. Let's find Robbie together as a united front. You always have a choice. I hope you'll choose to let this go for now."

"Consider it done but not forgotten." He grabbed her and pulled her close. "I will tell you that I'm not interested in immortality or the Griffin's power. I'm only interested in you, the most unpredictable woman I've ever known," he said against her lips. He nibbled on her lower lip. Gently parting her mouth he deepened the kiss, tangling his tongue with hers. Desire fueled him. He wanted to take her again, right here on the seat of the ATV. The timing was wrong. He pulled away to grab the helmets.

"What happened when you flew to the peak? You looked like you hit a wall."

"It's an invisible barricade to keep us from getting to Robbie. It must be magical. We'll have to find a way around it."

"Hop on behind me. We'll inspect it when we get there. Let's get this done."

Megan put on the protective gear and snapped the band under her chin while she waited for him to do the same. When he was ready she climbed on, wrapping her arms around his waist. After the rain, the trail could be slippery and she didn't want to fall off. "I'm ready."

Brody turned the switch and pushed the button to start the ATV but it didn't roar to life. The only sound was the click of the button as he tried to start it. "Damn! Hop off."

She climbed off. Looking out into the moonlit night she saw the silhouette of trees, their tops swaying gently. She inspected the bushes and trees on the ground. Nothing appeared to be out of the ordinary.

She inhaled deeply. The killer's dirty stench lingered on the air. She couldn't tell if it was left from when she'd dropped him or if he'd come back during the storm.

The flashlight's beam bobbled in the darkness as Brody inspected the ATV. He lifted the seat and shone the flashlight inside.

"We're walking." His voice was laced with a controlled anger.

"What's wrong?" She leaned in to get a better look. The battery was missing. This had to be the Mangler's doing. "I can't believe he did this," she seethed.

"It's a game to him. We're going to have to beat him at it." He removed the backpacks and other supplies from where he'd tied them to the ATV. He handed one to her and loaded everything else on his own body. "Here's where your psychic abilities come into play. I need you to turn on your powers while we're climbing. Let me know if you sense anything. This path leads straight up to the top of the mountain. The forest is on both sides and in some places it drops off like a cliff. We might run into wild animals so make sure you're aware of the surroundings. We'll walk side by side as much as possible."

He held up a rope. "If I have to go in front, we're tying ourselves together with this. I don't want the Mangler trying to abduct you like he did before."

"Okay. Let's go." She walked with him on the old, overgrown road, shining a flashlight in front of her.

They moved forward in silence except for the crunch of sticks beneath their shoes. Megan scanned the area, searching for any indication the Mangler was close by. The forest held only positive vibrations.

Soon the climb became monotonous. Megan's thoughts began to wander. In her mind's eye she saw Robbie lying by a rock sleeping. His tummy growled and he shivered in his jacket. My baby is hungry and cold. She tried to look around the area where he slept but only saw a few rocks and cave walls. The scene vanished.

A knot formed in her throat. She swallowed, her eyes stinging with tears.

Megan? Asari called to her. *You must hurry,* broeistar, *the Monocath grows impatient.*

We're walking up the mountain now. I hope to find the cave before lunchtime, she thought.

Look for the twisted oak. It resembles a staircase.

Asari?

Yes, broeistar?

She started to ask more about Soul Merging but decided against it. *Never mind.* She broke the connection. A warm sense of belonging enveloped her like an embrace.

The heavy thud of Brody's shoes plodded against the ground to her right side. She couldn't get the possibility she'd Soul Merged with him out of her mind. Even though he'd denied feeling differently, she wondered if she'd broken the most important rule of the Talgorians.

Did I mate for eternity without the human's permission?

Fear had kept her from asking Asari for details about the mating ritual.

If only I had someone to ask.

An image of herself as a child sitting on the stool in Auntie Faye's pharmacy flashed through her mind. Auntie Faye had always been open-minded and nonjudgmental. Maybe Varici would know if she'd broken the rules. *Her reaction might be worse than Asari's because she's a Talgorian Guardian.*

Worry refused to give her peace. She had to know for sure so she called out telepathically. *Varici? Can you hear me?*

Megan waited but no response came.

Maybe it was best not to know. She couldn't have betrayed Brody. He'd never want to live an immortal life with her but what if she'd given him no choice by unconsciously Soul Merging with him?

Suddenly she was aware of footfalls beside her. She stopped short and so did the new footfalls as Brody moved ahead. She looked over but couldn't see anyone. She psychically scanned the area. She discovered a large, powerful and very positive force.

You rang? Varici said telepathically.

Geez, you scared me, Megan whispered. *Why can't I see you?*
It's dark.

Megan rolled her eyes. "Now tell me something I don't know."

Use telepathy. No one can know I'm here.

All right. How can you be invisible?

Varici chuckled. *Another special ability of Guardians. What's wrong? Your tone sounded urgent.*

"Megan! Catch up!" Brody shone his flashlight back at her and waited.

"I'm coming!" she yelled as she started toward him.

Can you tell me exactly what happens when you Soul Merge?

Why do you need to know about that right now?

Megan glanced beside her even though she couldn't see Varici. *I think I may have Soul Merged with Brody.*

What? Why would the two of you have sex when your son is in danger?

It's not what you think. Megan shook her head. *The Monocath tricked me. I thought I heard Robbie in the woods but it was the Mangler. We fought and I transformed into the Griffin during the battle. He cast a spell on me so when I changed back I wouldn't have any strength or be able to shift again. The only way I could regain it was by making love with Brody. He restored me but now I'm afraid I Soul Merged with him.*

What made you think so?

There was a brilliant white glow all around us. He said my eyes turned yellow.

Did you see an aura around both of you?

I don't think so unless the white light was it.

Anytime a Talgorian has sex the aura is white. When we mate to transform one to our race, it changes to a bluish golden color. The human can only take on our shifting characteristics and immortality when the aura forms and simultaneous orgasm happens within it. If you didn't experience both of these things you didn't transform

Brody.

Thank God! I was so worried and hesitant to ask Asari. I wouldn't knowingly do that to Brody.

What if he chooses to be your eternal mate?

Megan stopped in front of Brody and lifted the light to his chest. His worried frown and scowl told her all she needed to know. *He'd never agree and I wouldn't ask him to.*

You don't give your Key enough credit.

I could never ask him to give up his race, his mortality, basically his whole life just to be with me. It wouldn't be fair to him. I just can't do it.

Then use your abilities. Look inside and see how he feels about you.

Never. I don't read people unless they ask me.

Yes, you do. Varici laughed. *When you need to know, you look. We all do. It's part of the Talgorian defenses. It doesn't mean you share the knowledge. You haven't looked yet because you're afraid of what you'll find in Brody's heart.*

I don't want to know. He's tried to talk to me about us but I can't hear what he thinks. Not now. Not until Robbie's safe. Then it won't matter.

In the end you may be surprised.

"Don't lag behind again, Megan." Brody grabbed her hand and held it tightly. "Stay with me or I'm tying us together."

Megan nodded. "Okay."

They took a few steps and Brody stopped. "Did you hear that?"

"Hear what?"

"Footsteps other than ours." He moved the beam of the flashlight all around them.

I have to go... Follow your heart, Talgorian Griffin. It will not lead you astray.

Thank you, Varici.

Varici's warm embrace wrapped around her shoulders for a

few seconds before it disappeared.

That's what I'm here for. Be safe.

"I didn't hear anything, Brody." She unclasped his hand.

"What do you sense?"

Megan noted Varici had gone and didn't find any other presence nearby. "There's nothing here. It must have been an echo."

"Don't take chances, Megan. With you lagging behind the Mangler could have grabbed you again. This guy isn't giving up. He's sneaking around us. Stay aware. You looked like your mind was somewhere else."

She couldn't tell him it was. His concern was endearing. It made her feel warm inside. "I'm sorry. I was thinking about everything."

His expression softened. "We've got a couple of hours of hiking left until daylight. I know you're running on little shuteye. Do you need to rest? Are you hungry?"

"I'm fine for now. Let's keep going for another hour before we rest and eat. I'll need strength to face the Mangler again."

Brody nodded, taking her hand. "Sounds like a plan. Come on."

Relief washed over her. She hadn't changed his life forever. "Brody?"

"Yeah?"

He sounded tired.

"I'm glad I didn't change you back there. I wouldn't do it to you on purpose."

"I know, ladybug. I know." He led her along the path and up the mountain.

Megan sensed someone behind them. She looked over her shoulder. She didn't notice the man shadowing their movement along the forest's edge.

CHAPTER FIFTEEN

"HOLD UP A MINUTE." BRODY SHONE THE LIGHT further up the path.

Megan looked at the rocky debris rising like a hill in front of them. She flashed her own light to the side and joined it with his beam, illuminating the area. A few trees stuck out of the dirt, which covered large portions of the trunks. The opposite side of the path dropped off into nothingness. All that lay in front of them was night sky. "Mudslide?"

"Yeah, it's old. Probably happened during the rainy season last fall. I better check it out. I knew this trail would take us by the cliffs but I didn't think about mudslides this time of year. If I remember correctly, the path should turn in a couple hundred feet." He took off the rope, wrapped it around a tree and tied it around Megan's waist. "I'm going to make sure the path is passable. Don't move from here. Do you sense anything or anyone around?"

"No but I think he's blocking me. A couple of times I thought I felt someone nearby but when I scanned I didn't pick up anything. I haven't figured out how to penetrate his defenses yet." Megan frowned into the darkness. "Be careful. It looks steep."

Brody nodded and moved slowly over the rocky incline. She kept her light on the area even after he was out of sight. A little while later the rope tightened around the tree, pulling her toward it. "Brody!"

She waited. When he didn't respond she did a psychic search

for him.

And couldn't find his spirit.

"That's it. I'm coming after you, Phelps." Megan braced herself against the tree to keep the tension and untied the rope from her waist and tied it tightly to the section already wrapped around the tree. Grasping the nylon she held on and followed it toward the rocks.

It suddenly went slack in her hands. She lost her balance and fell backward onto the hard rocky dirt. She took a deep breath, wrinkling her nose when the Mangler's disgusting odor assaulted her nostrils. She jumped up. "Brody! Answer me!"

A scuffle sent pebbles falling.

She waved the flashlight around to find the source of the sound. Brody emerged over the mound of dirt and rocks and stumbled toward her.

"Brody!" She ran up the dried mudslide. Grabbing his arm she supported him. He stumbled back to the path. "What happened? Are you all right?"

"We'll have to stop here until morning. There's a drop-off on the other side. It's too difficult to navigate in the dark."

Megan shone the light toward his face but he turned to look at the path behind him.

"Any sign of the Mangler?" he asked.

"I was coming after you because I smelled his stench. He must be somewhere close by. It's not safe to stay here. We'll find another way around this." She untied the rope from the tree and coiled it for storage.

"Let's camp here and head out at first light."

"Are you sure you didn't hit your head back there?"

"Positive."

"Well, I *could* eat." Megan tied off the rope. Dropping it to the ground she pulled the backpack from her shoulders and sat it down in front of her. Squatting down, she looked for food.

"So could I." His voice dropped an octave. His words were laden with desire.

The undertone in his innuendo gave her pause. She ignored him. "You have food in your backpack."

"I was thinking of something sweeter." His pack landed on the ground beside her. He opened it and started pulling out items. "Oh look! There's a blanket in here too. Should I spread it out?"

"Sure." She took a water bottle, opened it and drank deeply. Didn't he remember he'd packed the blanket? "We've got what, another hour until sunrise?"

"Probably." He laid out the blanket, handed her a ration pack and opened one for himself. Then he sat down and patted the spot beside him. "We'll be able to see better once the sun's up. Lie down."

"Don't you mean sit?" The hair rose on the back of Megan's neck. She looked to the edges of the forest. Apprehension crept along her spine.

"Of course. Silly me. I'm sorry. Please, sit down."

Megan set the flashlight on end so the light shone around them. She studied Brody in the glow. Something wasn't right. His actions were a little too prissy and flirty. A small cut bled near his temple. "You're hurt."

"It's a small wound. It'll heal quickly."

"Really? How quickly?" Suspicion caused her to question this was even the real Brody. She couldn't locate his essence even though he sat right in front of her.

He glanced at her, bit a piece of beef jerky and looked away. "I don't know. A week or so. I can't really tell how deep it is."

She leaned over, picked up the light and examined the wound closely. "It's not too bad. Are you feeling okay?"

"Yes. Why do you ask?"

"You seem a little…distracted."

"I am." He faced her. "Megan, about what happened in the

truck. Do you think we Soul Merged?"

She stared at him. Her senses went on high alert. Instinctively she put up psychic blocks.

This couldn't be Brody. He had always respected her need to talk about things when she was ready but now, he was pushing a topic they'd agreed to discuss after they found Robbie. Besides, he'd already told her he didn't think they had so why bring it up again?

They try to trick our females into Soul Merging with them. It is imperative we are always aware of their illusions and we never let it happen. Megan remembered Varici's words.

The Mangler must have used magic to change himself so he'd look like Brody. She couldn't let him know she'd figured out his game. Her pulse quickened.

"Yes, maybe it was. You said we'd become one." *How can I get away from him?*

"I think, maybe we should try again." He put a piece of dried fruit to his mouth and sucked. He licked it all around, eyes glued to hers and popped it into his mouth. "To be sure. Don't you?"

There is no way in hell.

She had to escape. Brody would never act like that or ask her to Soul Merge with him. The Mangler may have made himself look like Brody but his actions gave him away. "If you think we should."

He chewed on the fruit and washed it down with water, then poured it over his face. "Ahhh, that feels wonderful. What are we waiting for?"

Brody had told her to conserve the water. Now he drenched himself in it, wasting a whole bottle. She forced a smile. A whiff of his stench assaulted her. "I have to go potty first."

"Go potty?" he laughed. "Since when do you talk like a child?"

"Since I had a child." *A child you took!* She stood. "I'll only be a minute."

He handed her a napkin from the ration pack. "Here, you'll

need this won't you?"

"Yes." She reached to take the napkin from him but he grabbed her arm. "Don't be long, precious."

She froze at the pet name. The wrong pet name, which solidified her suspicions. The clammy touch of his long thin fingers sickened her. He'd murdered so many people with those hands.

"You won't even know I'm gone." Megan said, forcing a smile as she backed away from the blanket. "Why don't you get ready for me? Maybe I'll even surprise you and come back naked. Would you like that?"

His eyes gleamed. "Very much."

She turned and forced herself to walk slowly into the woods. She wanted to run, to get away from him as fast as possible. She couldn't without raising suspicion.

The Mangler must have blocked Brody from her.

Where in the hell was he? Or worse. What if the Mangler had killed him? The thought sent a sinking feeling to the pit of her stomach. Brody couldn't have died.

He's hurt because of me, again. I should have come alone. I have to find him.

Another spicy male scent assaulted her. She turned to watch the Mangler through the trees. Was someone else out there?

If she could figure out how to break through his defenses she'd find Brody and Robbie and this whole ordeal would be over.

The Mangler glanced back to where she'd entered the forest. "Precious?"

She cleared her throat. "I'll only be a few minutes, Brody."

He looked away, stood and walked around the blanket. The flashlight beam shone straight up into the night.

"Show yourself," he growled. "Make it quick."

A tall man emerged from the darkness into the light. He wore a long overcoat and had long dark hair.

Zangar? Megan silenced a gasp with her hand. *Why is my*

martial arts teacher here? If he's a Monocath, why didn't he try to kill me over the past four years?

"The king wants to see you, Alten. Now."

"No. I'm going to Soul Merge with the Griffin."

Zangar laughed. "You've got a better chance of getting pregnant."

"She finds me attractive as the ranger. She *will* Soul Merge with me." Alten glared at Zangar. "What does the king want?"

"You're using the magic too much, the Source is weakening. You must return to the lair or Megan will break through your defenses."

"She's not strong enough."

"Don't underestimate her, Mangler. If she figures out she can get through your magic on the astral plane you will lead her to the lair. Once there, she could find where the Source is hidden." He dropped his voice to a whisper. "Do I have to remind you what will happen if a Talgorian gains command of the Source?"

"I told you not to call me Mangler!" Alten growled and spat at Zangar's feet. "She'll never figure it out. She's a stupid woman. Besides only one Talgorian is prophesized to take command of the Source. We will kill any who try. I doubt they even know of its existence."

"Again, you underestimate her. Megan Cassidy may be a lot of things but she's not stupid."

"You're jealous because you want her for yourself."

Zangar's gaze left the Mangler and went into the woods. Megan swore Zangar looked right at her. "The Griffin is not my destiny, regardless of how beautiful she is or any feelings I have about her." He faced the Mangler again. "She is your Prophecy and you must succeed. Now get moving."

"After I've Soul Merged with her."

"No. Now."

Alten widened his stance, fisted his hands. "I said *after* I've

Soul Merged with her. Leave before you're discovered."

"I am your superior. You will leave and go to the king immediately."

"If this causes me to fail in my mission it will be your head the king has for breakfast."

Zangar pulled a dagger from inside his coat. "Do I need to take you to the king myself?"

"I'm going." Alten looked longingly toward the forest. "I was looking forward to devouring that sweet piece of—"

The dagger's point pressed against Alten's neck. "I said now."

Alten jerked back, spat at Zangar and disappeared into the forest.

Zangar watched him leave before looking toward Megan.

He gazed into the trees where she hid. Confusion crossed his face.

Is he torn between our friendship and his duty? Megan thought.

Her heart kicked up another notch. He must be a Monocath. Why else would he be out here in the middle of the woods at this hour meeting with a murderer? He even wore a sword on his back.

She'd trusted him in the past. He'd gotten rid of the Mangler, given her the way to get through the psychic blocks and told her about the Source. Now he stood there waiting for her to make a move. She took a deep breath and left the forest.

She stopped several feet from him. "Zangar."

He bowed slightly and looked up at her. "Talgorian Griffin."

She stopped. "Are you going to kill me?"

Zangar advanced, closing in on her. "I could you know."

"I know. But will you?"

He stroked the back of his knuckles against her cheek. "So beautiful."

"We've been though this before, Zangar. I'm not interested in a relationship." She took a step back. When he'd asked her out on a date after class, she'd made it clear she only thought of him as a friend, not a romantic interest.

"I'm not coming on to you. Simply stating a fact."

"Are you one of them? A Monocath?"

"I can't reveal my true nature to you."

"Why not?"

"It would put you in danger." Zangar lunged at her.

Megan quickly spun away then faced him again, ready to attack.

"Excellent. You haven't lost your edge."

"You're a good teacher." She relaxed her stance. He was testing her. "What is the Source?"

"I cannot tell you."

"Why are you helping me? You can at least tell me that much."

"I didn't." He shrugged. "I was merely stating a fact to Alten. We are not allowed to assist those associated with the Prophecy. It is not my fault you overheard." He smiled, moving backward toward the forest.

"Damn it, Zangar! Whose side are you on anyway?"

"The only side I can be on, Talgorian Griffin," he said and disappeared into the forest.

Megan stood there for a moment. Zangar was her friend and martial arts instructor. He'd never given her any reason not to trust him. In fact, before seeing him here, he was the one person who she had trusted besides Carmela. Was he really a Monocath? Or was something else going on here?

She had to find Brody. She couldn't waste any more time wondering what Zangar was up to. She picked up the flashlight. The beam died. Repeatedly pressing the on-off button didn't do a thing. She looked at the sky and noticed it was a filtered gray instead of pitch black. Sunrise wasn't far off.

She dug through Brody's pack, found another flashlight and switched it on. She put the supplies and blanket back inside the packs. She'd have to come back for them later.

What if Zangar is right? Could I break though the Mangler's blocks on the astral plane? It's worth a try.

She lay down on the ground. She disengaged her soul from her physical body and rose into the astral plane. Glancing back to make sure she was connected to her body by a silver cord, she focused on Brody. Moments later she sensed him. Relief surged through her.

Thank God he was alive!

On the astral plane, she moved over the mudslide, into a valley and along the forest's edge. There! By the tree. She zoomed in closer.

Brody lay unconscious. His hands and feet were tied, blood pooled around his head.

Megan jerked back into her body so fast it hurt. She jumped up and stumbled over the mudslide, the flashlight beam bouncing in front of her, praying for dawn to arrive. The old mudslide disappeared over the side of a cliff and into a small valley. She slid to a halt. It hadn't looked this steep on the astral plane. How in the world was she going to get down there without killing herself?

Then she remembered.

Ah, hell. What good is it to have immortality and shapeshifting abilities if I can't use them? She stripped out of Brody's clothes and laid them in a pile. Drawing the totem to her, she shifted into the Griffin.

Pouncing from the dirt she soared up into the air, made a circle and coasted down into the valley. Brody was three hundred yards ahead. She swooped lower, gliding toward him, the occasional beat of her wings echoed through the valley. She landed with a soft thud beside him.

This flying is getting easier every time.

She glimmered and knelt beside him. "Brody, can you hear me?"

She struggled with the knots at his ankles. The Monocath's rope seared her hands. He must have put a magic spell on them.

"Finally!" She threw the fraying cord aside and untied the one on his wrists, tossing it aside too.

The gash on his head oozed blood. Crap. She needed the first-aid supplies inside the backpacks.

"Come on, wake up." She shook him gently.

He groaned. His eyes flickered open.

"Atta boy. How are you feeling?"

Brody sat up. "Like I've been hit by a truck."

"It was the Mangler's magic."

He looked up at her as he rubbed the side of his head. "Where are your clothes? Did he hurt you?"

"No, I glimmered to get to you quicker but I have to go back to get the packs. It'll only take a minute."

"Is he here?"

Megan shook her head. "Will you be okay?"

"Yeah." He rubbed the other side of his head, felt something sticky and looked at the blood on his hand. "Bastard."

"Don't worry, we'll get him. I'll be right back then we have to talk." She didn't give him time to answer but glimmered while walking away. She soared into the air, out of the valley and to the backpacks. She dived down, grabbed both packs in one claw and scooped up her clothes in the other. Moments later she was back at Brody's side.

"See, I told you I'd be quick," she said, after she'd transformed. She retrieved the first-aid kit and took out bandages, antiseptic wash and a tube of antibiotic cream. "We need to clean this up."

"I'm fine. It's a long hike to the top of this mountain."

"Stop being so macho." Kneeling beside him, she squirted the antiseptic on a gauze pad and wiped the blood from Brody's face. Flashlights weren't necessary in the early morning light.

Warm fingers clenched around her wrist. Megan glanced at him but kept cleaning the wound. "Sorry. I'm trying to be gentle."

"Megan." He pulled her hand away. "Stop."

She looked into his eyes. "Am I hurting you?"

"Not exactly."

"What's wrong?"

His eyes roamed down. "Could you please get dressed?"

"I'm sorry. I was so worried about you I forgot." The blood rushed to her face.

"It's okay." Brody smiled. "I'm enjoying the view a little too much."

"Here, hold this." She handed him the gauze pad, gathered the clothes and dressed. "Satisfied?"

"Not really but I can wait. What did you want to talk about?"

"Zangar." She knelt again to finish cleaning the wound.

"What's Zangar?"

"Not what but who. He was my martial arts instructor for four years. For a while he thought he was in love with me. He was nice enough but I wasn't looking for a relationship."

Megan glanced at him, noticed the questioning look in his eyes and quickly continued. "When you disappeared over the mudslide the rope tightened and went slack. I thought you'd fallen. I was coming after you when you returned."

"What? How could—"

"It only took a few minutes for me to realize it was the Mangler. He used magic to look like you so I would Soul Merge with him. I knew you'd never ask to do that. He was acting…well, he was creeping me out with the way he came on to me."

"Did he…" Brody tried to stand.

"Let me get something on this." Megan took a couple of self-adhesive bandages from the kit. "I realized what had happened before he could make any moves on me. I used the bathroom excuse to get away. I sensed another presence so I watched him for a few minutes from the woods. I wanted to see if I could figure out a way to break through his psychic blocks. Zangar arrived and sent him back to the Monocath King. Okay, you're finished."

"Thanks." Brody touched his head. "Why did he do that?"

Megan nodded. "There's something called the Source which supplies the Monocaths with their magic. Zangar told the Mangler he was draining it."

"Asari never mentioned a Source of magic."

"Based on their conversation, I don't think any of the Talgorians know." She put the materials back in the kit, returned it to the backpack and handed Brody a half-full bottle of water. "Zangar wouldn't tell me what it meant."

"You talked to him?"

"I had to. He knew I was there. He warned the Mangler that if I figured out the astral plane was the key to breaking through the psychic blocks I'd find the Source." She sat down facing Brody. "I don't know if he's friend or enemy. He wouldn't tell me. He didn't deny being a Monocath. I traveled to the astral plane to see if what he said would work. It did and I was able to break the Mangler's block on your life force. It's how I found you. It's how we'll find Robbie."

"We need to talk to Asari. Can you contact him?"

"Yes but I'm going to ask him to come here. I want to tell him about the Source in person. I'll do that first and then I want you to watch my body while I search for Robbie on the astral plane. Maybe I can get an exact location and directions to him like I did with you."

"Is the astral plane unsafe?"

"When I astral travel my soul is temporarily out of my body. Normally I wouldn't worry but with the danger we're in, I would feel safer if you were protecting me. Are you feeling up to it?"

"Sure. Let's get it done. The sun's starting to rise." Brody drank from the bottle, closed the lid and threw it into the backpack.

"If I find Robbie we'll fly there. As the Griffin, you could ride me and it will save a lot of time."

"As much as I'd love to ride you," Brody said, tucking a stray strand of hair behind her ear and tracing her bottom lip with the pad of his thumb. "You've already changed a few times in the last couple of hours. I don't think you should do it again so soon."

Tingles warmed her lip with his touch. She drew in a shaky breath. "Very funny. Now stop because you're making me hot."

"I bet you're nowhere near as hot as I was watching you tending my wounds in the buff." Brody leaned in, kissed her on the lips. "We're adults who can wait, not the teenagers we once were who lost control over the slightest touch."

"So you say." Megan scooted away from him. She looked up toward the rocky top of Monocath Mountain. "I don't want Robbie under the killer's control any longer than he has to be. He must be so scared. He won't understand what's happening." Tears stung the back of her eyes. The mountain blurred out of focus. She blinked several times, fighting back the tears.

"We can't risk the Mangler losing his temper and harming Robbie either. Right now he's consumed with you. We have to keep it that way to have an advantage."

"I know but it doesn't make this any easier."

"I never said it did." Brody squeezed her hand. "What do you need me to do?"

CHAPTER SIXTEEN

MEGAN FOUND A GRASSY AREA TO LIE ON.

"Will you see the Mangler while you're doing this?" He didn't know much about astral travel and wanted to keep the risks as low as possible. "I'm not sure this is a good idea."

"I've astral traveled many times. Finding Robbie on that plane will save us a lot of time later. If the Mangler put blocks around him like he did to you this will be the only way to get through." She lay back and gazed up at him.

She looked beautiful with her hair flowing all around her. He should have known she would be this brave. What a fool he'd been to let her go. "We can track Robbie. I'll be able to find him."

"I know you could. Why do you think I came to you? Besides being Robbie's father, you're the best tracker in West Virginia. While the Mangler's magic is weak, I can try to locate Robbie before Asari arrives."

He looked down at her hand when she squeezed his fingers. They were so small next to his. "If you get into trouble, what can I do?"

"If you need to bring me back, touch me gently but only if we're in danger here. Don't touch me for any other reason, because you might bring me back before I find him." She smiled up at him. "I'll be okay, Brody."

He trusted that she would be.

"An hour. That's it." He glanced at his wrist. "Then I wake

you."

"An hour it is." She closed her eyes and released his hand.

All he wanted to do was protect her, rescue Robbie and have a normal life with his family.

Who am I kidding? We can never have a normal life. Megan is the Talgorian Griffin, a mystical animal of legend, part of a Prophecy that will save an immortal race or doom it to nonexistence. She is in a fight for our son's life and her own. The stress would make any other woman crack but not Megan. She has handled every obstacle thrown in her path with fire and determination. Most of all she hasn't given up.

He found himself counting her respirations. Her breathing seemed too slow.

Uneasiness snaked along his spine. He was suddenly aware the forest sounded abnormally quiet.

He tore his gaze from Megan to examine their surroundings. He glanced at his watch. Only ten minutes had passed? *This is going to be the longest hour of my life.*

He had to get his mind off the time. How could they outwit the Mangler? He wanted Megan dead but yet he wanted to Soul Merge with her first, thus ensuring the survival of the Monocaths.

The way he had danced and tipped his hat indicated either severe immaturity or mental instability. Maybe both.

He rubbed his forehead. The wound ached and his head was following suit. He retrieved some pain relievers from the first-aid kit and swallowed the pills without water.

Megan was right. Robbie must be terrified. He was so young to be in these horrific circumstances. *He needs me in his life and I need him.*

There'd been so much he'd missed. Robbie's first steps, his first words, playing catch. His heart ached with the thoughts. There were so many regrets, all because of misplaced blame. What a lesson this whole situation had turned out to be. Now, he might not even get to know his son because he'd let hurt and anger keep him from the one he loved.

Megan may not ever agree be part of his life again but he damn sure wanted to show his son a father's love.

Megan's arm spasmed.

Brody jumped. He stared at her. Had something gone wrong? The Mangler had come to her in a dream after all. What would stop him from fighting her on the astral level? She was defenseless there. He couldn't protect her.

Not that he'd done a very good job of protecting her so far.

He saw a movement in his peripheral vision. Asari and Varici, holding hands, appeared a short distance away.

Was this what it meant to be the Key? That he could see movement in energy fields?

Brody glanced at his watch again. Fifteen more minutes.

"Megan called for us. Is she all right?" Varici knelt beside her.

"Don't touch her." Brody stood up. "She's on the astral plane looking for Robbie. I gave her an hour."

"She takes a great risk." Asari said. "How long has it been?"

"Forty-five minutes."

"Has she moved at all?" Asari bent down beside Varici.

"Just her arm." Brody knelt at Megan's other side. "She said this wasn't dangerous."

"She didn't know. The Monocaths often use the astral plane for indirect attacks. If she were thrashing about I'd worry." Asari stood. "Varici, please watch Megan. Brody, come with me."

Brody followed Asari a few feet away to a large pine. "Have you discovered how you can assist the Griffin?"

"No…well, maybe…hell, I don't know."

"You are like this pine." He drew an invisible line down the bark with his finger. "There are many layers making up the exterior." He broke a piece of the bark off the tree. "When you look further, you see each section is layer upon layer."

He handed the smooth, lighter colored bark to Brody. "These are the places which cannot be seen unless you peel away the outer layers. Humans are often afraid to look at their flaws and mistakes or to learn from them. When they do, great change is often brought about. As the Key you need to look at your hidden layers. When the time is right, you will know what to do for the Griffin. She will need you. She cannot defeat the Monocath without you."

Brody rubbed the piece of bark between his thumb and fingers. "Why am I the Key?"

"It was foretold. My daughter was a Keeper and a Seer. She saw the Griffin's Key as a dark-haired man of a certain bloodline whose parents died in a car accident, a man who would father the Griffin's children and banish her from his life."

"Why do you speak of your daughter in the past tense?"

"She was with us when my wife was murdered. She fled but we never found her and she has never returned to us. For nearly a thousand years we have searched the world but have been unable to locate her. We have already lost Phoebus, her betrothed, in the search. I cannot believe the Monocaths killed her the same day they killed my wife. Sometimes, faintly, I sense her but I can't locate her. I only know she lives."

"I'm sorry, Asari. It's terrible for all of you."

Asari nodded. "The search has been difficult. Not knowing what happened to your child."

"I know how you feel, now that I'm in the same position." Brody looked back to the bark in his hand. "I don't understand the bloodline part. I'm not royalty, psychics aren't in my family. What did you mean?"

"You are an excellent tracker with a knack for understanding nature. Does that mean anything to you?"

Brody shook his head. "I spent a lot of time in the woods growing up."

"Your great-great-great-grandmother used the name Marda

Hamel. Her real name was Ireth Telemnar. She was, by birth, an Elfin Princess."

"You're telling me I have Elfin blood in my veins?"

"It's the truth."

"You've lost your damn mind, Asari." He flung the bark into the forest. "That is the most ridiculous thing I've ever heard."

"As ridiculous as Megan being the Talgorian Griffin?"

"Look at me. Do you see pointy ears? I can't do magic, I'm a normal human being."

"Ireth married a human. As the generations passed the amount of Elfin blood in each offspring lessened. You are from her line, your parents died in a car accident, you have dark hair and you are the father of the Griffin's child. When you sent Megan away we knew for sure you were her Key. As the Key, you are entrusted with assisting her to fulfill the Prophecy. My daughter was a very accurate Seer."

Brody thought it for a moment. "Weirder things have happened in the past twenty-four hours. I have noticed I can see ripples when any of you change."

"There, you see. It is because of your Elfin blood. Most humans can't see them."

"Asari, come quickly." Varici called.

They ran to her side. She pointed to a purple mark appearing on Megan's neck.

"Wake her." Asari said.

She took Megan by the shoulders and shook. "She's not responding. Do you want me to go in?"

"Let me try. She's had a mark like this before." Brody knelt, grasped her shoulders and jostled her. "Megan, time's up."

"Varici, get ready to go get her," Asari said.

"No, wait. I'll bring her back. I'm the Key after all. Let me try."

"Hurry. The mark is getting darker."

"Megan, it's not me. You're not with me. It's the Mangler. He's confusing you. Do not Soul Merge with him."

"What are you talking about?" Varici sat beside Megan. "If you think she's about to Soul Merge with a Monocath, I'm going in, prophecy or not."

"You said love was part of being the Key right?"

"Yes but this isn't the time to debate your feelings for her."

Brody lifted Megan from the ground and kissed her. "Come on, Megan. Tell the difference." He kissed her deeply.

Come back to me, Megan. Don't let him win. He tried to project the thought into her mind.

He broke the kiss and looked at her lying limp in his arms. He laid her down and hung his head. "Go get her, Varici."

Brody stood and walked a few steps away. He'd thought for sure his love would have revived her.

What in the hell was the Mangler doing to her?

Jealousy ripped through him, sweat broke out over his forehead. How could he fail to bring her back? Maybe his love wasn't strong enough to save her. Did he doubt? Was he questioning his feelings for her on a subconscious level?

Varici lay down beside Megan and closed her eyes.

MEGAN STEPPED FORWARD INTO THE ASTRAL PLANE, separating her consciousness from her physical body. She looked down at Brody glancing between her body and his watch. Confident he would keep her physically safe, she faced ahead.

The mountains stretched out in front of her. It was amazing how the world looked the same as it did in the physical realm. In this dimension she could see farther and travel faster. She searched for the staircase oak. It was halfway up the mountain. Imagining herself flying, her arms down by her side, she zoomed toward the tree. She passed it to travel deeper into the forest.

A glowing dome of red came into view. Was this the force

keeping her from reaching Robbie on the physical plane? High above the trees she slowed to a stop in front of it. Extending her arm she touched the pulsating color. Her hand went through the red field. She withdrew it. Nothing happened. She floated through it to the other side. Speeding along she saw a small clearing with a cave come into view.

She dived down to the entrance. Traveling beyond the light of the entrance she found Robbie lying inside a cage. He shivered in his sleep and curled up tighter. Megan's heart sliced in two. She wanted to stay with him. He needed her protection but she couldn't give it to him in this dimension. She had to get back.

She turned to leave the cave and came face-to-face with Zangar. He stared in her direction as if he could see her. *Impossible.* She drifted around him toward the mouth of the cave. He turned, his eyes following her.

Can he see me? She wasn't sure. She could only hope Zangar had grown to care about Robbie a little bit during the past four years that she had been taking martial arts classes. Robbie had only been two when she'd signed up for the first class and she'd enrolled him for his fourth birthday at Zangar's insistence. If he cared at all for Robbie, maybe he wouldn't harm her son.

She zipped into the sky above the trees and through the red barrier toward her body. A powerful force blindsided her, slamming her off course. She saw a man's body fly past her. She lost control, spinning and plummeting to the ground. The impact jarred her astral body sending spikes of pain into her.

Something's wrong. I've never experienced pain on the astral level before. She looked around to see who had collided with her.

The Mangler stood several feet away with a scowl on his face.

Shit! What's he doing here?

"You don't play fair!" he growled.

Before she could move he dived on top of her. Grabbing both of her arms he yanked them high above her head. Pain shot along her shoulder blades. Holding both of her wrists within his large hand he pinned her legs with his knees. Megan thrashed about, trying to knock him off but he didn't budge. Claustrophobia closed in around her, snatching her breath, pressing down on her body. She fought to get him off, kicking and screaming.

His free hand found her neck, squeezing like a vise. She jerked her head back and forth but his strong grip on her neck held her to the ground. She searched for the Griffin within. Its essence was gone.

"You can't hurt me! This is my astral body," she choked the words out. It was hard to breathe. She gasped for air. She'd never been aware of breathing in this dimension before.

He muttered strange words under his breath.

Megan struggled, twisting and turning, trying to slide her legs out from under him needing to escape.

His forehead touched hers. His greasy hair hung in her eyes. Thick fingers dug harder into her flesh. "Your physical body will feel the effects. Without air, it will die."

Black eyes full of evil intent bore into hers. His lips crept into a grin.

No! No! No! Megan bucked against him. Her vision blurred.

"How does it feel to die?" His laughter hit her in the face.

Come back to me, Megan.

Brody? Was that his voice? *Help me!*

Her astral body betrayed her. It stopped moving even though she commanded it to fight.

Don't let him win.

The tender caress of Brody's lips warmed her mouth. She unfocused her eyes and froze in place. Playing dead, she pushed the panicked fear aside. Her love for Brody swelled in her heart.

The Mangler couldn't hold her in this dimension if she didn't want to stay. She wouldn't allow it. She imagined her astral body turning to vapor.

"You lose this round, Mangler," she said from the misty cloud.

His furious screams droned into the distance as she zoomed back to her body and Brody.

MEGAN JERKED, HER back arched and she fell back on the ground with a gasp.

Varici sat up. "Megan, are you okay?"

"Fine…just give me a minute." She opened her eyes. "Where's Brody?"

"I'm right here." He knelt beside her.

She sat up and hugged him. "Thank you."

"I didn't do anything. I tried but it didn't work. You should thank Varici."

"It wasn't me," Varici said. "I hadn't even started to astral travel when she came back."

"I found Robbie." Megan released him.

She faced Asari. "You owe us some answers, Your Majesty."

CHAPTER SEVENTEEN

MEGAN RUBBED HER TEMPLES. ASTRAL TRAVEL HAD never given her a headache before. It had never been this intense either. She looked up at Asari.

"Why didn't you tell me the Monocaths used the astral plane?"

"I didn't think you would attempt to go there. Why did you?" Asari crossed his legs, covering his knees with his hands.

"I went because Zangar told me it was the only way to break through the psychic blocks the Mangler had put up. I thought I could find a quick path to Robbie. It worked."

Asari and Varici shared a quick glance.

"What was that look about?" Brody sat beside Megan. "What haven't you told us?"

"This Zangar. What did he look like?" Asari asked.

"Tall, long dark hair. A scar on his cheek and neck. He looks the same as he always has."

"You know him?" Asari raised a brow.

"He's my karate instructor." A sharp pain streaked through Megan's head. She pressed the palms of both hands against her temples. "Geez…"

"Are you in pain?" Varici asked.

"This headache came out of nowhere."

"Did you close the gateway?" Varici reached over to lay her hands on Megan's.

"I closed it. I've never had my head hurt like this after astral travel before."

"It's a Monocath spell." Varici moved Megan's hands out of the way, placed her palms on either side of Megan's temples and chanted a few words. The mark on her neck got lighter and disappeared. "Better now?"

"Wow. What did you do? The pain's gone." Megan pulled her knees to her chest, wrapping her arms around them. "The odd thing is Zangar was with Robbie when I found him. He was standing guard. He could be the Mangler's guard. What do you think, Asari?"

"I don't know. Did you see anyone else with him?"

"He was alone. I don't know if Zangar is my friend or an enemy. What do you know about him?"

"Zangar was born Talgorian but became a loner shortly before we were ambushed. I've always believed he betrayed us. I have heard he frequents the Monocath lair so he must be one of them now."

"If you're right and he did betray you, why did he tell me how to break through the Monocath's psychic blocks?"

"I don't know," Asari said. "Varici, do you have any thoughts on this?"

The Guardian shook her head.

Megan sighed. She might as well get the rest out in the open. "Zangar isn't the reason I asked you to come here. Have either of you ever heard of the Monocath's Source?"

"I've never heard of it," Varici said.

"Neither have I," Asari said. "What is this Source?"

"I had an incident with the Mangler and Zangar interrupted. Zangar told the Mangler that the Monocath King wanted him to return to the lair because he was using too much magic and draining the Source. Zangar said the Mangler knew what would happen if a Talgorian gained control of it."

"It can't be." Asari's face drained of color.

Varici wrapped an arm around his shoulders and held on to him with her other hand. "Don't get your hopes up."

"What are you two talking about?" Megan asked.

"I think I know." Brody watched Asari. "You said your daughter was a Keeper. What did she keep?"

"You have a daughter?" Megan asked.

Asari looked down, cradled his head in his hands. "It can't be. Not this."

"What did she keep, Asari?" Brody said sternly.

"Easy does it, Brody. If what we think is true, this will be difficult. He's searched for her for a long time." Varici rubbed the king's back.

Asari raised his head. "Trulanta, Talgorian Princess, was the Keeper of Magic."

Megan gasped. "Your daughter is the Monocath's Source of magic? Why would she go to their side?"

"I can't believe she went of her own free will. They must have known she was a Keeper and took her prisoner to tap into the power." Asari stood and walked away from them.

Megan watched Varici and saw the pain reflected in her face. Then it hit her—Varici was in love with Asari. She glanced at Brody to see if he'd noticed but he stared after the king.

Megan reached over and touched the other woman's arm. "Go to him, Varici, he will need your strength."

"Spoken like a true Talgorian." Varici smiled and followed Asari.

"What happened on the astral plane, Megan?" Brody asked. "Did you Soul Merge with the Mangler?"

"No, he wasn't after sex this time. He wanted to kill me for figuring out how to get around his blocks. He choked me and was shouting words I didn't understand. I'm surprised he didn't bruise my neck."

"He did. That's how we knew something was wrong. We could

see the bruise forming. When Varici healed your headache it disappeared."

"He's very strong. It'll be difficult to defeat him." Fear and uncertainty edged Megan's voice. She stood up. "Come on, that son of a bitch has Robbie in a cage. I know the way. We'll fly there."

"You must not change again," Asari said from behind her. "Not until you face the Monocath in the final battle."

"Why not?" Megan whirled around. "We can get there faster. I want our son safe with us."

"I understand. It's not so simple now. Trulanta's magic is powerful. If she is the Source, she's supplying all Monocaths with magic. They can channel all of her magic into one Monocath—the Mangler. If they do, it will be impossible to defeat him. You must not let them sense your presence. Imagine a dome of white light around both of you and visualize mirrors covering the light to reflect their probes. It is the only way to sneak up on them. If you glimmer you will alert them to your presence. Trulanta can kill you from afar with just her magic. I don't think she's on their side but I can't be sure."

Megan picked up her backpack and slung it over her shoulder to put it on. "Fine, I'll do it your way. Besides, I saw a red field in the astral plane that I couldn't get through as the Griffin on the physical plane."

"It must be magical," Varici said.

"There is only one reason Trulanta would be held against her will for this long," Asari said. "I'm going to speak with the League. If she is with the Monocaths, I shall do everything in my power to release her. As you are risking your life to save your child, I will do what I must. I will contact you if the League answers my questions about Trulanta."

"What's the reason?" Brody asked.

"I cannot say until I am sure."

"Both of you should eat before you continue. Your strength is waning." Varici stood beside Asari and took his hand. "Be safe."

The air surged and they disappeared. Megan put the rest of their things in Brody's backpack. "Let's get moving. I figure it should take us a couple of hours to hike to the cave."

Brody took the supplies from her hands. "No. You're going to do what Varici said and take a few minutes to eat. What good will you do Robbie if you're so tired and weak you aren't able to fight at your best? I want him to live, Megan." He cupped her face within his palm. "I want you to live."

Megan's heart leaped. She wanted to look away but his gaze held her. He cared if she lived or died? Reality set in. Of course he did, she was Robbie's mother after all. "We'll eat but make it fast."

"Let's think this through," Brody said. "If we go running up there, we're sure to take you to your death. A strategy will enable us to defeat him."

Just as I thought. Megan took out a ration pack, handed it to Brody and opened one for herself. "You're right. You're the cop. What do you have in mind?"

"Hang on a second." He lifted the radio out of the utility belt. "Lewis, you copy?"

"It's dead," Megan said.

Brody looked at the radio. "I've got a backup." He retrieved the replacement from the backpack and switched out the battery packs. It didn't work.

"Maybe all the fluctuations in the magnetic fields around us drained them." Megan sat down and bit into a piece of beef jerky. "Man this stuff is dry."

"You need the protein."

"If I can get it down." She drank some water.

Brody sat beside her and opened the ration pack. "Can you create the shield Asari mentioned?"

Megan nodded. "Creating it isn't hard. Keeping it constantly around us is. I can do it though."

"Tell me about Robbie. What does he like?"

"Music, video games and his red racecar blanket. He wants to be a racecar driver when he grows up." She smiled softly. "At least that's his career choice at the moment. He's already been through the policeman and fireman stage." What if he never had the chance to grow up? Her vision blurred with unshed tears. "He loves Gummy Worms and corn on the cob, even though he has a hard time eating it because he lost his teeth late and the front ones haven't grown back yet." She chuckled and her voice cracked. She dabbed at the corners of her eyes with the neck of her shirt. "I usually cut it off. He'll eat the corn and suck on the cob."

"Yeah? How funny. I suck on the cobs too." Brody gazed at her, a wishful, faraway look in his eyes. "Can he ride a bike?"

"With training wheels. He likes the little three-wheeler he can sit in and peddle better. He's almost outgrown it though. He's going to be tall like you." Handsome too. Robbie was his father's son, in looks and in character. She slowly chewed another bit of jerky considering the two of them. Robbie was honest, logical and determined. Like Brody. Her heart swelled with pride. "Did you know if you measure a child when they're two and double it that's the height they should be as an adult? If it's accurate he should be six foot three."

"Fascinating. He'll be taller than me."

"He loves to go fishing, hates peas and likes to draw. There's so much I could tell you. What else would you like to know?"

"What was his first word?"

Megan took out a piece of dried fruit, inspecting it before popping it in her mouth.

"Well, what was it?"

She looked up at him through watery eyes. "Dada."

His heart hammered against his chest. Delight brought a smile to his face. "Dada? Really? Wow."

"I think, on some level, he knew this was going to happen to us. He's told me several times Daddy would find him if he was ever lost."

"I will find him, Megan. We'll do it together. We'll save him."

She swallowed. "That's why, when it's time for me to fight the Monocath, I want you to stay out of the way. Robbie needs you in his life if something happens to me."

"Nothing is going to happen to you." He took her hand and gave it a squeeze.

"You don't know for sure. I've seen the vision and it's not pretty. Since you're the one who wants a plan, this is it. If it looks like I'm going to lose, you take Robbie and run. The Mangler couldn't care less about him. He uses the children as bait. It's me he wants." She pulled her hand away. "I don't want Robbie witnessing my death."

"I'm not leaving you with the Mangler. We're in this together."

"We will not die together. I want my son to have a life, to grow up and be the wonderful man I know he'll be. I want him to know love and have children of his own. You need to be with him, to teach him how to be a responsible adult. Promise me Robbie will come first. You have to protect him at all costs."

"I can't leave you to face a killer alone."

"To protect Robbie you'll do whatever needs to be done. If it means leaving me behind to save him, you must." A tear crept down her cheek. "Promise me, Brody. I need to know Robbie will be taken care of if I die." Her voice shook.

"I don't like this." Brody couldn't let her face possible death alone. Damn it. He didn't want her to die. He didn't even want her to fight the Monocath.

"We may not like it but these are the cards we've been dealt. We have to do what's best for our son."

"I know." Brody ran a hand through his hair. "Okay, I promise."

"Thank you." Another tear ran from the corner of her eye.

And sliced his heart in two.

"Damn it, Megan. Come here." He pulled her close and wrapped his arms around her. "We're together. I'm your Key. That makes us strong. Both you and Robbie will be fine. I have faith in you."

The strong arms holding her brought comfort. She relished his strength, the warmth of his breath against her flesh.

She tugged from his embrace. She ate the last piece of fruit from her ration pack and took the top off the water. She didn't want to talk about his faith in her or let the conversation turn to their past. "Let's get going."

"In a minute. Listen, we don't rush in. Slow and sure is the best way to get close. If you use the shield of mirrors we should be able to get right next to Robbie before the Mangler realizes what's happening."

"The shield will keep the Monocaths from sensing us but it's not going to make us invisible."

Brody stared at her and blinked. "I knew that."

"Sure you did." Megan grinned and then drank the water.

He picked up the trash from his ration pack. "It's too bad all I can do with this Elfin blood is see ripples."

Sputtering and coughing, she spat the water out of her mouth and pounded her chest until the choking lessened. "What...what did you say?"

"Asari said my great-great-great-grandmother was an Elfin Princess who married a human. When you glimmer or when Varici transports from one place to another I can see the ripples of energy around you. Other than that it doesn't do me much good."

"Are you serious?"

"I didn't believe Asari either. I guess anything's possible at this point. I'm tired of fighting a losing battle. It's easier to believe what I'm seeing than to keep questioning everything."

Megan stood and filled her backpack. "Well, Mom was almost

right."

"About what?"

"When I was a little girl I used to say I was going to marry a prince. Mom would always correct me and say Elf. It was a running joke between us." She heaved the pack onto her back and secured it. "Since we were almost married, Mom was almost right."

"Interesting." Brody picked up his pack and flung it on. "I don't understand how this guy, Zangar, fits into the puzzle. We can't trust him."

Megan looked at him. "I've known him for years. He's never given me a reason not to trust him."

"You saw him with the Mangler."

"Does it mean he's a Monocath? Something about his involvement with them doesn't feel right."

"We can't trust him for that reason alone. Understand?"

"Yes." She adjusted the pack. "You're the only one I trust right now, Brody."

His gaze met hers. He wanted to say so much, to hold her, to be all she expected of him. "Which route did you take on the astral plane?"

"I went over the valley right there." She pointed to a steep incline. "Then straight up the mountain until I came to this bent tree shaped like steps. The cave is to the East

and near the backside of the mountain. There are two markers on the way—an old porcelain bathtub near the red barrier and a broken table with bloodstains on it. Once we get to the table the cave is about a hundred yards beyond in a small clearing. The old shack the Mangler is using as a hideout is between the table and the cave."

"How long do you think it'll take us to get there?"

"Ten minutes if we fly. Two or three hours if we walk."

Brody grabbed her hand. "You don't give up do you? Asari said you can't change or we'll give away our position. We walk."

. . .

LEWIS PRESSED THE radio for the fifth time. "Chief, come in. What's your twenty?" He released the button and waited.

No answer.

"Where are you, Brody?" he muttered. He'd been trying to make contact for the past hour. Something must be wrong or they were in another cave like before. It wasn't like the chief not to report in.

He watched the last of the cars pulling away from the accident site. The three men who had been trapped inside were *en route* to the hospital. They'd been shaken up but not badly hurt. These mining cave-ins happened more than the national news reported.

He sat on the trunk of the patrol car and motioned for Gamby, the leader of the search and rescue team, to come over. Gamby was dirty and wet, his hat holding back the snow-white hair hanging in ringlets to his shoulders. It looked bleached blond but the color was natural. He was growing it out to donate for a cancer patient's wig. It was an admirable thing for a young man to do.

"Have you heard from Brody?" Gamby asked as he approached.

"Not a word. We've got to get up there. He wouldn't have asked for backup unless he really thought he needed it." Lewis nodded to a group of Clarkston officers huddled together, leaning over the hood of a black sedan. "What's the latest with them?"

"I think they're planning to go after Ms. Cassidy." Gamby adjusted his hat. "I overheard Lieutenant Randal say he wants to use her as bait. They think something is going down in Clarkston. Said the city is crawling with Feds."

"Where's Hatcher?" Lewis asked.

"Asleep in his car."

"Wake him up. I'm leaving him in charge of the station."

Gamby whistled. "Brody's gonna be pissed."

"He'll get over it. Hatcher's competent when he wants to be. I'm not staying behind on this one." Lewis clipped the radio back to his utility belt. "I'm going to talk to Randal. You follow Hatcher to the station and bring back supplies from the stockroom. Grab all the filled backpacks and several ropes. We'll leave from here so hurry up.

Radio the rest of the S & R team to meet us at this location. The men who were here last night went into town to eat breakfast. They're beat so only call on them if you can't get the second team together."

"Yes, sir," Gamby saluted.

"Cut the crap and get busy. It's been a long night and I've got a feeling today will feel even longer."

Lewis watched Gamby strut to his truck. He always walked as if he would pounce on something at any second. Reminded him of some large cat. Lewis waited while the two men spoke. Gamby climbed into his vehicle and pulled out behind Hatcher. Lewis flagged Gamby down as he drove by. "Bring coffee."

"You got it," Gamby said through the open window.

The truck rumbled past.

Lewis took his cell phone from his pocket. Scrolling through the saved numbers he found the one he needed and pressed the green connect button. Several of the Clarkston officers looked over at him, saw him watching them and turned back to their papers on the car.

"What's up?" A voice on the other end of the line asked.

"I'm gonna need you and your chopper. Can you meet me?"

"Of course. Where?"

"Same place as last time."

"Consider it done. See you in a few."

Lewis flipped the lid shut as he walked over to the group of men huddled around the car like a football team. "You boys going after Ms. Cassidy?"

Lieutenant Randal straightened took him by the elbow and pulled him away from the sedan. Lewis jerked his arm free.

"Exactly where did she run off to with your chief?" Randal asked, his tone low.

"They went up to the Ridge. The last time I heard from them they were headed to Monocath Mountain."

"What's she doing? Following one of those *psychic visions* of hers?"

"I expect so." Lewis crossed his arms over his chest and noticed Detective Archer, who he'd met during his interview in Clarkston, watching them from the sedan. "Why is it such a problem for you?"

"You're joking, right?" Randal laughed. "You really believe in all that crap?"

"It doesn't matter what I believe. Why are you going to use her for bait?" This guy had a definite power trip going on. His annoying attitude was pushing Lewis to the edge of his patience. "It's a risk you don't need to take."

"She's already agreed. Now I have to find her. The Feds believe the Mangler will make a move within the next twenty-four hours. Since the killer has her kid, we know he's coming after her."

"Why? What evidence do you have to support this?"

"It's not your concern. You take care of your minimal staff in this sleepy little town. We'll handle the investigation within our department. Tell me how to get to this mountain."

"You arrogant jerk. Your department isn't the only one in the country even though you think it is. Our chief is out there too. This Mangler has murdered each of his victims in these mountains— what makes you think he'll change now? He's already left evidence he's here by blowing up Megan's car. Why would he return to Clarkston to look for her?"

"Watch your step, boy. We have our reasons and I'm not at liberty to discuss them with you. You're lucky I've seen how hard you've been working the past few hours or I'd have your badge for insubordination. Now, which way is that mountain?"

Lewis rubbed his face. This guy was definitely on a power trip. With the chief out of contact, he needed every man available searching, including the Clarkston team. "Sorry, it's been a long night. Tell you what, I'll do one better. I'm taking our S&R team up to Monocath Mountain to look for Brody. I might not agree with your methods but we both want them found. The more people we have looking, the faster we'll find them."

"Why are you searching for them?" Randal asked.

"Because I've lost contact with Chief Phelps and a killer is on the loose in these mountains. We can call a truce and work together or you can go your way and I'll go mine. I really don't care which it is."

"You've got spunk boy." Randal chuckled. "I'll get my team ready." He yelled at one of the men as he sauntered back to the sedan. "Detective Archer! Change of plans."

CHAPTER EIGHTEEN

MEGAN GRABBED BRODY'S ARM AND PULLED HIM closer. "Hide between those boulders up ahead. We're being followed," she said softly.

Brody quickened his pace up the old road. When they reached the huge rock he stepped inside the large fissure, pulling Megan with him.

"What's going on?" he whispered.

"I'm not sure. It scurries, like a squirrel."

"Are you sure it isn't a squirrel?"

Megan glared up at him.

"I was just asking. Is it the Mangler?"

She shook her head. "No. Wait."

Seconds turned to minutes.

"It's coming. Three o'clock."

Brody looked in the direction she indicated.

"I don't see anything."

"Patience."

A short man wearing camouflage walked into the roadbed. He carried steel traps over one shoulder and a bulging bag on the other.

Megan glanced at Brody.

"Poacher? Auntie Faye told me there was a problem with them lately."

"Yep. I'll be right back."

"No," she whispered, grabbing his arm, "you stay here. You can catch him later."

"I can't tell who it is."

"Wait."

They watched the man hurry toward them, head bent as he zigzagged along the road, until he finally looked up. Brody tensed beside her.

The man didn't see them as he crossed to their side of the road and went deeper into the forest. He stopped at a boulder and bent down. Moments later he stood with a dead animal. Once the animal was bagged and the trap reset, he started back down the mountain.

Brody practically growled in anger.

"Who *was* that?" Megan asked when the man was out of sight.

"Larry Tate. Our local animal rights activist."

"Are you serious?"

"I'm afraid so. At least I know who to bring in for questioning about the poaching problems."

"Unbelievable. Auntie Faye told me he was searching for the poachers. I guess he doesn't practice what he preaches."

"Obviously not." Anger boiled inside. If there was one thing he hated it was the illegal killing of protected animals. Addressing this issue with Larry would be the first thing he did when he returned to work. He glanced at Megan. If he returned to work.

Megan followed Brody from the cover of the boulders as he headed for the trap.

Picking up a tree branch from the ground he shoved it into the center of the trap, hitting the pad at the bottom and knocking it loose. Once he'd sprung the trap he pulled out the pin that held it together. He put the small metal rod inside his backpack. "He's not going to use this one again."

"Good."

Megan, behind you.

Asari? she thought, as she turned around.

The crevice in the boulders where they'd hidden had changed into a cavern entrance with Asari standing in its center.

"Asari's back, come on." Megan touched Brody on the arm.

She hurried to the Elder. Brody's footsteps sounded right behind her. "What's going on?"

"Come inside."

A torch protruded from a sconce on the wall. Asari changed the entrance back into a boulder after they entered.

"Why are we hiding?" Brody asked, stopping near the flame. Flickering shadows jumped around the cavern.

"Some things cannot be spoken of above ground. The earth protects us from the Monocath's telepathy. I come to you because I have met with the League and have the answers to your questions."

"About the Source?" Megan asked.

"It is as I feared," Asari said. "Trulanta was taken against her will."

Pain and anger reflected in his eyes.

"I'm so sorry." Megan rubbed his upper arm.

"We'll rescue her after Robbie." Brody's voice lowered. "What happened?"

"She cannot be rescued."

"Why not? If she's being held against her will she can be rescued." Megan planted her hands on her hips. "No one should be kept against his or her will."

"It is not so simple." Asari crossed his arms over his chest. "Trulanta is very powerful. As the Keeper of Magic she has abilities wizards have longed to tap into. There is only one who can release her and he is trapped within the sun. The League said when the planets align the Sun will release his essence back into his body. It only happens once every two thousand years."

"When is the time up?" Megan asked.

"I'm not sure. I need to research our historical records to find out when the last one was. It has been almost a thousand years since the murder of my wife and my daughter's disappearance. I've asked the League many times in the past to tell me how to find Trulanta but they always refused to answer. The instigation of the Talgorian Prophecies is the only reason they have told me anything now." He walked to a rock formation and sat down.

The pain reflected in his eyes made Megan want to hug him. She knew exactly how it felt to have your child missing. She couldn't imagine dealing with those stressful emotions for a thousand years.

"Trulanta was captured by the Monocaths during the ambush and they have held her prisoner since. I've always thought Phoebus died. I have been unable to connect with him since he left to search for Trulanta."

"Who's Phoebus?" Megan asked.

"Trulanta's betrothed. The League has informed me he is not dead. His body sleeps in a state of magical suspension in Trulanta's prison under her protection. His essence can only be returned to his body during a solar eclipse when the planets are aligned."

"Why?" Brody asked.

"Trulanta refused to become the Source of the Monocath's magic. So they captured Phoebus and tortured him to force her to agree. She didn't give in until Phoebus was near the brink of death. When faced with living an eternity without the one she loved, or saving him and being held prisoner she chose to save him. Using magic she preserved Phoebus' body and captured his essence within the sun."

"All elements must be in agreement for his return. Trulanta will not be free until Phoebus is safely at her side. The Monocaths didn't understand the spell Trulanta cast so they have no control over when Phoebus is released. The League said she knew this when she evoked the spell and is planning her escape. I know my daughter too well. The love she has for her betrothed is everlasting."

"This is terrible, Asari." Megan knelt beside him.

"It seems like forever." He grasped Megan's hand and lifted her as he stood. "When the time comes we shall defeat the Monocaths for all eternity. They will pay for taking my daughter."

"If Trulanta is the Keeper of Magic, why didn't she use it to save herself and Phoebus?" Brody asked. "It isn't logical to me, not that any of this is."

"I do not know and the League would not tell me. It is strange indeed. My daughter is a fighter. Saving Phoebus is the only reason she would be in this situation."

Asari looked at Megan and Brody. "You must be careful of the magic. She manipulates it but it controls her. The Monocaths have kept her prisoner a long time." He frowned and rubbed the back of his neck, looking away. "I do not know how she will react now that the Prophecy has begun. I have tried to contact her telepathically but I cannot."

"We'll be careful," Megan said. She touched his shoulder. "I wish I could ease your pain."

He tipped his head to gaze into her eyes. "Thank you for your concern."

"Is there anything else we should know?" she asked.

Asari shook his head. "If I discover more I'll be in contact."

Megan lifted her palm to the rock door and opened it. Asari left them and walked deeper into the cave. She motioned for Brody to go out first and closed the structure behind them.

Funny, Asari had trusted her to get the door right without waiting around to make sure she did. Her heart swelled with pride in his acceptance. Maybe being the Griffin wasn't such a bad thing after all.

"Let's get out of here." She stepped in front of Brody and started back toward the road.

The morning sun rose higher in the sky, heating the air. A

trickle of sweat slid between her breasts. The shirt stuck to her chest and back. She tugged at it, creating a draft against her moist skin. The morning mist covered the ground, giving this section of forest an eerie feel.

Megan looked over her shoulder. Brody followed a few yards behind. A reflection shone in her eyes. She peered deeper among the trees. She drew on her abilities to see if someone followed them. Scenes of scary movies flashed through her mind's eyes. Her heartbeat pounded as she held her breath, imagining some monster jumping out of the trees.

Get a friggin' grip! This is real, she told herself, releasing the breath. *Where is the staircase oak anyway?*

"What were you looking at?" Brody caught up to her.

"I thought I saw a reflection in the trees."

"Where?"

Megan pointed into the forest. "It looked like sunlight reflecting off a mirror."

Brody stared in the direction she indicated. Moments later another flash appeared. "There!" He pointed. "I see it. Do you sense anything?"

She did sense something but it wasn't clear. She looked around. Several hundred feet up the mountain a rock formation jutted out from a steep cliff. On top of it stood a

man, his long overcoat and hair blew in the breeze." She grabbed Brody's arm. "Look! Up on the cliff."

The man held a mirror into the sun, sending reflections into the sky.

"It's Zangar," Megan said. "What's he doing?"

"Morse code, I think." He watched the flashes for a minute. "No, not Morse. Similar. I can't understand the message."

"Let's go find out what he's up to."

"Not a good idea. We don't know much about this guy. He could be a Monocath."

"Maybe. Maybe not." She started back up the trail. It narrowed as the ground became rockier.

She kept an eye on Zangar as she climbed. Was he signaling to the other Monocaths that she was almost to the cave? Or did he only use the karate class to get close to her? Why not turn her and Robbie over to the Mangler long ago? She couldn't imagine a close friend betraying her like this, it had never happened before.

"Megan, stop!" Brody said in a loud, urgent whisper.

She froze. A black bear shuffled up the path ahead of them. Brody's arm circled her waist from behind.

"Don't move. If he sees us, we back away slowly. Make lots of noise and hold your arms up in the air to appear bigger. Whatever you do, don't run. He'll see you as prey."

"Should I change?"

"No."

Zangar flashed the mirror at the bear. It stood on its hind legs and growled. It looked down the trail at them, lowered its body with a thud and lumbered into the woods.

Megan looked up at Zangar. He bowed to her and walked away from the overhang into the forest. "I think Zangar is on our side."

"Why would you think that when the evidence points to him being a Monocath?"

"He sent the bear away."

"He was with the Mangler. He can't be trusted."

"I don't know. We should talk to him. Find out what he knows."

"He didn't tell you before, what makes you think he'll tell you now?" Brody released her. "There are only two people we should trust. Asari and Varici. Anyone else may have ulterior motives."

Megan frowned. He was right. She wondered why Zangar sent the bear away. Or how he did it unless the bear was a shapeshifter. "Zangar was Talgorian. Asari didn't give us a reason why he thought he changed sides. What would drive him to defect?"

"You've always tried to see the good in people. I know Zangar was your friend before this happened. People change, Megan. Sometimes they choose a dark path, other

times they go from bad to good. And some regret their past and try to make things right. I know I regret our past."

She looked up into brown eyes filled with concern. He tucked a stray lock of hair behind her ear. His palm slid down her cheek, caressing her skin. He searched her face, his eyes darkened.

"I know we said we'd wait until this was over to discuss our past relationship but my actions caused a great deal of pain. You, Robbie, even me. I was too young and stupid to realize it. I'm sorry."

Her eyelids fluttered closed. She drew in a deep breath. She'd wanted, no needed, to hear this from him. "It was a long time ago, Brody. We were both young."

"That doesn't make it right. Can you forgive me?"

"Yes, I forgive you." She released the pain his betrayal had caused. "I don't want you to have regrets. Things happen in life, which we don't understand. Our breakup was one of them. It forced me to grow up for our son."

She saw pain in his eyes. Pain she'd caused by being honest. Standing on tiptoes she reached up to plant a quick kiss on his lips. "No worries, okay?"

"No worries." He ran the coarse pad of his thumb across her bottom lip. He longed to have her in his life again. Leaning in, he kissed her, lingering over the sensation. She parted her lips and he deepened the kiss. Warm arms wrapped around his neck. Pressing the small of her back he brought her against him. She pulled away first, her ragged breathing made him want her more. "You taste so sweet. I was a fool, Megan. A damn fool."

"Okay, Mr. Fool, let's get up this mountain," she said, trying to lighten the mood. She pulled from his grasp. "We've got work to do."

"I'll go in front. The path is getting rough."

"Let me lead. I can handle it. I'd feel better if you were watching my back."

"Yeah, that's a problem," he said in a low voice full of desire.

"Deal with it."

Megan stepped carefully around the large rocks lying in the path. She glanced over the side. Good thing she wasn't afraid of heights. This truly was a cliff. "I wonder if the bear was an Elder? Remember one of them shifted into a bear?"

"The Elder was a grizzly not a black bear. Don't talk, Megan. Focus on the path."

"Oh. I didn't realize they were different breeds." She pointed ahead. "The trail is blocked with rocks up there. We'll have to cross them."

"I've got a bad feeling about this. We should go back. Find another way around."

"For crying out loud. Before we backtrack, I'll change and carry you over."

"Asari said—"

"I know what Asari said." Frustration edged her voice.

"It's not the only way. You could levitate the rocks from the path. You forgot your other abilities."

Megan stopped to rub her eyes. Fatigue bore down on her. Keeping the light around them, the physical exertion combined with the lack of sleep—it was a miracle she could remember anything. Making love with Brody had restored her once before but she'd been under a spell and couldn't glimmer. It wasn't something they could do again now. "You're right. I did forget I could levitate things. I'll move them now."

She bent over, threw some rocks out of the way and positioned her feet on the ground between larger stones. Straightening up she surveyed the boulders ahead.

"Brody, look!" she said. Her eyes grew wide and her face lit up in excitement. "It's the staircase oak! We're close to Robbie."

She raised her arms, flung the rocks aside and ran down the clear path.

"Megan! Wait!" Brody shouted.

She was being reckless.

Again.

Brody ran after her.

He didn't know when it happened. One minute she ran in front of him, the next she was falling off the cliffs.

"Glimmer, Megan!" he screamed at her.

Brody stared in agonizing disbelief as she landed with a loud thud on a large, flat-topped boulder at the bottom of the cliff.

A tremor shook the mountain.

He looked down at Megan. She was immortal, she had to be all right. He couldn't live with himself if she wasn't. He jerked the rope off his shoulder. "I'm coming, Megan! Hold on!"

He looked for the best possible route to her. Tying the rope to a tree he created a seat around his legs and hips.

The earth shook harder.

Brody looked down again. The boulder she landed on sank into the ground. He watched in horror as it disappeared into the earth, leaving a black hole in its wake. He started rappelling off the cliff when suddenly the trembling stopped.

He looked down to see the boulder back in place, as if it had never moved.

Megan was gone.

CHAPTER NINETEEN

BRODY HUNG FROM THE ROPE, STARING DOWN AT THE boulder where Megan had been. Despair tore at him. Where in the hell did she go? How could she vanish into the earth? Unless...

Could the boulder be a secret entry?

I'll have to figure out how it opens and find her. He dropped further down the rope.

"Where is the Griffin?" a male voice said from above.

Brody looked up to see Asari and Varici standing on the trail. How could he tell them he'd failed to keep Megan safe?

Some Key I turned out to be.

"I don't know!" he yelled up at them, rappelling further down the rope.

When he reached the bottom, they were waiting for him.

"We felt the quake." Varici said. "Where's Megan?"

Brody recounted the incident to them, while searching the boulder for some sign that would lead him to Megan. "I don't how it happened but I'm sure she's underground. Is this part of your cavern system?"

Asari shook his head. "The entry where I met you before was the end of the west side of our network. If an underground cavern is being utilized here it belongs to the Monocaths."

Varici looked over the craggy area in wild-eyed panic. "I cannot sense the Griffin."

"She's under this boulder. I'm telling you, it lowered into the ground with her and came back up without her." Frantic, he moved rock after rock, stomped against the stone. There has to be a switch or something."

"You don't understand." Varici rubbed the back of her neck. "Guardians can sense their charges regardless of where they are. Even if she's underground I could find her. I can't feel her anywhere."

"Damn it." Brody flung a rock at the boulder. "This wasn't supposed to happen. How could I lose her?"

"This must be a secret doorway."

"To what?" Brody's tone rose in frustration. "The Monocaths?"

"I've never known the Monocaths to live underground. They prefer their lair, which is a village hidden at the top of Monocath Mountain," Asari said.

Varici cocked her head to the side. "Where exactly did she land?"

"Here." Brody stepped to the spot. "How could a village exist on the top of this mountain without anyone knowing about it, Asari?"

"Magic."

Varici pressed her ear against the boulder. "I can't hear anything. There isn't a vibration. It must be magically protected."

"What if the impact of Megan's fall was the trigger?" Brody stared up the cliff, rubbing the back of his neck. "If one of you could levitate something and drop it from where Megan fell, maybe the weight and velocity would cause the same reaction."

"I will do the levitation." Varici looked up at the two men. "There is one similarity we should consider."

"What?" Brody and Asari asked in unison.

"I cannot sense Megan or Trulanta, yet we believe they're both alive. This boulder may be the gateway to a Monocath prison."

. . .

A soft moan escaped Megan's lips.

By all rights I should be dead. She stretched slightly to see if she could move.

Opening her eyes she blinked against the darkness. This place smelled of damp dirt. The constant sound of trickling water echoed around her. *How did I get in a cave?* The last thing she remembered was hitting the boulder.

She lay on something soft. She sat up and saw it was a bed tucked into a smaller area with three walls. Someone had made the frame out of tree branches. She swung her feet to the side. A faint, flickering glow softly illuminated a larger section of the cavern.

"I wouldn't stand yet," a male voice filled the cavern.

It was difficult to tell which direction the voice came from. Megan looked around. Torches placed in sconces along the walls lit the area.

She found him kneeling by an underground stream, his back to her—naked to the waist, bending forward. She heard him splashing in the stream.

A birthmark filled the small of his back slightly above the waist of black leather pants. A spiral within a triangle within a circle.

He has the mark of a Talgorian Guardian, she thought.

"Who are you?" Megan tried to stand but collapsed back onto the bed. Her muscles were so weak. She didn't fear the man in front of her but what was he doing? "Where am I?"

The Guardian stood, squeezed water out of a cloth but didn't look at her.

"Why won't you answer me? What's going on here?" She tried to stand again and fell right back onto the bed. "What's wrong with my legs?"

She stared at him, waiting. Long dark hair hung past muscular, broad shoulders and chest, which led to a slim waist. Bulging biceps, tanned skin. Definitely built for battle. Were all Guardians built like warriors?

He walked across the room to a table. A black shirt hung over the back of a chair. He pulled it over his head and picked up a bowl from the table. The fabric clung to him like a second skin. Torchlight flickered over his face, revealing a scar from his cheek to neck.

"You've taken quite a fall." He faced her. "Your body must heal."

Zangar. She hadn't recognized his voice before.

A surge of relief sung through her. *I knew there was no way he would have switched sides. But a Guardian?*

It had never crossed her mind and Asari never mentioned Zangar's position within the Talgorians.

He strode toward her with the bowl in his hands.

She tried to stand again and failed.

"Stop exerting yourself. Your body needs time to repair itself." Placing the items on the bed he bent down to remove her shoes and then stood. "Lie back."

"Why?" Tension filled the air. Why was she feeling so uncomfortable around him suddenly? "You're really Zangar right? Or are you the Mangler in disguise again?"

"Scan me." Dark eyes bore into hers. "Look for the light. The essence of a Monocath is dark and evil. You'll never find the light in them. It's how you can tell the difference."

She tapped into her psychic sense to read Zangar. His essence practically glowed with a radiant light filled with positive energy. It was Zangar all right. Her trusted friend and teacher. She lay back on the bed, sinking into its softness. She gazed up into his eyes. "Now what?"

He bent over, caught the waistband of the pants she wore underneath his fingers. "Raise up."

"No way! You're not taking off my pants!" She pushed his hands away. She sat up too fast. Dizziness overtook her for a second. She closed her eyes to stop the room from spinning

"Whoa…"

Zangar took her by the shoulders and gently laid her back on the bed. "I have an herbal salve which will speed your recovery but I must apply it."

"I don't have on underwear."

He chuckled.

She opened one eye to peek up at him. "What's so funny?"

"You're embarrassed for me to see you? It's not like I've never seen you naked."

"That was one time. If you hadn't run into your school's women's locker room after Robbie it wouldn't have happened." The blood rushing to her face stung. "You've got some explaining to do. Why didn't you tell me you were a Guardian when I met you in the woods?"

"I couldn't speak of it."

"And why not? Which side are you on anyway?"

"The only—"

"One you can be." She finished the sentence for him. "I know already. Help me up. I feel too vulnerable down here."

He eased her into a sitting position and sat beside her. "If you don't let me apply the salve it will take you several days to regain your strength. By then it will be too late."

"I need answers first. Where are we?"

"In my home."

"You live in a cave? I thought you had an apartment on Coldway and Pine."

"When I'm in the city, yes." Zangar ran a hand through his hair. "There's much you do not know."

"Teach me."

"I'd be honored, Talgorian Griffin." Zangar grasped her hand.

She jerked away. "Don't call me that. You're my friend, call me Megan like you always have."

"Okay, Megan." He bowed his head.

"How do you know I'm the Talgorian Griffin anyway?"

"I saw your birthmark the day I saw you naked."

"You've known about this for three years and you never said anything? You could have prevented this from ever happening if you'd told me." She turned away. Feelings of betrayal coursed through her. Maybe Brody was right. Could she really trust Zangar?

"You were protected. It was not my place to tell you."

Megan stared at Zangar. A soft tender look reflected in the depths of his eyes. Could she believe him? Trust him? "How do you know so much about me, this Prophecy and the Talgorians if you've left their ranks to join the Monocaths?"

"I didn't know when we first met. When I saw your birthmark I conferred with the Celestial League. Do you know who they are?"

Megan nodded.

"They told me all about you. I decided to do my part by pushing you to hone your skills."

"You're with the Monocaths. You talked to The Mangler like you were one of them."

"His name is Alten." The muscles in Zangar's jaw clenched. "It's his fault the Prophecy began. Until now, the Talgorians have managed to stay hidden from the

Monocaths for centuries. We are a peaceful people who do not enjoy killing. It is a duty resorted to only when necessary to ensure the survival of our race. Every Talgorian and Monocath knows the Prophecy will escalate the war between our people. It will not end until one race is obliterated.

"You really hate him don't you?" It was obvious in his tone, in the tightness of his jaw, that he did.

"I hate him for involving you and Robbie in his quest to prove his worth to the Monocath King."

"I don't intend to lose." Megan patted his knee. "Why will it take me so long to heal without the salve? I thought we were immortal. Shouldn't we heal immediately?"

"It depends on the injury." He picked up her hand and turned it over, inspecting both sides. "A cut, broken bones, they heal quickly. Look at what happened to you. Your back was broken when you fell. It's healed now, minutes later."

"My back broke in the fall? I didn't feel any pain when I woke up."

"When we have traumatic injuries, passing out is a defense mechanism to block out the pain while you heal. Not only did you break your back but you broke your neck, this arm and that leg." He touched each appendage. "I think a couple of ribs too. The healing process is fast, in your case it took about five minutes before you started moving again, which told me the bones had healed. When we have substantial damage it drains us. We become weak. The salve will complete the healing process. Otherwise it would take several days to recoup after such a severe event."

"Wow. Guess immortality is a good thing, huh?" Megan stared at him, her mouth agape. If she'd been human she would be dead.

"You could say so. I guess it depends on your perspective." He looked across the cave.

A sense of loneliness wrapped around her. Emptiness in Zangar's existence. She laid a hand on his. "Thank you for being my friend."

He grinned and the feeling disappeared.

"Tell me how I got underground. Did you bring me down here? Where's Brody?"

"The boulder you landed on is a control switch. The impact triggered it, lowering both you and the boulder into the Earth. I removed you from the boulder before it returned to the surface. I suppose Brody is up there wondering what happened to you."

"That's not good." Her stomach clenched. Knowing Brody, he might fling himself off the ridge to see if he could obtain the same results. If he did, the impact would surely kill him. "Especially since

I came to him for help."

"Why would you go to him?"

"He's Robbie's father."

Zangar nodded. "Are you going to let me put the salve on you?"

"Can't I do it?"

"Only a Guardian can apply the salve. Its properties will transfer healing energy from my spirit to you during the application."

"Whose Guardian are you?"

"I am sworn to secrecy so I cannot say."

"You're so frustrating, Zangar."

"Always have been—"

"Always will be," she finished. "Fine. Put the gunk on me. Let's get it over with."

He smiled. "You hate not being in control don't you?"

"Wouldn't you?"

"It drives me crazy."

"There's one more thing I have to know."

"What's that?"

"Which side are you on? For real, no games, no cryptic messages or half-finished sentences."

"I'm on your side, Talgorian Griffin. I mean, Megan."

"I believe you."

Zangar laid her down on the bed, then hooked his fingers in the waistband of her pants. "Lift."

She tried to lift her hips. "Whoa, I can't. I can sit up so why can't I lift my hips? This is weird."

Zangar slid a strong hand under the small of her back and raised her up enough to slip the sweatpants down to her hipbone in the back. "It's probably part of the healing process. I've never broken my back so I can't know for sure."

He lowered the front of the pants enough to expose her

birthmark.

She looked up. "You never intended to take them all the way off did you?" She'd misjudged him.

"Of course not. I just wanted to see you sweat." He dipped his fingers into the bowl and took out a big glob of an orange-colored lotion. "This might be a little cold at first but it will warm as I massage it in."

"You have to massage it in?"

He chuckled and lifted one brow. "That's how it works."

Zangar put the salve over the birthmark, rubbing in slow circular motions. Warmth from the mixture radiated around the birthmark and then spread through her body.

Megan closed her eyes. The herbal cream's heat crept inside her, seeping down to the bone. It brought with it strength and rejuvenation. The weakness fell away, leaving her feeling refreshed and full of vitality.

Zangar's hand slid up her stomach to settle between her breasts. Her heartbeat grew stronger as it pounded in her ears.

Megan opened her eyes. An aura of golden light radiated from Zangar. His dark eyes were slate gray. Moments later he slid his hand back down to her stomach. The aura faded and his eyes darkened. Looking down at her he removed his hand.

"Better?"

"Definitely." She sat up and hugged him. "Thank you, Zangar."

"You're most welcome." He kissed her cheek. "It's time to go now."

Megan stood, feeling ten years younger. "I really wish I knew whose Guardian you are," she said, adjusting her waistband.

"Follow me." Zangar smiled. "I'll introduce you."

He walked past the table and across a small natural bridge over the stream. The damp smell of earth clung to the air. She'd always thought Zangar had an earthy scent. Now she knew why.

As they walked she noticed the walls in this part of the cavern looked different from any she'd seen. Large oval objects shimmered and sparkled in the glow of the torches positioned along the passageway. "Where are we going?"

"You'll see." Zangar turned around a bend. For a moment Megan lost sight of him.

She followed, entering a huge cavern, bright with light. A large fire burned in the center of the room. It wasn't like any fire she'd ever seen. Blue, gold, red and silver flames licked the air. Megan stood by the entrance, looking for Zangar.

Where did you go? She asked him telepathically.

Come to the fire, Megan.

She took cautious steps toward the flames contained within a bowl-like formation. She walked around it, looking past the strange fire to a living area. Zangar sat on a long leather couch.

"What is this place?" Megan asked.

"Prison," a female voice said.

Megan's gaze rose above Zangar into the cavern's dark recesses. A woman stepped into the firelight. She wore a long royal blue gown with a low oval neckline. A gray insert from the bodice to the hem sparkled with silver studs. Fiery red hair curled down to a narrow waist. Her alabaster skin reminded Megan of a porcelain doll. Full ruby lips matched her hair, accentuating vivid green eyes.

"Who are you?" Megan froze in place.

"Talgorian Griffin," Zangar said, "meet Trulanta." He stood took the woman's hand and led her toward Megan.

"Trulanta? Asari's daughter?"

"You know my father?" A smile lit up her face.

"I met him recently." Megan smiled back. "He's looking for you."

"I have brought him much pain." Trulanta frowned.

"He loves you very much." Megan said.

"Soon, I shall see him again. The time is almost at an end."

Megan looked to Zangar. "Are you Trulanta's Guardian?"

"He is," Trulanta answered. "Because you are his trusted friend and the Talgorian Griffin, I have a gift for you."

"You do?" Megan's defenses were up. As much as she wanted to trust these two, her experience with the Mangler had left her skeptical.

"You worry too much, Griffin." Trulanta laughed.

"I forgot you could read my thoughts." Megan's cheeks warmed.

"You have been through a lot in a short period of time but your Prophecy is drawing to a close. Know you can trust me." Trulanta released Zangar's hand to take Megan's. "Love is the most important emotion to Talgorians. We will do anything for those we love."

She pressed her palm flat against Megan's.

"You're right." Megan's skin stung. She glanced down when Trulanta's palm moved to the back of her hand. The imprint of a dagger was seared into her flesh. "What did you do?"

"You are now armed against Alten, whom you call the Mangler. You may only use it once. Place your palm flat over his heart and he will die. If you miss, the magic will be lost."

Trulanta curled Megan's fingers into the palm of her hand, speaking magical words.

"Thank you." Megan wondered at her kind gesture.

"I hate the Monocaths for forcing me into their service. For harming Phoebus." Trulanta released Megan's hand. "Where is your Key?"

"We were separated when I fell. He's probably going crazy trying to find me."

"Zangar, please bring the Key to me."

He nodded and exited the cavern.

"Sit down, Griffin. Rest until he returns." Trulanta sat on the couch, motioning for Megan to take the other end.

Megan sat. "Tell me about Phoebus. He must be special for you to give up a thousand years of your life and switch loyalties to protect him."

"I am loyal to the Talgorians. The Monocaths may use my magic but I will turn the craft on them and they will suffer much pain when I am once again in complete control." Trulanta laid an arm across the sofa back. "I couldn't bear to lose Phoebus. He is the love of my life. The only verbal contact I have with him now is through Zangar who sends mirror messages each day. Come I will show you."

Trulanta stood, grabbing Megan's hand and pulling her from the couch as she walked by. She led her into a darkened area of the cavern. Trulanta raised her arm, lifting Megan's arm up too. The area in front of them was illuminated with a soft amber light.

There in a glass case was a tall, muscular man, his long dark hair reached past his shoulders. He wore a band around his forehead. His eyes were closed. He had angular cheekbones and full lips. He was dressed in a loose-fitting shirt, leather pants and knee boots.

"I talk to him every day. I wish he could respond. Maybe you could come to visit me once you've rescued your son. You know the way."

"Do I have to break every bone in my body just to come see you?"

Trulanta raised an eyebrow.

"As much as I'd like to, I don't know if I can. I've seen my death at the Mangler's hands."

"Remember the Prophecy and have faith in your Key. Come." Trulanta raised her arm in the air. The magical light around Phoebus went out.

"Where'd you go? I can't see anything," Megan said.

A soft laugh echoed. "Griffin, tap into yourself."

Megan allowed the Griffin to rise through her. Gathering its essence, she focused on tapping into the Griffin's vision. She could see Trulanta standing in a narrow passage, watching her.

"See, that wasn't so hard. You must remember you are the Talgorian Griffin. You are vulnerable when you forget."

Megan stood still. She hadn't realized until this moment but she did forget about her new abilities. "You're right. I'll make more of an effort to remember." Megan followed Trulanta out of the passage and into the main room. "This must be a hard life for you."

"It will be worth the time alone when Phoebus returns to me."

"There is one thing I don't understand. If both Zangar and I can leave, why don't you?"

Trulanta lifted her hands toward the walls. "See those shimmering designs? Those are dragon scales. They keep me trapped within these depths through my own magic. During the planetary alignment the spell I was forced to cast will break and the scales will lose their power to hold me. Phoebus will return to his body and we will seek our revenge on the Monocaths. They will try to stop us, of course but they don't know I gave the spell a specific duration when I cast it. I've had a thousand years to plan our strategy."

Male voices echoed from outside the entrance. Moments later Zangar returned with Brody by his side. Worry etched Brody's features. Megan watched him scan the cavern. When his gaze rested on her, his brow relaxed and he rushed across the room to gather her in his arms.

"Are you all right?" He kissed her forehead.

"Now I am, thanks to Zangar and Trulanta." She stepped from his embrace.

"It took some convincing but Zangar told me what happened to you. When he said you'd told him I was Robbie's father, I finally believed he was on your side." Brody wrapped his arm around Megan's waist. His gaze took in the room, stopping on the other woman. "You must be Trulanta."

She smiled. "I saw you as the Griffin's Key over a thousand years ago."

"I'm not sure what I'm supposed to do as Megan's Key."

"You will know when the time comes." She addressed Megan. "My gift to you is not only the magical dagger on your palm. I have asked Zangar to lead you to your son. After this, you must rely on your own abilities. Remember the Talgorian Prophecy, 'When the Monocath kills in pairs, the Griffin and Key together must seek the salvation of the innocent. In this quest only four exist, no other shall assist. The Griffin, Key, Monocath and child—good and evil shall collide. Only change will bring acceptance. Only fire will end the rampage. Only love challenges death'."

Megan considered the Prophecy for a moment. Faith and hope filled her. "How can I ever thank you? For everything?"

Trulanta shook Brody's hand and then grasped Megan in a tight hug. "Visit me when this is over. I'll have Zangar tell you the way in so you don't have to break your bones every time."

Megan wished they could indeed be friends. Regardless of how sure Trulanta was she would survive, Megan knew death waited for her.

She'd seen it, sensed it coming for her.

"Remember to use the Griffin's essence, even when you may not think you need it," Trulanta said, stepping away. She nodded to Zangar.

"This way," Zangar said, exiting the room. Brody and Megan followed.

At the end of the passageway Megan turned to look at Trulanta. Eyes filled with sadness stared back at her.

Did Trulanta see her death too? Or was it her lonely existence reflecting in those big green eyes?

Megan waved goodbye and followed the men.

CHAPTER TWENTY

MEGAN ADJUSTED HER VISION TO THE GRIFFIN'S SO SHE could see in the cavern's darkness outside Trulanta's prison. Brody's flashlight bobbled in the darkness as he directed the beam in front of her feet. He waited several yards ahead.

"Walk with me," Brody said, motioning Megan ahead of him.

"Where's Zangar?" she asked.

"He's probably up ahead. You can't see him in the dark."

"I'm using the Griffin's sight. I still don't see him."

Brody grabbed her arm, stopping her from walking any further. "I don't like this."

"They're on our side," Megan said.

"How do you know for sure? The Mangler changed into me didn't he? What if this is all a ruse to get us deeper into this cave? What if we can never get out?"

Megan thought about what he said. Doubt seeped inside. What if both Trulanta and Zangar had defected to the Monocaths. Was she that gullible? A pawn in their game? Did looking for the good in people make her blind to evil? She called out telepathically, *Zangar, where are you?*

About a hundred feet in front of you. I'm trying to get this torch lit. Turn to the left of the angled stalagmite"

"He's trying to light a torch. Come on."

A scraping noise echoed behind them followed by the sound of footsteps.

"We're too vulnerable in here," Brody said. "We should backtrack, find the way out, if there is one."

"How did Zangar get you down here?" Megan pulled from Brody's grasp, turning to face him.

"He did the thing Asari and Varici do. You know, when they appear out of thin air."

"What makes you think we can find a way out? If he brought you here by glimmering as only a Guardian can, there's no way we'll get out."

"Zangar is a Guardian?"

She nodded. "Trulanta's."

Brody looked behind them, shining the light into the darkness. It revealed only the sparkling cavern walls. "These walls are different."

"Dragon scales." Megan took his hand. "They keep Trulanta here."

"How?" Brody asked.

"I don't know. She said they do."

"I think the noise is Zangar." Megan said. "It sounds like it came from behind us because of the way the cave echoes."

At the end of the passageway was a small room. A large, leaning stalagmite filled the center. She went around it, Brody close behind.

The passage turned around a small bend. They found Zangar bent over a torch. He looked up as they approached. Megan scanned him, looking for his light, to make sure he wasn't the Mangler in disguise since he'd been out of their sight.

Still don't trust me, Megan?

It's not that...

Don't worry. I understand. I'd do the same in your shoes.

Zangar stood. "I don't suppose either of you has a lighter on you? Mine is out of fluid."

"I do." Brody removed the ever-present rifle and backpack

from his shoulders, dug inside and handed a navy lighter to Zangar.

"Thanks, man." Zangar flicked the button down and held the flame underneath the rag soaked in pitch, wrapped around one end. The flame grew until the entire end of the torch blazed. Zangar handed the lighter back to Brody. "Much better."

Brody put the lighter in his pants pocket. With Megan in front of him they followed Zangar through the cave. Several times Brody thought he heard footsteps behind them. He glanced over his shoulder often until they stopped at a dead end.

"I thought you were taking us to Robbie," Brody said.

"I am. The Mangler is keeping your son in another cave on the other side of this wall. I will transport you over there but then I must leave. You will be on your own."

Zangar ran his fingers down Megan's cheek. "Remember Griffin, you hold the power to kill him in the palm of your hand. If the magic fails, you will have only your Key and the Griffin to rely on."

"I understand." Megan kissed him on the cheek. "Thank you, Zangar."

Zangar's smile for Megan held a hint of sadness. He turned to Brody. "Keep her safe, Key."

"I plan to," Brody said, a hint of jealousy in his voice.

"Alten is a crazy one. Don't call him Mangler unless you intend to provoke him. He hates the name." Zangar wedged the torch between two stones and held out both hands for each of them to take one. "It is time."

THEY GLIMMERED INTO complete darkness on the other side of the rock wall. Megan tapped into the Griffin's eyesight.

"Your Prophecy awaits." Zangar released them and disappeared.

Megan grabbed Brody's hand. "Don't let go of me."

"I want to get the flashlight out of the backpack."

"No. If the Mangler is in this cave, he'll see it. I don't want him to know we're here. I'm tapped into the Griffin so I can see in the dark. Follow me." Megan put a shield of protective white light around them. How she knew which way to go, she wasn't sure. Maybe it was the essence of the Griffin driving her, or because Robbie was so close.

She followed passage after passage until a dim light indicated the cave's entrance was ahead. Two torches stuck into the cavern walls flicked light over a small cage with thick steel bars.

"Robbie…" she whispered. He looked so small curled up on the metal floor.

She scanned the cave for the Mangler's evilness. Nothing. It was safe for the moment.

Megan jerked Brody's arm, pulling him behind her, as she ran to Robbie. She released Brody's hand to kneel in front of the cage. A sob of joy escaped as she looked at him. He was dirty but, as far as she could tell, he hadn't been hurt. She reached through and touched her son's legs. "Robbie, honey, wake up. It's Mommy."

Sleepy eyelids fluttered open.

"Shush, honey," Megan held her fingertips over his soft lips. "Stay quiet so he won't hear us."

A smile brightened his face. He jumped up, stuck small arms through the bars and around Megan's neck, squeezing tightly.

"I'm going to get you out. Go to the back."

He scooted to the furthest corner. Megan tapped into the strength of the Griffin. Robbie's eyes widened as she pulled the bars apart.

"Mommy, your eyes are yellow," he whispered.

"I know, sweetie, come here." She reached in to get him and pulled him out of the steel cage. He buried his head against her neck.

Tears streamed down Megan's cheeks, a sob choked her. "Did he hurt you, honey? Are you okay? I'm so sorry, sweetie. I tried to get to you sooner but I couldn't. I love you, Robbie, I love you so much." She rocked him, lifting him into her lap, squeezing him as tears streamed down her face.

Robbie pulled back to look up at her. "Don't cry, Mommy. I was really scared but I tried to be my bravest. Sometimes it was hard 'cause I wanted you. He sounded mean and scary."

Megan hugged him tight, kissing his forehead. "You've been very brave. I'm going to need you to be brave a little longer, okay?" She held him at arms length to look at him.

Robbie nodded his head in agreement. He looked past Megan to where Brody stood. "Hi, Daddy. I always knew you'd come for me."

Robbie's words plunged into Brody's heart almost breaking it in two. He walked over to his child, knelt down and stuck out his hand. "I'm very happy to finally meet you, son."

Robbie looked at Brody's palm, then into Megan's eyes. He grasped the large fingers and pulled up from her lap, flinging himself into Brody's arms. "I love you, Daddy."

His eyes misted as he held Robbie close. This was his child, his flesh and blood. He'd never expected such immediate acceptance from his son much less a declaration of love. The feeling didn't compare to anything he'd ever experienced before. Love for your child. "I love you too, Robbie."

Megan watched father and son, her heart swelling with joy. They'd be okay. Even without her, they would have each other and love.

Another tear trickled down her cheek.

"Robbie," Megan said. "I have to have a talk with the man who took you. I want you to promise to be brave. Stay with Daddy okay? He'll get you to safety. I love you with all of my heart for now and eternity."

Robbie's eyes welled up. "Zangar told me about the Prophecy. You can have my bubble of white light. You'll win, Mommy. You gotta win."

She didn't know he knew. His unconditional love washed over her. Hugging him against her chest, Megan kissed him on the cheek and stood. "Take care of our son, Brody."

"Mommy! No! I changed my mind." Robbie clung to her leg. "Don't go. Don't leave me!"

She reached down and picked him up. His arms clutched her neck. Sobs racked his small body.

"Honey, it'll be okay." She wiped the tears from her face. Pulling him back she looked into his brown eyes and smiled. "Remember when Zangar taught us how to defend ourselves? He said Mommy was the best student at the school, right?"

Robbie nodded between sobs.

"I can take care of myself if I need to. Don't you agree?"

"Um-hum but I don't want you to go."

"Sometimes we have to do things we don't want to do. I don't want to leave you but I have to, honey." She wiped his tears away. "Be a brave boy for me?"

"Okay."

She sat him on a rock and gave him a kiss. She started to walk toward the light at the cave's entrance when strong hands grabbed her waist, twisting her around. Firm lips found hers, hungry and filled with passion. Brody broke the kiss to whisper against her lips, "You're not going out there alone."

She shook her head. His finger covered her mouth when she started to speak.

"I'm your Key remember?" Brody turned to Robbie. "Son, it's very important for you to do exactly as we ask. I want you to stay right here behind this rock." He pulled off the backpack. Digging inside he took out the last bottle of water and a ration pack. "You sit here and eat this. We'll come back for you in a little while."

Robbie dug into the food. Brody rubbed the top of his head as he stood. He turned to follow Megan. Several feet away from Robbie he ran into an invisible barrier, knocking him backward.

"Dammit, Megan! Take this wall down!" He hit at the field with his fists. A hollow sound echoed around him.

She looked back over her shoulder. "I'm sorry, Brody. I can't. I love you."

Turning away, she walked out of the cave's entrance and into the light.

"Nooooo! Megan!" He punched the invisible wall so hard the skin over his knuckles split. Blood sprang from the wound. There was nothing he could do. She had locked him inside with no way out. Damned hardheaded woman! In angry frustration Brody kicked at the invisible wall. He couldn't do anything but wait.

Brody turned to his son. The boy's features were his own but maybe he'd inherited Megan's abilities. "Robbie, do you know how to break this shield?"

"No." He spoke around the food filling his mouth.

"Do you know how to speak to people in your mind?"

Robbie nodded. "Me and Mommy do it all the time."

"Can you ask her to take down this wall?"

"Okay." He cocked his head, looking up at the ceiling, his eyes a bit unfocused.

He reminded Brody of Megan.

"She said no. She loves me too much to let me get hurt. She said tell Daddy it will be okay."

Brody hung his head, releasing a deep sigh of frustration. "Can you try to talk to someone else?"

MEGAN BLINKED AGAINST the bright light outside the cave. She allowed her eyesight to return to normal.

She hid behind a large boulder to survey the area. This place was the one in her psychic vision. They'd bypassed the Mangler's red dome by coming here in the caves. The old shack sat on the other side of the small clearing. Vines covered the exterior wall facing her. A dead tree lay across what used to be the front yard.

She searched for and found the Mangler's darkness inside the old shack. Maybe she could sneak up on him, take him by surprise. He wasn't aware of her presence, yet.

Who am I kidding? The only weapon I have is the magic knife on my hand. If I miss his heart... She should have taken Brody's rifle. No. It would have been too hard to get it off his back without a fight.

She might not have a gun but she did have the ability to manipulate energy. Her confidence rose. She used creative visualization to put a shield of white light around herself.

She crept around the perimeter of the clearing, staying behind the trees. She stopped when she found an unobstructed view inside the old shack.

The sound of rotating helicopter blades filled the air, a car horn blasted, a train rattled down its track. *What in the world?*

Megan looked around and realized her senses were on high alert. The noises came from far away. She forced herself to ignore them, intent on hearing the nearby sounds.

A movement inside the shack brought her gaze back to the window. The Mangler stood with his back to her. He leaned over a makeshift table. He wore an oversized dark flannel shirt with a hood and tight black jeans. *Like he wore in the vision.*

The grating sound of metal against flint filled her senses, echoing in the forest as he sharpened a knife. Whistling, he raised the blade into the air, turning it from side to side to observe his handiwork.

As it had in the vision, dark, negative properties swirled around him. He sliced the blade through the air. Megan sensed the satisfaction in him as he thought about killing her. She shifted her position to get a look at his face but he turned away.

He pulled the hood over his head with bony fingers. Dirt or dried blood soiled the area underneath his long fingernails.

Turning toward her, he walked outside the shack, raised his arms and began to waltz alone.

"Time to dance, Megan," he said with a laugh, deep and hollow, its evil intonation echoing through the forest.

"You wanted a challenge, Mangler," Megan said, stepping from behind a tree and into the clearing, "you've got it."

"Well, looky, looky, looky. What have we got here? I didn't expect my victim to come to me but here you are." His singsong voice sounded screechy and off-key. He continued his lonely waltz.

"I will not be your victim, you will be mine. You know only one of us can survive. I plan for that someone to be me," Megan said loud and clear.

The Mangler stopped waltzing to jerk the hood from his head, revealing a hollowed, sunken face, gaunt and malnourished with bulging bloodshot charcoal eyes. His thin lips spread into a wicked grin baring yellow rotten teeth.

Damn, he is one ugly Monocath, Megan thought.

"Do not be so sure of yourself. I've almost had you several times," he laughed. "Maybe I *should* have you before we fulfill the Prophecy. Last chance, Talgorian Griffin. Let me slip into your sexy body and get my rocks off for a while. Soul Merge with me."

"Only in your dreams."

"Almost in *your* dreams you mean. Why don't you let me have a little taste? Let me have one long slow lick between those creamy thighs, before I slam into you, taking your abilities and become the Griffin myself. What do you say?"

"I say you're disgusting and gross. I'll never Soul Merge with you, *Mangler.*"

Stalking, he inched closer, circling. He reminded Megan of a tiger readying for the kill.

Only this time I'm ready for you.

She matched his stride, stepping sideways in sync with him watching his every move, physically blocking him from getting past her to the cave where Robbie and Brody were protected inside the barrier. Her family's life depended on using every survival skill she'd ever learned from Zangar. This was why he'd pushed her so hard in class. He'd prepared her for this battle.

The crunch of rocks under her feet silenced as she stepped onto a small grassy area. She tried to create a barrier around the Mangler like the one she'd placed around Brody.

"Don't waste your time, sweetheart." He laughed. "I'll walk right though your little psychic wall."

Which meant he could walk right through the one she'd created inside the cave.

"You bastard," she growled the words at him. Fury rose from deep inside.

"You finally got something right."

Bright sunlight streamed into the clearing. The Mangler slanted the knife and reflected sunlight struck her eyes, blinding her.

She moved out of the glare, blinking against the yellow spots left in her field of vision. Glancing around for a weapon, she spotted a thick, long stick near the forest's edge. She looked back at the thin man.

Dark, stringy hair hung to his shoulders. The antique scabbard with sword clattered on his back. A knife casing was strapped around his leg. The ancient weapons still looked out of place with his modern clothing.

He lunged forward.

Megan met him halfway, palm flat and aimed at his chest. He saw the mark on her hand and turned at the last minute. Her palm hit him on the shoulder. Blood poured from the magically inflicted wound.

"Where did you get magic?" The Mangler spat the words.

"My secret."

He lunged again.

She ducked and rolled. The hard rocks dug into her back. She sprang to her feet and ran to the clearing's edge. She grabbed the stick she'd spotted earlier and whirled toward him.

His lips curled, eyes narrowed as a low growl rumbled from him. He crouched down. The evilness in his leer radiated outward. His darkness surrounded them. He shifted his weight to one foot and tapped the flat side of the knife blade against an open palm.

Megan sprang forward, swinging the stick. He turned away, taking the blow across the scapula, sending a bone-jarring tremor up her arm. The sword in the scabbard rattled. She pivoted, whirling around to add power to the movement and swung the stick full force at his head. It cracked when she connected.

Shaking his head he took a step back. He grabbed at the stick, missed and fell back several more paces under her assault. She landed blows on his arms and head, driving him away from the cave.

Laughter rumbled deep within his chest as he rotated.

Megan knew what to expect because of the visions. He would cut her hand if she didn't retreat. Instead of hitting him again she jumped back.

Hot searing pain sliced through her stomach.

She looked down. The knife was sticking out of her. When had he flung it?

This isn't how it happened in the vision.

He jerked the stick from her hand and slung it into the forest. "Did you really think I'd let you win? If I can't Soul Merge with you I will absorb the Talgorian Griffin's essence when you die, making my people stronger. You will submit to me one way or the other."

Wrapping his fingers around the hilt of the knife, he pushed it down to her hip then jerked it out. The noise of the blade pulling out of her flesh caused a wave of nausea. The pain was unbearable. She bit back her scream so Robbie wouldn't hear.

She stumbled backward, the taste of bile in her mouth, searching frantically for another weapon. The blood flowed between her fingers and down her side.

This can't be happening.

Robbie emerged from the mouth of the cavern.

Where in the hell is Brody? He was supposed to be watching our son!

"Get back inside!" Summoning all her strength she jumped forward putting her body between the murderer and her son. "Robbie! Go now!"

"Mommy!" Robbie, overwrought with tears, stared at her before darting inside, disappearing from her peripheral vision.

She turned her full attention to the Mangler. He grabbed her shoulder before she realized he moved.

A scream escaped when an intense burning pain pierced her abdomen again. She gasped. Gurgling sounds came from her throat. She clutched both wounds. Sweat broke out across her forehead and another gush of warm blood filled her hands. Her life force ebbed, flowing from her with the blood.

Megan stared down at the red stains soaking her ripped clothing. The second stab had left a wide gash splitting her abdomen open. She fell to her knees and looked up at the Mangler.

Death was upon her, waiting to take her essence and give it to the Monocaths.

Robbie and Brody appeared in the mouth of the cave. She tried to put a shield around the opening but she didn't have the strength.

Horrible images—people mangled and mauled—bombarded her mind. She saw the Mangler following the Monocath King during Asari's ambush, Trulanta rejecting his advances, his own people and their constant doubt. His anger at the way he'd always been treated consumed the deranged thoughts with a determination to prove his worth to all of them. He spun away. Long strides carried him toward Robbie and Brody.

Megan screamed, "No!"

Brody herded Robbie back into the cave, aimed the rifle and fired. Again and again he shot the gun until he ran out of ammunition. The Mangler kept stalking toward him, pausing for only a moment with each bullet hit.

Brody charged the Mangler, swinging the empty gun as a weapon. The Mangler flung Brody against a tree. He crumpled to the ground. Robbie emerged from the mouth of the cave, crying. "Mommy!"

"Go inside, Robbie. Hide! Don't let him find you!"

He disappeared once more into the darkness.

The Mangler stopped. Slowly he turned, bringing his enraged gaze back to her. "I've changed my mind. I'll kill the man quickly and the boy very slowly. I'll make him suffer so much you'll hear his screams in the afterlife. First, you die."

He shoved the hunting knife into its sheath and slid the sword from its scabbard.

Megan forced herself to crawl toward the cave.

The Mangler ran up to her, kicked her to the ground and onto her back.

In two swift strokes he slashed an X across her torso from shoulders to hips. Megan's screams sliced the air. He yanked her onto her knees raising the sword above her head.

If he kills me, I can't protect Robbie.

If he kills Brody, Robbie will be alone.

I can't let him hurt them.

Love and protectiveness for Robbie and Brody washed over her, filling her until she thought her heart would explode. Rage at the Mangler for kidnapping Robbie deepened and fought for a place in her heart. She called on the Griffin.

Her vision expanded. Colors became more vibrant. Something

shifted inside. She embraced the mystical beast within. Its powerful essence burst forth. She heard the ripping of fabric as she glimmered.

Her dark wings beat the air, giant talons dug into her assailant's shoulders, lion's claws ripped his chest open. The flurry of motion spun her out of control. Her anger with the Mangler surged into a rage.

You will not win. I won't let you harm my child.

The Mangler disappeared beneath her attack.

BRODY STOOD AT the mouth of the cavern. He'd never seen such an assault. The Griffin shredded the Mangler's skin, ripping him apart, marking an X across his chest.

The Mangler lay in a heap of flesh and blood on the ground. The Griffin shrieked and stumbled. Brody ran to her. "Change back, Megan. You've killed him."

She didn't change. She watched the prey.

What's she waiting for? Brody thought. He didn't dare leave her side to retrieve the rifle and more ammunition.

The Griffin shrieked beside him. He looked up to find her staring at the Mangler. Brody followed her gaze.

He was standing up.

How could he restore himself like this? It's impossible!

What did the Prophecy say?

Think! Think!

Only change will bring acceptance. Only fire will end the rampage. Only love challenges death. They die like we do, with an X and decapitation.

He heard the words in his mind more than remembered them. Looking up at Megan he finally knew what his role as Key was. He ran inside the cave and returned to Megan with one of the torches.

He slid his hand along the Griffin's neck and looked into its yellow eyes. "I love you, Megan. I've always loved you, even when I blamed you for everything wrong in my life. I'm not going to live without you. When this is over, I want you to Soul Merge with me so our family will be together forever. I want to be yours for eternity."

Brody faced the Mangler, who was now standing, sword in hand but unable to walk. Brody charged, his heart full of love for Megan, torch blazing. He rammed the fire into the Mangler's chest. The Mangler dropped the sword. Brody grabbed it.

"I love you, Megan Cassidy, Talgorian Griffin!" he screamed, swinging the blade. The Mangler's head dropped to the ground, his body followed.

God, I hope that worked.

Brody stumbled backward. A gray cloud rose from the Mangler, forming into a whirlwind of power above his body. Brody stepped further away. The Griffin reared on its hind legs as a lightning bolt of power surged from the whirlwind. The shriek of the eagle sounded through the forest as the bolt struck it in the chest. She shifted during the electrical shock.

"Megan!" Brody yelled.

She lay naked on the ground. Robbie bolted from the cave.

"Mommy!" he cried, grabbing her around the neck.

Brody heard the thick thrumming of a helicopter as he stumbled toward his family.

He inspected Megan. He couldn't believe she didn't have a cut on her body. He'd seen her bleeding to death and now all the wounds she'd received before shifting were healed. He carried her to the mouth of the cave. Retrieving the backpack he found some extra clothes and dressed her.

The whirling of the helicopter grew louder.

"Robbie, stay here with your mom."

Brody ran outside. The helicopter appeared over the trees. He waved his arms in the air, shouting to get their attention.

Deputy Lewis hung out of the open side door. Brody motioned to an area where they could land. The gale from the blades blew up the dirt around the rocks outside the cave as it landed.

When the aircraft settled, Lewis jumped out and ran over to where Brody waited with Megan and Robbie. "You okay, Chief?"

Brody nodded. "The Mountain Mangler is over there. Dead."

Lewis looked in the direction Brody indicated. "Good." He looked back to Robbie. "So you must be Robbie. How are you?"

"I'm fine now. Mommy and Daddy are here." Robbie smiled. "Mommy won. She fulfilled the Prophecy."

Lewis' gaze met Brody's.

"The Talgorian Prophecy is real," Brody said.

"I know." Lewis grinned when Brody's eyes widened. "Come on, let's get you guys out of here."

EPILOGUE

MEGAN WOKE WITH A START AND SAT UP. HER WHOLE body ached. She expected to be in the forest, protecting Robbie from the Mangler. Instead she found herself in Brody's bed. The alarm clock said five fifty five a.m. *Identical triple digits. Three fives are the sign for transformations, new beginnings and a fresh life. Just what I want.* She smiled and threw back the covers.

Cold air chilled her naked body. Noticing a robe at the foot of the bed, she got up and wrapped it around her. Barefoot, she padded out of the room to search for Robbie and Brody.

She looked over the balcony into the living room. Brody was stretched out on the couch with his eyes closed. The lavender envelope she'd given Deputy Lewis lay on his chest. The letter she'd written was clasped in his hand.

She'd poured her soul out in the letter, knowing it might be her last communication with Brody. She'd told him of her anguish because of their breakup and the trials of raising Robbie alone. She'd included a list of Robbie's likes and dislikes to help Brody raise Robbie when she was gone. She'd even told him how much she loved him. Of the dreams she'd had over the years, of following his career, secretly loving him, wanting so much to be with him again and being afraid to face him because of his harsh words. She'd spoken from the heart.

What had he thought when he'd read it?

He opened his eyes, saw her and ran upstairs. Wrapping her in an embrace, he hugged her tight. "Megan. I'm sorry I wasn't there to help you raise Robbie. You did a great job. He's a wonderful boy," he whispered against her neck. He pulled back to look at her. "I was so worried. You've been asleep for two days. He rested his forehead against hers. "I will make you happy, if you'll let me."

"Oh I'll let you." She smiled at him. "In fact, I'm going to hold you to that statement," she said.

"It's a promise."

"Where's Robbie?" she asked.

"In his room." He took her hand and led her to a closed door. He twisted the knob and pushed it open. Robbie lay in a full-sized bed, asleep.

Megan went to the edge of the bed and sat down. She looked into his round face. She ran her fingertips through his tousled hair, down his soft cheek. She watched the steady rise and fall of his chest. She worried how this ordeal had affected him as she watched him sleep. Leaning forward she kissed his temple. "I don't want to wake him. Poor baby must be worn out."

"He is." Brody took her hand. "Come on, we've got some unfinished business."

He led her from the room, quietly closing the door behind them. Back in his bedroom he shut and locked the door.

"What are you doing?"

He untied the robe's sash. "I'm claiming you. I love you, Megan. I want to be with you. Forever." His lips found hers. The kiss was soft and gentle. He slid the robe off her shoulders. It fell to the floor. "I want you to Soul Merge with me so we can be together for eternity," he said against her mouth. "If you want, we can get married as humans too."

"Brody." She pulled back. She couldn't believe he meant it. He must be relieved that she hadn't died, just as he'd been when he kissed her after the Mustang blew up. "As much as I love you, as much as I want to marry you, I can't ask you to give up your mortality for me. Soul Merging isn't reversible."

He planted kisses on her face, trailing down her neck. The brush of his lips seared her skin. Her senses reeled as he showered soft kisses across her shoulder. Her body reacted, heating, aching under his touch.

"I want you, all of you." He scooped her into his arms and carried her across the room, stopping beside the bed. "You say you love me. Do you mean it?"

"With all of my heart and soul."

"Prove it." He laid her down on the light blue comforter.

"You're sure?" She gazed into his eyes. Love looked back at her.

"Absolutely." He stared into her eyes. "I've never meant anything more."

"What about your belief in my psychic abilities. You know it's a problem between us."

"After what we've been though how could I not believe in them?" He traced the edge of her face with his fingers. "I believe in you, Megan."

She wanted this so badly. Wanted him for all time. "I need to read you. I can't Soul Merge with you unless I'm sure."

"Go for it." He smiled.

She opened the psychic door allowing her empathic self to look into his soul. Powerful love touched her heart. It wrapped her in sincerity. His word was truth. He loved her, all of her. His desire to become Talgorian, to be hers forever, was strong and pure.

His mouth continued its exploration, moving down her shoulder to her breasts. He held them in his hands, flicking his tongue over one nipple while rolling the other between his forefinger and thumb.

She arched her back. Brody switched his mouth to her other breast. The cool air hardened her wet nipple. She needed to feel his skin on her. Reaching up she pulled the hem of his shirt over his head. He rose, jerked it off and flung it across the room. She unzipped his pants, shoving both pants and underwear past his hips. His erection

sprang forth. Megan took him in her hands and stroked the length of him while Brody kicked off his pants.

He drew her against him. She straddled his knees and the soft curls of chest hair rubbed against her nipples, stimulating them even more. He pulled her earlobe into his mouth and suckled. Lifting her into the air he buried his head between her breasts. He kissed her abdomen as he laid her onto the bed, his wet warm tongue traveled down her body.

He pressed her legs apart. "So beautiful." He lowered his head. She quivered when his warm breath caressed her skin. The anticipation of his tongue touching her made her pulse throb. Her breathing quickened, became shallow.

Gentle fingers parted her flesh. His tongue laved her slick heat. She opened her legs wider as he kissed, licked and sucked. He plunged his tongue deep inside driving her into a frenzy.

"Come here." She pulled him into her kiss. She reached down, feeling the silken shaft, hard and throbbing for her. She wiggled, positioning him at her entrance. "Are you ready?"

"Most definitely." He smiled at her. "I love you, Megan."

"I love you too." She lifted her hips and took him inside.

He moved in her, slowly at first, her slick hot heat clamped around him. The pressure built and he quickened the pace.

"You're sure? Positive you want to Soul Merge?" An ache grew inside Megan, demanding release.

"You're the most hardheaded woman I've ever met. I want to be one with you in every way, Talgorian Griffin."

She allowed the essence of the Griffin to release, rising in her, filling her until it wrapped around both of them holding them together as one. Brody thrust into her as the aura turned white, glowing around them.

Her emotions blended with his until she couldn't tell where she stopped and he began. The white orb of light turned to a deep shade of blue with an aura of gold. She heard the cry of an eagle and looked up at him. Brody stared down at her, his eyes a vivid yellow.

He thrust into her, gliding his body against her tender flesh until she was on the edge of orgasm. Her body tensed, she rolled her hips to meet his urgency. Her body clamped against him, tightening the pressure as the friction took her closer still. Sweat glistened between them. Panting, she wrapped her arms and legs around him. "Now, Brody, now."

Her body quaked and quivered with his as they climaxed together. The tension burst up and out of her as pulsating contractions drew Brody deeper inside. His release exploded inside her, warming her canal with his seed. He held her against him. Their labored breathing filled the room.

A golden blue light exploded from Megan. Its aura wrapped around them. Her soul merged with his, the essence of the Griffin embraced him, filling him. Brody leaned heavily against her. Suddenly his back arched. His deep baritone yell echoed around her. A golden-blue arc of light jumped from her chest to pierce into his heart.

His body arched back, shaking from the impact of the light.

Oh God, what have I done? she thought.

The aura dimmed and Brody collapsed on top of her. His heart pounded against her ribs.

Worried she'd hurt him, Megan stared at Brody's face, waiting for him to open his eyes. "Brody, are you okay?"

He raised his head and slowly opened his lids. Eagle eyes stared back at her. He smiled. "We are one, my love. I am yours for eternity."

. . .

Hours later, over breakfast, Megan explained to Robbie what had happened in terms he could understand. He thought it was cool they were Talgorians and couldn't wait until he went through his own ceremony.

There was a knock on the front door. Brody answered it to find Asari, Varici and the Elders waiting outside.

"What's going on?" Brody asked, allowing them entry.

"I see we have a new member in our midst," Varici said, shaking Brody's hand she smiled at Megan. "You couldn't ask for a better mate."

"Why are you here?" Megan asked.

"The League decided Robbie should go through the transformation ritual now. While the immediate danger to you is over, we are at war with the Monocaths." Asari shook Robbie's hand. "What do you think, son? Are you ready to become the Hawk?"

"Oh boy! Can I Mommy? Can we do it now? Pleeease?"

"Are you sure it's okay?" Megan glanced from Asari to Varici. "He's only six years old, not even close to ten yet. It's too soon, he's too young. This could be really bad for him. After all he's been through I don't want to put him in any more danger."

"He'll be fine. This is one of those rare circumstances we told you about." Varici said. "Come with me, Robbie."

"Do we have to go to the cave?" Megan followed her son. "Are you sure he'll be all right?"

"Right here in the living room will do and yes, he'll be fine." Asari took paint from an Elder and marked Robbie's face.

"It's easier for the younger ones," he said to Megan. "Robbie needs protection now that the Monocath's know of your existence. He must change."

"You do as Asari says." Megan ruffled his dark locks. Bending down she squeezed him in a hug and kissed him. "I'll be right here."

"Okay, Mommy." He looked up at Asari. "So do I get to fly now?"

"In a few moments." Asari chuckled. "Here's what we're going to do. First, you need to undress."

"I get to be nekkid? Oh boy! Mommy never lets me be nekkid." He stripped out of his clothes, throwing them onto the floor, laughing and singing, "I'm gonna be a nekkid hawky, I'm gonna be a nekkid hawky."

"I want you to imagine yourself as the Hawk." Asari said, still smiling at Robbie's excitement. "Pretend to change your body into the Hawk. You will feel a shift inside. We will all add our force to yours when you glimmer the first time but you need to wear this cloth so our energy can join with yours. Then you'll get to do it by yourself. After you glimmer alone you get to fly to complete the ritual. That's all there is to it. Are you ready?"

"Oh boy, yeah!" Robbie said, jumping up and down. "I get to use the force! That's so cool!"

"What are we waiting for?" Asari smiled down at Robbie and laid the cloth over his shoulders like a scarf.

He took Varici's hand as the Elders danced and chanted around him so Robbie started to dance too. Still singing, *I'm gonna be a nekkid hawk, I'm gonna be a nekkid hawk, I am the hawk,* his song turned into screeches. The hawk stood in the middle of Robbie's scattered clothes and the cloth, lay piled on the floor. The hawk flapped its wings and hopped up and down.

Megan laughed and it turned into a sob.

"Are you all right?" Brody whispered in her ear. He wrapped his arms around her.

"I'm so happy he's alive," she said, leaning her head against his shoulder.

"Try to shift by yourself," Asari said.

Robbie appeared for a split second before he became the hawk again.

"There is only one thing left." Asari faced Megan. "He must fly."

Brody opened the sliding glass door leading to the outside balcony.

"I'll go with him." Megan undressed and laid her clothes on the couch. She turned to Brody. "Are you ready for your first flight?"

"No time like the present." Brody undressed. "Do I have to go through the transformation ritual too?"

"You gained the ability from Megan, so you do not need the ritual. We're here if you need us. Ask in your mind and we will hear," Asari said. "Imagine yourself as the Griffin and allow it to guide you."

Megan walked onto the balcony and glimmered. Robbie glimmered to human form and back into the hawk. He strutted over to stand by Megan. *This is fun, Mommy!* Brody imagined himself as one with Megan. He remembered feeling the Griffin consuming him when they mated. He allowed the same sensation to flow through him again. He heard Meagan in his mind.

I love you, Brody, she said.

His muscles ached to stretch. He gave himself over to the need. His vision expanded to encompass the entire room.

You did it, Daddy! Let's fly, Mommy!

Robbie flapped his wings and lifted from the balcony into the air.

I'm coming. You first, Brody.

He tested his wings, flapping them and pushed off the balcony. Lifting upward he followed Robbie.

Megan turned to look at Asari. *Thank you my friend and you too, Varici, my protector. My family is complete now.*

She turned away and propelled herself into the air. Each powerful thrust brought her closer to Robbie and Brody until she flew beside them. She dipped and soared, playing with them as they tried out their new bodies.

Varici grasped Asari's hand. "Don't you love happy endings?"

"More than anything." He gave her hand a squeeze, watching the family fly into the misty gray of early-morning light.

Keep reading for a paranormal romantic suspense short story by Melissa Alvarez writing as Ariana Dupré, which is a prequel to *Talgorian Prophecy*.

TALGORIAN DRAGON

Also available as an ebook from Adrema Press

DRAKAR HOLKINVERG SNIFFED THE DAMP NIGHT AIR, tracking the faint aroma that led him farther into the city and away from his sanctuary in the nearby mountains. Snowflakes floated toward the hard ground, and ice crunched beneath his heavy boots. The city lights grew closer as he followed the scent that drew him, called to him, only stopping now and again to inhale, ensuring he was on the right path.

She was near. The light floral fragrance, like roses after a summer rain, filled his senses, deepening in its bouquet with each step. A tinge of fear and desperation clouded the scent.

Drakar paused high upon a hill at the edge of the forest. Down below, the Magdoli Bridge crossed over the slow moving Cantar River near the outskirts of Karsburg. The town was alive with celebration. Even from this distance, he could hear the thunder of premature fireworks and the shrill squeal of noisemakers. The townspeople's laughter and loud voices drifted through the night as they celebrated the coming New Year.

A new year…a new life.

He listened intently, focusing on one small sound, until the noise of the city faded away and the rhythm of her heartbeat pulsed through him. He felt it as his own, its quick tempo pounding in an adrenaline rush. He scanned the area until he saw her.

Gwyn.

Love surged through him at the sight of her. She'd always held an immense power over him.

She stood alone at the highest point of the bridge in the shadows of dim streetlights, clutching the railing while leaning over the edge, staring into the icy water of the Cantar River. She swayed from side to side, lifted her face to the sky, then looked back into the river. Her energy enveloped him, thrusting forward a desire he thought he'd never feel again.

It had been too long.

Her short black hair, straight and cropped at one length just below her ears, fell forward blocking her face, yet he knew every line, every angle. Wet from the falling snow, her hair glistened a blue black in the glow of the streetlights. A short coat covered the slim body that he knew was underneath. She leaned over the rail.

She was going to jump.

Not on my watch.

Shifting the energy fields around him, he moved to her side in an instant, leaned over the rail, and followed her gaze into the dark depths of the Cantar. "You don't have to do this."

She spun toward him, fists drawn." Get away from me."

"You don't have to do this, Gwyn."

"You're not taking me back," she yelled, running a few yards away from him. She threw her foot over the rail and climbed. "I won't go back!"

Drakar grabbed her waist and pulled her off the railing. She kicked and punched at him.

"Stop, Gwyn! I'm not taking you back. Don't you recognize me?"

She pushed against him, still struggling to break free, her eyebrows furrowed. Anger radiated from her.

Of course she didn't recognize him. He'd grown a beard and wore his hair long. You could barely see the tattoo across his forehead and cheek that marked him as Talgorian. He no longer wore the fine robes of an aristocrat but now donned the heavy clothing of a huntsman. He didn't look anything like the pale, skinny youth he'd been when they fought the Monocaths together. He'd seen her die that day. Her life force had faded as the arrow pierced her heart. Devastated he'd lived in a self-imposed isolation for the past two years, lost in grief after her death. Wandering from place to place, living off the land, had changed him into a powerful warrior.

Drakar's heart went out to her even as anger coiled in his gut. He would destroy the Monocaths for making her suffer, for driving her to this point.

"I don't know you." She pushed harder against his chest, increasing the distance between them. "Let go of me."

"Are you sure about that?" He pulled her closer.

"I would remember you." She stared up at him, her body stiff and stretched as far away from him as she could get within the circle of his arms.

"I've changed." He ran his fingertips along her temple to calm her, losing himself in the depth of her dark eyes. "Let me refresh your memory."

He crushed his lips against her mouth. She hit his shoulders, struggled to break free but suddenly stilled and parted her lips, allowing him entry. He gripped the back of her neck, deepening the kiss, tasting the sweet elixir of his future mate. Her body melted against him.

Drakar broke the kiss. "Spark any memories?"

Her eyes brightened, a soft smile played on her lips. "Drakar?"

He smiled back.

"Drakar!" She threw her arms around his neck and hung on tight. "I've missed you."

"And I you, my love."

Her body pressed against him, her scent tempted his control.

"Why did you leave me during the battle?" She pushed away. "If you'd protected me, I wouldn't have been held captive by the Monocaths for the past two years."

And there it was.

He hadn't protected her as he'd promised.

"I saw you die, Gwyn. I had no idea any Talgorian could survive an arrow through the heart, an X across the body and decapitation. How *did* you survive? Did you complete the transformation ritual? "

"I'll never be able to complete the ritual," she said. "They didn't decapitate me. The Monocaths took me to their prison and made sure I healed. They wanted to use me to get to you but when they went looking for you... they told me you vanished."

"I did." He grasped her hands, looked out across the Cantar then back at her. "It doesn't have to come to this. I won't let you jump now that I know the truth and have found you."

"They're coming after me and this time, they will kill me. They saw my birthmark. During the transformation ritual I was just scared to shift...to glimmer...but now... I know why they want me, and I can never fully be Talgorian." Her eyes clouded. "You have no idea what I've been through or what they plan."

"Had I known before this morning that you were still live I would have come for you. I'd have saved you from the hell they put you through. King Asari contacted me telepathically after your Guardian sensed your life force. I immediately came to find you."

"You've been looking for me all day?" She stared at him, her mouth gaping open. "Why didn't you just contact me telepathically?"

"We tried." He smoothed her hair and caressed her cheek with the back of his fingertips, noticing the snowflakes sticking to her eyelashes. "Asari couldn't contact you. I've tried every single day for the past two years even though I saw you die. Even your Guardian thought you were dead. I don't understand how we all lost contact when you were still alive."

"Dragon scales."

"I don't understand."

"The Monocaths lined the prison room they kept me in with dragon scales. They said it was the only thing that could keep my captivity secret."

"*That doesn't explain why I couldn't contact you this morning,*" Drakar said telepathically. When Gwyn didn't respond, he repeated the sentence out loud.

"I don't know. Try now."

"I just did. You didn't hear me. We'll ask Asari. He'll know what to do."

Gwyn stared at him. "They've been looking for you. They seem to think that our combined shifting abilities would enable them to defeat us, and that the scales of a Talgorian dragon will give them an undefeatable power."

"That will never happen."

"I know. I'm not shifting to finish the ritual, and you'd never turn your back on our people." Gwyn moved out of his arms and turned back to the railing, looking out over the dark water below. "I don't blame any of you, Drakar. It's my fault that I was captured."

"You were protecting that little girl. What you did then was heroic. What you're about to do now, isn't."

Gwyn hung her head, sighed and then looked back at him. "Give a girl a break, will ya? You found me when I was resting, not contemplating suicide. I've been on the run all day, I haven't eaten. If I can survive two years in a Monocath prison, I sure as hell am not going to jump into some icy cold river and drown myself."

Drakar burst out laughing. "There's my girl! Come on, let's get out of here."

"You will not be going anywhere, Dragon."

Drakar pushed Gwyn behind him as he turned to face the menacing voice. Two men stood at the edge of the bridge closest to Karsburg, dressed for battle and carrying swords, lances and other weapons. The Monocaths still preferred the weapons of ancient times.

"Monocaths," whispered Gwyn from behind him. "The one in the black skin is Marden, the leader. His magic is pure evil. The other five are his pawns. They all work for Narvon, who is more evil than Marden. We can defeat these guys."

"You're not taking Gwyn, Monocath."

"Then we'll take both of you," said a voice from behind them.

Drakar whirled around, positioning himself so that Gwyn was

between him and the railing, as he faced the man who had spoken from the other side of the bridge. Twenty Monocath warriors stood shoulder to shoulder blocking the path into the woods.

They were trapped at the highest point of the bridge, with no way to escape.

One man stood in front of the rest, sword drawn, a long cape covering his body, a hood shadowing his face.

"Narvon." Gwyn spat out the name in disgust. "You bastard. I'll die before you take me again."

"With my magic, you didn't even hear me approach, so yes, I will capture you again." Narvon pushed the hood back. "But you will not die, Gwyndolyn. You will shift, become the beast within, and I shall have your head. For with it, and the scales of a Talgorian dragon, I'll create a magical potion that will put an end to all Talgorians and then you will all die now that you've brought the dragon to me."

"You're a liar, Narvon." Gwyn said. "I'd *never* help you harm my people."

Narvon motioned to the men on both sides of the bridge. "Take them."

The men rushed toward the center of the bridge, screaming and yelling.

"It's now or never, Gwyn. Glimmer with me."

An explosive burst of air threw the men backwards but Gwyn stood in the quiet of the storm and stared up at Drakar. He stood in all his glory, a giant blue and silver dragon, the current of air from the powerful beat of his wings held the Monocaths back. He looked down at her, his glowing silver eyes held hers for moment before enormous teeth gently placed her on his back. She gripped the base of his wing and dug her toes between the scales. Her foot slipped and she almost fell before regaining her footing. The Moncaths shouted and threw lances and rocks as Drakar spit bursts of fire over them. When he leapt upward in flight, pain pierced through her shoulder.

As Drakar soared high into the air, Gwyn glanced over her right shoulder. A lance stuck out of her body. Drakar flew higher and out over the forest, leaving the Monocaths behind. The air current pushed against the wooden shaft, causing the blade to move upward through her flesh. Gwyn gritted her teeth against the pain.

She shuddered as agonizing spasms tore through her. Beads of sweat rolled down her face, yet she shook with cold shivers. Waves of nausea washed over her. The sticky warmth of blood flowed down her back, soaking her pants. Sudden weakness threatened her hold on Drakar. If she lost her grip from this height. . . She pressed her forehead against his scales and sent him a telepathic message, *"Drakar, I'm hurt. Please land now. I can't hold on much longer."*

WHY HADN'T GWYN glimmered? Drakar felt her slight weight on his back as he flew through the hidden pathway to his cave. He'd known that as a ten-year-old, when they'd gone through the transformation ritual, she'd been afraid to complete it by changing into the giant snake, indicated by the birthmark on her thigh. At twenty-two, she should be over that fear, unless the Monocath's threat to wipe out the Talgorian race kept it alive.

Drakar landed in front of his cave, looked back at Gwyn and saw the lance protruding from her shoulder.

Anger surged in him. Why couldn't he ever keep her safe?

He moved her from his back to the ground in front of him, then glimmered back into human form. The air was frigid against his naked body.

Gwyn groaned and tried to sit up. "Get this thing out of my back, Drakar."

He knelt beside her and grabbed the wooden staff. "Ready?"

She nodded, and he yanked the blade from her flesh and threw it into the forest. She grimaced in pain.

He picked her up. "Wrap your legs around me."

He carried her deep into the darkness of the cave until he reached a dead end. He placed his palm against the rock wall and it slid to the side, revealing a high ceiling room, a low burning fire and handmade furnishings. Once inside he closed the hidden entrance and sat Gwyn in front of the fire. "I need to look at that wound."

"You should get dressed first." Gwyn looked up at him, then down the length of his body before turning her dark gaze back into his eyes. "You're definitely not the skinny boy I fell in love with."

Drakar grinned. "I grew."

"Yes, you most certainly did." Gwyn carefully shrugged out of her coat while he dressed. "I haven't been injured since they captured me. It doesn't feel like I'm healing." Gwyn unbuttoned her shirt and tried to get her arm out.

Drakar kneeled beside her. "Let me help you, Gwyn. You don't have to be so damn independent."

He slid her uninjured arm out of the sleeve and then gently removed the fabric from over the wound, leaving her back bare. The deep gash in her body still bled. He gently wiped away the blood with her ruined shirt.

Something *was* terribly wrong.

"You're right, you're not healing. What did the Monocaths do to you when you were in captivity? You've lost your telepathic and healing abilities."

"They took care of my wounds and constantly threatened me, you and our people, but they never touched me again." She glanced over her shoulder. "Are you going to have to sew me up?"

Drakar studied the uninjured left shoulder blade. It looked misshapen, raised up a little, and had a slight half moon scar. "Did that arrow go through your left side?"

"No, the right, just like now."

"You've never had an injury to your left side?" Drakar ran his hand over the misshapen part of her back. Damn if it didn't have the shape of one of his scales.

"No, never."

"I think the Monocaths put a dragon scale inside of you, Gwyn."

She stared over her shoulder at him. "A scale? That's what's been blocking my telepathic abilities? Son of a bitch!" Gwyn pounded her fist against the floor. "Take it out. Now."

"But you're not healing."

"Cut it out of me." She pulled a small knife out of the side of her boot. "Use this. While you're in there, look for a small piece of silver that looks like a coin. If you find one, take that out too."

"What is it?" Drakar took the knife, rose and walked to the fire.

"I'm not sure," she said as he dropped to a squat and held the blade over the flame to sterilize it. "I once overheard Marden say that it would prevent both Talgorians and Monocaths from healing if embedded in the flesh. He was threatening one of his men with a slow painful death and an end to his immortality by using a silver coin."

"And if it's removed, you'll heal?"

"I hope so. Or you'll have a lot of sewing to do."

"This is really going to hurt Gwyn." Drakar knelt beside her. "Are you ready?"

"As ready as I'll ever be." She removed the leather belt from her pants, stuck it between her teeth, and nodded for him to start.

Drakar worked quickly. Five minutes into the procedure Gwyn passed out. He was surprised she'd lasted that long. He found the scale easily and slid it from underneath her skin. The silver coin was there too, but embedded deeper in muscle. It took a few moments but he was able to cut it out as well. Once removed, Gwyn's body immediately began to heal. Soon it looked as if she'd never been injured, even the scar was gone, but she hadn't woken up.

He put the scale on the table, washed the blood from her back and removed the blood-soaked pants, before putting her in bed. As he covered her, he noticed the Talgorian birthmark on her outer thigh. It was no longer the snake that he remembered but was now a beast with nine heads and the body of a dragon.

The Hydra.

Now he understood.

Both the Monocaths and Talgorians considered the Hydra to be a source of intense magical power. If a head were severed, she'd grow two back in its place. The Monocaths could wreak havoc on the Talgorians by using pieces of one of the Hydra's decapitated heads in their magical rituals. And with his scales…

"*That's why I can't change,*" he heard Gwyn's voice in his head, "*Narvon wants to use me, kill you for your scales, and eliminate our race.*"

Drakar studied Gwyn. She pushed herself up, holding the blanket to cover herself, and sat facing him. She'd always seemed to know what he was thinking. Apparently, that hadn't changed. He picked up the red and purple scale from the small bedside table and handed it to her as he sat on the edge of the bed.

"They used a scale from the Dragons of Belmere, the most evil of all dragons. The Monocaths must have bewitched it to block your telepathy. My scales wouldn't block our communication."

Gwyn examined the scale from all sides. "I don't understand why Narvon must have your scales if he's already using these."

"I was taught that my scales, when burned with the head of a Hydra, would create a living mist that would seek out and kill every Talgorian." He reached over and tucked a stray lock of Gwyn's hair back into place. "As far as I know, I am the only Talgorian dragon and you are the only Hydra."

Gwyn frowned. "So we can never be together?"

"I've never stopped loving you, Gwyn. I mourned you for two years and I'll be damned if I'll let you out of my sight again now that I have you back. Of course we can be together. We're stronger together than apart. That is, if you still love me."

Gwyn yanked him to her. "You crazy dragon. How could you even wonder if I still love you?" She kissed him hard, then turned the kiss into a playfully soft seduction, talking between kisses. "I love you more now than ever. I've fantasized about you day and night, hoping you'd come for me while I planned my escape. You're stuck with me, broeistar."

"Forever, beloved." Drakar kissed her deeply, then pulled back to look at her. "How did you escape?"

"I didn't. A boar mauled my guard's child. I healed his son and in exchange he let me go in the middle of the night."

Drakar smiled, holding her face between his hands. "I'm glad he did. I've missed you."

He lay down beside her on the bed, pulled her close, enjoying the taste of her lips on his, the floral scent that was uniquely Gwyn. Her arms wrapped around his neck, her pulse vibrated through him as his own. He kissed her shoulder, the curve of her neck, moving toward the rise of her...

"Gwwwyyynnn . Ruuunnn!"

The voice screamed through Drakar's head. He looked up at Gwyn. Her eyes were wide with fear. She pushed him off her. "Get up! That's my mother."

"Aaauuughhh," the woman screamed, *"Narvon is after you. Run, Gwyn, run!"*

"I'm coming, Mother." Gwyn scrambled out of the bed. "Give me clothes. We have to save her."

"No, Gwyn. Get as far from here as you can. Narvon can never have your power."

Drakar rifled through his wardrobe and found a smaller sized shirt and pair of pants that he no longer wore and threw them on the bed for her. *"Asari, did you hear that? What's going on?"*

"It is Corenth, Gwyn's mother. Narvon has invaded her home, hoping to draw out Gwyn. She sent the message to everyone to protect Gwyn." Asari said telepathically. *"I know she is with you. Take her far from here, Drakar. Narvon is mad."*

"I will."

Gwyn, fully dressed, placed her knife back in her boot. "I'm going to rescue my mother. Don't even think of stopping me. For two years Narvon has threatened my family and now he's followed through. I will save her whether you help me or not."

Drakar saw the determination in her eyes and knew it was pointless to argue.

"Asari isn't going to like this." He grabbed a coat and handed it to Gwyn. "Put this on."

He stripped, put his clothes in a big canvas bag and slung it over his shoulder. "Now we fly."

GWYN WATCHED THE cliffs from her childhood rise on the horizon. From Drakar's back she could see parents' home at the edge of the forest facing the largest cliff. Landow Mountain's snow covered top disappeared into the clouds behind the cliffs. Her mother had refused to move after the Monocaths killed her father.

"Land behind the house in that clearing," Gwyn said telepathically. *We'll walk from there."*

Drakar dove down toward the open field. *"Hang on."*

He dropped the canvas bag to the ground, landed, and once Gwyn slid to the ground, glimmered to shift back into his human form and quickly dressed. "Follow me."

"I should lead. I know this forest better than you," Gwyn whispered. She pushed ahead of him and moved with stealth through the trees for several minutes. "The house is right up here."

Drakar grabbed her elbow and moved in front of her. "You

can't just go barging in there. Stay behind me."

"Not happening, dragon-boy. I've got the left side of the house, you take the right. We'll communicate telepathically."

Drakar growled in frustration as Gwyn moved quickly through the forest to the other side of the house. She'd given him that name when they were kids. He loved her independence but she could be reckless, especially when it came to family. If anything happened to her now...

Gwyn disappeared from view around the side of the house. Hidden within the edge of the forest, Drakar changed his position until he had a clear view of the front door. Gwyn stood there, knife pulled, confronting Narvon who had his arm wrapped around Corenth and a blade pressed against her neck. Blood soaked Corenth's clothing where Narvon had cut an X across her body. The X combined with decapitation was the cross of death for an immortal Talgorian.

"So much for working together, Gwyn."

"Stay back, Drakar. I don't want you in danger too. I'll handle this."

"Like hell you will. What did they do to you in that prison? You've turned into some kind of vigilante."

"I protect my own. Always have."

That much was true, but Drakar wouldn't let her do this alone. He walked out of the forest and into the standoff.

"Messing with me is one thing, but to pull my family into this is going too far."

Drakar stood fifteen feet away. "Let her go, Narvon."

"I will as soon as Gwyn shifts and gives me one of her Hydra heads."

"That'll never happen." Gwyn took a step forward. "Just glimmer and get away, Mother."

"Gwyn! Did you forget I shift into a turtle?"

"Yeah, a snapping turtle! Bite him and we'll rush him while you

heal."

"Having one of her heads isn't going to help your plan, Narvon." Drakar said. "You'd need my scales, and I'll never give you one."

"Oh, but you already have, mighty Drakar." Narvon laughed. "When you made your big escape from the bridge Gwyn nearly fell off of your back. She dislodged a scale, which we now have in safekeeping." He patted his chest to indicate that the scale was on his body.

"I'm tired of this game." Narvon whistled and Monocaths poured from the house, surrounding them. He drew the blade across Corenth's neck just as she glimmered and fell to the ground.

"You son of a bitch." Drakar rushed him, as did Gwyn.

Narvon flung the blade, piercing Drakar in the chest. He staggered forward, and then fell back against Gwyn, who lowered him to the ground.

Gwyn stared at her mother and Drakar, both lying so still. Rage burned through her. She thought about the last two years, her escape, finding Drakar again. She'd lost too much at the hands of the Monocaths and this monster, Narvon.

"Now you will do as I say and change into the Hydra. I will have one of your heads."

"Not before I have yours, Narvon."

She'd done everything in the Talgorian ritual except the final step, glimmering into the sign of her birthmark. Now it was time to finish it. "You should be careful what you ask of me, Narvon. It may be the death of you." She looked around at the Monocaths surrounding them. "It could be the death of you all."

Gwyn felt the rage grow inside of her, she drew the glimmering energy close and felt the change as her body grew and distorted into the powerful Hydra. She held her breath as her clothing fell to the ground. She picked them up with her foot and threw them over Corenth's and Drakar's faces. She grabbed

Narvon, covering his face with her foot, inhaled deeply and with all nine heads, blew her breath over the Monocaths surrounding them. She watched them drop to the ground in death from her poisonous breath. She then turned her heads to Narvon, who stared at her in terror.

"More than you imagined?" Gwyn hissed the words from all nine mouths at once. "I want you to choose a head, Narvon. If you can hold your breath long enough to cut it off, you can have it. If not, you die."

She pulled the blade from Drakar's chest by biting the handle with one of her mouths and gave it to Narvon. She placed him on the ground. He took the blade and swung at the head closest to him. Blood spurted from the cut, covering his face and body. Her wound immediately healed.

"I hope this was worth the two year wait, Narvon. You do know that my blood is as poisonous as my breath and will eat the skin from your body, don't you? Now give me the scale."

"Never." Narvon inhaled and died instantly, saving him from the horrific pain of her acid blood burning away his flesh.

Gwyn removed the scale from Narvon's shirt and placed it beside Drakar, then glimmered back to human form. She uncovered her mother.

"Are you okay?"

"I'm fine. Is it safe to glimmer now?"

"Yes."

Corenth glimmered and looked at Drakar. "Is he okay?"

"He's probably still healing. I'm going to check him now."

"I'll go dress and bring your clothes." She hurried inside the house.

Gwyn knelt beside Drakar, picked up the dragon scale and placed it on his chest over the wound. Maybe having all parts of him together would help him heal faster.

"Drakar. Wake up." She held his face between her hands,

leaning down she kissed him. His lips felt cool against hers. She kissed him again, and again, urging him to wake up.

Finally he kissed her back. His arms wrapped around her and pulled her close to him, deepening the kiss. Then he opened his eyes and drew back. "Are you all right?"

"I should be asking you that, dragon-boy."

"I'll be fine but you know I hate that name."

"You know it means I love you."

"I love you too, Hydra-lady."

Gwyn laughed at his teasing and sat up. "Come on, I have to get dressed."

Drakar looked at her, "I don't know about that. You look fine to me."

"Later. Besides, look where we are. What would my mother say?"

"She'd say you two need to hurry up and Soul Merge before anything else happens. It's a new year. You should start a new life together." Corenth threw some clothes beside them. "Get dressed Gwyn and both of you come inside. I've already contacted Asari. He's sending people to clean up this mess and to get a full report from you two." She walked back into the house.

Drakar sat up. "I want us to be mated forever, Gwyn. Will you Soul Merge with me when we get back to the cave?"

"You know you're going to have to move out of there, don't you?"

"You didn't answer my question."

Gwyn wrapped her arms around his neck and kissed him, giving him a taste of what was to come, full of passion and promise. She broke the kiss and smiled. "I wouldn't have my New Year start any other way, dragon-boy."

Keep reading for an excerpt from a contemporary paranormal romantic suspense novel by Melissa Alvarez writing as Ariana Dupré.

NIGHT VISIONS

Now available in print from Adrema Press

PROLOGUE

Slayton Homestead
Southern Central Virginia
August—early 1800's

THE BLISTERING HEAT OF THE MIDDAY SUN WAS NO match for the fire burning within Theodore Slayton. Thunderheads rose in the crystal blue sky, a sure sign of turbulent storms to come. Not even a driving rain would cool his angry suspicions.

Small puffs of dust rose around the hooves of the dappled gray stallion fidgeting beneath him. Theodore clasped his legs against the horse's body to still the animal as he studied his overseer's house.

He adjusted his wide-brimmed hat and squinted into the sunlight. This two-story home would be his undoing, he was sure of it.

Theodore inhaled the still air, so thick and hot it hung like a weight inside him, adding to the heaviness already in his heart.

Glancing down the dirt road, he saw Mary, his wife of three months, running toward him. He gripped the reins tighter. Why hadn't she listened? He'd told her to stay at the main house while he confronted Clyde. If the rumors he'd heard were true, she was putting herself and their unborn child in danger by coming here.

Her wild impulsive streak would get her into trouble one day. She could be a spitfire, that Mary! She'd always said, "You'll be mine Theodore. One day I'll make you love me as I love you. You'll see." Now she had his heart. No doubt she thought she could protect him. The woman had such daring, such boldness. She was a handmaiden, beneath his status in the eyes of the community, but she had the spirit of a queen. The love she felt for him, the loyalty and devotion—it was a small wonder he felt like a king among men.

A moan escaped through the open window on the second floor, disrupting Theodore's thoughts. His body went rigid and he pressed his lips together. He knew that sound well—a woman in the throes of passion. He glared at the window, his jaw clenched.

He'd talk with Mary later. Right now, there were more urgent matters.

The growl vibrating in his chest threatened to become a full-blown scream of fury, but he pushed his anger down, struggled to remain silent. *I need proof.* There would be hell to pay if he found his younger sister Ruby inside with Clyde.

He glanced down the road at his beloved. He must surprise them before Mary arrived.

Theodore dismounted so quickly his horse shied. He didn't bother to tether the animal before he slipped into the house and began to climb cautiously up the wooden stairs.

When he reached the bedroom door, he stopped. He knew in his heart what he would find. Was he ready to face it?

He gathered his courage, twisted the knob and stared through the partially opened door.

What he saw enraged him.

No woman would ever tarnish the Slayton name again. His grandmother, in her youth, had done that job quite well enough, taking every man she fancied to her bed. It took years for the Slayton name to gain respect again, after the damage she had inflicted on the family reputation. Theodore would not allow his sister to repeat his grandmother's mistakes.

"I love you, Clyde."

His sister's throaty words exploded inside Theodore's head.

He slammed the door back against the wall. His voice boomed, deep and ominous, belying his small stature. "You love him, little sister?"

Ruby's eyes widened in shock. "Theodore!" she gasped, pulling up the cotton blanket to cover her nakedness.

Clyde leaped out of bed to face Theodore's rage silently. His eyes, narrowed with contempt, the only indication of his feelings.

"You only love him as Grandmother loved her men!" Theodore's voice pulsed with fury. "Get away from my sister, Clyde, and leave my property at once!"

"No." Clyde's voice was eerily calm. His steady gaze locked with Theodore's even as he grabbed his pants, jerked them on and fastened the buttons. "Ruby and I belong together. You can't make me leave."

"I'm the owner of this estate," the other man snarled, advancing toward Clyde. "You work for me. Now get out."

An insolent smile curved Clyde's lips. He took a step closer to Theodore, stopping the other man in his tracks. "You sold this house to me. I'll quit, but I'll never leave my home."

"Then I'll make you pay for spoiling my sister's reputation and our family name." Theodore charged, fists swinging.

Clyde stepped out of the way to miss the blow. "You'll make me pay?" He laughed derisively, "You're half my size. You've got it wrong—"

Theodore swung again. Clyde pushed him away.

The smaller man crashed against the edge of a table, scattering its contents, before hitting the wall with a loud thump. Immediately, he doubled over and fell to the floor. His voice, when it came again, was low, "Curse you both!" Then his eyes closed and he became eerily silent.

"Oh, no," Ruby whispered, turning wide-eyed to her lover. "You've killed him!"

"I didn't push him hard enough to kill him," Clyde responded, struggling to keep the worry out of his voice. He looked at Ruby. The shock in her pale face was unbearable, so he turned his gaze back to her brother. "He's out cold, that's all." Pulling on his shirt, Clyde kept an eye on Theodore. *He can't be dead.*

"I'm not a murderer, Ruby," he said, his tone anxious. He walked over to where Theodore lay in a crumpled heap. "Get up," he ordered, pushing the smaller man's shoulder with his foot.

Theodore's limp arm thudded against the wooden floor. Mumbling, he shifted slightly.

Clyde squatted down. "What did you say?" His brow furrowed at the sight of Theodore's pale skin, the slow trickle of blood that oozed from the corner of his mouth.

Theodore turned his head and stared up at him with a look of pure hatred, but Clyde saw the life ebbing from his glazed eyes.

No! Not this... Panic filled him. *Please. Don't die.*

With great effort, Theodore spoke louder. "I'll haunt you—I swear you will pay..." He grimaced in pain as death claimed him.

Clyde stared at the smaller man's chest, waiting for the steady rise and fall that never came. Finally, he pressed his fingers against Theodore's neck. He looked at Ruby. "There's no heartbeat," he said in a choked voice.

"Are you sure?" Ruby shuddered as she got out of bed and quickly stepped into her dress.

Clyde frantically searched for any sign of life in Theodore. Picking up the man's wrist, he pressed his fingers to the pulse point. Nothing. He hung his head. "He's dead, Ruby."

He stood to shove his feet inside his boots, was silent for a long moment, as his mind raced. "We've got to think this through," he said at last. "I could say I found him in the woods, thrown from his horse—an accident." He turned toward her. "When I tell you about it, later, when other people are there, you'll have to act surprised and upset. Do you understand?"

"Yes, I understand," she replied, her voice hollow, tears

streaming down her face. Aimlessly she searched for the sleeves of her dress while staring at her brother's body. "He died thinking that I'm like Grammie. I wish we had told him that we got married."

Clyde heard the helplessness in her voice, saw the pain in her eyes and rushed to her side. He ran his hands down her arms to steady them before he twisted the fabric that hung around her waist to reverse it.

Trancelike, Ruby allowed him to dress her, then stepped into her shoes. She stood in silence as Clyde's trembling fingers fumbled with the small buttons on the back of her dress.

"We'll only keep our marriage secret a little longer. You know we didn't tell Theodore because he'd never approve of you marrying me, his employee, even though he did the same. He wanted you to marry into money."

When the last button was in place, he slipped his arms around her waist, pressed his face into the long brown locks that cascaded over her shoulders and held her tight. "Are you all right?"

"No, Clyde, I'm not." Her voice was flat, empty of emotion. "How can I be all right, when my only brother's dead?"

Clyde held her close. "I'm sorry, Ruby. I'm so very sorry. I never meant—" How could I have killed anyone, especially my wife's brother? He took a step away from her. "Go wait for me outside. Please."

Without looking back, Ruby left the room.

Sighing deeply, Clyde lifted Theodore's lifeless body over his shoulder and followed her. Outside, he laid the corpse over the dappled gray stallion. His wife was already halfway down the dirt road that led back to the main house, so he led the heavily laden horse into the forest alone.

When the hoof beats faded, Mary moved from behind the hallway curtains. She had darted behind the thick green fabric just before Ruby entered the hall. *If Clyde could kill Theodore so easily, surely he'd do the same to me and my unborn child. They must never know that I witnessed Theodore's murder.* Her face stained with silent tears Mary caressed her abdomen, the last link to her husband.

"Theodore," she whispered in anguish, then stepped into the bedroom where, just moments before, her one true love had met his end.

Water from a white washbasin dripped down the side of the small table and splattered against the matching pitcher overturned on the floor. The bed was disheveled, the sheets a rumpled mess.

If only I'd arrived a few moments earlier, Mary thought miserably, *I could have done something, anything, to save him.*

"My love, my life," she choked between agonized sobs. She knelt on the floor where Theodore had fallen, murdered in cold blood. Her stomach twisted and curled, threatening to release itself. "Why did this happen?" Her body shook with the depth of her sorrow. "You'll never even know our child, Theodore," she whispered through her tears.

How could this have happened? She had never known her own father and now that joy had been taken from her baby in a manner so horrible she almost couldn't bear it.

Too exhausted to cry any longer, she dropped her head into her hands. What would happen now? Ruby and Clyde were each in their own way cruel, despite what Theodore thought of his younger sister. Separately, they had already hurt her family in ways she could not forgive. Now this. Who knew what other terrible things they would do as husband and wife.

"I'll make them pay," she said to the empty room, her voice forceful and distinct. She raised her head high and wiped her tear-stained cheeks with her fingertips.

I swear...you will pay... Theodore's dying words echoed in her mind.

Only one person could help her now. She stood, walked out of the house and headed for the woods.

The lush greenery of the forest streamed by as she ran. The squirrels twitched their tails and scuttled out of her way. She barely noticed the woody scent of pine or the fragrance of wildflowers in her hurry to reach the cave.

She had approached this clandestine place once before, but fear had made her run for home. She knew the rumors that were whispered everywhere. The gypsy witch would grant you favors, but the price was very high—part of your soul was demanded in return.

Mary paused to catch her breath beside the stream that flowed alongside the cave. In her grief and desperation, she was sure its gurgling song whispered her name.

"Come inside, Mary," a low voice vibrated from the inky blackness.

Mary stiffened in alarm. Thieves were known to hide in the woods. "Who are you?" She stepped back, surprised that her voice sounded strong and clear.

"The one you seek. No thief am I."

A wave of uneasiness washed over her. How had the voice known what she'd been thinking? She hesitated, thought of Theodore and knew that this time she had to go inside. She willed her feet forward and cautiously entered the dank, dark cave.

Cool air caressed her sweaty skin. The cave's musky scent sent a rippling shiver and then a shudder through her. As her vision adjusted to the darkness, she focused on the glimmers of candlelight flickering along the rocky crevices in the walls. A stone table grew upwards from the earth. On top were four unlit candles set apart in an imaginary square. Inside the square were a white candle, a large empty bowl and several small bowls containing what looked like salt and herbs.

Mary stared at the table. Fear struck a chord inside her. She'd made a mistake in coming here. Suddenly, a scratchy hardness bumped against the back of her knees and she whirled around. She saw no one, but a hand-hewn wooden chair sat on the ground behind her.

"I've been waiting for you." The disembodied voice filled the cavern. "Please rest. Running is dangerous for the child you carry."

Mary searched the shadowy depths. Where was the owner of this smooth, measured voice that surrounded her? It was as if the cave itself spoke her innermost thoughts.

"How did you...?" With a slight waver, she sat on the edge of the chair. "Are you the gypsy witch I seek?"

"Yes, I am the one, Mary. I already know your secrets. I know you want to make the lovers pay for killing the father of your child."

Mary's mouth dropped open, her pulse quickened and her gaze darted nervously about. Glancing back at the table, she noticed a double-edged knife lying beside the bowls. Had it been there a moment ago? At the sight of it, she fought against the desperate feeling to flee this evil place.

No, no! Clyde and Ruby must pay. She grasped the edges of the chair with both hands in anger and called out, "Show yourself!"

"Say what it is you ask of me."

"A curse. A curse on those who killed Theodore Slayton."

"There is a price, Mary."

Her head dropped. Her pockets were empty. "If it's money you want, I have none with me," she said. Sighing heavily, she stood to leave.

"It isn't money I require."

The rumors came flooding back and Mary's heart quaked. Did she dare ask? "Then... What?"

The gypsy witch stepped from the shadows into the light and stood insolently in front of her.

Mary gasped. Her hands flew to her mouth to silence the scream that threatened to burst from her. She scrambled backward into the darkness, to hide. "You're...a..." Her mind whirled. This couldn't be right.

Candles flamed to life around her.

Speechless, Mary gazed up at the gypsy seer.

He was gorgeous. His long hair, the color of a raven, fell across his shoulders. His white shirt hung open to expose a tanned and muscular chest. His unblinking smoky gray eyes scorched into hers, as if he could look right into her soul. The candlelight danced over his handsome features. Opening his mouth slightly, he ran the tip of his tongue sensuously across his full lips.

Mary stared in disbelief. "But... You're a man!"

Hadn't others who visited this cave told her she would find a woman here? She searched the recesses of her memory, suddenly realizing that she'd never heard anyone describe the gypsy witch.

"Surprised?" The seer's tone was arched.

Mary ignored his question. She had already experienced so many terrible things today and now this...

It was too much. Her emotions were spinning out of control still Theodore must have his revenge.

Stay strong, Mary. Fearing for her soul she asked, "What do you require in payment?"

"A kiss."

A kiss? A wave of dizziness buckled her knees, her body swayed. Kiss the devil himself? Kisses were the last thing on her mind. How could she kiss someone else? Her kisses were only for Theodore. But this was for him—she must do this for her husband, whose dying words still echoed in her ears.

"Is there no other way?" she asked, lifting her chin in defiance. "Do you not wish to take my soul instead?"

Mary's body burned under the gypsy witch's intense inspection, as he slowly looked her over until his gaze finally locked with hers. "A kiss is what I require." He took a strand of her hair, curling it around his fingers, awaiting her reply.

Revulsion grabbed at the pit of her stomach at the thought of kissing something so evil. Could she bring herself to do it to revenge her beloved husband? Yet, he hadn't asked for her soul or her child, only a kiss. "In return, you will curse all those who hurt Theodore Slayton?"

He stilled and scrutinized her face. "Are you sure of what you ask?"

In her mind's eye Mary saw her sister's mangled body, broken and violated by a group of rogues the day after Ruby had banished her from the farm because she had flirted with Clyde. She saw her mother's stooped shoulders, weighed down by years of overwork under Clyde's rule. Then Theodore's brilliant smile nearly broke her heart.

"Yes, I'm sure."

"You understand this affects several families?"

"Yes."

He released her hair, slid his hands across her shoulders and down her arms until he grasped her hands. "You must be certain."

Her body trembled at his touch. "I want them all to pay." A tear inched down her cheek still she stood tall. "I'm positive."

The gypsy witch blinked and all four candles on the table burst into flames, drenching the cave in a bright light. He moved quickly, pulling Mary near. With his free hand, he grabbed some salt from a bowl and sprinkled it on the ground around the table, enclosing them inside a circle. Releasing her, he took herbs from the smaller bowls and dropped them into the large one, chanting words she didn't understand.

"What language are you speaking?" she asked.

"The Romany of my ancestors." The white candle flickered to life. He turned to face her, a mocking smile played on his sensuous lips. "Now…payment."

Mary closed her eyes for a brief moment. "Forgive me, Theodore," she whispered.

She went to him, stood on tiptoe to reach his mouth. As she lightly held his shoulders for balance, she felt hard muscles ripple beneath her hands. A brush of her lips against his and she stepped back, releasing him.

His eyebrows lifted. "That's it?"

Mary nodded. "It was a kiss, as you required."

"That's not payment." He grabbed her around the waist, pulled her hard against his body, held her tight as he crushed his lips to hers.

Mary struggled against the fire inside him, pushing at his shoulders, but it was no use. He filled her with his unholy passion, until she surrendered beneath him, relinquishing with a deep shudder all the goodness left in her soul.

He broke the kiss and then stared at her. "That's payment."

Seizing her hand, he ran the knife blade across her spread palm. She screamed in pain. When did he grab the knife? She tried to wrestle free but his grip was relentless. He held her hand above the bowl. Three drops of her blood dripped onto the herbs inside. Only then did he release her.

She pressed her bleeding hand against her breast, her pulse throbbing through the wound. The gypsy witch reached over and in one deft movement sliced off a lock of her hair.

"What are you doing?" She cried out, grabbing at the shortened strand.

"This is the curse you place on all who harmed the one you love. You are the main ingredient. One drop of blood for each of the three who can break the curse, a lock of hair and spit bind the potion together. Now spit."

"What?"

"Spit in the bowl, Mary."

She did as he commanded, then wiped her chin with a sleeve, her gaze glued to his blazing eyes.

Once more, he took her bloody hand into his own and placed

the mixing stick in her palm. Wrapping his fingers around hers, he slowly stirred the potion. He closed his eyes and spoke in a soft songlike lilt.

> *In answer to harm done to you,*
> *I put a curse on love that's true.*
> *Never shall the lovers gain,*
> *Instead to them comes only pain.*
> *Until the three shall meet as one,*
> *All joined by family once unknown,*
> *The souls of those who live today*
> *Shall walk the lands and never stray.*

Mesmerized, Mary watched his eyelids flutter open. He lifted the stick from the bowl and laid it on the table. Taking a handful of potion, he sprinkled it over the candle flames and closed his eyes again.

> *The gifts of sight I now bestow,*
> *The virgin shall dream, the sister shall know.*
> *To the secret one I give,*
> *Visits from others who might have lived.*
> *Two hundred years, no more, shall pass,*
> *Before these three find true love at last.*
> *When the three bind blood to blood,*
> *The curse I place shall turn to love.*
> *The souls I capture by my hand*
> *Will then be free to leave the land.*
> *But if true love is never found,*
> *The souls will ever walk the ground.*
> *When at last the time's at hand,*
> *They will meet in the circle of trees you plant.*
> *Then they shall see all that is true,*

Why love was lost, avenged by you.

The gypsy witch raised his eyelids to look at Mary. His smoky gray eyes were now pitch black. The four candles on the table dimmed then went out. He reached over, snuffed out the white candle and picked up the double edge blade.

Mary cringed.

He whispered more words of his ancestors, then, bending down, he placed the blade into the earth and cut through the salt, breaking the circle. Straightening, he turned to Mary, then reaching out, he ran the pad of his thumb across her cheek, removing a single tear.

"It is done," he whispered.

Mary blinked and, in the next moment, she was standing in her kitchen, a knife in one hand, the palm of the other cut and bloody.

How did this happen? She dropped the knife, grabbed a cloth and pressed it to the open wound. As she did so, she recalled the details of the curse and that she must plant a circle of trees deep in the forest.

She stood for a moment searching her thoughts. She frowned, then shook her head. No matter how hard she tried, she could not remember what the gypsy witch looked like. What difference did it make? She'd carried out Theodore's dying wish.

Suddenly overwhelmed from the pain of the loss of her husband, the emotional turmoil of the day and the pain in her hand, Mary collapsed on the floor. Lying there, brokenhearted, she buried her head in the bend of her elbow and let the emotions pour from her, mourning her loss with sobs and tears. *Oh, Theodore! You're gone. You're really gone.*

Without Theodore, all that was left in her life was sorrow and despair. Not even the thought of her unborn child could console her.

CHAPTER ONE

Old Slayton Homestead
Present day

THERE WAS NOWHERE TO HIDE.

Angie Benton watched the young woman running through the forest. As she fought the brush and bramble, her torn clothes ripped even more.

She tripped over a tree root and fell to the ground. Quickly, she struggled to her feet while leaves caught in her hair and briars slashed her arms, drawing blood.

Angie could feel the woman's terror—like a knife slicing through her own heart.

Just then a man appeared. Angie, watching from a high perch in the trees, trembled. What now?

Jaw clenched, eyes narrowed, the man opened and closed his fists repeatedly as he tramped toward the frightened woman. His shirt was unbuttoned, revealing the sweat glistening on his heaving chest. He looked so angry, so hostile. She could even hear the fury in his strong, deliberate footsteps.

The woman heard him too and looked over her shoulder.

Angie gasped. The woman's face was her own!

Horrified, Angie watched the woman who could be her twin run into a clearing, then pause and look frantically around. She could feel her desperation and when the other woman sprinted across the meadow toward an old shack, Angie experienced a jolt of hope and a burst of energy as she mentally followed her twin.

Arriving breathless at the cabin, the woman jumped onto the porch, pushed through the broken door and ran into the first room on her left.

Angie spotted an exit at the back of the shack. She willed her twin to find it and escape that way. Instead, the woman ran wildly through the house in terror, searching for a place to hide.

Entering the kitchen at last, she didn't run out the back door as Angie willed. Instead, she crouched in the corner behind an antique hutch.

The old pine floors creaked as if under a heavy weight.

Angie screamed, "Run! Run!" But the twin didn't move.

The man's footsteps moved methodically through the dilapidated old shack, searching, slowly, room by room.

Still her twin waited motionless, until, at last, the footsteps left the house.

Tentatively, the young woman stood up and glanced around. Inching toward the back door, she looked through the screen and out the side windows, surveying the yard with wide, frightened eyes.

All clear.

Cautiously, she opened the door and slipped out. With her back to the yard, she quietly closed the door behind her, then spun around to make a run for it.

And crashed right into her pursuer.

A loud whistle pierced Angie's hearing. What on earth was happening?

Someone was pulling her from her perch. Someone had a grip on her biceps and searing stabs of pain were shooting through her arms.

She looked up and stared into the angriest blue eyes she had ever seen.

Eyes belonging to the man she'd just seen outside the cabin door.

Her heart pounded. *How had she become the woman she'd been watching?*

The man's sandy brown hair hung over his face in wet strands, its blond highlights still noticeable. Sweat beaded across his brow. He clenched his jaw against chiseled cheeks and he tightened his grip by digging his fingers deeper into the soft flesh of her arms.

Angie jerked her body violently, but could not break his hold. Wave after wave of terror crashed through her. She had to escape!

"Angie!" he growled.

She snapped her head back to look up at his angry face.

A flash of light in her peripheral vision caught her attention and she turned to see someone, shadowed by trees, leveling a gun at them.

Angie froze. As if in slow motion, the muzzle of the gun moved until it was pointing straight at her. She heard a booming blast, so loud it hurt her ears. *Oh God, I'm going to die, she thought in terror.*

The man with the sandy hair whirled her around, using his body to shield her from the oncoming bullet. Suddenly, his face contorted, his back arched and his grip on her arms loosened, then released, as he fell to the ground.

Angie watched him land in a crumpled heap at her feet. She'd barely had time to take this in before she felt something hard and cold jab into her back and an arm clench around her neck, forcing her to look skyward. She heard a deep, raspy, laugh behind her as a man dragged her backward, knocking her off her feet with a quick pull, his laughter intensifying.

Angie struggled frantically with the gunman. She was so desperate, so frightened, that several seconds passed before she noticed that the man who had come between her and the bullet was no longer there.

Where had he gone?

The pressure increased against her throat.

Angie twisted and turned, trying to break free, trying to find the man who had saved her before.

But it was useless. He'd disappeared and the more she struggled, the more her assailant tightened his hold.

Then the realization hit her. The sandy haired man was dragging her across the yard. Somehow, he'd captured her.

A gunshot rang out.

Fire burned through her chest. The man pushed her and she sank to the ground, feeling her life ebbing away.

ANGIE'S EYES FLEW OPEN. She didn't dare move as she peered into the inky blackness.

Where was he?

Who was he?

Propping herself up on one elbow, she covered her racing heart with her hand. Her nightgown, wet with sweat, stuck to her chest. Even the sheets were soaked.

The dream terrified her.

He terrified her.

Those angry blue eyes, crystal clear and light as the sky, still seemed to be staring at her, so full of intense emotion she couldn't look away. She tried to swallow but her parched throat tightened until she thought she might choke.

Shaking her head to clear it, she slipped out of bed and headed through the darkness to the kitchen for something to drink.

It isn't real, she reminded herself. *It's just a dream.*

A dream that followed her, tormented her, caused so many sleepless nights, more lately than ever before. And it was always the same. She was an outsider looking in, unable to do anything to help.

Except this time, for the first time, she had watched herself. That worried her. She didn't have a twin.

She reached for a glass, filled it with cold orange juice from the fridge. She drank deeply, then set the glass down on the counter with a thud.

It would not be like the other times when she had been a dream observer. She simply wouldn't let it.

When she dreamed of Aunt Martha's death before it happened, she'd told herself that it was only a coincidence. And her dream about the accident that left her great-uncle paralyzed? Same thing. And the time when—

"No!" The sound of her own voice startled her. She hadn't meant to speak aloud.

Angie knew the truth in the depths of her soul, but she would not, could not, admit that her "observer dreams" came true. Aunt Martha called them prophetic. But she was wrong. She had to be.

Angie licked the juice from her lips and glanced at the stove clock. Five a.m. There was no way she would ever fall back to sleep now.

"Might as well start the day," she said with a sigh. She went into the bathroom, turned on the shower and peeled off the clammy gown. The scent of lavender soap mixed with the silky warmth of the hot spray had a calming affect, but still the dream haunted her.

Stepping out to dry off, she tried hard to think of something, anything, other than the nightmare but it consumed her thoughts. Still unsettled, she selected her clothes and dressed, then checked the mirror to make sure everything matched.

The store doesn't open until ten, she reminded herself, dabbing lavender perfume behind her ears and on her wrists. I could complete the jewelry inventory and submit reorders.

The house creaked and she jumped in fear.

"All right, that's it!" she yelled at the walls. *No way is this stupid dream going to take over my life!*

She wasn't about to screw up after all the years of hard work she and Aunt Martha had put into The Variety Vine. She would not lose her focus now. Together, she and her aunt had made the store one of Dansburg's most successful gift shops. She'd practically grown up in the store, until she decided to become an interior decorator—a job she'd given up the moment Aunt Martha willed the business to her.

Angie picked up a scrunchie, pulled her hair into a ponytail and went into the kitchen. Still thinking about all the work she needed to do at the store—and the dream—she toasted a bagel, then spread cream cheese inside.

I better go in early, she thought, pushing the dream to the recesses of her mind.

Grabbing her breakfast and briefcase, she headed out the door.

ANGIE PARKED HER sport utility vehicle in front of The Variety Vine at exactly six a.m.

The store had been converted from a family home years ago. "The old Randall house", people used to call it. Sitting off the road with no other buildings in sight it looked eerie with the sun dawning behind it. A misty fog surrounded the wisteria vines that covered the front porch banister and crept up the round columns to the roof.

Angie climbed out of the SUV and brushed the breakfast crumbs off her shirt. Grabbing her briefcase, she locked the vehicle and headed toward the store.

She saw the web, shimmering with sunlight through droplets of dew, just before it touched her face. Too late, she dropped her briefcase, jumped off the steps and frantically pulled the web from her eyelashes and hair.

"Uugghh!" She shuddered, spotting the spider. "Nasty little

creatures."

Using a long branch, she removed the remaining web, including the spider and tossed the stick under the tree.

Aunt Martha's favorite rocking chair sat on the front porch, gently swaying back and forth.

That's odd, thought Angie. *How is it moving? There's no breeze.*

Dismissing the chair, she sorted through her keys for the one to the store, but before she could place it in the lock she heard a voice behind her.

"Angelina."

She froze, feeling a cold chill quake through her body. Impossible!

"Angelina, sweetie," the voice said again.

She forced herself to turn around.

There in front of her stood Aunt Martha. She was smiling at her as though her ghostly appearance were the most ordinary thing in the world.

Oh God! Oh God! Breathe Angie!

She pressed her back against the door and inhaled deeply. *Good. Breathing's good.*

Sweat broke out on her forehead and her stomach clenched.

Aunt Martha looked beautiful. Her long dark hair flowed unrestrained around her shoulders.

She never wore her hair like that in life. Well, maybe when she was young, but she always worn it in a bun around me.

The apparition seemed to be waiting for her to speak, but Angie, her throat tight with fear, couldn't form any words. *Geez…what do you say to a ghost anyway?*

She cleared her throat. "H-Hi." The word was a mere whisper.

"Oh, honey, I scared you," her aunt smiled but made no move to hold or comfort her as she had always done when she was alive.

"Yes, you did," Angie said, finding her shaky voice, struggling to remain calm. She couldn't take her eyes off the woman in front of her, the woman she'd loved like a mother.

"I'm so sorry. Look, sweetie, I don't have much time." Martha's smiling face darkened. "You must be careful, Angelina. Danger is near."

"What do you mean, Aunt Martha?" Angie said frantically, losing the battle for calmness. Why would she, of all people, receive a warning from the dead?

"Remember your dream and be careful," Martha replied, her face still serious, her voice low. "Things happen in threes, Angelina. You must be aware of what's going on around you. That's all I can say. I love you, sweetheart."

"I don't understand, Aunt Martha."

Angie blinked. In that split second, her aunt disappeared.

She looked to either side of the porch. Nothing. Her feet were frozen in place. Inside she shook with fear. What would come next?

But no more apparitions appeared and no strange sounds met her ears. The air around her was unusually still.

Then the realization hit her full force. A real ghost had just visited her!

Angie turned around quickly and tried to unlock the door. The keys fell from her trembling hands, clanking onto the wooden porch. Scooping them up, she used both hands to steady the key as she placed it into the lock. When it turned she scooted inside, slammed the door behind her and leaned against it.

Her heart hammered against her chest. She took several deep breaths in a desperate attempt to calm herself.

Exhaustion. That must be it. Her beloved aunt had died three months ago and since then she had taken on so many new responsibilities. All those late nights and long hours were finally affecting her, causing hallucinations.

Bewildered, she walked down the hallway. Dropping the briefcase on her desk, she fell into the leather executive chair and then rubbed her eyes.

"It must be Friday the thirteenth or something," she muttered, looking at her desk calendar for any reason not to believe in Aunt Martha's visitation. Monday the eleventh of June. She shook her head to clear it.

No, she couldn't dismiss this as easily as she'd dismissed the rocking chair. Aunt Martha had returned to warn her that she was in danger. Angie knew in her heart it was true. What kind of danger would bring her aunt back from the dead?

Pull it together girl, she thought after several minutes. *You have work to do.*

She got up, went behind the register and began taking jewelry out of the storage bins.

After spreading the pieces across the floor behind the counter, she started counting. At first she jumped at every little noise, but the work was exacting and soon she was immersed in it.

Slow, deliberate steps thudding against the wooden floor brought her back to the present with a jolt. Had she been so engrossed that she hadn't heard someone come in? She glanced at the clock on the wall behind the register. Eight-thirty.

She still had an hour and a half before the store opened and no morning meetings were scheduled. Her brow knit into a frown of concentration as she tried to remember if she had locked the front door.

She heard the footsteps again, closer now, as though someone were approaching the counter. My God, they sound like the ones in my dream. Angie put her hands over her ears for a moment. *Stop it. Stop it!* she admonished herself. *Don't be so silly. This has nothing to do with the dream.* She closed the storage bins, certain now that she had forgotten to lock the door and would find a customer waiting at the counter. Wanting to look her best, she pulled the scrunchie from her hair and laid it on a shelf under the register.

"How can I help you?" she asked, as she stood then turned around, wearing her most welcoming smile.

She was alone in the room.

"Hello?" she called. "Is anyone in here?"

She ventured into the hallway of the old house. Her heart beat faster—her palms began to sweat.

When she saw the man in the art room, his back to her, she froze and held her breath. His build reminded her of the stalker in the dream. He was admiring one of the paintings on display.

God, Angie, now you're really getting paranoid. She let out her breath as the panic ebbed. He's just an early customer. She had left the door unlocked after all.

"Good morning. Welcome to The Variety Vine. If I can help you find anything just let me know," she said to the man's back.

"This is an exquisite piece," he replied, admiring an oil painting of a winding river bordered by large trees. The magnificent colors of the changing leaves were captured in the glistening hues of the artist's paint.

"I think so too. That part of the Dan River, with those large stones, is near the bypass and Memorial Park. Are you familiar with that area?"

She waited, but the man didn't respond. *Must be the quiet type,* she thought, taking in his broad shoulders and narrow waist. His white tailored shirt was tucked into tight blue jeans that hugged his round behind and long, muscular legs. He stood about six inches taller than her five-foot-nine-inch frame.

Great body, she thought. Wonder if his face is as striking?

"Local artists made all the pieces in this room," she said in hopes that he would look at her. "I like to showcase their work and of course, offer them the supplies they need to do it."

He wandered over to one of the tables and, with his back still to her, picked up a picture of Angie, taken by a local photographer. "Interesting," he muttered.

Was he responding to her statement or the photo? As he studied it, her stomach gave an odd flutter.

"Are you looking for anything special?" she asked, rearranging the paints and brushes behind him. Why hadn't he looked at her yet? Maybe he was just rude. The way he held the framed picture made her uneasy and she really wanted to finish the jewelry inventory before opening the store.

I'll just tell him we're closed and to come back after ten, she thought. Taylor, her assistant manager, would be in then and Angie wouldn't be alone with this man.

"No, but I think I'll take this," he said, turning to her.

Angie gasped. The paintbrushes slid from her hands and crashed onto the floor.

Aunt Martha was right. Everything always happened in threes. The dream, Aunt Martha's spirit and now—this.

The blue eyes weren't angry now, but sparkled with humor as a grin inched toward those chiseled cheekbones. His sandy hair was dry, not wet from sweat, the blond highlights were even more noticeable as strands slipped across his forehead toward his eyes. His lips were full, his nose straight. She hadn't noticed either of them in her dream.

Unable to move or speak, Angie just stared at him.

"You're the woman in the picture." It was more of a statement than a question.

She nodded her head, tried to take a breath and couldn't. She would suffocate before he could kill her. Her eyes felt like they were going to pop out of her head at any second. Ripping her gaze from his face, she bent down to pick up the paintbrushes only to drop some again.

He walked to her side and knelt to help her. "I must say, you're more beautiful in person."

Angie used her hair as a shield against him. Her hands trembled, betraying her fear. Maybe he didn't notice, she thought.

When she gathered the last of the brushes, she forced herself to look at him and smile.

He's a customer handing me paintbrushes, nothing more.

"Thank you," she said, more calmly than she felt, as she accepted the items he held out to her.

The slow innocent brush of his fingers against hers made her stomach tighten but it wasn't in fear. Not this time. Never in her twenty-six years had such a slight touch confused her so.

Oh, no. Am I attracted to him? The sudden thought made Angie cringe. *I must be out of my mind! How could I be attracted to someone who stalks me, terrorizes me, night after night, in my dreams?* Sure, the nightmare man had saved her from a bullet, but he'd shot her himself at the end, hadn't he?

Hadn't he?

"Did you want the picture?" she asked abruptly, standing up.

"Do you come with it?" He stood too and smiled, revealing brilliantly white straight teeth. He moved toward her.

"Uh, no." She took two steps backward. He is handsome.

Stop it, Angie, stop it! a voice inside her said. *Stay away from him! He's dangerous!*

Through her renewed terror, Angie heard the man say, "Then I guess, for now, I'll just take the picture. Perhaps it will be different some other time. Unless, of course, you're married."

"I'm not," she said and then instantly regretted revealing anything about herself. She shoved the paintbrushes into a mug, took the picture from him—making sure their hands didn't touch again—and walked down the hall to the register.

"Boyfriend?" he persisted, following her.

"Maybe."

"My name's Jared Maxwell."

"Angie," she replied, stepping behind the counter to ring up the picture. She collected his money and then folded the top of the bag. Holding it out to him by a corner, she forced yet another smile. "Thank you, Mr. Maxwell."

Jared wrapped his large hand over hers as he took the bag. Their gazes locked and, suddenly, against her will, against her fear, Angie felt drawn to him. Those ocean blue eyes smoldered. Her gaze dropped to his full lips.

Wonder if he's a good kisser? she thought, her pulse quickening. Oh, no, stop it, Angie.

Jared reached out with his free hand to caress her cheek lightly. Angie stilled at his touch. Then he ran the pad of his thumb over her bottom lip. A festival of butterflies danced inside her as she watched Jared's blue eyes darken even more.

What was wrong with me? Fantasizing about the man who attacks me nightly in my dreams.

Jared leaned toward her.

He's going to kiss me!

No, this cannot happen. Angie jerked back, pulled her hand from underneath his, releasing the bag, ending the moment and breaking the spell.

The clock ticked. Time hadn't stopped after all.

Jared grinned as he picked up a business card from the counter. "Angelina Benton, Proprietor of The Variety Vine. Well, thank you, Ms. Benton. I hope we'll meet again soon."

"Angie," she spoke on a breath, "everyone calls me Angie."

"Until next time, Angie." He smiled, lightly running his fingers down her forearm. Then turning away, he walked down the hall and out the door.

As soon as he left, Angie ran over and turned the lock. She sank into a nearby chair, one hand absentmindedly caressing the place where his fingers had trailed down her arm, the other to her lips. A soft smile briefly lifted the corners of her mouth before a frown took its place.

She didn't know what to think. Every night, she ran in terror from this man and she certainly never expected to see him in her store.

Who am I kidding? She sat back hard in the chair. *I've always known he'd come after me one day.*

The electric current of his touch. His smoldering blue eyes. She had to put these things right out of her mind. Because they drew her to him—to the one person in the world who absolutely terrified her.

If she had anything to do with it, Angie decided, the "next time" he had mentioned would be never.

CHAPTER TWO

JARED MAXWELL JUMPED INTO HIS RED MUSTANG convertible, slammed it in reverse and backed out of the driveway.

What in the hell just happened back there? He had never been so entranced by a woman before, especially one he'd just met. God, he'd wanted to taste her lips and almost did before she'd pulled away. *What were you thinking, Maxwell? You, Mr. Confirmed Bachelor, put those playboy ways behind you a long time ago.*

It was her eyes. They captured him, connecting him to a long-lost friend. Could this be the woman he had searched for his entire life?

Had he even been searching?

A boisterous laugh exploded from him, full and unrestrained. *Love at first sight? Nah, it couldn't be, could it?* He'd never believed in it before, but now he was certain that this was another secret he'd have to keep.

When he'd spoken with Alan Harland, the attorney in charge of the estate, the lawyer had said the property wasn't for sale because the new owner was in mourning. Out of respect, Jared had kept his distance, even though he remained determined to purchase the twenty acres someway, somehow.

If only he had stopped by three months ago when he'd first inquired about The Variety Vine, he could have gotten to know Angie and convinced her to sell by now.

Jared chuckled again thinking about it and shifted into third gear. Spotting the silver SUV in front of the old converted house and finding the door unlocked had been pure luck.

Only now he wanted more. Not only did he need the property, he also wanted the woman who owned it.

Why did she stare at me in absolute horror? He frowned as he shifted gears again. Her reaction was one of fearful recognition, but he was certain they'd never met before.

Many times women reacted to his looks with surprise or desire. There was a time when he'd been flattered, now he found it irritating. Until today, he'd never come across a woman who'd been afraid of him. He realized Angie's fear was genuine and he just couldn't figure out why.

Angelina Benton in the flesh sure had complicated his plans. He hadn't even considered that he might find her attractive, from the silkiness of her hair, the fullness of her body when it tugged against her shirt, to the gentle curve of slim hips flowing into lean, long legs. Or that he would want her more than he'd ever wanted another woman in his life.

It's more than just a physical attraction you know, a small voice murmured in his mind.

Jared shook his head to clear away the thought. In a brief moment, this woman had stirred up feelings he'd never experienced before but he would have to deal with them later.

Picking up his cell phone, he dialed the office. He couldn't afford to let a woman, even such an intriguing one, distract him from his work. Not now.

"Maxwell Development and Realty," said a chipper voice.

"Good morning, Sandi," Jared said to his secretary. "Do I have any messages?"

"Let me check. How did your meeting with Tom McNichols go?"

"I listed the farm and already have a buyer in mind."

His half sister, Terri Logan, had always talked about owning land near a small town like Dansburg, away from the hustle and bustle of Richmond. Since McNichols' acreage was eight miles from his own farm, Jared had decided to convince Terri to buy it, but if she refused, he'd just give it to her as a birthday present. He could afford to, after all, thanks to both his shrewdness in business and an enormous inheritance from his grandfather. Then, once he'd bought the two properties that bordered his land from the current owners, Sam Slayton and Angelina Benton, he would have accomplished all he set out to do when he moved to Dansburg. He'd own the original Slayton estate and he'd have his sister nearby.

"That's great news. Let's see, you have two messages from your sister, the bank called and Mr. Harland wants to reschedule your meeting until nine tomorrow morning."

"Okay. Will you contact Harland and tell him I'll be there?" He glanced at the clock on the dash. Eight-fifty. "What time did Terri call?"

"Consider it done. Um… She spoke with the answering service around ten last night and again at seven this morning."

"Thanks, Sandi," Jared said, steering the car from the hard surface road onto the mile long dirt driveway to his house. "I'm mending fences on the farm today and you know the cell doesn't work out there. I'll check in when I get back to the house. If Terri calls again make sure you ask her if everything is okay."

"No problem, we'll hold down the fort."

"I know you will," Jared said. "Talk to you later."

After Sandi said goodbye, Jared pressed the off button and gripped the wheel tighter with his left hand.

This wasn't like Terri. He couldn't remember the last time she'd called him that late—or that early. Something must be wrong. She had struggled too much since her husband divorced her unexpectedly, then left town a year ago.

He dialed Terri's number again. If only she'd quit being so

stubborn and accept his help. This time he wouldn't give her a choice. That farm was a done deal whether she liked it or not. Besides, he would enjoy having her and the kids close by again.

Jared listened to Terri's phone ring as he drove between rows of large oak trees. Their intertwined branches created a canopy that shaded the road from the sun.

Where the heck is she? Four rings and she still hadn't answered. He rounded the gentle curve to see his two-story home tucked between large oak and maple trees. The deep green shutters blended well with the natural setting and the rocking chairs on the open veranda seemed to preserve it in an earlier time.

He left a message and disconnected as he drove to the back of the house, parked and put the convertible top up.

He noticed three of his prized Angus calves in one of the paddocks. They'd escaped through some damaged fencing yesterday. Luckily old man Carson down the road had housed them in the barn after they'd wandered onto his property. Otherwise, he would have lost them for sure. The inspection and repairs he'd put off couldn't wait any longer and would take all day to complete.

Inside the house, Jared snatched the portable phone off its stand in the kitchen and dialed Terri again as he headed upstairs.

Again, no answer. *Dammit, Terri! Where are you?*

Jared changed into a work shirt and old jeans, then went back to the kitchen for something to eat. Maybe he should take a road trip instead of working. It was only a two-hour drive to Richmond and he was starting to get worried. It wasn't like Terri to call and then vanish. He slapped two sides of a sandwich together as the phone rang.

"Hello? Terri?"

"Hey, handsome," said a southern drawl.

"Terri, where in the hell have you been?"

"At the grocery store."

"What?" he said, pouring a glass of milk. "I'm over here, worried sick because you called last night and at seven this morning and you're *grocery shopping*?"

"Don't get your pants in a wad, bro, I'm fine. I called your work number because you didn't answer any of your other phones."

He let out a sigh of relief. "I sat out on the porch late last night, thinking. I didn't hear the phones."

"You mean scheming, right?"

"Ah, you know me so well," he teased. "What's up? Why didn't you leave a message?"

"I did. Anyway, guess what? Devin lost his first tooth."

"No kidding?"

"No kidding. Kevin's sooo jealous, he's wiggling his tooth to make it looser." She laughed, hesitated, "And... I was lonely and wanted to talk to you."

"Have you heard from Paul?"

"No. He's vanished without a trace since the divorce. It's just that, well, since you moved to Dansburg, I've missed you. So have the twins."

"Yeah, it's been six months. Time flies, huh?" Jared leaned against the kitchen counter. He'd been so busy relocating the company that he hadn't even been back to Richmond. It took dedication and a constant effort to keep his edge against the local competition. "I think I should take a week off and come visit."

"I've got a better idea since I know you'll feel guilty about leaving your business. I'm taking vacation the week of July Fourth. Maybe we could spend it with you?"

"Just in time for your birthday..." Jared grinned, then purposefully blocked all thoughts of the farm. "Sounds great. Squeeze the boys for me."

"Okay."

"And don't scare me like that anymore."

"Of course I will. What's a sister for if she can't scare her brother every now and again?"

"Well then, since you're fine, I guess I'll talk to you later," Jared said, thinking of her birthday present. Remembering his sister's telepathic abilities, he quickly imaged a big brick wall between them.

"Jared, is something wrong?" asked Terri. "I feel like you're hiding something from me, blocking me out."

Jared quickly said his goodbyes without answering her question and put the portable back in its stand.

Whew! He'd almost slipped up. "I'll keep blocking you, sis," he muttered as he left the house, "until I surprise you with the deed to your new farm."

After gathering his fence-fixing tools and readying Thunder, Jared rode his horse down the dirt road.

There were still places he had yet to see on his two-hundred-and-eighty-acre farm. If he had time later, maybe he'd do some exploring.

Beginning with the perimeter, he rode until he found the two sections that needed mending.

Hours later, when the work of repairing the damage the calves had caused was finally done, Jared switched his sights to the interior, tracking along one barbed wire fence until the spiked metal cornered on a tree.

He looked up to see that he was on the edge of a meadow. Far across the field, he spotted what looked like a tired old shack. *I haven't seen this before.*

He trotted the stallion across the field, tethered him and went inside.

The dank mustiness of dust and cornhusks filled the air. In one room an old armchair served as a home for field mice. A broken bookshelf lay across the middle of the floor. Torn, faded drapes clung against the windows.

In the second room, a stained, old mattress leaned against a decrepit chest of drawers. Rain had dripped through a large hole in the roof, warping the old wood. Cornstalks, stored for cow feed, filled the entire left side.

Jared walked down the hall and opened the door into what looked like an old kitchen. An icebox, its bottom hinge broken, door ajar, stood beside a handmade table. In the opposite corner was an antique hutch, remarkably well persevered.

I can restore that hutch, he thought as he went through the back door and down the three concrete steps and *use those cornstalks as feed.*

A small building, painted red, stood at the forest's edge behind the house. An unusual noise came from inside, like glasses clinking together. Jared tried to open the door but it wouldn't budge. Finding no other way inside, he made a mental note to bring something to break the door open when he returned.

This little house, shack and meadow were a great discovery. A few repairs and they'd be perfect for storage of the fescue or corn he would plant in the meadow next spring.

Someone had stored the corn in there recently, he thought as he untied the reins. He'd ask around to find out who was using the old house. Jumping astride his horse, he rode across the meadow to finish his fence inspection.

As Thunder's hooves plodded out their monotonous rhythm, Jared's thoughts once again turned to Angelina Benton.

"ANGIE, I JUST don't know what's gotten into you," said the town gossip, hands on her hips.

"I'm fine, Mrs. Turner." Angie smiled at her customer. "How's Kimmie? I haven't seen her in a while."

"Oh, you can't evade the question by asking about my daughter." Mrs. Turner adjusted her glasses, allowing her to look over them at Angie. "I swear you're just a-shakin'. Now, tell me what's wrong, sugar."

"Really, I'm fine." Angie had learned to keep her thoughts secret when she and Kimmie were still in middle school. Mrs. Turner meant well, but she could spread a rumor faster than a rocket could burn fuel. She could also irritate Angie faster than most. Angie had learned to control her temper over the years, at Aunt Martha's insistence, but some people could still set her off like a wild fire.

"Well, now that's got to be the biggest lie you've ever told. What would Martha say?" Mrs. Turner took Angie's chin, twisting her head from side to side. "Just look at those circles under your eyes. It's not natural I tell you, not natural at all."

"I'm closing up in five minutes," Angie said, pulling free of the older woman's grasp, while picturing a calming scene of the beach in her mind. She'd gotten stuck working alone all day. Now all she wanted was a good long soak in the tub, away from the memories of today's events, without losing her temper on top of it all. "What can I help you with?"

"You can confide in me, Angie. I know you don't have anyone to talk to since Martha passed, bless her soul."

Angie stared at her. Damn it if the woman wasn't right. She hadn't had anyone to talk to since Aunt Martha died.

But before she said anything, she remembered the time when Kimmie had a crush on her best friend, Eddie Harland. When Eddie had turned down Kimmie's advances, Mrs. Turner told everyone that Angie had stolen Kimmie's boyfriend. What a mess. She'd barely survived that one without losing a lot of friends.

Wonder what Eddie's up to? He hadn't written or called in months, since the winter semester started at Virginia Tech. But then again, neither had she.

Angie clenched her teeth, forcing a smile. She was worn out. Sales had been slow, but the customers demanding. "You know,

Mrs. Turner, I just received these cool paintbrushes. I know how much you love to paint. Would you try them out for me? Let me know what you think of them before I purchase more?"

"Oh, I'd love to, dear. This store always carries such unique merchandise. Made Martha a celebrity, you know." Mrs. Turner dug in her oversized purse, pulled out a picture and shoved it in Angie's hands. "Have I shown you my grandson's graduation picture? How much do I owe you for the brushes?"

Angie glanced at the picture. A young man with blue eyes stared back at her.

The memory of Jared Maxwell's icy blue eyes flashed through her mind for the hundredth time that day. How could the monster of her nightmares have come to life in the body of a gorgeous man? Was he somehow connected to the appearance of Aunt Martha's spirit and the warning she'd given?

I really need to get out of here. "Your grandson is very handsome," Angie said, handing the picture back to Mrs. Turner. "Why don't you just let me know how the brushes work out? No charge."

"Oh, thank you! He is a cutie pie, isn't he?" She put the picture back in her purse then folded her arms across her chest. "You go ahead and lock up, dear. I'm going to wait for you to finish. A pretty girl like you shouldn't be walking out alone at night you know." Mrs. Turner looked Angie in the eye. "And neither should I."

Angie couldn't help the grin that spread across her face. "Just let me count the drawer and we'll leave. But I only have to walk as far as my car, Mrs. Turner."

"I know that," answered the older woman. "But you can't be too careful."

So the two left the store together. Angie shivered as they walked across the porch where Aunt Martha had stood early that morning.

Reaching her SUV, she waited for Mrs. Turner to get into her car before climbing inside. She waved goodbye through the window, let the older woman pull out of the driveway first, then followed but turned in the opposite direction.

When she passed Sam Slayton's farm that bordered her property, her car lights flashed over the red "Sold" sticker on the real estate agent's sign.

How odd. Property never sells that fast around here.

Sam had just passed away yesterday. She'd never expected his property to go on the market and sell within twenty-four hours. She'd thought about buying the farm herself when she'd seen the For Sale sign go up yesterday. An additional two hundred acres would substantially increase the value of her place but the expense had made her hesitate and now it had sold.

She would ask long-time friend and attorney, Alan Harland, if he knew who'd bought it during their meeting the next morning.

When she arrived at home exhaustion settled over her. Going into the bathroom, she ran hot water for a bath, praying that when she went to sleep that night, her dreams would not be filled with Jared Maxwell.

Now her attacker had a name and that name spelled fear.

An uncontrollable shudder ripped through her body. It wasn't like her to be so edgy all the time and she worried it was already affecting her work.

As the steamy water filled the tub, she poured in the lavender-scented bubble bath.

It was time to put this dream in the past. If Jared Maxwell wanted to harm her, she couldn't stop him. She would just make sure that she stayed well away from him, that's all.

She stripped down and put her feet in the hot water. With a sigh, she lowered her body into the tub, letting the calming effect of the heat and fragrance wash over her.

Ah! Exactly what I needed.

Soaking in the bath, she closed her eyes and tried to forget the day for a while. But images of Jared's blue eyes and the way she felt absorbed in them kept invading her thoughts.

He's a playboy, she thought, remembering his flirtatious actions in the store. Well, maybe he hadn't given her any real reason to think that, but after the way he'd touched her lip, he *must* be a man who'd use and then leave a woman with a broken heart.

And she wanted a man who didn't play games—someone loyal, kind and strong. Jared didn't seem to be that kind of a man, despite the swarm of butterflies he'd set loose in her.

She wondered yet again if she would ever meet a man who would sweep her off her feet. Maybe she'd set her standards too high and it was just her destiny to die a virgin.

But Jared had looked at her so intensely. With a fire she could see in his eyes and feel in his touch.

Despite herself, she imagined Jared gathering her in his arms and placing a passionate kiss on her lips. As she fantasized how her own lips would part beneath his, emotions stirred within her that had nothing to do with fear.

"I must be insane," she whispered before sinking under the water, trying to wash the images from her mind.

CHAPTER THREE

JARED ROUNDED A CORNER IN THE HALLWAY THEN slowed his steps to enjoy the incredible view in front of him. Angelina Benton stood in front of Alan Harland's dark-glassed office door, where gold lettering proclaimed him Attorney and Counselor-at-Law. She twisted the handle, glanced at the silver watch on her wrist, then, cupping her hands beside her eyes, she peered inside. Her jeans hugged her hips as she bent over. Her thick dark hair, pulled into a ponytail by a blue scrunchie, lay down the middle of her back and then slipped over to one side, its silky highlights reminding him of moonlight shimmering on the Dan River at midnight.

This is a welcomed surprise, he thought as he stopped behind her. "Good morning, Angelina."

Angie, obviously startled by his voice, jerked around to face him.

"And how are you this fine day?" he added, watching her bright smile fade and brows knit together.

"What are you doing here?" Angie snapped. Crossing her arms, she set her mouth in a straight line of indifference. Her big brown eyes, slightly widened, betrayed her fear.

"I have a meeting with Mr. Harland," Jared said casually, walking closer to her. "And you?"

Angie stepped back, tripping against her briefcase on the hall floor.

Jared studied her. He had to think of some way to set her mind at ease about him, to convince her that he could be trusted, or he'd never persuade her to sell him her property. Before he could do that, he had to figure out why she seemed afraid of him.

"I'm meeting with Alan too." Her firm tone surprised him, belied the emotions in her eyes.

Jared raised an eyebrow and smiled at the tall, lithe woman. *Interesting, she's fighting her fear. She's also looking very intriguing in those tight jeans and sleeveless, scooped necked blouse.* The shirt's top button had popped loose, allowing him a glimpse of the tempting flesh underneath. He felt his reaction to her stirring in places that were better left alone.

Seconds later, her slender fingers pushed the pearl button through the buttonhole.

He lifted his gaze to find her glaring at him. Turning away, she crossed her arms under her breasts, which made them lift and swell in the dip of her shirt.

Damn!

It was obvious she wanted to be left alone, but didn't she realize the effect she had on him?

He didn't consider himself an impulsive man, but he wasn't about to let this moment, or this woman, pass him by again.

I'm probably going to regret this later. Jared reached out and took her hand in his. "Angie," he whispered, the softness of her palm warmed his hand. The silence in the hallway was deafening as he looked into her eyes. He couldn't help but wonder what was going on behind those wide brown orbs.

Angie could only stare at Jared. The touch of his hand had sparked up her arm like an electrical current, catching her breath. She'd never imagined Jared would touch her.

Again.

She glanced down at his large, strong hand engulfing her smaller one, his tanned skin sharply contrasting her fair complexion. She allowed her gaze to travel up his arm, his suit unable to hide the muscles underneath. The cut of the jacket made his shoulders and chest look even broader and tailored down to his narrow waist.

When she realized the direction her eyes wanted to travel, she looked back up at him. His eyes were smoky blue, deep, dark and full of desire. His full lips beckoned to her.

The images she'd envisioned during last night's bath came rushing back. As much as she wanted to fight him, run from him, the desire to feel his lips touch hers was overwhelming.

Are you crazy, Angie? Get a grip. He's a stalker! This isn't a dream!

She couldn't move as Jared cupped his free hand under her chin, lifting her face closer to his. The blue of his eyes was deeper still and she saw the danger flicker through them, like the eyes in her dream.

She trembled at the memory.

The pad of his thumb slid over her lips, parting them ever-so slightly. His head tilted toward her.

Angie, realizing that he intended to kiss her, jerked her hand from his grasp. Pressing both palms firmly against his chest, she pushed him away. "Don't ever attempt that again, Mr. Maxwell."

"I just—" he began, then his eyebrows furrowed together.

"I am not a piece of meat," Angie interrupted, "to be ogled by some playboy used to getting his way with women."

Glaring at him, Angie noticed that his still-lustful gaze held a hint of embarrassment. *Good,* she thought, *maybe standing up to him had set Jared Maxwell straight.*

At the sound of fast approaching footsteps, Angie moved further away from Jared, picked up her briefcase and looked toward the sound.

"Sorry, I'm late," Alan Harland said as he walked up to them, shook Jared's hand and then kissed Angie on the cheek. "I see the two of you have met."

Angie looked to Alan, raised an eyebrow. "What happened, Alan? I've never known you to be late for an appointment."

A grin plastered to his face, mischievous glint in his eye, Alan unlocked the door and let them into his office.

Had he been late on purpose? Angie thought, holding the door for the older man as he went into the office. "It looks like I'm underdressed but I've got to go into work after our meeting, Alan."

"You look beautiful in anything, besides you didn't need to get all fancied up for me." Alan grinned, flipping on the light switch to illuminate the room. "I'm sorry to keep you both waiting. I had to stop by the post office. I swear, the lines there just get longer and longer."

"Where should I wait while you meet with Ms. Benton?" Jared asked, closing the door behind them.

"I need to speak with both of you." Alan entered an office attached to the reception area, took off his jacket and hung it on a wooden coat rack.

"Both of us?" Angie glanced at Jared then stared through the open door at Alan. *Was her long-time friend playing matchmaker or was this another of his projects?* "Together?"

"That's right. Come on in, have a seat." Alan motioned toward the maroon high-backed chairs facing his desk and then busied himself gathering paperwork and laying it across his large mahogany desk. "Oh, Angie, before I forget, Eddie called last night. He said to tell you hello."

"Tell him hi when you talk to him again, since he never calls me anymore." Angie scooted back in the huge chair. Her belt squeaked against the leather as she settled into it. She tilted her briefcase against the chair leg.

She thought about all the times Alan had tried to involve her in some project or another over the years, while fixing her up with a "nice man" who was also helping out. She'd been more than willing to help him in the past, putting up with his attempts at playing Cupid, since she loved him like a father. But this time, she'd have to pass, especially if it involved Jared. From the sound of it, that was exactly what he had in mind.

"So what's going on, Alan? I thought we were just rescheduling the meeting I missed yesterday. This doesn't involve Mr. Maxwell."

"There were some other developments yesterday afternoon. I needed you both here so I could do this once and get it over with."

"This sounds interesting," Jared said, as he took the window seat beside Angie.

Angie glowered at Jared but he just grinned in response, so she turned to Alan, who was now sitting behind his desk. "Well, whatever it is, I don't have time to take on any additional projects right now. You know how busy I've been with the store."

"Yes, I know, but this involves The Variety Vine."

"What do you mean?" she asked.

"The Slayton estate bordering each of your properties sold yesterday," Alan said.

"I noticed that," she said, studying Alan.

"I've heard the rumors about that farm being haunted," Jared said. "Do you think they have a factual basis?"

Alan nodded. "I have a letter Ruby wrote to her son that proves how Theodore died."

Most of Dansburg's residents knew the tale of Ruby and Theodore, but Angie wondered why Jared was so interested in those old stories. "What does this have to do with us, Alan?" she asked impatiently, her voice strained.

Alan tapped a pencil on the desk and leaned back in his chair. "Did you know that Sam Slayton passed away the day before yesterday?"

"Yes, I heard," Angie said, "and I thought it strange that his estate was sold within twenty-four hours of his death. I mean his funeral's tomorrow."

"I didn't know," Jared said.

Alan nodded. "Well, the sale went exactly as Sam willed it."

"Which was?" Angie asked.

"The original plantation totaled five hundred acres and included your farm, Jared and Angie's twenty acres." Alan set the pencil aside. "The Slayton's went through some hard times and sold your properties off from the original estate. But, they included a clause, which followed all future sales."

"Is this the clause to ensure the unity of the original estate?" asked Jared.

Alan nodded and pulled out a sheet of paper, yellowed with age. "In the clause, it states that if the last Slayton died without an heir, the main estate would be combined with the other two farms to unite the original property."

Angie took the paper from Alan. The hand written part at the bottom grabbed her attention so she started reading it.

Alan continued, "The owners of the other two farms would inherit fifty percent ownership of the union of all three properties. Sam knew that he wouldn't have an heir and added to this clause three years ago."

"Oh God!" gasped Angie. Her hand flew to cover her mouth. "Alan, please tell me this isn't true."

Leaning forward to prop his elbows on the desk, Alan watched Angie. "Yes, it's true but this is a good thing, Angie. Now each of you owns half of the original estate. That's two hundred and fifty acres each. You just have to complete all of the requirements."

"I don't think I remember all of the details," Jared said. His hand stopped beside Angie's. "May I?"

Trembling, Angie gave him the document, "You knew about this?" she confronted Jared.

"Yes, didn't you?"

Angie shook her head. "Is this even legal? Can someone sell

property with conditions attached?"

"Yes it is. The buyers knew about and accepted the Slayton's conditions when they purchased the property," Alan said. "Would you read the clause aloud, Jared?"

"Sure. Mr. Slayton's addition states—" he looked down to read the clause, .Upon my death, all three farms which made up the original Slayton estate will be deeded as one property. The current owners of the two separate farms must live in the homestead located on the main property while it is renovated into a bed and breakfast inn that will honor the Slayton name. Should the parties succeed in creating a fully functional inn, they will each retain fifty percent ownership in the land, buildings and businesses associated with all three properties. However, if either party refuses to participate, then both parties forfeit their original investments. The original five hundred acre Slayton estate will then be sold at private auction to the highest bidder who agrees to the creation and continued success of the Slayton Bed and Breakfast Inn."

Angie stared at Jared in disbelief.

He looked up. "This works for me."

Panicking, her breathing becoming ragged, Angie turned to Alan. "No, this isn't possible, Alan. You never mentioned this to me before today."

Alan looked alarmed. "Angie, I'm so sorry. Martha knew about this clause. I just assumed she'd told you at some point." Concerned, he stood and came to her side.

"No, she never said a word. Why do we have to live there? Why would Sam concoct such a ridiculous situation for all the owners? I just don't understand," she whispered, searching his face for some sign that this was all a big, bad joke.

"Sam was eccentric. Who knows why he came up with this? But he did and it's legal and binding. You have to follow his instructions exactly or lose your property and the business." Alan crouched down. "Angie, are you okay?" He took her smooth hands in his wrinkled ones and looked at her intently. "You look pale. Would you like some water?"

Angie nodded, then took a deep breath while Alan went to get the drink. She looked at her hands shaking in her lap. "I can't believe Aunt Martha didn't tell me," she whispered.

"I knew this was always a possibility," Jared put in. "It really is a good investment if you think about it. We can each have our homes, you can still run your store and now we'll both own more property and have a new business to share."

Angie was sure her eyes were going to pop out of her head from staring at Jared so much. There was no way she could live in the homestead alone with him. It was the entire summer, when one day would be far too long to be confined with the man who terrorized her nightly in dreams.

Alan came in and Angie took the glass of water he offered and sipped.

"Better now?" Alan asked.

"A little," she said weakly as Alan returned to his seat behind the desk. *How will I...how can I share a house with this man? Why did the clause say we must live in the homestead? Just my luck.*

"Okay, there's also a trust set up with enough funds in it to finance the renovation and for start-up money for the inn."

"How much?" Jared asked.

"A little over a million dollars."

"*What?*" Angie and Jared said in unison.

"Yes, over a million."

"Why would he do that, Alan?" Angie scooted to the edge of her chair and sat the water glass on Alan's desk. "If Sam had that much money, why not just renovate the place himself while he was alive?"

"I don't know, Angie," Alan answered. "Like I said, Sam was eccentric and very proud. It's unconventional and he never gave me a reason why he wanted the estate handled this way. Maybe he thought this would create a legacy just as the haunting rumors keep up interest in the Slayton place. Whatever his reasons, I'll be working with you to ensure the inn's success. The way I see it, between the three of us, we have the skills to make it work."

"Why would you want to help us?" asked Jared.

"I was Sam's lawyer for many years. He made me the executor of his estate, but not in the traditional sense. I agreed that in lieu of payment as executor, I would be paid when the renovation was complete. I don't collect any money until you open for business. As you can see, I too have a stake in the inn's success."

Angie slid back in her chair, gripping her hands together. She might as well find out all the details if not participating meant losing the store. "What skills are you referring too, Alan?"

"You gave up your interior design career in Roanoke to come back here and run The Variety Vine after Martha's death. You could offer your redecorating expertise and work on the interior of the homestead," Alan said, then turned to Jared, "Your background is in developing subdivisions and selling real estate, Jared. You could contribute your construction and real estate knowledge to aid in the remodeling of the house and other areas of the property. I will handle the marketing to ensure we have guests for the inn."

"I'm sorry, Alan," Angie said, "there's no one I can trust to run The Variety Vine."

"What about Sharon Brady? She used to help Martha run the store," Alan suggested. "I'm sure she would love to help out."

Angie looked between Alan and Jared, then stared at her quivering hands, all the while tugging on her bottom lip with her teeth. *I'm out of excuses and I can't tell Alan about the nightmare.*

She glanced at Jared. The muscle in his jaw worked as he stared, deep in thought, out the window, rubbing his palms against his knees.

"You know, Angie, it will be interesting to see if you have one of those dreams."

"What do you mean?" Jared asked.

Angie shook her head slightly to quiet Alan. *Don't tell Jared about my dreams.*

"Angie's known in these parts for having dreams that come true," Alan told Jared.

Great. Just great! She glared at Alan but he didn't even look her way.

"She can see in a dream what will happen in the future and she has seen the past too. I'm hoping that, after spending time in the house, she will dream about Theodore Slayton." Alan leaned back in his chair. "Then we'll know if his ghost indeed haunts the place. Local folk know about her dreams and would back up her predictions as true, thus making the Slayton Bed and Breakfast more intriguing to ghost hunting visitors."

"Do you believe her dreams come true?" Jared asked.

Geez! Now they are going to talk about me like I'm not even sitting in the room with them, thought Angie. *God I hate this! Why did Alan have to bring it up?*

"She doesn't flaunt her gift." Alan's gaze settled on her and Angie gave him the *hush* look. "You still have a hard time accepting it, don't you?"

Without waiting for a response, he turned back to Jared. "She has helped many people by telling them about her—what did Martha call them? Oh, yes—prophetic dreams. She helped me and now, my friend…I'm a believer."

"What dreams of yours came true?" Jared asked with genuine interest.

"I just dream and sometimes it happens," she said.

"Is there something in the dream that lets you know it will come true?" Jared pressed.

"I don't know what you mean," she lied. *Like I'd ever tell you about my observer dreams.*

"Do you dream in color or see a symbol that let's you know

this dream is different from a normal dream? A sign which means this dream will come true where another one without the sign wouldn't come true."

No way would Jared Maxwell ever know that she watched the dream happen night after night until it came true. That was private. The only person she'd ever told was Aunt Martha. "There's not a sign. Some of them just come true, that's all."

"Hmm, you have a unique gift," Jared said. "My sister, Terri, has a similar ability. It's hard for her to talk about her paranormal experiences too. I bet the two of you will get along great."

Angie studied Jared and tried to figure out if he was teasing her or being truthful. He probably thought she was a freak now. People usually did when they found out about her dreams.

It didn't matter what he thought of her anyway and she doubted if she would ever meet his sister. What she knew for sure was she would never sleep under the same roof with him, especially since the horrific dream continued each and every night. If the past had taught her anything, this would not end until the dream came true in life."

"I've drawn up all the necessary paperwork," Alan said. "All you have to do is sign and we can start today. Both of you can move into the house tomorrow."

"I'm in," Jared said.

"Great!"

Angie looked at the contracts Alan slid across the desk, one for each of them and panicked.

"I'm sorry, Alan. I just can't do it," she said, pushing the contract back toward him. *I can't risk putting my life in jeopardy by living with Jared Maxwell.* After the episode in the hall, her life wasn't the only thing at risk—her virginity was too!

"Why don't you just admit the truth, Angie," taunted Jared as he looked over the contract. "You're just afraid to sleep in a haunted house—with me."

That's only the half of it. "Riiigght," she said, drawing the word out in an attempt to appear unaffected by the whole situation, "haunted houses. Why would I be afraid of staying there with you?"

"My dashing good looks?" Jared teased.

What an ego. "I am not afraid of you, Mr. Maxwell."

"Then prove it," Jared grinned, signing his name across the bottom of his contract and handing it back to Alan. "Take a risk, Angie. Or are you afraid of ghosts?"

"No, Casper doesn't scare me. I just don't have to prove anything to either of you." But, come to think of it, if she said yes but needed time away from him, she'd have five hundred acres at her disposal. There would be workers there during the day that could protect her and she could get people she knew to hang out with her if she felt threatened. It was just the nighttime. How could she sleep in the same house with him at night?

Alan sighed. "Angie, if you don't participate, I'm legally bound to put the property up for auction. You'll lose The Variety Vine. Think of Martha and all the work you two put into that store."

Jared touched her...again. He gently took her chin, trying to turn her toward him, but Angie resisted. He tried again and this time she looked over into those blue eyes.

"No, you don't have to prove anything to either of us but don't lose your store because of fear. You've barely looked at me since our little fiasco in the hallway. I think you're worried that you wouldn't be able to handle yourself alone with me, away from the world and you know it."

She pulled her chin from his grasp, surprised at Jared's boldness. Then, her anger at the unfairness of everything that had happened in the past three months caught up with her. She narrowed her eyes. "How dare you!"

"Listen you two," Alan interrupted, "the renovation could be completed a week before the new convention center opens, if it's started immediately. We could book guest reservations beginning on September first, if we're on schedule. I know the deadlines are short and you will work long hours each day, but this way you could both meet the conditions of the clause over the summer and move on with your lives."

"You have to be kidding me, Alan." Frustrated and angry, Angie grabbed his desk and leaned forward. "Do you honestly believe the house can be ready before the convention center opens? I just don't see it all coming together that fast."

"I'm game. I think we could do it," Jared told Angie. "If you know how to work hard."

"Are you insinuating I'm not a hard worker, Mr. Maxwell?"

"No, I wasn't insinuating anything. To be quite honest with you, I don't want to lose my property because you're afraid to commit."

Angie's knuckles whitened as she clenched the desk. *How dare he? What an insufferable, arrogant man!* Grinding her teeth together, she glared at Jared. *Control, Angie. Do not let your temper get the better of you.*

I'll show you, thought Angie, looking between the two men. *Dammit! I might be afraid, but I'll hide my fear from you, Mr. I-Wasn't-Insinuating-Anything, so you'll never know. I can handle anything you can dish out and I'll throw it right back at you, tenfold.*

At least I hope I will.

It was a risk. A big risk that could put her in grave danger, especially after the warning Aunt Martha's ghost had given. Angie knew she had to do it. She owed Aunt Martha that much. She couldn't lose her aunt's most prized possession just because she gave up before she'd even tried.

Maybe, if she agreed, she would actually be able to understand Jared's role in her dream. Had he saved her from the bullet or was he the one who stuck the gun in her back?

The mix of emotions that this man and this situation caused in her made her shake inside, made her temper flare. Instead of her usual angry outburst, Angie looked Jared straight in the eyes, accepting his challenge. Then, her gaze still locked with his, she took a deep breath, released the desk and extended her hand toward Alan, palm up.

"Give me the contract, Alan. Where do I sign?"

To be continued...

Night Visions is available at online book retailers and can be ordered from a bookstore near you.

Photo by Isabel Barney

Melissa Alvarez is a multi-published, award-winning author. She writes nonfiction under her real name and paranormal romantic suspense as Ariana Dupré. She owns Friesian horses, Barock Pinto horses and German Shepherd dogs with her husband and together they are successful breeders of champions. She enjoys reading, spending time with her family and horses, and designing book covers when she's not writing. Melissa lives in sunny South Florida. Visit her online at MelissaA.com for updates on new releases or at BookCovers.Us or BookCoversGalore.com if you're an author in need of a cover designer.